LIZ MISTRY moved to West Yorkshire in the late 1980s. Her gritty crime fiction police procedural novels set in Bradford embrace the city she describes as 'Warm, Rich and Fearless' whilst exploring the darkness that lurks beneath. Yet, her heart remains in Scotland, where childhood tales of bogey men, Bible John and grey lady ghosts fed her imagination.

Her latest work, The Solanki and McQueen crime series is set around West Lothian, where she uses the distinctive landscape, historic heritage and Scottish culture as a backdrop to her hard-hitting yet often humorous stories.

Struggling with clinical depression and anxiety for many years, Liz often includes mental health themes in her writing. She credits her MA in Creative Writing from Leeds Trinity University with helping her find a way of using her writing to navigate her ongoing mental health struggles. The synergy between creative and academic writing led Liz to complete a doctorate in creative writing researching the importance of representation of marginalised groups within the genre she loves.

Her husband, three children and huge extended British Indian family are a constant support to her. In her spare time, Liz loves visiting the varied Scottish and Yorkshire landscape, travelling, listening to music, reading and blogging about all things crime fiction on her website blog, The Crime Warp.

You can connect with Liz here:

Website: lizmistry.com

𝕏 (Twitter): LizMistryAuthor

f: https://www.facebook.com/LizMistrybooks

Also by Liz Mistry

The Blood Promise

LIZ MISTRY

ONE PLACE. MANY STORIES

HQ
An imprint of HarperCollins*Publishers* Ltd
1 London Bridge Street
London SE1 9GF

www.harpercollins.co.uk

HarperCollins*Publishers*
Macken House, 39/40 Mayor Street Upper,
Dublin 1 D01 C9W8

This paperback edition 2024

1
First published in Great Britain by
HQ, an imprint of HarperCollins*Publishers* Ltd 2024

To my mum and dad who, although they never saw my books published, would have been so proud.

Also, to my niece, Jaina, whose journey through sight loss has been inspirational, and to Guide Dogs UK and all who support them.

Prologue

Inverness

15 years earlier, 14th December

The stench as the constable kicked in the door – rich and meaty and dense, like a felled stag, its carcass left to rot in the summer sun – should have been warning enough that what was to come wouldn't be pretty. But being only eighteen and his first day on the job, his naiveté sent him blundering into an unimaginable situation with his guard well and truly down. Such was life.

With his sergeant sweet-talking the neighbours and his own eye on the end of the shift, all he wanted was to get this done, go home, shower and relax with his girlfriend. All day he'd listened to Fletcher the Belcher burping and belching his garlicky way through this never-ending shift and he'd had enough.

'What you waiting for, laddie? Get in there and see what's going on.' Sergeant Fletcher's tone was dismissive as he played to the crowd of wifies, hanging off his every word, each of them desperate for a bit of excitement to end this blisteringly cold winter's day.

With one hand over his mouth, he used the other to locate the light switch and allowed himself a smile when he found it just inside the door. His smile vanished when he pressed it and nothing happened. Reluctantly, he stuck his head half through the door into the darkness beyond. The smell seemed to thicken and encapsulate him, gripping him by his throat and dragging him forward like an unwieldy alien into its belly. Behind him, the Belcher continued to laugh and joke with the neighbours – their voices drifting to him as he took his phone from his pocket and found the torch app.

'She's an alky, you know, Sergeant Fletcher?' The voice of a fifty-a-day woman kicked off the litany of criticisms.

'Keeps that house a fucking disgrace – pardon my French. And those weans? Well, listen here to me . . . they're always filthy and I'm not even sure she feeds them half the time.'

'Aye, you're not wrong there, Margo. The number of men coming and going at all hours . . . She makes Gina Costello down the road look like a saint.'

The constable blocked out their moans and navigated the steps up to the lobby landing. Typical of many council houses, this one sat atop another – a sort of two-storey flat. When he tried the door handle, it turned. Halfway up the stairs he realised his heartbeat had increased. Despite his outward bravery, he was a wee bit off kilter. What if something bad was in there? *Yeah right. Nothing ever happens in Westhill in Inverness. Not a sodding thing!*

His torch cast eerie shadows round the sticky lino stairs. He shook his head and, ignoring his inner misgivings, ran up the last few steps to the door. Again, he hesitated, observing the half-glass, half-wood entrance. He inhaled, gagging as the pernicious air hit the back of his throat. He gipped. *Get a bloody grip, man. Last thing you need is the Belcher telling everyone back at Burnett Road that the Rookie upchucked and can't handle himself.*

He tucked his mobile under his chin, extracted a pair of crime scene gloves from his pocket and pulled them on. He hadn't expected to need them when he reported for duty that morning, but he was glad he'd pocketed them. After all, that was something they drummed into you at Tulliallan, the police training college: be prepared. The gloves made him feel equipped – like he'd created a barrier between himself and whatever he was about to face. Like their presence covering his hands protected his entire being. He grinned. Maybe the gloves were *his* superpower – not that Glove-Man had quite the same ring to it as Spider-Man.

Emboldened by his newfound courage, he opened the door.

'You not in there yet, lad?' the Belcher's voice echoed up the stairs.

Gie me a bloody chance, ye auld scunner.

The Belcher, clearly enjoying his position as king of his immediate surroundings, wasn't done mouthing off. 'Bloody bairns. Nay stamina, nay oomph. Can't get decent coppers these days.'

Of course, that elicited a chorus of twittering giggles, which made the younger officer's ears burn. Tight-lipped, he chuntered under his breath. 'Arrogant sodding fat slobby bastard. I'd like to see him pulling his weight for a change. Bloody lazy git.'

Lips narrowed, he stepped through the gap, his torch illuminating an uncarpeted hallway. There was a door to either side of him – bedrooms no doubt – and straight ahead at the end of the hall was the living room, probably with a minuscule toilet recessed to the left. He danced the beam over the area. Dark smears trailed along the stained wallpaper. It looked like shit. Now he came to think of it, excrement was one of the overpowering aromas present. His mother would have a fit if she could see him in this midden. With the top door open, the smell was more intense and had taken on other unidentifiable odours – none of them pleasant.

With the Belcher's wheezes and muttered curses indicating he'd finally entered the stairwell, the constable stepped into the lobby, cast his light first to the right, then the left, then back to the right again. *Right it is!* He pushed the bedroom door open and a gust of chilled air burst through the gap. He snaked his hand in and searched for the light switch – again no response, so he resigned himself to the fact that the entire house was without electric.

With his nose scrunched up, he directed his torch beam in small increments over the room, trying to get a sense of what was inside. A stained double mattress occupied most of the floor space with a pile of ragged covers bundled on top. A rickety sideboard stood to one side. Two of its three drawer spaces lay empty. Strips of sodden wallpaper snaked away from mouldy walls and accounted for part of the stench; the other was the bucket of eye-watering human waste that stood near the broken cupboard. *Oh, fuck this is boggin'!*

Intent on slamming the door shut against the stench, he edged away but as his light jiggled over the room, movement from the bed made him jump backwards, anticipating a large and jaggy-toothed rodent about to attack him. A pair of unblinking, unflinching eyes gazed at him. It took only a second to register the creature's shorn blooded scalp, their hollowed-out cheeks and blue-tinged skin. In their tiny hand, the creature-child held an open ring-pull tin with a spoon sticking out the top. No wonder this wean cowered under the few thin covers on the mattress. It was freezing.

An icy blast hurled through the inch-wide gap at the bottom of the window and the thin curtains wafted listlessly in the arctic breeze. The kid's eyes were dark and expressionless, and the constable wanted to grab the child up and run from the room. Then, another head appeared, followed almost immediately by a third. Three children stared at him, yet said nothing. He tried a faltering grin – still no reaction. Maintaining his distance so as not to appear threatening, he widened his smile. 'You're okay now. I'm a police officer and you're safe.'

Still nothing. No nod, no flicker of movement, just that sad, dark, scary stare from all three of them. He cast his mind back to his police training, but nothing he'd learned at Tulliallan had prepared him for this. He turned his head to the open door and

4

spoke in an urgent half-whispered shout. 'Sarge, you need to get up here.'

The Belcher's reply was faint and his words sent a chill down the constable's spine. 'Help. Chest pain. Need an ambulance.'

*The younger officer closed his eyes. Really? Sodding really? My first day and my sarge is about to cop it on me **and** I've found three kids huddled up in a cesspit of crap? Could my day get any worse?*

The neighbour with the smoker's rasp said, 'I've phoned 999. I'll stay with him, son.' Her voice dropped to a cooing simper. 'You're all right, Fletch. You'll be okay. Help's on the way.' Then: 'What the hell's that bloody stink?'

Hoping she referred to the stench drifting downstairs rather than anything produced by the Belcher, he heaved a sigh of relief. One problem sorted for now, but he still hadn't found the mum. He raised a finger to his lips. 'You three stay here. I'm going to find your mummy and then I'll get you out, okay?'

No response. But he'd no time to wait. Backing out, he closed the door behind him and turned his attention to the room on the left. As he reached for the doorknob a shiver trickled up his spine and the hair on the back of his neck stood on end. He wasn't into all that psychic sixth sense sort of shite, but his unease persisted. Despite the cold, sweat pulled under his armpits and his gut felt like a horde of maggots had taken up residence. *Pull yourself together. You're in charge now that auld man Belcher's wheezing like a fucking hippo on the stairs.* A grin twitched his lips. 'Not bad for my first day on the job, eh? De facto sergeant and not a full shift done yet.'

He inhaled and promptly regretted it when he ended up coughing up his guts. Vomit burned his throat, but he swallowed it down and as if pulling a plaster off, barrelled against the door using his full body weight and stumbled into the worst nightmare of his life.

With the sound of blue bottles thrashing against him in their efforts to escape the confined space, he dropped his phone, plunging the room into near darkness. That was a relief, because the last thing he *ever* wanted to see again was that bloated moving thing on the bed.

Heart pounding, he shooed the flies away, before diving down. Thankful for the gloves, he snatched his phone from the cesspit at his feet. He closed his eyes and stifled a sob. *I didn't sign up for this.* Then, he remembered the traumatised kids in the next room, and he counted to three. *This* was the reality of the job. It wasn't all sausage and egg floury rolls and haggis suppers. It was about helping folk and he'd never met anyone who needed his help more than those three wee mites next door.

With the sound of sirens competing with the Belcher's laboured breathing, he stood up and cast his torchlight once more on 'the thing' on the bed. It was worse than he'd first thought. A person – a dead person, probably the kids' mother – lay there with her tongue protruding. However, that wasn't the worst thing. This was something incomprehensible. A sight he'd never forget. This would feature in his nightmares for a long time to come.

He turned, ran from the room, slammed the door behind him and dived back into the one opposite. The children hadn't moved, so he yanked one of them onto his back, another up to grip his neck and the third into his arms. Their feet skimmed the wooden floorboards, as he half-dragged, half-carried them down the stairs, past a heaving, still-belching Belcher, and into the frozen night.

Day 1

Chapter 1

'Can you just *stop* for a minute with the clack, clack, clackety clack, clack? You're doing my head in, Queenie.' Detective Constable Jasmine – Jazzy to most folk – Solanki, glowered through the windscreen of the undercover police car and into the freezing gloom beyond. 'I thought you were told not to do that anymore, anyway. Not after you nearly had that bloke's eye out. Health and safety or something.'

When Queenie's clackety-clacking didn't let up, Jazzy sighed. With the start of a headache tugging at her temples, she reached up and released her ponytail, allowing her waist-length hair to cascade down over her shoulders, before pulling her hat back over it.

'Well, well, well, if it isn't a Simone Ashley lookalike.' Queenie stared at Jazzy. 'You look ten years younger with your hair down like that. No idea why you'd want to keep it tied up like Miss Trunchbull.'

Jazzy glared at her. 'Firstly, Simone Ashley's hair is curly and mine is as straight as a die; secondly, whether my hair is tied up or loose, I look nothing like Miss bloody Trunchbull.'

'Aye, well. I'm not so sure about that, JayZee.'

Jazzy had only been working with the older detective for a few days and already she was learning that Annie 'Queenie' McQueen was a law unto herself, so she resigned herself to a noisy overnight stakeout. A quick glance at her phone told her it was just after 1 a.m. – only five minutes later than when she'd last checked. This was going to be a long, uncomfortable night. 'Can't you do it quietly then?'

'I'm only knitting, for God's sake, JayZee.' Queenie delivered both syllables of the nickname she'd given Jazzy, as if about to perform a rap and, because it was dark and Queenie wouldn't notice she'd got a rise from her, Jazzy rolled her eyes. *How original.*

Oblivious, Queenie continued, 'I'm not making a racket and my knitting needles are hardly lethal weapons, are they?'

Jazzy reserved judgement on that one. From where she was sitting, they were definitely lethal *and* she'd seen the report from 'needle-gate' and knew at least one person who'd agree with her. If Queenie didn't let up with the knitting soon, Jazzy might be tempted to prove just how lethal the damn things could be.

But Queenie ranted on. 'It's not like I'm toting an AK-47, is it? Or a Heckler and Koch or even a Sig SG 550.'

Stifling a sigh, Jazzy rubbed her eyes, undecided which pissed her off the most: the incessant clackety clack or the way Queenie emphasised her observations with a trio of needless and exaggerated descriptors. In an attempt to blank out the racket, she looked out the windscreen again. Snow was falling thick and fast, blurring their visibility, and if Jazzy didn't regularly swish the wipers across the screen, they'd lose visibility of their target. Not that Queenie seemed bothered by that; her entire focus was on the woollen monstrosity she was creating. The annoying clackety sound increased in tempo as Queenie chuntered on, her needles keeping pace with her mouth.

'Besides, you'd be glad of them if we were set upon by a group of rabid youths . . . or dogs . . . or drunks . . .'

*God, not **again** with the trio of exemplars. Can't take much more of this.* 'Okay, okay, I get it, Queenie. Just don't . . .'

'Aw nooooo!' Queenie's tortured yelp made Jazzy jump. 'You and your bloody distractions. I've gone wrong.'

Queenie reached over, flicked on the interior light and groaned. 'Look what you've done, JayZee. Look what you've made me do. You and your damn yap, yap, yappity yapping. This was a gift for my other half, you know, and you've bloody spoiled it. Look at the state of it.'

Exhaling through clenched teeth, Jazzy glowered at the bright orange thing Queenie held up. Despite her annoyance with the woman, Jazzy couldn't stop a smile forming. As if the colour of the garment wasn't hideous enough, it was misshapen with random holes all over. Even in her wildest imagination, Jazzy couldn't imagine what it should look like. However, it was neither the colour nor the holes that caused Queenie's current distress. It was the fact that one arm was at least three inches longer than the other. Jazzy frowned. 'Aren't you supposed to knit each of the component parts of the jumper separately?'

'Hmph – what do you know about knitting? I'll have you know this is a special all-in-one pattern. I adapted it from a kid's one I made for my nephew.'

Wondering how *that* jumper had turned out, Jazzy leaned across and flicked the light off. 'We're supposed to be keeping an eye on the suspected cannabis farm, not advertising your failed knitting attempts and giving them a heads up that we're here. No lights. Besides, surely knitting in the dark is responsible for the mistakes in that thing.'

Queenie snorted, but ignored Jazzy's comment. 'Like the tossers in the Argy Bargy are going to be capable of anything. They'll be so spaced out on the auld ganja, woozy on the weed, zonked out on the old pot, they wouldn't notice if we rode up there on a rainbow-coloured unicorn.'

'Yeah, I get it, Queenie. It's a thankless task, but we've got our job to do.'

'Yeah – stuck in the arse end of nowhere, surveilling a bunch of hapless dopeheads who think they're above the law, whilst every other damn team in the district has something gritty to get their teeth into.'

Queenie had a point. This was a pointless exercise. Everybody knew that the residents of Stùrrach – a ramshackle village a stone's throw from the more respectable and much larger village of Fauldhouse – were generally left to their own devices and for good reason. As long as any illegal activities didn't spill over into the wider community, they were usually ignored rather than take up valuable police time chasing up grievances that nine times out of ten were kicked out of court due to lack of evidence.

This begged the question: why had she and Queenie been sent there tonight? Was it yet another punishment devised by DCI Dick – the dickless wonder – to hammer home their demotion to D team? Bastard even opted not to call them C team, just to punch home the fact that he considered them dunces. Or busy work to keep their nebs out of the real investigations that seemed to fully occupy teams A and B? Jazzy suspected Dick's vindictive streak had led to both those decisions. Never had such a small man carried such a large chip on his shoulder – but Jazzy wouldn't dwell on his motives. No matter how irritating this stakeout was, she'd do it to the best of her ability, despite being lumbered with gob-shitey Annie McQueen.

Stùrrach was more of a hamlet than a village – a grouping of rundown houses on either side of a potholed road whose focal point was the aptly named Argy Bargy pub. Rumour had it that a clan of Sturrocks settled there centuries ago and became closed off from the other small villages around when leprosy took hold. Jazzy had no idea whether that was true or not. However, it was undeniable that the Stùrrach residents were, if not exactly feared, then certainly distrusted and avoided by their closest neighbours in the larger village of Fauldhouse. The two villages were divided by no more than twenty metres of overgrown land, which the locals called the Badlands. On the Stùrrach side old cars minus their wheels, rusting washing machines and fridges formed a sort of impromptu barrier to civilisation.

Unfortunately for West Lothian and Borders police, and specifically Jazzy and Queenie, the big bosses in Police Scotland didn't view the increased presence of these reported activities in quite the same way as the Fauldhouse locals, particularly when a glut of weed and meth amphetamine seemed to be barrelling its way to towns and cities throughout West Lothian and beyond. Which was why Jazzy found herself freezing her arse off in a malodourous police pool car, with a fellow newly demoted DC she barely knew and had no desire to get to know.

Her annoyance was compounded by fear that at some point on this cold, dreich, snowy night, Queenie would bring up the very thing Jazzy was determined to avoid discussing – the incident that had caused her own demotion from celebrated detective sergeant of the month to lowly constable, in the space of a few weeks. Jazzy sensed Queenie's eyes on her and wished they were anywhere other than in the confines of the car.

With the inevitability of a fast-moving tide, Queenie stuffed her knitting into the bag by her feet, crossed her arms under her ample bosom and turned sideways towards Jazzy. 'Sooo. We all know *I* was demoted for what has become known affectionately throughout the district as "needle-gate", but *nobody* seems to know why you're now a DC instead of the well-respected DS with a career trajectory set to orbit the entire galaxy of a month ago.'

Jazzy's lips tightened. She'd no intention of sharing *that* with Queenie. It had been in the brass's best interests to keep the real reasons behind Jazzy's demotion quiet, but it rankled that the newspapers had exposed her. However, the fewer people who knew the cause of her demotion the better. In a different world Jazzy might have been inclined to challenge the sexism of it all, but in the present circumstances, she'd elected to keep her head down and her mouth shut. That didn't mean she was oblivious to the rumours flying around about her, and neither it seemed was Queenie.

'Hmph, word is that you and the chief super are at it. You know, up to the old rumpy-pumpy, humping like rabbits, forn-ee-cay-ting?' Queenie drew both arms back and jerked her hips twice in quick succession. 'Me? I don't see it, myself. Old Waqas Afzal goes more for the petite, cutesy sort of lass, the OMG I can't do a thing for myself sort, the wimpy, woopy, woosy sort.' She sniffed and raked her eyes up and down Jazzy's frame. 'Not a big brawny thing like you with an attitude that a personality transplant would have trouble shifting.'

Jazzy opened her mouth to take issue with the 'big, brawny' description, but then clamped it closed again. It was true she was taller than most of her fellow officers and she was a bit heavy round the hips and her boobs were what her auntie Lillie described as generous, but still . . . she wasn't going to get drawn into a discussion about her relationship with the chief super. The personality jibe was a bit much, though. Especially coming from pint-sized Ms Porcupine beside her. It wasn't as if Queenie was the most tactful or best communicator around. Abrasive was how Jazzy would describe her new partner. Loud, prickly and objectionable. No way would Jazzy confide in Annie McQueen. No bloody way.

'Nearly half-one now, Queenie. You want to doze for a while? It'll be a long night if we don't grab some kip, and there's no need for us both to stay awake all night.'

Queenie's lips pursed, then shaking her head she opened the car door letting in a waft of icy air. 'Just going for a wazz and then I'll have a wee nap. You should go for one too. This fricking cold goes right to yer bladder. I've bagged the back of that fridge-freezer for my urinal; that way the piss runs downhill. You can crouch down by the auld settee or the jacked-up car. Your choice.'

As the door slammed behind her partner, Jazzy became acutely aware of a pressure in her own bladder. If she was going to feel comfortable watching the pub, she had no option but to leave the relative warmth of the car when Queenie got back and freeze her arse off. Maybe she should have opted for buying some of those Tena pads her mum kept going on about.

Chapter 2

There's something to be said for creeping around in the early hours of the morning – unseen and unheard, a ghost. It's like *I'm* the only person in the world. Like the world and everything and everyone in it is at *my* disposal. As if I'm superhuman – a god, a hero! That thought tickles me as I touch the amulet I keep on a chain round my neck. I always wear it. Its presence helps me focus on the wider implications of my work. Some might say I'm more devil than god, more anti-hero than hero – it's just . . . nobody knows it yet.

I sidle through the streets, sticking to the shadows, avoiding the cameras like a fox on the prowl. With my hoodie pulled up over my hair, I look like any old junkie out trying to score a deal in the underbelly of society. The snow's getting heavier now and it's bloody freezing, so there's really nobody about.

Up ahead, in a doorway near the Argy Bargy, a light flicks on, illuminating two silhouettes. Probably two manky auld fuckers doing it. *Get a bloody room, yeah?* But it's just a couple of kids from the pub having a fly smoke.

I watch them for a bit, but my mind's focused on another job. I edge into the shadows of the Badlands and head towards the dark shape on the other side of the wasteland. Everything's falling into place. Every one of my little machinations is beginning to

16

bear fruit and the two in the car are exactly where I planned for them to be. They're parked away from the streetlights facing the Argy Bargy but keeping their distance. I cast my eyes down the road and smile. From their position, they're almost invisible from the Stùrrach side, but they can see everything going on near the pub. They're coppers, keeping an eye on the only gaff where the snow is melting off the roof.

I snort, and shake my head. Dead giveaway if you're growing grass. It's good for me though. It shows my plan's in place. If these two pigs are stationed where I intended them to be, then there's less likely to be any coppers driving round the house I'm targeting four streets over. I slink into the dark, knowing that my black clothes and the heavy snowfall will provide enough cover for me to leave the area undetected.

I slope down the alley that leads to Azalea Close, dodging the used needles and condoms that are becoming covered by the snow. At the end of the alley, the houses are nicer – all sectioned-off drives with big cars on them adjoining their well-sculpted front lawns. Posh gits in posh houses. Kings of their castles, looking down on the rest of the world. I turn right heading straight for number eighty-three, pretentiously called The Hedgerow. It's a detached five-bedroomed house with two BMWs parked on the drive. I know this house so well that I creep past the red car by the hedge without setting off the motion sensor lights.

If I wait, just – I check my phone – another twenty minutes, the motion sensor will be deactivated; but I won't wait. Not tonight. Crouching down, welcoming the way the hedge and the car shelter me from some of the wind, I blow on my hands for a couple of minutes. Got to keep my fingers heated. I'll need them to be nimble in a bit. When they're warmer, I head off for my other little job and cast a silent nod towards The Hedgerow as I go. I'll be back before they know it and boy will they wish I wasn't.

But first, I've got another job to do and now I know the pawns are in position it's all systems go. Tonight is going to be explosive.

Chapter 3

Discordant snuffles followed by seconds of blissful silence, abruptly broken by rough guttural snorts played on repeat. It did Jazzy's head in and she was beginning to regret offering to keep watch whilst Queenie slept. If the sounds from her mouth were bad, the ones from her backside were the real killer. She took farting to a whole new level, filling the police car with noxious fumes, forcing Jazzy to crack the windows every so often. She was gross. At least if Queenie was sleeping, she wasn't hassling Jazzy, which was why she hadn't wakened her yet. Besides, she wouldn't sleep. No matter how knackered she was, Jazzy couldn't snooze on a stakeout. It was part of her overzealous nature. A symptom, according to her therapist, of her past experiences and one that she needed to work on if she ever wanted to form meaningful trusting relationships.

Jazzy scowled. She wasn't keen on forming relationships of any description and trusting ones seemed a step too far. Last thing she needed was folk inserting themselves into her life and making demands on her time. No, she was perfectly fine on her tod. Besides, she *had* relationships. She had her mum and dad, didn't she? And Elliot. That was more than enough. How many relationships did her therapist expect her to maintain? Jazzy suspected the answer was a number significantly higher than three.

She glanced at her watch. Nearly half two. God, it had been a long and freezing night. Layers of clothing and the fleece blanket she'd wrapped around herself, cocoon style, hadn't taken the edge off her numb toes and fingers. She glanced at Queenie. How could she look so restful? With her mouth hanging open, her short spiky grey hair peeking out from under an appallingly misshaped bobble hat – which Jazzy suspected she'd knitted herself – Jazzy would waken her at first light.

For the last hour, Jazzy had intermittently cleared the windscreen of snow in order to peer through the dark abyss that was the Badlands. So far there had been no nefarious activity near the Argy Bargy, unless you counted the kids leaving the pub at closing time. They'd indulged in a drunken snowball fight that ended when they skited across the potholed street using their arses as sledges, whilst belting out a tuneless chorus of 'Frosty the Snowman'. Laughing, they'd split up to enter three of the houses closest to the pub.

Shortly afterwards, the pub's lights had gone off, leaving Jazzy bereft. Somehow, the glow from the pub had created the illusion of warmth. Now, with only the snow turning to drizzle and the gloomy moonless night for company, a shiver hurtled up Jazzy's spine. She drew her blanket tighter and wondered if she could risk putting the engine on to heat them up. Another one of Queenie's lethal farts rent the air and Jazzy groaned, covering her nose with her hands as she opened the window.

Thankfully the vibration of her phone against her thigh offered a distraction. Recognising the tone as the one from her motion-activated home security system, Jazzy dragged off her glove to access the notification. After being alerted a few times over the past week by a fox stealing through her back garden to access the children's play area and the fields adjacent to it, she looked forward to seeing what Mr Fox was up to tonight. She pressed play on the most recent recording. The light above her back door was on, activated by movement from the far side of the fence surrounding her garden. Rather than the fox with its baleful eyes and limp tail, a figure dressed entirely in black sidled over the lawn area leaving footprints in the snow.

Jazzy brought the phone closer to her face and pressed pause, her heart hammering a tattoo against her chest. On instinct her fingers searched for the small glass Ganesh statue she carried in her pocket. Running them over its familiar contours soothed her as she studied the hunched figure wearing a hoodie pulled completely over his head. Wrapped around his mouth was a scarf or balaclava. Dark glasses or goggles covered his eyes. As fear surged through Jazzy's body, the colour drained from her face.

Shit! It had been months – almost a year since the last time. Certainly, before she'd moved to her small house in Bellsquarry and installed her security system. In all that time there'd been no suspicious activity and she'd been lulled into believing her torment was past. *Stupid, stupid, stupid!*

Still holding the Ganesh, she struggled to maintain her composure. Her peripheral vision darkened and she fought to stop the flashback to another time – a time when she was scared and alone. A time in the darkness with footsteps coming up the stairs. She screwed her eyes shut and willed herself to remain in the present. After a few moments, the fog lifted and with a trembling finger she pressed play again. The dark figure walked closer but because of the way he'd hunched his shoulders and scrunched his upper body it was difficult to use her fence for a height comparison. He could range between five foot five and six feet or so tall. From experience, Jazzy knew that the white rectangle he held contained a card – a birthday card. A birthday card for her.

Beside her, Queenie shuffled, rolled to the side so her head rested on the window and settled down. Whilst Jazzy was amazed at how deeply her partner slept despite the nipping cold, she was also relieved. She needed time alone with her thoughts to process what her security system had captured and although freezing her

20

arse off in a smelly police car near Fauldhouse wasn't ideal, if Queenie remained asleep it gave her time to think.

Regardless that she'd be in dereliction of her duty, the urge to head straight home was strong, but that was something she couldn't risk if she wanted to keep her job – particularly in light of her recent demotion. Her two-bedroomed house in the sleepy village was ideal for her and she'd made it her home. A stone's throw from West Calder in one direction and a similar distance away from her work in Livingston police station, it was more than just a house. It was her sanctuary.

Under her breath, she cursed herself for being stupid enough to let her guard down. For being naïve enough to grow too attached to one area and putting down roots that would be impossible to yank up without a great deal of emotion. She should have committed to her previous nomadic life. A year here, six months there, eighteen months in the next place. The mistake she'd made this time though was a cardinal one. A pulse throbbed at her temple and her breaths came in quick, panting succession. As she tried to grasp control, a wave of dizziness made her close her eyes and groan deep in her throat. *Shit, I'm losing it.*

Forcing herself to sit upright, she slowed her breathing down until each breath became a measured razor cutting up her oesophagus, and as it left her mouth, it steamed the air in front of her. She began to count, slow and easy, and as she did so the dizziness eased and the pain in her throat faded. Haring home would be pointless. The dark figure would be long gone. She focused on the sounds around her. The faint rustle of leaves in the trees and the drips from the branches above landing on the car roof as the snow melted. A far-off owl hooting over the fields to her right and, louder than everything else, Queenie's relentless racket. *Thank God she didn't witness my moment of weakness. It would be all round the team by lunchtime.*

Jazzy bit her lip. No, that wasn't true. Queenie was a character – an annoying one, definitely – but she wasn't mean for the sake of it. Not in Jazzy's limited acquaintance with her, anyway. Still, she was glad the older woman hadn't seen her in this state. She exhaled and when she was sure she had herself under control she pressed play on the recording again and watched it all the way through this time.

The dark hooded figure in the weird goggles tramped over the lawn to the back door and jogged up the steps. He glanced at the camera before giving a jaunty wave. *Cocky little bastard!* The 'bastard' wore gloves, which meant there would be no fingerprints on the envelope – just like before. He tucked it behind the planter on the top step. Now he was so close, she realised the envelope was sealed in a plastic food bag. He glanced at the camera again, blew a kiss from his masked face and retraced his steps.

What could Jazzy do? She couldn't report it without dredging everything from her past up again. There was no overt threat to her. Yes, it was decidedly dodgy to turn up dressed like a ninja in the dead of night to deliver a birthday card. But it wasn't illegal. The card would be unsigned like all the others. She'd hoped her creepy stalker had got tired of his games, but now he'd found her again. How she wished she could identify him and, although this recording was the first time she'd laid eyes on him, there was no guarantee that he hadn't paid someone to drop the card off. She couldn't get dragged down the rabbit hole of assuming this was her actual stalker.

That he'd deliberately allowed himself to be spotted delivering the envelope concerned her. Was he escalating? Was this the next step in a campaign that till now had seemed disturbing, yet somewhat benign? Who was she kidding? She knew the statistics on stalkers and they weren't good. There was no such thing as a benign stalker. What Jazzy needed to do was work out a plan of action and get to the bottom of this. Good job being on the D team meant she'd plenty of time to do just that.

Using her relative solitude, Jazzy zoomed in on the figure at various points on the recording, desperate to spot something that would identify him, but no matter how hard she looked, there was nothing. As she'd done before, Jazzy scrolled through a list of suspects in her mind and finally settled on Dwayne Taggart again. The Taggart family had been through enough. Jazzy had been involved in the investigation into his sister, Lucy's, rape. They'd caught the rapist, but he'd got off because one of Jazzy's officers had been bribed to lose the evidence.

Understandably, the family were angry. Dwayne had threatened Jazzy at the court and it was shortly after that the mysterious cards had begun arriving. The only other course of action Jazzy could take was to pull in some favours. She rummaged in her bag and grabbed another phone – a burner that was unregistered to her and shot off a text with the footage attached.

Jazzy: Got another one. Can you check it out?

Within five seconds, her burner phone vibrated with a reply:

Chapter 4

It was sooo warm all wrapped up under her duvet that Imogen Clark was in no rush to get up. Then, she remembered – it was her birthday and the desire to throw the duvet aside and jump out of bed was strong, but she resisted. Her mum had plans for a 'special birthday breakfast' and had warned Imogen that she'd better not leave her room until they called her down. She wished they'd hurry up though. She needed a wee and she really wanted to see her presents. She snuggled deeper under the duvet and smiled. This was going to be the best day of her life. She could feel it in her bones.

For the past fortnight, every time plans for her birthday celebrations were mentioned, her parents had joked, 'Sweet sixteen and never been kissed'. Little did they know that she wasn't *quite* as innocent as they thought and that tonight was *the* night when she'd dump her innocence once and for all. All her friends had done 'it' over the summer holidays. But, cautious by nature, Imogen had resisted. Then, she and Danny Banik had become a 'thing' and she was ready. Yes, he was older than her and at first, she'd found it hard to believe that this gorgeous twenty-one-year-old could possibly be interested in her. He'd wanted to do 'it', but she'd wanted to wait and he hadn't put too much pressure on her – not really.

Her friend Gloria had done it in the back of her dad's car with her next-door neighbour. Stupid cow hadn't used a condom, which resulted in weeks of 'Oh my God what if I'm pregnant' conversations, till thankfully, her period had arrived. Stupid cow had promptly celebrated by buying a box of condoms with her pocket money and proceeding to shag any boy in sight.

Danny had agreed to take things slow – make it special. That's why older boys were so much more sophisticated than the kids from school. The only downside to their relationship was her friends – making up stories about him. Imogen frowned and a familiar stomach flip had her reaching for her phone. Surely the rumours about Danny shagging Gloria, and that university student from the Halloween party Imogen had missed were all lies. *None* of the things they said about him were true. Danny had sworn on his mum's life and Imogen believed him.

Propping herself on one elbow, she reached for her phone and scanned notifications, looking for one from Danny, but although loads of her friends and her family had posted on her Facebook and Insta or messaged her, there were no birthday wishes from her boyfriend. She glanced at the time and quashed the flicker of unease that had settled like wiggly worms in her gut. It was still early and she knew that Danny wasn't a morning person. Most days he barely got up before lunch. His message would come later and that would be fine.

Still, she'd expected her mum and dad, wearing party hats, to burst into her room as usual at half-six, blowing cardboard whistles and pulling poppers accompanied by Stevie Wonder's 'Happy Birthday'. She smiled. They must still be making things perfect for her special birthday breakfast. *After all, it's not every day a girl turns sixteen is it?* Conscious of the ever-increasing pressure on her bladder, Imogen distracted herself by scrolling down her phone, smiling and laughing at the birthday memes and photoshopped birthday photos of her with friends and family.

Her smile faded as she realised Danny still hadn't posted a soppy greeting anywhere. Had she missed it? She scrolled back up to the top of her notifications and took her time searching for the one message that meant more than any of the others. But no, it wasn't there. Her earlier excitement trickled away like an hourglass emptying. Her shoulders slumped and she wanted her mum's arms round her holding her tight, the familiar scent of her perfume soothing her. Even though her mum didn't like Danny, she'd tell her that he'd probably got caught up in something. Flicking the duvet back she got up, shoved her feet into her slippers and wandered over to the window.

It was snowing – hard enough to make her think of that stupid Christmas film *Love Actually*. None of her friends admitted to liking it, yet for the past three weeks, they'd watched it together at least once a week. She glanced at her phone again and frowned – 6.45 – what was keeping her parents? This was *so* not like them. Imogen padded over to the door and put her ear to it, listening for signs of activity. Nothing! The house was silent. It was like she was home alone.

She cracked the door open and listened. Again nothing. This was crap. First no message from Danny, then her parents were taking the piss, leaving her upstairs on her own on her special birthday and she really, really needed to wee now. *Sod them!* She flung her bedroom door open till it banged against the wall and strode down the hall to the loo, hoping that her mum and dad would hear and come for her. She yanked the bathroom door open and slammed it closed behind her. *Surely, they'll hear that!*

More comfortable after her wee, Imogen opened the door, certain she'd hear her parents bickering at the bottom of the stairs over who should go first. But again, she was met by silence. Her nose crinkled. *What is that awful stink?* She crept along the hallway, past her parents' room. The door was ajar and their king-size bed was made, the stupid throw cushions precisely placed by the pile of pillows – just as it was every morning. So where were they?

Her stomach clenched as she peered downstairs. The smell seemed stronger now, yet she couldn't identify it. 'Muuum, Daaad. Can I come down now?'

She leaned over the banister and caught sight of a sliver of light from the kitchen. The door wasn't closed. A concrete block lodged in her heart as silence resonated round the house. Imogen tried to swallow, but her throat was too dry. She tried again, before edging to the top of the stairs. 'Mum, Dad. What's going on?'

A draught floated up from below. Goose bumps sprung along her arms and a flicker of unease started behind her neck and made its way down her spine and into her wobbling legs. *Come on, Imogen. You can fucking do this. You're sixteen now – practically an adult, not a wimpy kid.* Forcing herself to breathe slowly, she tiptoed down another couple of stairs, willing her mum to appear from the kitchen. When she reached the bottom step, the smell was more intense. The breeze was stronger now and she realised the back door had been left open. Maybe her mum and dad were in the garden.

A reluctant smile twitched her lips. It would be just like them to build a snowman for her. It wasn't often it snowed on her birthday, and that was just the sort of thing they would do. Why hadn't she thought of that before?

Easing her clenched fingers from the banister, she momentarily regretted letting go when her legs wobbled. Catching her balance, she edged towards the open kitchen door. 'Please, God, let everything be okay.'

She closed her eyes, placed a shaking hand against the shiny paint and pushed the door wider. Before stepping through, she opened her eyes. Her scream when she saw the scene that greeted her pierced the silence . . . and then she turned and ran down the hallway where she struggled to unlock the front door, finally managing and falling out onto the snow-covered path.

Not stopping to breathe or to register the ice on her bare feet, she jumped up, ignoring the tears streaming down her cheeks, and took off over the road to where her neighbour Mrs Patel was de-icing her car.

Chapter 5

Beside her, Queenie stirred and sat upright. Rubbing her eyes, she farted and wiped a streak of saliva from her cheek.

Nice. Jazzy, under cover of opening the driver's side window, cleared her phone screen. She'd spent the last four and a half hours alternating between watching the security recording and tossing her phone back onto the dashboard in frustration, only to pick it up and start the process again seconds later. Her contact hadn't got back to her. Twice she'd had to leave the relative warmth of the car to face the elements and empty her bladder. Of course, none of that was Queenie's fault, but that didn't stop the pulse of resentment settling in her jaw. She could have wakened the other woman at any point. Instead, she'd chosen to simmer in the cold frustration and suppressed energy of enforced inactivity.

She cranked the window wider and looked at the Argy Bargy, hoping Queenie would get the hint and keep quiet. Chance would be a fine thing!

'What's the time?' Queenie peered through the windows at the impending daylight, looking like a rotund dormouse leaving hibernation.

'Nearly half-six.'

'You didn't wake me?'

With a round of slow claps, Jazzy resumed her scrutiny of the silent pub opposite. 'Well observed – you should be a detective.'

'No need to get arsey, Solanki. It wasn't *my* job to wake up, it was yours to wake me. You said you'd give me a couple of hours' kip and then we'd swap. Not my fault if you've gone all martyr, all poor wee me give me a sainthood, all pity me, I'm so hard done by, now, is it?'

Queenie was right. She'd done nothing wrong and Jazzy was being a prize bitch for taking her frustrations out on her. She turned, all set to apologise when Queenie farted again.

'Fuck's sake, Queenie. What've you been eating?'

'Greggs ran out of sausage rolls so I went for one of them vegan ones – bloody toxic for the digestive system. Shame really cause they taste damn good.'

Fingers pinching her nostrils, Jazzy rolled her eyes.

'What were you doing on your phone, JayZee? Looking at porn?'

Jazzy nearly choked on her own spit. Of course, Queenie, sitting sideways on the seat, a crater of sleep lines meandering down one cheek and a grin on her lips, had anticipated Jazzy's outraged reaction. 'Now, now. No need to get your breeks in a fankle, hen. I'm joking.'

She sniffed and scratched her armpit, glancing round the pool car with a puckered brow. 'Mind you, I've no doubt you wouldn't be the first officer to indulge in a fly-solo encounter during a stakeout, if you get my drift.'

Unfortunately, not content to let the euphemism stand on its own merit she elected to elucidate it. 'You know what ah mean, eh? A wee wank, a juicy jerk-off, a torrid todg . . .'

'Queenie!' Jazzy's tone was sharp enough to earn a sulky tut from her companion who then crossed her hands under her breasts and lapsed into silence, glaring out the passenger-side window. *Thank God for that.* Jazzy wasn't sure she could cope with any more of Queenie's nonsense and was happy to sit quietly.

Even on such a short acquaintance, Jazzy should have known better. Queenie was irrepressible.

With a dramatic shudder, the older woman bounced round to face Jazzy. 'Doesn't bear thinking about, does it? I mean who the hell knows what forensics would find if this car was a crime scene?'

'You mean if I was goaded into using one of your knitting needles to eviscerate your brain?'

Queenie ignored Jazzy. 'They'd have a field day . . .'

'. . . I'd stick it right up your nose and into your skull cavity . . .'

Queenie still ignored her. '. . . Just imagine all the bodily fluids soaked into the upholstery . . .'

'. . . I'd plead self-defence, you know?'

'PUS – that's what they'd find – Puke, Urine and Spunk – P.U.S!' Queenie, head bouncing like a nodding dog's, grinned.

'I reckon I'd get away with it too. Bound to be loads of folk who'd testify in my defence. Loads of . . .'

'Get it, JayZee? P.U.S. Puke, Urine, Spu . . .'

Her musings interrupted, Jazzy slapped her hands on the steering wheel. 'For crying out loud, Queenie, can't you just shut up? Just for a single, solitary, isolated nanosecond?'

'Humph. You're no fun, you know? A young lassie like you should have a bit of humour in her bones . . . even if you've got crap taste in men. I mean, Afzal? For God's sake, he's old enough to be your da.' Queenie slapped her hand to her forehead. 'Aw, Yuck. You weren't indulging in a wee bit of phone sex with auld Afzal, were you? I mean . . .' Queenie shuddered, her face scrunched up like a discarded crisp poke.

But Jazzy had had enough. Queenie's obsession with the rumours surrounding her relationship with the chief super were doing her nut in. 'Stop. Right. Now. If you've got nothing kind, nice or informative to say then just don't speak, okay?'

'You're not the boss of me, JayZee Solanki.'

Although she issued the words in a sing-song tone, Jazzy was well aware that Queenie had taken umbrage. Lips set in a tight line, her chin tilted just enough to express her annoyance, Queenie leaned over and extracted her knitting from the bag at her feet. Jazzy sighed. Even the annoying clickety clack of her partner's needles was preferable to her immature mutterings.

Queenie lasted less than five minutes before breaking her silence. 'Anything to report, hen? I mean, I presume nothing much happened when I were in the land of nod, but . . .' She shrugged.

About to chastise Queenie for calling her hen, Jazzy paused, reconsidered and instead provided a succinct update on her overnight observations of the Argy Bargy pub. 'Not a sodding thing – as we expected. The Stùrrach lot aren't daft. They probably made us as soon as we rolled up and we all know this was a punishment more than a fact-finding operation. The only thing I saw was three lads prancing about in the snow before going home. Not long after that the pub lights went off. Nothing since.'

'So, what's got you all crabbit, then? Something to do with what you were looking at on your phone?'

Did the woman never miss a bloody trick? 'Candy Crush, that's all. Lost a life because your farting distracted me – addled my bloody brain, it was so noxious.'

'Náy chance. Your face is tripping you. Something's up!'

Fortunately, Jazzy's mobile vibrated across the dashboard and when she answered it a grin twitched her lips. As their boss, DCI Tony Dick, spoke, Jazzy interjected only with short sentences. 'Yes, boss.'

'No, boss.'

'Straight on it, boss.'

'No, we won't fuck up.'

'Yes, she'll leave them in the car.'

'Don't worry, we're on it.'

Queenie raised her eyebrows. 'Well, you gonna tell me what dickhead said?'

With a triumphant grin, Jazzy gathered up her hair, dragged it back into a ponytail, engaged the clutch, executed a skilful three-point turn and sped through the snow. 'Looks like we're off weed farm duty for now. Caught ourselves a murder a few streets over and, because A and B teams are tossing off elsewhere, we're the only CID team available. This could be our chance to come back in from the cold.'

She flicked her wipers on high as snowflakes flurried before them. 'In more ways than one, with any luck.'

Queenie glanced at her watch and released a blast of air that steamed up in front of her. 'It's nearly half-seven now. Our shift ends at eight.'

'And? You've had nearly a full night's kip, Queenie. Don't you dare fuck this up for me.' Jazzy's tone was snippy. If getting back onto major crimes rather than babysitting a weed farm in the freezing cold meant working double shifts for the next three months, then that's what she'd do.

Queenie sighed. 'If I'm going to be working a double, this better be a juicy serial killer murder at the very least – or an organised crime assassination, or a multiple murder with loads of victims . . .'

'Aw, shut up, Queenie. FYI, it's a double murder and, if the rumours are right, you don't do too well with murder crime scenes, do you? Threw up at your last one, I heard.'

Queenie glared through the blizzard. 'Dodgy bacon butty – that was all.'

Chapter 6

'Oh my God.' The words slipped like a wisp of frigid air from Jazzy's lips as she stepped up to the door leading to the Clark family's kitchen. She stood stock-still as her brain tried to make sense of the macabre tableau before her.

As Queenie stepped close enough for her breasts to jut against her colleague's back, her breath tickled her ear. Standing on tiptoes she peered over Jazzy's shoulder and for a few seconds – long enough to scan the room and take in every ounce of the depravity that had been acted out there – the pair were silent. Then, the force of Queenie spinning away from her followed by a muffled 'Aw Jesus', propelled Jazzy forward. As Queenie stumbled out of the house, hands over her mouth, a desperate wail seeping out from under them, Jazzy grabbed the edge of the door with her gloved hands to steady herself.

With the sounds of Queenie's heaving gips by the crime scene tape trailing after her, Jazzy exhaled a few times, then blocked out everything else as her eyes once more swept the scene. There was only ever one chance to view a crime scene like this intact. One opportunity to view it before the CSIs got truly stuck in and, despite the sensation in her belly like moths fluttering against a light, Jazzy focused on what the scene could reveal.

The bloody slaughterhouse stink didn't bother her. In fact, it wasn't often that she was affected by the dead body stenches that sent other officers – like Queenie – running down wind, hands over their noses and laboured hurling sounds gathering in their throats. That didn't mean that she was immune to the destruction of a human life. On the contrary, the gut clenching had already begun. This was her chance to get in the zone, to imagine what the killer had done, what steps he had taken to stage the scene, how he'd subdued his victims, how he'd gained entry to the property and what his motivation was.

According to Franny Gallagher, the head CSI, the scene had been minimally disturbed prior to being sealed off, apart from confirming death and setting out treads so the scene wouldn't be compromised as people worked. Franny had realised that this wasn't a run-of-the-mill scene and for that Jazzy was grateful. She was aware that what she was witnessing right then was precisely what the killer had wanted the victims' daughter to see and that could indicate that the killer's motivation was personal.

Blood spatter dappled the walls leaving trails drizzling down the paintwork to pool on the floor. The Clark parents, Bob and Shirley, were propped on chairs opposite each other at a beautifully decorated table complete with birthday bunting, sprinkles and party poppers. In centre place stood a decadent, lush chocolate cake complete with a *Happy 16th Birthday* banner and rose petals scattered all around. The candles had burned down to the icing, making multi-coloured lakes across the surface.

The normality of the birthday table up till that point had a mocking feel to it and a cold dread snaked up Jazzy's back. Her breath caught in her throat as she stared in horror. Right then she wished she could join Queenie outside. In fact, she wished she could be back in the car outside the Argy Bargy pub at the edge of the Badlands, the clickety clack of Queenie's knitting needles or her incessant snoring doing her head in, rather than here in this abattoir confronting her wildest nightmare. With closed eyes she tried to banish the memories that flooded her mind in an explosion of colour and smell and noise and fear, but when the images came, they always came with a vengeance over which she had no control. Unable to dislodge it, Jazzy sank into the memory, reliving it for the umpteenth time.

Her heart hammers and her hands shake as she pushes the door. She doesn't want to go in there, but she has to see for herself . . . has to know what's behind the door. The stink hits her as soon as it opens. She stumbles backwards, her hand covering her mouth and nose as she coughs, blinking to overcome the urge to spew her guts. What has she done? She's responsible. She knows that and she doesn't know what to do. Her torchlight darts around the room, casting creepy moving shadows on the walls. Tears stream down her face and her knees quake. She can barely stand up but she's come this far and she needs to see it through because this is her doing.

As the yellowy light lands on the figure, she gasps. It's moving – alive. Has she made a mistake? Can she redeem herself, before it's too late? She lunges towards the bed, towards the heaving, undulating lump that lies there and, as the beam tracks the length of the form on the bed, she opens her mouth to ask if she can help, to ask what she should do, but the words remain lodged in her throat as she blunders backwards away from the writhing mass. Sobs gather in her throat as she tries to make sense of what she sees – clothes pegs, lots of them, on the nose, on the ears, on the lips.

The buzzing increases in volume as her movement alerts a Mexican wave of flies to her presence. They swarm around the room, leaving glistening cauldrons of wriggling maggots in the bloated face that is turned towards her. She drops her torch and in an instant the room is dark, but still the incessant buzzing attacks her ears. She screams, batting her hands about her head as if the bluebottles are attacking her, as if they could mistake her living, breathing body for the dead one lying on the filthy bed.

'DS Solanki. DS Solanki! Are you okay?'

The voice penetrated Jazzy's thoughts and she realised that

she'd covered her head with her arms as if it had been real. Shite, why did that intrusive memory have to choose this particular moment to kick in? She hadn't had a full-on vision for a while and clearly the crime scene, combined with the shock of seeing her stalker return, had triggered this one, and being caught like this was embarrassing. Last thing she wanted was more gossip about her. Not for the first time she cursed her post-traumatic stress.

Come on, Jazzy, pull yourself together. No weakness. Not here. Not at a bloody crime scene and especially not when you're trying to claw your way back up the ranks. With a quick breath to ground herself, she risked a weak smile at the young police officer and in a voice that wobbled only slightly said, 'Fine thanks. Just needed a moment. It's' – she wafted her hands towards the table – 'a lot.'

Judging by the officer's dubious frown, he wasn't convinced, but then neither was Jazzy. *Am I okay? Probably not.* Not if she had allowed herself to be transported back to *that* scene. Not if she could see it as if she were reliving it again and certainly not if it had her cradling her head in her hands to protect it from imaginary blowflies. Not that she'd admit that to anyone. She forced herself to observe the kitchen again. This time she would be detached and professional. No letting her past experiences rattle her. She wasn't a child anymore.

Rather than study the scene as a whole, Jazzy focused on the bodies. Both Bob and Shirley's heads had been detached from their torsos and placed before them on what would once have been pristine white plates, at the table where they now sat. Their heads faced the kitchen door, almost like gargoyles standing guard on the grotesque scene. Had the killer relished the thought of Imogen finding her parents like that? Or had he some other reason for such precise positioning? Sometimes there was no rhyme nor reason for a killer's actions, but in this instance, it felt deliberate, which in turn increased the chances of it being personal to the Clark family. Whether to Imogen, one of the parents or the whole family, Jazzy had yet to determine. It was too early to make any broad, sweeping assumptions.

As she worked, the tightness in her chest and the squirming in her gut faded and she became more convinced that it was designed to torture and destroy the Clarks. The big question remained – was it specifically *this* family that had been targeted or would any family have done? More importantly who would be the next victim? Everything about this crime scene shouted that there would be another similar crime if they didn't catch the killer soon. This sort of detailed, ritualistic murder was rarely an isolated event.

She paused, allowing that thought to mature. This couldn't possibly be the opening gambit for their killer, could it? The detail of this scene yelled practice and skill, not a first outing. But then why wasn't this killer on their radar? She cast her mind back, but she could remember no similar crimes in recent years. That was something she'd mull over in more detail later.

Beheadings were rare and, in the confines of a detached house in a small hamlet like Fauldhouse, these two were even more shocking. However, that wasn't the most disturbing aspect of the scene. What was more shocking and what had triggered Jazzy's earlier reaction was the 'scene setting'. Clothes pegs had been attached to each victim's nose, ears, lips and fingers. Kitchen utensils protruded from their ears – wooden spoons and chopsticks, lengths of fresh spaghetti – presumably either brought to the scene by the killer or retrieved from the fridge – trailed from their mouths. A multitude of cuts – slashes really – covered their bodies and a blood-smeared apple corer lay next to the single eye, which had been gouged from each head. An open tin of beans had toppled over leaving a glutinous mass of orange mixing with the blood.

All of this indicated that the killer had spent time with the victims, possibly before, during *and* after the killings. At the sight of the beans, Jazzy's stomach flipped and, again, she thought she might have to follow Queenie from the house. Ever since she was a child, she'd been unable to eat beans. The very sight of them had her gut contracting and their sickly-sweet smell made her nauseous. Even walking along the bean aisle in a supermarket was torture, although her therapist had encouraged her to try it. Dots of sweat popped out across her brow as Jazzy struggled to concentrate.

She looked away from the orange mess, but what they landed on was worse – the killer had scrawled messages in blood across the victim's foreheads. *For you!* on Mrs Clark's and *Happy Birthday!* on Mr Clark's.

Jazzy's breath hitched and for a crazy moment she wondered if the whole scene was directed at her, but how could it be? The thought rattled in her brain like a loose screw as she flashed back to the black-clad man delivering a rectangular envelope – a birthday card – to her home earlier. She was rattled and thinking irrationally. Thrusting those thoughts away, she considered the messages.

Those had to be directed at the daughter. The killer must have known Imogen would be the one to discover her parents. Now that *was* truly malevolent.

But still, Jazzy's gaze returned to the spilled beans and the pegs. She shook her head and tutted. There were only a few logical answers to the question. Either the messages were specifically aimed at the daughter, Imogen, or they were for the police, or they were for some other random person connected to the killer. An homage, of some sort? Perhaps the entire scene was designed to terrorise the general public, which of course when word got out, it would. The words written in blood were ominous and threatening and Jazzy's heart went out to the daughter. She knew from personal experience that this would have a long-lasting effect on Imogen Clark. How could it not?

There were so many questions juggling for supremacy in Jazzy's head – but for now, she moved to the wider crime scene. The kitchen was clearly the hub of the Clarks' life. The fridge was covered in photos that portrayed a loving family of three – fridge magnets taken at various attractions, scrawled shopping lists and notes attached to the doors. A family planner filled to the brim with activities planned for each of the three family members was filled in different handwriting and in different colours and liberally adorned with love hearts and kisses. A healthy aloe vera plant sat on the windowsill, next to a chubby resin Buddha, and the sink was filled with used baking utensils.

A muddle of shoes tumbled from a wooden crate by the door and three hooks with a pile of coats on each indicated that the family regularly came and went through the back of the house. This flash of insight into the family hardened Jazzy's resolve and she silently promised to find who had taken such enjoyment from destroying them.

Judging from the extensive blood spray, the Clarks had been alive when the beheading had occurred, which again prompted many questions: how could two able-bodied adults be overcome like that? Had they been alive but incapacitated in some way? Did they know their killer? How had Imogen not heard anything? That last point raised suspicions and Jazzy would keep an open mind on that. No weapon had been discovered at the scene so far, although an extensive search in the surrounding area had only just begun. Hopefully the post-mortem would give them more of an idea of what kind of sharp-edged object could do this amount of damage.

She studied their hands, which rested on either side of the plates containing their heads – pegs stuck on the end of each finger, like Edward Scissorhands gone wrong. Jazzy saw no signs that they'd been tied up, but a forensic examination would determine that. Perhaps the killer had brought a weapon to force them into submission, or had they been drugged? And if so, how? The backs of both victims' heads were a mass of matted blood, so it was reasonable to assume that they had been hit over the head at some point. Again, the PM would clarify if that had been enough to knock them out. Hopefully they had been unconscious when the actual beheading took place.

Directing her question to Franny, the CSI manager, Jazzy nodded towards the closed kitchen door. 'Was it locked?'

'Nope, we're assuming the killer left that way – might even have entered through there too. The front door alarm was on, although the motion sensors were disengaged. No idea whether it was the Clarks who set it like that or the killer. In the snow we found footprints with blood traces in the tread, but of course this damn blizzard is doing a grand job of obscuring things. Touch and go if we'll get a decent print, but we've got images at least and we'll do our best despite the weather. Maybe when Dr Johnston arrives, he'll be able to tell you more.'

Jazzy hoped Lamond Johnston, the pathologist, would arrive before the powers that be designated a senior investigating officer and sidelined her from the case. She nodded. Franny was an excellent CSI and the scene was in good hands. With a mental note to have CCTV, home security footage and a canvas of the back and the front of the house underway before the SIO was appointed, Jazzy began to consider what the victims themselves could tell her.

A shudder rattled up her spine as she studied Bob and Shirley Clark. What sort of monster would do this to two people about to celebrate their daughter's birthday? What would make someone leave this scene so carefully set out for a young girl to discover? At sixteen, Imogen Clark would carry that with her forever. In a little corner of Imogen's heart, a frisson of fear would always remain. She'd find it hard to trust and to feel safe ever again and the life she had imagined for herself when she went to bed last night would be irrevocably altered.

Which brought Jazzy back to a persistent niggling thought – a question that would have to be addressed sooner rather than later. One that would be on every officer's lips and one that made a solid weight form in Jazzy's gut because she didn't want to go there. She never wanted to go to that sort of place ever again. Still, she had to consider why the girl hadn't been wakened by what took place downstairs. Surely there would have been some noise. Hadn't her parents cried out when confronted by the intruder – unless of course it was someone they knew? Or perhaps they were told that if they made any noise their daughter would be next.

Jazzy hoped that Imogen Clark would be available for interview soon. Time was of the essence and although her heart broke for the girl, they had a job to do.

Aware that the sickly fluttering sensations in her gut were making their way up to her chest, Jazzy took a deep breath and entered the kitchen fully, taking care to stick to the metal treads. 'Franny, your team can start processing the perimeter of the room, I want to have a last look round, then I'll get out of your hair.'

Two unidentifiable members of the forensics team – one with a camera, the other carrying a tool kit – entered behind Jazzy as she stepped forward. This sort of scene got to everyone and an absence of the usual crime scene banter showed how much everyone was affected. As she was currently in disgrace, Jazzy wouldn't be allowed to keep this investigation as her own, but she'd damn well hand over a full and accurate report to whichever poor sod inherited it.

Behind her, someone entered the room and Jazzy was relieved to recognise Dr Johnston. A tall man, certainly almost as tall as Jazzy herself who nearly hit the six-foot mark, he was prone to stooping. Whether this was because he spent a lot of time with his head angled down to hear other people's muffled mumbles behind their crime scene masks or some other reason, Jazzy didn't know. 'Hey, Doc. I'm glad you're here. This one's bloody and dark and very disturbing.'

Lamond Johnston pulled his mask over his nose, his grey eyes moving from Jazzy to the two dead bodies at the table before he replied, his voice deadpan. 'Didn't know we were invited to a party, Jasmine. Whose birthday is it? Yours?'

Behind her mask, Jazzy offered a half-hearted laugh and hoped he wouldn't notice the way the blood leached from her cheeks. She'd long since giving up telling him to call her Jazzy, so throwing off her disquiet at his birthday comment, she shrugged and stepped aside so he could approach the bodies. Whilst he focused on the dead couple, Jazzy cast her eyes round the room. The daughter had been taken to St John's and was being treated for shock, but PC Conrad Lee, the first attending officer, had managed to ask her a few questions before the paramedics sedated her. According to him, Imogen had been waiting, as per the family tradition, for her parents to escort her downstairs for her birthday breakfast. Her neighbour, a Mrs Sonal Patel, had, after checking that Imogen wasn't imagining things, phoned the police. Apparently, she hadn't disturbed the scene either.

Realising she could gain no more information from remaining in the kitchen, Jazzy left the CSIs and the pathologist with a: 'You'll let us know when the PM is, won't you, Lamond?'

Unable to shake the dark cloud that hung over her, Jazzy's mind buzzed with everything she'd learned. She had a lot to think about and needed space to sift through what was and wasn't relevant.

Chapter 7

Jazzy had taken two steps along the carpeted hallway when she heard her boss, DCI Dick's, voice. *Dick by name and dick by nature.* His piercing tone shattered the ambient soundtrack of CSIs intent on gathering potential evidence and processing the scene that presented as a hum of activity behind her.

'For God's sake, Queenie, don't tell me you puked your load again. You better not have compromised the crime scene, for it would almost – but not quite – break my heart to send you back to uniform. God, I'm not sure even the minions would bloody want you after needle-gate. Hardly your finest hour, was it?'

Jazzy felt a degree of sympathy for Queenie. Nobody enjoyed being rollicked in public, but being rollicked by DCI Tony Dick took the term to an entirely new ballpark – generally one that encompassed a five-mile radius and left a noxious atmosphere behind, long after the main event. Yep, definitely Dick by name and dick by nature. Taking a moment to order her thoughts and steady her nerves before facing her boss's scrutiny, Jazzy exhaled, flung her shoulders back and, throwing off the tiredness of her sleepless night, she raised her chin. She had the height advantage and she was prepared to use it.

Jazzy approached the front door, mentally ticking off each

action she had initiated in the absence of a senior investigating officer. Dickish Dick would scrutinise every one of them – not to make sure that the investigation was progressing as it should, but solely to catch her out. Prior to her fall from grace, Jazzy would have assumed the SIO role and fought tooth and nail to keep it. However, her demotion to detective constable meant that she was currently operating above her rank. She hoped that being the most experienced officer on site would earn her some leeway from Dick. After all, in the absence of a DS, he'd sent *her* here to oversee the scene. It wasn't her fault all the other major crimes teams were swanning off around the district, was it?

As she exited the house, she became aware of the man accompanying Dick. Crap! Chief Superintendent Waqas Afzal was the last person she'd expected to encounter here. Her feet faltered as she stepped down the stairs and onto the front path. Aware that her usual giveaway blush was rapidly warming her cheeks, Jazzy swallowed hard, wishing the ground would open and swallow if not her, then definitely the chief super. This public encounter would be scrutinised by everyone present and her blush would confirm their worst suspicions and add fire to the burning inferno of innuendo that followed her everywhere.

Both men were dressed in golf gear, although Afzal carried his green checked trousers with a lot more class than Dick did his pink ones. They'd probably planned on some indoor golf practice followed by lunch at Bistro 19 in Harburn later on. When she looked beyond the two men, she noticed that Afzal's BMW was parked down the road, thus explaining his presence at the crime scene. Jazzy yanked her hood down and pulled her mask away from her mouth, so it hung from one ear, and tried to ignore the fact that her heart was beating double time.

She sensed the eyes of every officer in the vicinity scouring her demeanour, trying to work out if the rumours about her and the big boss were true. Queenie was no exception. Her gimlet eyes lasered onto Jazzy as she simultaneously shuffled backwards as if distancing herself from her partner – or maybe she was just standing down wind of Dick's overpowering aftershave. With her eyes fixed somewhere just to the right of her boss's head, Jazzy ignored the senior officer and greeted DCI Dick. 'Good morning, sir. I'm happy to talk you through what we've found and the actions I've instructed.'

Dick was short with a rounded, soft belly and he walked with the rolling gait of a man trying to bulk himself widthways to compensate for his lack of height. With a scowl he pursed his lips, causing his substantial moustache to wiggle under his nose like a caterpillar suffering an epileptic fit. 'I bloody hope you've got everything under control, Solanki. Those were my express orders to you not . . .' he glanced at his oversized, knock-off Rolex '. . . an hour ago, if you remember?'

Jazzy risked a glance at Queenie who, out of Dick's line of vision, rolled her eyes and alternated between making slashing motions across her throat and pointing first at DCI Dick and then at his companion, a maniacal grimace on her face. Uncertain whether her colleague was warning her to stop talking or directing her to kill both their bosses, Jazzy ignored her.

'Hear we've got a right one here, Solanki. A *beheading* and on *my* bloody watch to boot. Disgrace. It's a bloody disgrace.' Dick glared at Jazzy, his mouth curled up in a snarl as if she were personally to blame for the atrocities visited upon the Clark family.

Dick by name, dick by nature! If the circumstances had been different, Jazzy would have laughed out loud at her boss's horrified emphasis on the word 'beheading' and his farcical outrage. She glanced around, avoiding meeting the super's gaze and saw that a group of journalists were gathering outside the outer cordon at the end of the road. Having been scalded recently by their immoral tactics of using enhanced microphones to pick up private conversations, she edged closer to her boss and lowered her voice. 'If you want to come in, sir, I'll walk you and the chief super . . .' she flicked a quick glance at Afzal '. . . through the crime scene.'

Dick's moustache foxtrotted above his lip as he spoke. 'The bodies been removed, yet?'

Jazzy shook her head. 'Not yet. Soon as transport turns up and Lamond is happy for them to be transported to the morgue, I'll get on that.'

'Lamond? Lamond? Who the bloody hell's that?'

Dick knew exactly who Lamond was, but Jazzy took a deep breath, refusing to rise to the bait. 'The pathologist, Dr Johnston. His friends call him Lamond, because that's his name.'

'Hmph, ridiculous. The man's spent bloody years grafting to get where he is and he lets you lot call him by his first name. Familiarity breeds contempt, Solanki. You heard that saying? Not something I'll allow on my ship. That's how you lose the respect of your inferiors.'

Still conscious of Queenie's vomiting actions behind him, Jazzy swallowed the words that sprung to her lips – *Inferiors my arse* – and instead said, 'I thought that with no SIO on site yet, you'd like to see the victims in situ.'

Eyes narrowed, Dick growled. 'You're the temporary acting SIO, Solanki – *very* temporary, you know – and only because I've no one else free to take up the mantle. So, get those damn bodies out of there and *then* we'll go in.'

Jazzy's mouth fell open and a swell of anger started at her toes and gained momentum as it surged up to her chest and exited her mouth. '*Damn bodies?*'

The words left her lips in a soft but firm whisper and although she was aware of Queenie dancing up and down behind the two senior officers, repeating her earlier frantic 'cut it' movements, her anger would not be quelled. Her inability to rein it in was, if she'd taken a moment to consider, one of the reasons she was in her current position in the first place. Her voice increased in volume and she took a step towards Dick. '*Damn* bodies? *God*, you'd think you'd at least show some *respect*. The Clark family have been *destroyed*. A teenage girl's life has been *devastated*. She's seen her parents with their heads *removed*. She's a now an *orphan* and *you're* referring to them as "damn bodies". Don't you have even a modicum of decen—'

Superintendent Afzal interrupted her. 'I'm sure that DC Solanki is overwrought at what she's just witnessed, Tony. Who wouldn't be? I know I would.'

Jazzy opened her mouth to say, *He wouldn't be. Fucking DCI Dick clearly wouldn't be*, but Afzal wafted his hand at her and that, combined with Queenie's grimace, made her bite her lip. Huge gasping breaths clogged her throat and made her chest throb. She'd done it again. She'd fucking done it again. *When the hell will I learn?* Worse still though, now that Afzal had intervened, he'd added even more fuel to the rumour mill about their relationship and secondly, never mind Queenie ending up back in uniform, Jazzy would beat her to it.

She'd shot herself in the foot. She *really* wanted to be a part of this investigation, but no way would that happen now. Not when she'd argued so vehemently with her boss and criticised his attitude to boot. It was this stubborn, quick-to-anger attitude that had landed her partnered with Queenie. Now the pair of them would be traipsing the streets of Livingston like some bloody Little and Large throwback act.

Afzal threw her another lifeline. 'You've been on night shift all night, Solanki? You must be tired. Credit to you that you took this on so near the end of your shift. You should go and get some kip. When you come back later on – say 3 p.m. – we'll have an SIO in place, and I'm sure you and . . .' He turned to Queenie, a slight frown troubling his brow as he tried to place her.

'. . . DC McQueen, sir. You can call me Queenie.'

Jazzy looked on in amazement as Queenie all but genuflected in front of Afzal, her face all round smiles and bonhomie.

'Eh, aye, that's right.' Afzal directed the rest of his sentence at Jazzy, but kept his gaze firmly on DCI Dick. 'DCs McQueen and Solanki have done such a good job here, I'm sure they'll prove to be valuable assets in this investigation, isn't that right, Tony?'

Whilst Queenie punched the air and mouthed the words 'get in', Jazzy clenched her fists by her sides and tried to ignore the building frustration in her chest. What the hell was he playing at? Didn't he realise that he was fuelling even more tittle-tattle and making it harder for her to blend in with her co-workers? She was able to fight her own battles. There was no need for him to flounce in, throwing his weight about and infantilising her.

Chin up, she glanced at DCI Dick, expecting to see anger and resentment in his expression. Instead, he was studying her, a slight frown tugging his brows together, his face inscrutable. As she angled her body away from Afzal, effectively distancing herself from him, Jazzy met Dick's gaze without flinching. 'I'm sorry, sir.' She bit her lip for good measure and looked down. 'It's just the scene in there is bad – really bad. Obviously, I'm happy to do whatever is best for the investigation. I know swapping rotas can be a real pain. Queenie and I will work wherever you direct us to.'

Queenie's frown showed her displeasure, but Jazzy didn't care. This wasn't about her relationship with her partner – she had only worked with Queenie for a short time. This was about her reputation and she had to disentangle herself from the rumours linking her to the chief super. That was the only way she could gain the respect of her colleagues and the only way she could continue to work here in West Lothian and specifically out of the Livingston station.

However, Afzal wasn't finished, yet. He clicked his fingers and a smile spread across his face. 'Your teams are so busy with Operation Thistledown at the moment, maybe this is your chance to see some action, Tony. I know your remit is to coordinate major crimes, but let's face it, this is an emergency and it's good to keep your hand in. *You* can be SIO on this one and I'm sure these two officers are eager to redeem themselves after their unfortunate demotions. You can head up D team on this investigation.' He slapped Dick on the back, making the shorter man stagger a little.

'Show the youngsters you've still got what it takes, eh, Tony?'

For a nanosecond the silence was deafening, then DCI Dick nodded and smiled at his boss, the throbbing pulse at his temple the only indication of his annoyance. 'Sure thing, Waqas. Give me a chance to whip D team into shape, eh?'

'Well, that's settled then. Good job. I'm sure you'll solve this in record time.'

Jazzy had her doubts about that. In her experience, DCI Tony Dick wasn't a team player and she desperately wanted to pull the super to the side and beg him to give the SIO job to anyone but Dick. Fortunately, for once, sanity prevailed. However, there was no way she would let Dick fuck up this investigation. No bloody way.

A momentary flicker at his lips made Jazzy think that perhaps he could read her thoughts. As he continued to study her, his sharp eyes raking into her soul, Jazzy wondered if perhaps she had been wrong in her assessment of him. Perhaps *Dick by name, dick by nature* wasn't as vacuous as he first appeared.

He gave an abrupt nod. 'Okay, best start as we mean to go on. You and McQueen fill in your report from your surveillance in Stùrrach and from this scene then go get some kip. I expect you back at 3 p.m. sharp. There's a lot to do.'

'Shall I walk you through the crime scene before I go, sir?'

He laughed. 'I think the chief super and I are experienced enough to walk ourselves through a crime scene; besides the CSIs are here if we have questions.'

With an abrupt nod, Jazzy spun on her heel and strode back towards their parked car, Queenie jogging behind her.

Chapter 8

Jazzy's infuriation with her senior officers combined with disgust at the neighbours' ghoulishness sent a sharp punch of anger to her belly, and as she approached the crime scene tape she studied the gathering crowd and shuddered. The looky-loos may take great pleasure in standing on the perimeter of the crime scene, mugs of tea and mobiles in their hands, but they'd never have to see the horror that she'd just witnessed. Often, the perpetrator of a violent crime like this one returned to the scene, intent on getting as much gratification as they could. Sometimes they went so far as to inveigle their way into the investigation, usually as 'key' witnesses or the like. Of course, it was impossible to discern the onlookers' motivations just by sight; still there were actions that could be taken in case, further into the investigation, a link was made between an observer and the killer.

She turned to Sergeant Hobson, who was monitoring entry and exit to the crime scene. 'Get video of these idiots, will you, Wullie and repeat it every so often, so we don't miss anyone.' She lowered her voice. 'You know what they say about those sick fuckers returning to the scene of the crime.'

With a scowl at the excitable group on the other side of the tape, Wullie nodded. 'My bloody pleasure. They're doing ma head in with their nonsense – it's not a bloody West End show we've got going on here. Insensitive bastards, the lot of them. Leave it with me, I'll get one of the constables to do a wee trek around the perimeter to ensure we get them all on file. Just in case.'

He lowered his voice so only Jazzy could hear. 'You notice the journos have got wind of it too? At least two lots have turned up from the *Daily Record* and the *Scotsman* as well as a wheen of freelancers. They're doing the rounds questioning the neighbours and trying to entice one of the younger uniforms to spill the beans.' He puffed up his massive chest and grinned. 'But, I've got them too well trained. Their lips are zipped. There'll be no leaks from my crew – you can bet your arse on that one, DS Solanki.'

Jazzy blinked, a strange prickle in her eyelids. She knew that Wullie was aware of her demotion, yet had chosen to address her by her previous rank because he rated her. His show of solidarity was unexpected, yet appreciated. She reached over and squeezed his arm. 'Thanks, Wullie. I owe you one.'

But the big officer shook his head. 'Nay chance, boss. Just doing my job.' And he lifted the tape so she and Queenie could slip under it.

'What was all of that about? All that touchy-feely crap with Wullie? He's a married man you know, plus he's gay. You've no chance with him.'

Jazzy scowled and, refusing to give Queenie the satisfaction of a response, brushed past. But Queenie wasn't finished needling her. 'You couldn't have just gone along with the chief super, could you? You know, accepted his get-out plan gracefully, grabbed the olive branch with both hands, smiled sweetly and said thanks?'

Jazzy braked and spun round, glaring at Queenie. 'No, no and no. I won't accept a single thing from him, got it?'

Queenie blew out her cheeks and took a step back. 'Whoa. Yes, I get it. *Comprendez. Verstehen.* Understood.' She sidestepped Jazzy and marched through the slush to the pool car and climbed in without another word, slamming the door behind her.

'A disagreement between colleagues, DS, or should I say, *DC* Solanki?' The voice was smarmy and intrusive.

Jazzy turned and regarded the man standing behind her. She pegged him as a journalist as much by his well-worn suit and unzipped parka as by the latest iPhone gripped in his gloveless hand. 'You can ask what the hell you want, but all you'll get is "no comment".'

She made to sidestep him but, anticipating this, he shimmied in front of her. 'You're not really in a position to lord it over me, now are you? I mean not with your demotion and your relegation to the dunces' team. Who knows what other scandals a diligent reporter might be able to dig up about Jasmine Solanki, eh? Maybe it'd be in *your* best interests to give me a soundbite now, might be enough to keep me at bay for a while, if you get my drift?'

He moved closer, crowding her, the smell of peppermint fresh on his breath, and an upmarket cologne on his skin. Jazzy, nose to nose with him, took a moment to study his features – dark brooding eyes, heavy brows, clean-shaven – not altogether handsome, but not plug-ugly either. A slow sneer slid across her face. This was Philip Jamieson, the freelance reporter who was indirectly responsible for her demotion. He'd made a quick buck from eavesdropping on her private conversation with the chief super and selling the subsequent pictures of her slapping Afzal to the *Daily Record*.

God, I want to smack that smirk off your arrogant face! Aware of the interested observers nearby, some of whom were fellow journalists desperate for a headline, Jazzy contented herself with flexing her fingers – for now.

Both taller and wider than her, Jamieson edged even closer, his intent to intimidate, but what he hadn't counted on was Jazzy's stubborn inability to kowtow to anyone, far less the journalist who'd thrown her into the public eye for a while. Instead of backing off, she edged forward, her eyes glued to his, her breasts just skimming the fabric of his coat and, with a grin, she aimed her heavy boot at his foot and stamped down hard. 'Get out of my face, you little scrotum.'

A soft female northern voice made Jazzy turn her head as she backed away from Jamieson who was hopping about on one foot. A slender woman in a bobble hat and huge padded full-length coat stood, hands on hips, glaring at Jamieson. 'Don't tell me you're using your old tricks to try to get a rise out of a police officer again, Philip? It's reporters like you that give us conscientious ones a bad name. Why don't you slither back under your stone and let the rest of us report responsibly about this tragedy, eh?'

'Aw, fuck off, Ginny. Your sanctimonious crap's wearing thin. You're just jealous you didn't manage to snap those pics of her and her sugar daddy.'

Wullie, approaching Jamieson, used his bulk to force the journalist away from Jazzy. In a deep growl that brooked no argument, he said to Jamieson, 'If I see you anywhere near this scene, laddie, I'll haul you in. Got it?'

Jamieson glared at Jazzy then splayed his arms and backed off. 'Okay, okay, big man. I'll keep my distance, but I'll not be moving from here. It's my right to stand on a public pathway *and* it's my duty to report on this investigation to the public.'

'Aye, but you mind and stay away from the officers. If I see you hassling them, I'll make it my business to pull you in on obstruction charges.' As Jamieson sidled away, Wullie grinned at Jazzy before ambling back to his spot on the other side of the tape.

'He's an arse.' The swaddled journalist held out a hand. 'Ginny Bell – and I mean Jamieson, not your burly sergeant.'

Jazzy ignored her extended hand. 'I'm telling you the same thing I told Jamieson. No comment. There'll be a press briefing later, so you'll have to wait for that.'

'Oh, God, no. I'm not going to waste my time asking for a quote from you. I know it's too early for that. I just saw Fuckface Phil hassling you and thought I'd offer some moral support, that's all. You know, woman to woman and all that?'

With a shrug that implied 'whatever', Jazzy continued to the car. Journalists pissed her off at the best of times, but having to interact with two of them in a matter of minutes was pushing her patience too far. She yanked the driver's door open and got in, meeting Queenie's questioning gaze with an eye-roll. 'Bloody intrusive parasites. Don't ask.'

But just before the car door slammed shut, Ginny Bell's 'See you around, DC Solanki' rang out and, in her rear-view mirror, she saw Jamieson hovering, face like thunder, his fingers clenched into fists as he watched her.

Chapter 9

It's clichéd, I know – coming back to the crime scene, that is, but like plenty of other sociopaths before me, that's exactly what I've done. I've not come back to get my rocks off. Nothing as crass as that. No, I've come back to make sure that my plan is playing out as it should. Of course it is, and that's no more than I expect really. I mean why wouldn't it? My plans have a habit of unfolding like clockwork. They always have. Ever since I was little I was able to manipulate situations so that what I wanted to happen actually did. Society at large considers it a curse or a blight. Something that needs curbing, but they're wrong. It's a blessing, whether from above or not I'm still not convinced, but it's gift, nonetheless.

Once, a long time ago, when I was younger and less experienced at hiding what I really am, a therapist – a fat old guy with a paunch, halitosis and false teeth that wobbled when he talked – guessed my guilty secret. We skirted around my diagnosis for a while. It was like taking part in a macabre dance. I looked forward to our sessions.

He asked me about my necklace. Suggested it gave me comfort and, at the time, I just smiled. In those days, I didn't carry it for comfort. No, it was a reminder. A reminder of the betrayal.

56

Of course, over the years its significance has altered for me. It still reminds me of my past and my aims, but its familiarity is a comfort and God knows, I've had few of those over the years.

I stamp my feet, to keep the circulation going, glad of my gloves and jacket. It's exceptionally cold and even the buzz that Jazzy Solanki rolling up to the house gave, isn't enough to keep me warm. I watch as she goes in with her dumpy buddy in tow and a grin spreads across my face. Good job my scarf's round my mouth. No point in upsetting the equilibrium. I've learned that nobody likes those 'out of the box' jarring reactions. But, safe in my disguise, my mind's at liberty to imagine revisiting my work with DC Solanki like a fly on the wall.

She'll be by the door now, looking in at the scene, trying to get inside my head – good luck with that, Jazzy. Oh wow, can you believe it? The dumpy one's given up already. I laugh, but when I sense the punter beside me watching me, I turn it into a hacking cough and bang my hand on my chest, like that'll sort it out. At least Old Dumpy made it past the inner crime scene tape. Wouldn't do for a police officer – especially not one as experienced as DC Annie McQueen – to foul the scene. You'd think after what happened to her daughter she'd have a stomach of steel, but apparently not.

I sidle away further into the crowd and return to my musings. Jazzy will be wondering what it all means and, hopefully, my little homage will trigger all sorts of emotions, but will they spot the link? The thing I've brought to the scene and left there, looking inconsequential near the periphery, or will they focus on each carefully placed item, every perfectly orchestrated placement to the detriment of their understanding of me? Oh, I do hope so, otherwise where will I get my fun?

A stir at the periphery of the crime scene tape attracts my attention and again the temptation to laugh out loud is strong, but I hold it in as a flurry of uniformed offers fuss around, moving cars and making space for Superintendent Afzal's BMW. This is so much better than I anticipated. DCI Tony Dick and Afzal fall out of the vehicle, their stupid country club trousers visible below their coats showing that the old boys' network is still up and running. I shake my head. Pretentious arses. Still, their presence definitely spices things up and, right on cue, Jazzy comes out of the Clarks' house, her flushed face revealing altogether too much of what she's feeling.

Brilliant! I couldn't have planned it any better.

Chapter 10

The atmosphere on the drive back to Livingston police station was as frigid as the weather outside, the coldness accentuated by the clipped clickety clack of Queenie's knitting needles, reminiscent of icicles snapping and impaling unsuspecting victims. Judging by the venomous glances lobbed Jazzy's way, *she* was the prime candidate for having a skewer plunged through her skull. She only hoped Queenie wouldn't see fit to replicate 'needle-gate' with her. Several surreptitious glances confirmed Jazzy's worry that, in her anger, Queenie had forgotten that the sleeve she was furiously taking her frustration out on was already far too long. Jazzy hoped her colleague wouldn't notice her mistake until she had calmed down.

As the snow turned to a persistent drizzle, Jazzy took the A71 through West Calder, and past Bellsquarry, her home village. She'd checked her burner phone to see if she'd had a reply about her stalker, but it remained ominously quiet. Although that was frustrating, her mind was still full of her argument with the dick-less wonder, the crime scene and the fact that Afzal had thrown her and Queenie a bone. She navigated the myriad of streets that wove through residential areas of Livingston and headed towards the police station, which adjoined the sheriff courts. As she drove the tyres threw up mucky slush and the people scurrying about doing their day-to-day business looked frozen. Even the bright Christmas lights festooning some of the gardens as they passed couldn't lift the mood.

Caught at traffic lights, Jazzy rolled her shoulders in the hope of releasing the tension that exacerbated the throb at the base of her spine. She and Queenie had been on duty for five hours past their shift end and the seventeen hours on duty, combined with the previous sleepless day, left Jazzy's eyes grainy and her head almost too heavy for her slender neck. She longed to be back home snuggled up in her king-sized bed. Yet, after what she'd witnessed today at the crime scene, plus her nocturnal visitor and the subsequent clamour of thoughts, she doubted she'd be able to sleep anyway. Besides which, by the time she and Queenie had completed their paperwork and got back to their respective homes, it would hardly be worthwhile trying to catch some shut-eye. The most she'd manage would be a catnap, which would have to suffice for now. After all she was well used to operating on little sleep.

However, it wasn't just tiredness that troubled Jazzy. The entire crime scene was etched in her mind, like a zombie film gone wrong. It wasn't only the horrific brutality of the scene that had put her on edge. She'd seen scenes like these before and, although you didn't get used to them, you did somehow compartmentalise them. You had to or else you'd never survive in the job. No, it was something more than that, something on the periphery of her thoughts – a deep and hollow uneasiness that she just couldn't shift. She wished she could shelve the niggle that made her wonder if there was a connection between their stakeout at Stùrrach, her nocturnal visitor, the coincidence of a shared birthday and the Clarks' brutal murder.

As she set off again, Jazzy risked breaking the silence. 'What did you make of the crime scene, Queenie?'

Queenie's clickety clacking increased in tempo for a few seconds, before slowing down again. She sniffed and, with deliberation, looped yarn round the needles and continued to clickety-clack her way to an even more lopsided jumper. 'How am I supposed to know? I was only in there for a second, before that dodgy prawn salad from last night forced me to vacate the scene.'

Jazzy's lips twitched at the blatant lie, but rather than confront her partner, who was notoriously bad at holding down her lunch at the more gruesome crime scenes, she decided to reveal her trump card. 'You know as well as I do, Queenie, that in spite of your dodgy gut, you have a very peculiar skill that means you retain photographic impressions of a scene after viewing it for mere seconds.'

The clickety sounds halted with an abruptness that told Jazzy she'd hit her mark. Thrusting her needles and jumper onto her lap, Queenie edged round to glare at Jazzy. 'What the fuck? You been checking up on me?'

Jazzy grinned. 'You did your due diligence on me, Queenie. Raking up all that crap about my private life earlier wasn't fun – so you can hardly moan about *me* doing due diligence on you. When you're working nights with a new partner, especially in the arse end of nowhere, near an unpredictable community, it pays to know if you can rely on them. If they'll have your back in a crisis. Besides, it's not as if your highly superior autobiographical memory constitutes a national secret.'

'Hmph, maybe fucking not, but it's *my* secret to share – or not. *My* business, *my* private thing, not something to be handed out willy-nilly like tablet on bonfire night.' She paused, shrugged and continued to glower at Jazzy. 'Who the fuck was it?'

'Eh?'

'Which of the disloyal wee scrotes plied you with private information about me? Was it that wee bawbag Fenton Heggie? Useless wee scrote that he is. His heid's full of mince.' She paused and shook her head. 'Nah, Haggis. His head's full of fucking haggis. Heggie the Haggis heid. Haggis, that's what I'll call the disloyal wee arsewipe from now on.'

DC Fenton Heggie was a fairly new member of D team and was the butt of most people's jokes because he was so short. Jazzy had always found him to be reliable and what he didn't know about IT wasn't worth knowing. About to deny the boy's culpability, Jazzy was interrupted. 'Nah, I bet it was that useless gangly shite McBurnie. Back-stabbing bastard. Bloody Judas with a quiff. Brutus in brogues – it was him, wasn't it? You can tell me. I'll sort him out for gossiping like an auld wifie.' Her eyes flashed at Jazzy, her mouth twisted, her chin raised and pointy as her entire body trembled with anger and she dared Jazzy to deny it.

'No, of course not. Nobody told me. I've got eyes, you know, Queenie – and I can read. It was mentioned in the report about "needle-gate". Seems you got away with that stunt *mainly* because you cited your verified "Highly Superior Autobiographical Memory" as justification for managing to identify the culprit *months* after seeing him for a *nano*second as he fled the scene of a rape. *That's* what got you merely demoted rather than turfed out on your sizeable arse. Well, that and the fact that you copped to accidentally taking your knitting needle with you only because you were knitting whilst you should have been monitoring a block of flats in Craigshill for a suspected dealer.'

'You looked at my appeal? You went to the bother of chasing down the transcript of my appeal and then ogling it?'

Glad that she didn't have to meet Queenie's eye because she was driving, Jazzy shrugged.

'And what the hell do you mean – sizeable arse? My hubby describes my arse as pert, curvy . . . comfortably rounded. Not bloody sizeable . . . You should take a look at your own backside. You're not exactly Ms Sylph-like yourself. You might think you look like bloody Priyanka Chopra with your long thick lashes and plumped-up pouty lips, and hair down to your thighs, but you're carting some weight around the arse, hen. Anyway, what are you . . . bloody ten feet tall? Cheeky bloody cow disparaging *my* butt. If you laid off the bloody chocolate, you might not have such hefty hips.'

Jazzy had hoped her comment would divert Queenie away from the issue of her prying into her past record – not that she regretted it – it was useful to know that Queenie possessed such a skill. She just hadn't expected to have to reveal her knowledge so early in their partnership, but it was time now to wind things back in. If they were to work together they needed to be on speaking terms. Besides, over the last few hours, farting and knitting notwithstanding, the older woman was beginning to grow on Jazzy. 'Your hubby's right, Queenie. Your arse is just right – perfect some might say, as is mine, right?' She waited till Queenie gave a reluctant nod before continuing, 'But that's not what I want to talk to you about.'

She pulled into Hochsauerland Brae, which led to the police station. After driving through the barrier that separated employee parking from the public area, Jazzy edged the car into a bay, switched off the engine and turned to Queenie. 'Tell me your impressions of that crime scene, Queenie.'

'What, the high and mighty Jasmine Solanki – now a mere, newly demoted DC – wants *my* input? *You* want *me* to resurrect that bloody memory?' She exhaled a whoosh of air strong enough to steam up the windscreen. 'Don't you get what it's like for me, Jazzy? It's not a bloody stroll in Beecraigs Park, you know?'

As she thrust her wool into her bag, Queenie's voice lowered to the point that Jazzy had to strain to hear her. Not only that, there was a tremor to it that made Jazzy kick herself for upsetting the woman. 'I live with this *every* day. I can't just un-forget things and I have to work damn hard to compartmentalise the crappy stuff. I can't just drop a memory whenever I feel like it – you get me? It's exhausting. Dealing with them all, barricading them behind other nicer, more pleasant memories isn't fucking easy. That's why my face is as wrinkled as a chimpanzee's bahoochie. It's the bloody strain. It's a wonder Craig can bear to look at me.

He's a bloody saint that man. A bloody saint.'

She raised her head and met her partner's gaze, allowing the rawness of her emotion to slice Jazzy like a knife. Jazzy reached over and squeezed her arm. 'Shit, I'm sorry, Queenie. I didn't stop to think, I just—'

But Queenie interrupted. 'No, I know you didn't think. No fucker thinks.'

'I know, Queenie. I can see how it must be wearing. I should have been more sensitive.'

But it was as if Queenie had retreated inside herself, Jazzy's words not registering, so wrapped up in her anguish as she continued, 'And, you know what?'

She glared at Jazzy, her face ashen, her strangely spiky hair almost vibrating with the anger and frustration that played out across her face, making her shoulders shrug up till they almost touched her ears. 'It's the fucking pits, JayZee. The fucking absolute, abysmally dire, disgustingly frightening, horrifically gruesome pits. And . . .' She raised a finger in the air. 'It's not just that scene! Oh no, not a fucking chance that it's only that singular, isolated, barbaric scene that I have to contend with. Oh, fuckity doo dah no. It's *every* damn scene I've ever set eyes on . . . The car crash near Bellsquarry roundabout where the auld wifie with Alzheimer's lost her husband of sixty fucking years. She kept asking again and again where her Rabbie was. It's the decapitated kids at Linlithgow Loch and the way their parents fell to the ground in a heap when they heard the news. The pulped body of the old bloke over in Armadale, offed just so some scrote could buy MDMA . . . Every one of them comes flooding back into my head when I least expect it.'

She inhaled, her entire body shuddered and a single tear rolled down her cheek. 'Every sodding one of them lives with me.' Her head sank further into her body, bowed forward, and then without warning she began pummelling her head with her fisted hands. 'AND I CAN'T FUCKING UNSEE ANY OF THEM.'

Her breath came in huge rasping gasps that rent the air and made Jazzy wonder if her colleague's inner chest wall was gauged to shreds with each inhalation. 'I'm sorr—.'

'Don't you dare. Don't you fucking dare with the "I'm sorries". They mean sweet Fanny Adams to me. You're just like the rest of them; all you want is to use me and then when I make one little slip-up with a knitting needle – a slip-up that took a scrote off the streets, I remind you – you and the rest of your jumped-up, jacked-off, bloody tossing mateys – think it's all right to demote me, disrespect me and then, when there's something in it for *you*, you expect me to use my affliction like some sort of bloody superpower. It's just not on. Not fucking Bisto, not a bloody cream tea in The Thistles in Cauther, not a ticket to paradise – I repeat NOT EFFING ON!'

Jazzy nodded. 'No, you're rig—'

'Bang to rights, I'm right. Course I'm right.' Queenie slammed her hand on the dashboard, her head tilted away from Jazzy, looking sightlessly through the sludge to the dull, despairing car park. She crossed her arms over her chest and shivered.

Unsure whether to stay or get out of the car to allow Queenie time to calm down and compose herself, Jazzy stared out the windscreen.

'Right, what do you want to know?' Queenie's voice was low and husky, like she'd swallowed a tonne of razors and was being forced to regurgitate them one by one.

Jazzy's head spun towards her. The older woman stared blankly out the window, her expression unfathomable, apart from the shadow of pain that lurked in her eyes. Torn between her desperate need to see if Queenie felt the same way as she did about the crime scene and gutted at putting the woman through this, Jazzy bit her lip. 'You don't have to . . .'

'Yeah, dead right I don't . . . but I will.'

The two looked at each other for long seconds, then Jazzy gave an abrupt nod. 'First impressions – that's all. Just want to see if your thoughts tally with mine.'

Queenie inhaled, closed her eyes and flinched, her eyelids flickering, her lip trembling as she relived the scene from earlier. 'Not a crime of passion, though the fucker wants us to believe it is. Every bloody thing was done and presented precisely how he wanted us to see it, from the decapitated heads and mutilation, to the display of kitchen paraphernalia, to the birthday tea party thing, but especially those birthday messages.'

Her eyes sparked open. 'That poor kid – the daughter – she'll never ever have another birthday without seeing that scene, without seeing her headless parents presented to her like an abysmal birthday gift.'

Glaring into the torrent outside the car, lips in a grim line, Queenie nodded and exhaled. The silence between them grew until it was almost uncomfortable. Then Queenie hefted her body round till she was facing Jazzy again. When she spoke, her voice was almost soporific. 'But what I don't get, lass, is why *you're* so affected by it all – putting aside the fact that you want to worm your way back up to DS – it's more than that, isn't it? I might not have lasted long in that room, but it was long enough for that scene to be burned into my brain. It was also long enough to see that it knocked the stuffing out of *you*.'

Jazzy opened her mouth, but Queenie shook her head and wafted her hands in the air. 'Don't you fucking dare try to palm me off with a shedload of lies. Not after you made me relive that nightmare. No fucking chance, no way Jose, not a haggis in hell. Something about that scene was like a fish hook to the gullet for you and you owe it to me to tell me what.'

She spread her hands out palms up. 'We're a team after all, you and me. Queenie and JayZee. JayZee and Queenie. We're the Jazz Queens. That's what *we* are.'

Not even the ridiculousness of Queenie's words could raise a smile from Jazzy, but she had to say something. She glanced at Queenie. She barely knew this woman and had no real expectation that Queenie would work with her on this. That she'd relive the scene with her, yet she had. Jazzy wasn't used to trusting people – working with others. She had a reputation for being offish and cold, but maybe she needed to bite the bullet and just spit it out. 'It's my birthday today . . .'

Head to one side, Queenie scrunched her arms under her bosom and glowered at Jazzy. 'So, what? You want me to get Geordie McBurnie to sing you "Happy Birthday"? Or maybe his alter ego Misty Thistle might do it for you. She's got a cracking voice has Misty. Maybe that wee Haggis will bake you a cake? Heard he's applied for *Bake Off* and he does bring some cracking cakes into the office. Maybe he'll make you a chocolate one, eh? Or hear, do you want me to give you your dumps? Is that it? You want your dumps for your birthday?'

Jazzy gave a half-hearted shrug and opened the car door, avoiding catching Queenie's eye. Queenie's words had conjured up images that she'd tried so hard to suppress. Last time she'd been given her dumps was at school when she turned nine – before 'it' had happened. Umpteen 'friends' piled in to crash fists into her back, the knuckles of their middle fingers jutting out for maximum impact as they punctuated each punch with a number – *one, two, three, four, five six, seven, eight, nine, and one for luck* – before dancing off leaving her in the corner of the playground, tears blurring her vision, but with her head held high, as they taunted her like they did every other day.

Nobody wanted to play with the brown girl. Nobody wanted to play with the brown girl who smelled of filth and foost. Nobody wanted to play with the brown girl whose clothes were older than she was and whose brown mum was an alky. The brown girl with no dad and half-siblings that looked white because their dad was so pale and blond.

But it wasn't *that* memory that dominated her thoughts. It was the expectation of the unsigned card that had arrived on her birthday for the past five years – not to mention the occasional extra non-birthday-related ones that arrived at other times – and the knowledge that this year's had already been delivered. That it had arrived while the other major incident teams were active out of the area and she and Queenie were surveilling a pub not a quarter mile from where two people had been slaughtered. But how could she explain that to Queenie?

'Hey, hold on a minute, hen.' Queenie reached across the handbrake and grabbed Jazzy's arm before she could swing her long legs round and get out of the car. Queenie's grip was tight, stopping Jazzy in her tracks. The furrow across her forehead deepened into a crater and after long seconds, where Jazzy unsuccessfully tried to shrug off Queenie's gimlet grip, the crater smoothed over and a glint glimmered in the older woman's eyes. She snorted – a strange sort of half-laugh – the sort that cast a layer of doubt between them. 'You're not telling me that you think that' – she wafted her hands in the air in the vague direction of the Clarks' house in Fauldhouse – 'that you think *that* was meant for you. You actually believe that because of you, some sick bampot took a machete to the heads of those parents and displayed them at a table just so their sixteen-year-old lassie would find them like that on her damn birthday? That this was all planned to scare the goolies off of *you*?'

Queenie's lips turned upwards into a snarl as she ran the fingers of her free hand through her hair. 'Well, does that not just take the shortbread. You're deluded. Bloody hallucinating. In the proverbial cloud cuckoo land, that's where you are.'

Each of Queenie's accusations landed on Jazzy, piercing her like the metal slivers from a dirty bomb. She yanked her arm away, swung her legs out of the car and, cursing herself for letting her guard down, clamoured out. She was desperate to put as much distance between the two of them as possible. Her only excuse for her stupidity in bringing this up with Queenie was her exhaustion. A night shift in the freezing cold after days of insomnia, followed by the shock of that crime scene had left her vulnerable. Vulnerable *and* stupid. Stupid to think she could confide in Queenie, stupid to think she could share her burden with anyone, never mind a colleague. She might as well pack her locker up now and hand in her notice, for when this got out, she wouldn't have a moment's peace.

Queenie got out of the car and caught up with Jazzy. When she spoke, her voice was little more than a whisper, her tone softer, more like an adult to their crying child than the abrasiveness Jazzy was used to from her. 'Unless there's something more to this than you're letting on, hen . . . Is there?'

Jazzy paused, the chill air sharpening her mind as with a deep breath she met Queenie's eyes and shook her head. She scrunched her eyes closed. 'Just ignore me, Queenie. I'm exhausted. Night shifts don't agree with me. I'm just being stupid.'

Queenie stared at Jazzy until the younger woman felt an uncomfortable warmth trail across her cheeks. The bloody woman was a rottweiler. With a single step closer, she invaded Jazzy's personal space. Despite her lack of height, her annoyance shimmered around her, making Jazzy long to take a step back. But she wouldn't. *Show no weakness.* She'd learned *that* at a young age.

Glaring at her, Queenie said, 'You think I'm a bloody teuchter, do you, eh? Think my heid's zipped up the back, maybe? One raisin short of a currant bun? You young ones are all the same. You see me – an older officer demoted to DC who's never reached more than the giddy heights of sergeant – and you think "has been, never was". Your condescension rolls off you in waves and that pisses *me* off, let me tell you, JAYZEE.'

She jabbed at her temple, her stubby fingers, bitten nails and scraggy cuticles taunting Jazzy. 'Every sodding thing I've seen or experienced is up here, and that's . . .' the finger pointed to Jazzy's chest '. . . why I'll *always* know more than you. Got it?'

Shit! If Jazzy could go back and relive the entire drive from the crime scene to here, she would, and this time she'd stay silent. She'd allowed herself to let her guard down and now she'd alienated the one person who'd shown her a modicum of respect since her own demotion to D team. Would she ever learn to play nicely? Time and again, in her evaluations, that very point had come up and, time and again, she'd dismissed it as trivial. Her past made it hard for her to trust anyone. How could she when she'd been bullied by her birth mum, deserted by her birth dad, hated by her grandparents, shunted into foster care and separated from her siblings before finally being allowed to live with her beloved Aunt Lillie and Uncle Jiten, who she now called mum and dad? Right now, though, the urge to tell Queenie everything was almost overwhelming.

As if sensing her partner's quandary, Queenie let her hand fall to her side and took a backward step. Although her chest still heaved, her expression had softened, a small frown gathering in the middle of her forehead. 'I'm not your enemy, JayZee Solanki. If anything, I'm your friend – your only ally – and I suspect that it wasn't just being knackered that had you spewing all of that out, so, if that's the case, then you should bloody well tell your auntie Queenie *all* about it. It's you and me against the world, hen. You and me against the dickless wonder. You and me braving the tempest and don't you deny it. We're the Jazz Queens.'

For a moment Jazzy was tempted, then sanity prevailed. No way could she draw this wonderfully feisty woman into the quagmire of her situation. Unable to dislodge the lump in her throat caused by Queenie's olive branch, Jazzy couldn't speak so instead she offered a shake of her head and a rueful smile.

Disappointment flashed over Queenie's face, but she quickly recovered and with a shrug fell into step beside Jazzy as they walked into the headquarters. 'Okay, your choice. No grudges held here, but that doesn't mean I'm going to let you get away with the humungous elephant in the room. What I want to know about is Waqas Afzal,' said Queenie, referring back to their altercation an hour earlier by the car at the crime scene. 'You really banging him?'

Jazzy stopped and glowered at Queenie, whose grin took the sting from her words. The older woman splayed her hands in front of her and shrugged. 'Asking for a friend, like. I couldn't give two farts on a veggie night who you're shagging.' And with that parting shot, she marched ahead, her cropped greying hair glistening in the morning sun.

The smile was still on Jazzy's face as she followed her partner into the station.

Chapter 11

Together Queenie and Jazzy walked into the incident room and, as one, stopped just inside the door, allowing their gazes to wander the area and their tired minds and bodies to absorb the vitality that made this place like a second home to them. With A and B teams still AWOL, the room was occupied mostly by civilian operators and uniformed officers dotted around at various desks. Most were checking CCTV, processing data from the scene as it filtered in and doing background checks on the Clarks, their neighbours, acquaintances, colleagues and the like. They'd also check the system for new prison releases to the area.

The buzz in the room alleviated some of Jazzy's exhaustion and with the smell of coffee twitching her nostrils, she headed straight to the filter machine to snag a mug, catching snippets of conversations as she went: 'What time are the post-mortems scheduled for?' 'Anything on the CCTV in the locality of Azalea Close?' 'We've got home security footage from a couple of the neighbours' home security systems; I'll get on that.' 'I need background information on the daughter, like yesterday – school friends, teachers, and her boyfriend. Check her social media.'

Jazzy had agreed to write the Clark crime scene report – mainly because she had managed not to vomit and flee the scene within a matter of minutes – whilst Queenie dealt with their surveillance report of the Argy Bargy pub. Fortunately, because of the dearth of activity there, Queenie could blag it using the notes Jazzy had sent from her smartphone.

The reality was that Queenie's recollections of the Clark scene were more accurate than Jazzy's. However, it had been Jazzy who had spoken with the CSIs and the pathologist, as well as actually entering the room and studying the scene from a variety of angles. Besides which, Jazzy welcomed the chance to shuffle her observations into some sort of formal shape. That way she hoped to be able to dismiss her lingering fears that somehow the Clarks' deaths were linked to her stalker. It wasn't like Bellsquarry and Fauldhouse were neighbouring villages; still, Jazzy knew that the timings could work. In practical terms, both could have been the work of the same person.

Queenie had made valid points earlier and, outwardly at least, Jazzy wanted it to appear that she'd accepted the older woman's counsel. Internally though, her churning stomach and fogged mind told a different story. She wanted to get the briefing over with so she could escape with her thoughts to her home and discover what had been written on the card her stalker had left. Logic told her it was likely to be related to one of the bangers she'd had locked up when she was based in Edinburgh, but still she felt uneasy.

Twenty minutes later, DCI Dick, in a cloud of Invictus, strode past the desk where she was working on the final paperwork. His face was a thundercloud waiting to explode and drench any unwitting officers working nearby. On reaching the front, he yelled louder than necessary considering the size of the room and the fact that his blustering trip from the door had driven the occupants to silence anyway. 'Right listen up. We've got our number-one suspect. The girl's boyfriend. I want everyone focusing on this Danny Banik. The neighbours have said the girl was slipping out of the house at all hours to meet him at the corner of the road.

Seems the parents disapproved, so it looks like we've got a motive and two suspects; let's get this investigation moving.'

Jazzy blinked as she pressed submit on her paperwork to upload it to the shared server and then risked a glance at Queenie. Just back from stocking up on provisions from the canteen, Queenie paused, the roll with its flat sausage inside halfway to her mouth, brown sauce dripping onto the napkin she'd positioned on her ample chest. Jazzy jumped up, ignoring her partner's whispered, 'Shit a brick, JayZee, sit your backside down.'

'Excuse me, sir, but *two* suspects? I understand Danny Banik being one, but who's the other?'

With an exaggerated tut, Dick rolled his eyes and glared at her. 'Makes me wonder how you ever managed to get to sergeant level if you have to ask that, DC Solanki. It's the daughter of course. Imogen Clark is the second suspect. It's clear she was in an unsavoury relationship with an older boy. Banik is twenty-one, I believe, and her parents disliked him. We've seen it before and no doubt we'll see it again.'

Queenie tugged at Jazzy's sleeve to encourage her to back off, but Jazzy jerked her hand away. 'I mean it's fair enough to pursue that line of inquiry, but should we be giving it that much weight at this stage? It's very early in the day to narrow the parameters of the investigation, don't you think? We haven't yet got all the information from the house-to-house or the background on the victims and their contacts. The way the bodies were displayed should be factored in when considering motivation, and we have to exclude enemies from the victims' personal circle or work life or even a burglary gone . . .'

Dick's face became a mass of red with flashing eyes glinting like a lighthouse light in overdrive. 'Constable Solanki, as you and the rest of the team know, you and your sidekick are here only as a courtesy to do basic grunt work, *not* to question my investigation. I suggest you get your paperwork in order and head home. I want you and McQueen back at three to collate, log and order evidence, and to make yourselves available to assist the *real* detectives on this case. *Comprendez?*'

Then who the hell is going to do the investigation? echoed in Jazzy's mind. A and B teams were knee-deep in a three-pronged investigation that stretched south of the border, around a drug production factory near Linlithgow and upwards into the Highlands. So, by her calculations that left her, Queenie, DCs McBurnie and Heggie. Did Dick really think that McBurnie and Heggie had enough experience to carry this investigation on their own? Both she and Queenie had years of experience between them. Surely it was in his best interests to utilise that – at least until some of the others were freed up.

Before she could respond, Queenie dropped her roll on the desk, jumped to her feet and grabbing her coat with one hand and Jazzy's arm with the other said, 'We've just submitted our reports, sir. We'll be back at three.'

As a whispered conversation sprung up around them, she frogmarched Jazzy from the room muttering under her breath, 'Bloody dick, balls, scrotum, ballsack, bawbag, fucker. I'll get him back for this. Sidekick indeed. Bloody sidekick. Mark my words, the Jazz Queens will not let that stuck-up little dickless turd beat us.'

Despite her anger, Jazzy's lips twitched as the incident room door slammed shut behind them. 'Jazz Queens? Really? Jazz Queens? You really want to stick with that? You're not letting it go?'

Queenie's shoulders relaxed and she released her grip on Jazzy's arm, only to slip her arm through the younger woman's. 'We'll head home, grab some rest and be back here at three. But, there's no way we're going to confine ourselves to his narrow parameters, girl. There's a reason that tosser was promoted and it's nothing to do with time served and everything to do with keeping him tied up in paperwork so the real detectives can crack on. Which is why *I've* hatched a cunning plan. Soon as the briefing's done, we're going to recruit that Haggis lad and Geordie McBurnie to the Jazz Queens and we're going to make sure the important stuff gets covered, *despite* the dickless wonder.'

Jazzy leaned against the wall and massaged her temples. She was flagging big time and was conscious that she had things to take care of at home. Still, Queenie's plan was sound. They couldn't allow Dick to mess up this investigation, so recruiting the two underrated DCs to their gang seemed like their best shot. 'Not sure either of them will appreciate the code name Jazz Queens though, Queenie.'

Queenie bristled. 'Well, I don't get why not. Especially not Geordie – he's got his own drag queen act. You know . . . Misty Thistle. Got a cracking good voice too, has Misty. He'd be honoured to be part of our wee group, I'm sure. Now come on. They'll be heading to the canteen after the briefing; we'll catch them there and then we can go home.'

Against her better judgement, Jazzy dragged her carcass after Queenie's jaunty walk down to the canteen, wishing she had half the older woman's energy.

Chapter 12

'I don't get why you're the one doing the recruiting. Anybody would think you didn't trust me or something.' Queenie was sprawled over two chairs in the canteen, her bloodshot eyes giving her the look of a maniacal psychopath.

Eyeing with distaste the dried-up mince pie she'd bought, Jazzy rolled her eyes. She didn't want to have this argument with Queenie, but the fate of their plan lay in her convincing the older woman that she was best placed to negotiate a deal with McBurnie and Heggie. 'Course I trust you. It's not that. It's just . . . Well, it's a bit sensitive and . . .' Her voice trailed off, distracted by the sight of Queenie attacking her drink. With the relish of a two-year-old, Queenie slurped her extra-large gingerbread latte and proceeded to lick the cream from her lips with a furry tongue that made Jazzy want to heave. The woman was a bloody nightmare and now she was throwing her hat in the ring with both Queenie *and* two inexperienced DCs.

Unaware of her dismay, Queenie continued as if Jazzy hadn't spoken. 'I mean, everyone knows that I'm the queen of tact, the duchess of decorum, the lady of propriety.'

Really? Jazzy held up a hand. 'Define *everyone*, Queenie, because from where I'm sitting, those two lads are petrified of you. I've seen them leave the room when you enter. Only the other day, Heggie nearly spilled his drink over his laptop when you looked his way.'

Queenie snorted. 'That lad's a wuss though, eh? Needs a bit of tough love to set him on track. A bit of firm handling. A modicum of . . .'

'Queenie, *I'm* doing the recruiting, and if I fail then you can use your strong-arm tactics to convince them, okay?'

'Aye, all right then. You do the softly, softly, touchy-feely crap and I'll be your backup.' Her face brightened. 'Here they are now.'

The two young officers walked into the canteen. McBurnie, tall and gangly with a long narrow face that habitually hosted a sardonic expression, towered over his colleague. Geordie was a natural communicator and Jazzy had seen him extract information from the most reticent of witnesses; however, his sarcastic tongue often put him on the back foot with senior officers. Fenton Heggie, who Queenie had nicknamed Haggis, was a good six inches shorter than McBurnie and rounder all over, from his face to his torso. He wore a perpetual worried frown, which Jazzy suspected was the reason that many underestimated his skills. However, she knew that, given the space to concentrate, he had a keen eye when it came to spotting a bullshitting suspect.

Before Queenie had a chance to wave her hand to attract McBurnie and Heggie's attention, Jazzy grabbed it. 'No. You need to skedaddle. Go and sit over there and pretend to be normal.'

Chuntering under her breath, Queenie grabbed her drink and the remnants of Jazzy's mince pie and absconded to the back of the canteen. Jazzy stood and approached the two lads. 'You two okay?'

McBurnie nodded. 'Aye.' Then he lowered his voice. 'Bloody fuck-up that briefing though, eh?'

His words made Jazzy hopeful that her mission would be successful. 'Eh, about that. You think I can have a wee word with the two of you, after you've got your food?'

Heggie made a point of glancing behind Jazzy at the table she indicated before saying in what he clearly hoped was a casual tone but, in reality, was slightly raised in pitch: 'Just you, is it, Jazzy? Queenie not with you?'

Jazzy smiled. 'Just me. Come over when you're ready.'

She headed back to the table, ignoring Queenie's less than subtle gestures from the back of the room, and positioned herself so that the two detectives had no option but to sit with their backs to Queenie. When they'd settled with their sandwiches in front of them, Jazzy leaned forwards. 'I'm hoping I can trust you both?'

McBurnie took a bite of his tuna mayo sandwich and exchanged a glance with Heggie before nodding.

'Right. That's good, because I want to ask you what you think of DCI Dick.'

The two shared a look, then, between bites of their pieces, they took turns replying.

'Eejit,' said McBurnie.

'Right.' Jazzy nodded.

'Bawbag.' That was Heggie.

'Aye.'

'Plonker.' Back to McBurnie.

'Agreed.' With confirmation that all of them were on the same side, Jazzy leaned in. 'And what's your thoughts on his handling of the investigation so far? You know, the direction it's taking?'

This time Heggie took the lead, his frown deepened as he spoke and a flush darkened his cheeks. 'Too narrow a focus.'

McBurnie followed on, less animated, but equally scathing, encouraged by Jazzy's nods. 'No justification for restricting the investigation.'

Back to Heggie. 'He's stalling progress by waiting for the daughter to be well enough to interview rather than covering all the bases.'

McBurnie threw his half-eaten tuna mayo sandwich onto its wrapper and sighed. 'The idiot's not pushing things forward and exploring all possibilities. It's a disgrace, a bloody disgrace. We're never going to catch the fucker who did this if we wait for him.'

And *that* was exactly the sort of answer Jazzy had been waiting for. 'So, what actions would you two implement, then?'

Judging by the exchanged glances, this very thing had been a topic of discussion before. McBurnie picked up his sandwich and gestured to Fenton. 'You kick off, Heggie boy. I know you're dying to.'

Fenton snorted. 'Too bloody right I am.' He rubbed his fingers clean on a napkin, took a slug from his Irn-Bru can and settled back in his chair. 'Background checks on both parents . . .'

'And the lassie,' added McBurnie.

'. . . Aye, and the dad's business contacts.'

'. . . And the mum's work colleagues and the neighbours.'

'. . . The girl's teachers, her school friends, any clubs she goes to.'

'. . . Aye, and her social media.'

Fenton clicked his fingers. 'Then there's chasing up any known offenders in the area. And recent releases of known violent criminals from prison.'

'Extending the search for CCTV, home security, dashcam footage for the area.'

'Checking HOLMES 2 for similar crimes throughout the UK. Judging by the crime scene photos, that's not this fucker's first soiree.'

McBurnie studied Jazzy. 'But that's what you were trying to tell him before he relegated you to grunt work, isn't it?'

Jazzy nodded. 'That's exactly what I was trying to tell him. Which brings me on to the reason for ambushing you on your break. If he's only going to follow one lead at a time this investigation will stall. Agreed?'

Nods all round.

'So, what if we band together and investigate the leads he's *not* interested in. I mean, obviously he's right to look at Imogen's boyfriend and we can let him focus on that whilst we see if we can unearth anything else. That way, if he comes up blank, we'll have a direction to push him towards.'

McBurnie and Heggie didn't bother consulting each other before nodding. 'We're in.'

Heggie nodded. 'Aye, damn right we are. We'll be like the three musketeers . . .'

'Eh . . .' Jazzy tapped her fingers on the Formica table top. 'About that.'

Fenton's face crumpled and he closed his eyes. 'Aw no. You're not telling us that Queenie's part of this are you? That would be my worst nightmare. She *hates* me. Really hates me. The other day she called me a bag of mashed-up tumshies because *she* forgot her password. I mean she's a nightmare.'

'He's no wrong, Jazzy. She's not the easiest person to get on with, is she?'

Jazzy had to concede that they had a point, but she had to salvage this. She and Queenie needed the lads if this plan was going to work. 'I know she's a bit abrasive . . .'

'A bit?' Fenton's frown was sceptical.

'Aye, well a lot, but her heart's in the right place. It was her idea to recruit you two. Said she rated you highly and that your input would be invaluable.' Okay so that was an exaggeration. Queenie's words had in actual fact been something along the lines of: 'those daft wee turds will be better than a bucket full of cold sick, I suppose'. But now wasn't the time to share that. Over Geordie's shoulder Jazzy saw Queenie approach, so she sped up her placatory talk. 'She's a pussycat underneath the sharp tongue and she's a really good . . .'

'Well, hello there, boys.' Queenie thumped each of them in the back, causing Geordie to spurt out a mouthful of water on the table and Fenton to almost shite himself. 'JayZee brought you up to speed, has she?'

Heart sinking, dreading that here at the last hurdle when she'd almost convinced them on board, Queenie was going to mess it all up, Jazzy signalled for her colleague to shut up. But Queenie would not be closed down. 'Bet you can't believe you two are going to be part of the Jazz Queens, can you?'

This time, it was Fenton who sputtered. 'What? What did you say?'

Queenie beamed at him. 'The Jazz Queens.'

She pointed a stubby finger first at Jazzy, then at herself and then at each of the two men. 'Us four, the Jazz Queens.'

Geordie McBurnie jumped to his feet, shaking his head, his hands waving at either side of his head as if he was auditioning for a role in a musical called the Jazz Queens. 'No, absolutely not. That's a deal-breaker. I get enough stick from those homophobic bastards for Misty Thistle without being part of the dunces' brigade *and* being dubbed a bloody Jazz Queen. No way.'

Jazzy, torn between exasperation at Queenie's inopportune appearance and amusement at Fenton and Geordie's horrified expressions, grabbed one each of Geordie's and Queenie's arms and dragged them back onto their chairs. 'Stop it, both of you. Get a bloody grip. I'm too knackered to deal with theatrics right now. I know you get hassle for being gay, Geordie, and even more for your drag queen act, but this is more important than that. Besides—' She turned to Queenie, her voice stern. 'Queenie, we will *not* be called the Jazz Queens, got it?'

Queenie, looking like a petulant two-year-old who'd been denied a treat, grunted with a sharp nod and muttered under her breath, 'We will so be called the Jazz Queens.'

'As for you two, just bloody get with the programme, eh?'

Fenton exhaled, sending a waft of oniony breath across the table. 'If she at least tries to be nice, then I'm in. But only because I don't think I'll ever forget those crime scene photos.'

Geordie glared at Queenie, but nodded and offered a subdued, 'Me too.'

Jazzy exhaled and got to her feet, glad to have got that sorted. 'Right, I'm off to grab some kip. We'll see you two later. Just try and find out as much as you can in the meantime.'

With Queenie trailing behind, Jazzy headed off, then turned around and retraced her steps. 'By the way, get a hold of big Wullie will you? Ask him for the footage he took of the onlookers at the crime scene. See if you can ID everyone photographed and see if there's anybody there with no reason to be.'

As the door of the canteen swung shut behind them, Queenie said. 'You know we're still the Jazz Queens, don't you?'

Too knackered to argue, Jazzy sighed. 'I do, Queenie, I do.'

Chapter 13

Jazzy sat in her Mini and pasted a smile on her face. She'd already missed two of her mum and dad's calls and if she didn't want to be in their bad books she had to FaceTime them now. As the phone rang, she imagined her parents in their house in Portobello. Lillie would be baking her a cake because Jazzy had promised to head over there later. Now she doubted she'd have time. Her parents would be getting ready for their walk along the promenade with her mum's guide dog, Crumble.

'Happy birthday, Jasmine.' Two smiling faces appeared on the screen and proceeded to sing a mash up of Stevie Wonder's 'Happy Birthday' and the traditional one.

Despite her tiredness, Jazzy grinned. Neither were great singers, but the love they felt for her flowed over the phone. She needed that. After everything that had happened today, she needed that unconditional love. It filled the car and she could almost smell their familiar smell – aftershave and perfume tinged with incense. It symbolised home to Jazzy. 'All right you two, enough of that droning. Crumble doesn't need to hear that.'

'You okay, Jazzy, sweetie. You still going to make it over tonight?' Her mum looked hopeful and it broke Jazzy's heart to disappoint them like this, but with this ongoing investigation she couldn't guarantee her presence.

'I'm on a case – it's bad, so . . .'

'Och, don't worry, Jazz.' Her dad's understanding was immediate. 'We know how important your job is. You just come to us when you can. Your mum has your present wrapped up here waiting for you.'

Her mum chimed in. 'You sound tired, Jasmine.'

'Been up all night. Just heading home for a few hours' kip.'

'Aw, sweetie. You get off now and get some rest. We'll see you soon. Happy birthday, my gorgeous girl.'

When they'd hung up, Jazzy spent a couple of minutes composing herself. Those two people were her rocks. Despite Jazzy's grandad's disapproval they'd taken her in when she had no one else to look out for her, they'd sacrificed their relationship with her grandfather for her and they never made her feel guilty for that. As she wiped the tears from her eyes, Jazzy acknowledged that although she may have few relatives, those she did have meant everything to her.

She drove from Livingston to Bellsquarry on autopilot. Despite the phone call with her mum and dad, Jazzy was on edge, her nerves frazzled, her brain sluggish, yet she couldn't put that murder scene out of her head.

The Clarks deserved a dedicated investigative team prepared to explore every potential lead. For God's sake, they were only a few hours into the investigation and this was not the time to close down other leads. Narrowing the scope of the investigation at this stage was a massive mistake. She worried that this course of action might retraumatise Imogen. Although Jazzy's personal experiences differed from the girl's, there were parallels. If anything, what Jazzy had lived through – severe trauma, a foster system that was slow to accept her because of her colour and her dubious history, grandparents who rejected her because of her Muslim father, the incessant chipping away at her confidence resulting in her being so tightly wound – made her more

85

empathetic. Sometimes, she thought she would explode. A life-time of struggling to deal with a past that was hazy to her had taught her to survive; yet, although she had a therapist and she wasn't that frightened little girl anymore, learned behaviour and emotional responses were hard to control.

Hands gripping tight on the steering wheel of her boxy gold Mini Cooper hatchback, Jazzy focused on controlling her breathing. Tiredness, frustration and fear of what awaited her by the back door were affecting her judgement. She shouldn't have challenged the DCI in such a direct and public way. She'd done that twice now and her career wouldn't survive a third such occurrence. Thank God for Queenie dragging her from the room before she made things worse. If she'd had even a modicum of sense, she'd have controlled her emotions at the crime scene *and* she'd have waited till the end of the briefing – such as it was – to, in a calm and measured tone, request permission to follow a few leads of her own.

She slammed the heel of her hand down on the steering wheel and yelled 'Shite' into the empty confines of the car. That felt good – released some of the tension.

As she pulled off the Brucefield roundabout and drove onto her quiet street, she made a point of scoping out the area. Of course, her nocturnal visitor would be long gone, but it paid to be vigilant. Happy that no suspicious characters loitered nearby, she parked in front of her small two-bedroom ex-council house. With a reluctance she'd never experienced before on returning home, she opened the car door, braced herself against the barrage of arctic air that hit when she got out and jogged through her gate. As she inserted her key in the lock her heart picked up a pace. Again, she glanced around the street, but apart from Mrs Arthur battling with her umbrella against the buffeting sleet, the street remained empty.

As soon as Jazzy pushed the door open, her home alarm beeped with its five-second warning. The familiar sound grounded her a little. She knew her home hadn't been violated, for she'd have had a notification from the security company; nevertheless, the beeping alarm was reassuring. Without warning, her limbs became heavy and Jazzy recognised it as the result of holding herself tightly in check for so long. Since that damn envelope had been delivered hours ago, she'd been functioning on adrenalin. She slammed the door behind her, forced herself to plod to the alarm, pumped in her code and took two backward paces to lean against the door, with her eyes shut. Its solidity settled her, creating a barrier between her and the outside world. This was her domain, her sanctuary and as she relaxed, she sank onto the floor, her back maintaining contact with the PVC, as her bum landed gently on the carpet.

With the gentle clicks of the central heating system and faint excitable shouts of the primary school children cavorting in the playground next door for company, the tension seeped from her body. Here, at home in this small cosy refuge she'd created, she allowed herself to let her defences down – just a little. She closed her eyes, pulled her legs up to her chest and, holding herself in a vertical foetal position, rested her forehead on her knees. As she'd expected, the floodgates opened, releasing the emotions she'd held at bay all day. That was *her* coping mechanism – but only in private. There was no way she'd ever allow herself this luxury in company. *Show no weakness.* She'd learned that early and, even if others viewed her as cold and emotionless, this coping mechanism had served her well since her childhood.

As she sobbed, a small feline head butted against her thigh – Winky. She kneaded her fingers into the cat's fur before hauling him onto her lap and hugging him tight. He was more than a pet – he was her best friend and her confidant. He was the only creature, other than her mum and dad, that she allowed herself to be responsible for. She'd got him from the RSPCA as a kitten and every day she looked forward to hearing his plaintive meows on her return home and recounting her day to him – after all, who else could she tell? She savoured the softness of the tabby's coat for a long moment before releasing him. She had something to do and she couldn't delay it any longer. Scrubbing her face with her coat sleeve, she got up and followed the meowing pet through to the kitchen.

With her bag on the small round table that took up one side of her kitchen, she retrieved her burner phone from its zipped compartment, only then realising she'd still had no notifications from it. *Annoying.* She tossed it back into the pocket and rezipped it. *What the hell was keeping him?* She glanced at the back door as she poured some biscuits into one bowl and followed up with some wet food in another. *Winky first, then the envelope.*

Her security app showed that the garden was empty, but the image of her nocturnal visitor lingered. With a mental shake, she donned gloves and undid the heavy-duty chain, the huge bolt, and the five-lever mortis lock before yanking the door open. Peering through the billowing sleet, into the garden beyond, she felt foolish. *What am I – nine years old? Scared of the bogeyman?* Still, eyes narrowed, she scanned the small garden, probing the corner where she kept her water butt and the rose bush opposite, just to be sure. Only when she was satisfied did she bend down to retrieve the plastic bag containing the envelope that was tucked behind the plant.

Winky, taking advantage of the open door rather than having to endure the indignity of squashing through the cat flap, tried to slip out between Jazzy's legs. For no reason other than the sudden chill that went up her spine at the thought of Winky outside on his own, she yanked him back, eliciting a high-pitched mew of protest as she deposited him safely behind her. When she'd closed the door, she bent over and flicked the cat flap switch closed. 'Sorry, Winks, no outdoor forays for you for a while.'

Unperturbed Winky rolled over onto his back presenting a small all-white area of fur, which Jazzy dutifully massaged. 'It's only for a short time. Just till I feel sure, yeah?'

Jazzy settled at the table where she ate or worked when she brought work home. She was procrastinating, and that annoyed her. Her position at the table offered her a clear view through the kitchen window into the garden at one side and, with the kitchen door ajar, afforded her a direct view of the front door too. She hadn't intended to position her table in this way, but on the few occasions she'd moved it to the corner of the room, which would create more space, she'd baulked. *This* was where she felt comfortable and so the table stayed there.

Still with her gloves on, she studied the plastic sleeve. It was just a bog-standard generic A4-sized sleeve folded over to accommodate the A5 card inside. She had no doubt it would reveal nothing of forensic importance – no fingerprints, no DNA, no microfibres. He'd never left any trace evidence before, so why would he now? Jazzy frowned. That he went to such extremes to hide his identity had always been worrisome, but it was only now – after attending the Clarks' murder scene – that her worry had edged over into fear. Previously, when she'd received a card, her only confidant – bar Winky – had wanted to instigate an investigation. But she'd been reluctant. The other cards had all been posted to her workplace and she'd argued that loads of officers received similar communications.

'It comes with the job, Elliot,' had been her final word on the matter. It was hard enough being one of only a few officers of Indian descent in Police Scotland, without attracting more attention. So, she clung to her mantra: *show no weakness*, to cope with the crap directed her way. Still, she had hoped that, with this being the first time a card had been delivered to her home, Elliot would have responded by now.

She could hear his words as if he was standing right beside her. 'This isn't good, Jazz. This is stalker behaviour and you need to report it this time. He's visited your home, for Christ's sake. This is an escalation.'

She took some evidence bags from a drawer and, after

extracting the card from inside, she placed the plastic sleeve in one of them. Now with the pristine white envelope lying on her table, contrasting with the maroon tablecloth, the desire to just rip it up and toss it in the bin taunted her. 'Come on, Winky. Do I open it or bin it?'

Winky, licking his belly, one leg elevated, was no help, but that didn't matter. Jazzy had no choice. She *had* to open it. She couldn't dispel the niggle that told her its arrival now, followed by a horrific double murder two streets from where she was on surveillance duty, was too coincidental.

Fuck, fucking, fuck, fuck! Her name was written in capital letters across the envelope in black felt pen. From another drawer, she extracted the bundle of cards she'd received before and studied the writing. Each was sealed inside individual evidence bags. To her untrained eyes the writing looked similar. Previously, when she'd called in a favour with a handwriting expert, they'd confirmed that the likelihood of the writer being the same person was high. When the first few had been analysed they had come back with no usable trace DNA – no distinctive fibres, no stray hairs inside the envelope, nor fingerprints that matched to any on the IDENT1 database and nothing on the seal, except that which was expected from processing at Royal Mail and just a local postmark on them. The bastard was forensically savvy. Although she assumed this time would be no different, the personal delivery was an escalation and warranted all of the cards being reanalysed. *Nobody could be careful all the time, could they?*

In line with police protocol, Jazzy, using both hands, shoogled the envelope till the card fell onto the tablecloth, then deposited the envelope in a separate bag.

With the generic Hallmark card face down on her table, Jazzy flipped it over with the knife. When she saw the front, bile rose in her throat, her hand flying to her mouth. A picture of a tabby cat, almost identical to Winky, wearing a party hat and blowing a party blower was on the front with a generic *Happy Birthday* across the top. The tabby's white fur had been coloured red with a series of blood drops trailing down its chest. Black slash marks eviscerated the animal's throat and his eyes had been gouged out. There was no doubt that this was a threat. A warning of what would happen to her precious Winky if her night-time visitor ever got his hands on him. A wave of dizziness swept over her and as the colour leached from her face, she rushed to the sink and vomited.

After wiping her mouth, she returned to the table, glad that she'd had the presence of mind to lock the cat flap. With sweat beading her forehead, Jazzy slumped. She had nothing left in the tank. Not a damn thing – and if she was to be worth anything by the time she was due back at the station, she had to grab some sleep. First though, she had to finish securing the card. Placing Winky on the lino, she used the knife to flip open the card. Her heart skipped a beat when she read the message, again written in block capitals but in red this time. *FOR YOU! HAPPY BIRTHDAY!*

Jazzy's mind flashed back to the messages scrawled in blood over the Clarks' foreheads. *For You! Happy Birthday!* Could that possibly be a coincidence? Her tiredness made her doubt her own thought processes. Was there a link between the Clarks' murders, the shared birthdays and her stalker . . . more to the point, what was the link and what should she do about it? Elliot would say, 'Report it. You need protection and if there's a common thread between these incidents then it will be found.'

That came with its own problems. Jazzy had been a victim before. She knew what it was like to feel controlled and unable to make decisions for yourself. What it was like to have things done to you and for you, and she was reluctant to submit to that again. She'd no doubt DCS Afzal would pull out all the stops. He was a fair man and wouldn't tolerate a threat to one of his officers. But at what cost? Surrendering her privacy? Her darkest moments becoming open to public scrutiny? Her heavily guarded secrets becoming entertainment fodder for round the coffee machine?

She couldn't bear that. People viewed you differently when they considered you a victim, and Jazzy had struggled against that all her life. She wasn't about to relinquish control over that – not because of some sicko stalker.

Another voice – Elliot's? – insisted that she had to come clean. That the gouged-out eyes on the image and the timing of the Clarks' murders was too coincidental to be ignored. She sighed, and that was without him knowing about the sodding beans left at the crime scene. But Dick thought Imogen's boyfriend, possibly with Imogen – was the killer. That was a valid line of inquiry, but why then had Jazzy been so uneasy with it? Why had she so readily committed to working with Queenie and the others? Because she didn't want to risk being sidelined from the investigation, that's why.

She slid the card into another plastic bag and after removing her gloves, checked her phone. Still no message from Elliot. *What the hell is he doing?* Her finger hovered over the call button, then moved away. If he could, he would have been in touch. So, she sent a text to update him.

> *Escalated! Card with violated cat and threat. Possible link to my current investigation. Call me ASAP!*

She waited for a couple of minutes but when there was no reply, she dragged herself to her feet. She was safe. Winky was safe. There was nothing else to do, but go to sleep. She set up a cat litter tray, set the house alarm and fell into bed without removing anything other than her shoes.

Chapter 14

There's someone in there. Someone in that room with the thing. She has to open the door, has to rescue them, but she doesn't want to. She tries to scream 'Why are you in there again?' but her mouth won't open. Her bare toes knead the carpet as she moves from foot to foot, tears streaming down her face. She has to go in and see what's happening . . . then there's beans and pegs and a birthday cake and she's back in Fauldhouse. Now, there are three bodies: the Clarks and her mum. They each hold a tin of beans and are doing cheers to her as they sing 'Happy Birthday'. The Clarks' grotesque heads smiling at her from the table top, her mum's atop her maggoty corpse . . .

It took a moment for the ringing doorbell to penetrate Jazzy's nightmare and when she finally dragged herself from it, her duvet was wrapped round her body, trapping her in the bed. She struggled to free herself, the movement releasing a waft of pungent sweat, reminding her that not only had she tumbled into bed in the same clothes she'd worn for almost twenty-four hours, she hadn't paused for a shower either and now someone was at the damn door. She hesitated, trying to still her shaking body and force the images to fade. This wasn't the first time she'd had this sort of nightmare and it wouldn't be the last. Dissociative amnesia from a childhood trauma was to blame for the thought distortions that resulted in these episodes. This one though had been extra vivid and left her more exhausted than she'd been when she went to bed.

Finally, she stumbled to her feet, catching her foot in the trailing duvet and almost landed flat on her face in her haste to reach the door and stop the persistent bell pusher. Her head was fuzzy with the dullness of someone who was still half asleep, exhausted and who'd indulged in a mega crying fest a mere few hours earlier. Jazzy glanced at the clock and groaned. She'd barely had two hours' kip and, in an hour, she'd have to head back to the station. If this was an Amazon delivery, she'd hand the guy his balls in his hand.

On automatic pilot, she surveyed the hallway. Her home was secure and Winky was dozing in his basket, so all was right in Solanki world. At the door, a twinge of unease made her pause before answering it. She brought her security app up on her phone and studied the boy standing on her doorstep, finger extended to her bell as if determined to wake her. He was tall and skinny and, wearing only a flimsy long-sleeved T-shirt and a pair of jeans, he was severely underdressed for the winter weather. His hair was blond with a hint of strawberry and was tousled in all directions, as if he'd just got out of bed. A smattering of acne across his forehead told Jazzy that he was probably younger than she'd first thought.

Although she didn't recognise him, her interest was piqued by the tattoo visible on his neck just above the collar of his round-neck T-shirt. The calligraphic 'S' with a single vertical bar cutting it in half was reminiscent of a weird dollar sign, but it wasn't its beauty that intrigued Jazzy. She recognised the mark. This was the tattoo favoured by the Stùrrach residents – a sort of tribal marking.

As the bell chimed again, Jazzy considered her course of action. For some reason this young Stùrrach lad had punted up at her home and the only logical conclusion was that she and Queenie

94

had been clocked last night on the edge of the Badlands. That didn't explain why the boy hadn't confronted them the previous night or why he was standing on her doorstep now. Then it dawned on her. The wee shite had followed her. He'd followed her home and *that* was why he knew where she lived. Had he followed her from the Badlands to the Clarks' crime scene and then from there to the station in Livingston? It seemed so, because otherwise how would he have been able to follow her in her personal vehicle back here?

She paused, assessing his stature. This boy was too short and too skinny to be her stalker, which was reassuring. However, the thought that yet another unknown entity knew where she lived sent a spark of fear through her. The fear was quickly replaced by indignant rage, as he stopped pressing the doorbell and began hammering on the door instead. *What the hell?* Cheeky bugger, pitching up at her home – her safe haven – ringing her bell and hammering on her door.

Heedless of any personal threat, Jazzy disengaged the alarm, slid open the chain and yanked the door open. Surprise made the boy stumble backwards and land on his arse in the wet ground. *Serves him right.* He gawped up as if he hadn't actually expected her to open the door.

Hands on her hips, face scrunched into an angry challenge, Jazzy glared at him. 'You've got some explaining to do. So, get on with it.'

'Sorry missus, really sorr—'

'Name?' The word left her lips like a bullet and the boy flinched. 'Bbbenjy. My name's Benjy.'

Benjy? For God's sake, who the hell calls their kid Benjy? 'Your folks not like you much then?'

Benjy frowned, not getting Jazzy's sarcasm, and shook his head. 'No, my ma and da like me fine. I'm their favourite.' His lips flashed into a quick, uncertain smile as he shrugged and struggled to his feet. 'I'm their only kid though, so they got no choice.'

Although his attempt at humour almost brought a smile to her lips, Jazzy wasn't going to be won over too easily. She stuck to her usual interview technique of keeping her subject off balance by switching up the questions. 'You been following me?'

Although not strictly a question, Benjy treated it as such and nodded, clasping red cracked fingers in front of him as if he could ward off Jazzy's anger. 'We did, but then we went for a McDonald's breakfast and came back a wee while ago.'

In spite of herself, Jazzy felt a pang of pity for the lad, with his skinny frame and sore cracked hands. Uncertain how to proceed, her eyes drifted beyond him to a ramshackle car parked a few car lengths down from her own. It was scratched useless and the driver's door had clearly been replaced because, unlike the rest of the navy vehicle, it was a mucky, matte brownish colour. Jazzy frowned. The little scrote had followed her in that clap heap and she hadn't even noticed? She turned her attention back to the boy. 'Age?'

Seemingly following her chain of thought, Benjy began shaking his head as if the quicker he did it, the more she'd believe him. 'I'm sixteen, missus, but I didn't drive it. Honest I didn't. Ivor was driving.'

Jazzy stepped back into the house, grabbed her coat and slipped her feet into her boots. 'Come on then, let's meet this Ivor character and I swear, Benjy, if your mate Ivor doesn't have a valid driver's licence or if that car isn't MOT'd or has no insurance then you're in deep shit, got me?'

Benjy trailed after Jazzy, his face a mask of misery, his head bowed. As she neared the car, strains of Nirvana accompanied by wafts of smoke seeped through the half-open windows. Top marks for the music choice – Jazzy liked a bit of Grunge herself on occasion – no marks for the smoking. She sighed, grateful she couldn't detect the acrid stink of weed, because she really had no time to deal with a minor drug violation. As she was about to rap against the steamed-up glass, the door burst open and she had to jump back to avoid it smashing into her thighs. 'What the . . .?'

But her sentence faded away as a tall girl – young woman really, maybe late teens or early twenties – unfolded herself from the driver's seat. A cascade of wavy blonde hair trailed over her shoulders and down to her waist. She took one look at Jazzy's glowering face and shrugged. 'Told you it would be a waste of time, Benj. When have you ever heard of the polis listening to one of us? Come on, let's get home. It's freezing.'

As Benjy moved towards the passenger's seat, his eyes pleaded with Jazzy. *Shit!* Hoping she wouldn't later regret it, Jazzy made her decision. 'Okay, okay, I'll give you five minutes. That's your lot. But . . .' she gestured to the girl whose sullen glare had magically been replaced by a wide grin. 'I thought you said your mate was called Ivor.'

'He did. And I am. Ivor that is. Well, Ivory, if I'm completely honest, but who the hell wants to be called Ivory, eh?' She splayed her hands and, head to one side, shrugged at Jazzy.

'Not sure I get your drift, Ivor.'

With a typical teenage huff, Ivor, eyes wide and incredulous that Jazzy could be so out of touch, launched into a diatribe. 'I'm like, duh? When elephants and hippos are being decimated for *their* ivory, it's just *wrong* for me to carry a tag that encourages ivory poaching, you get it?'

Jazzy wasn't sure she did. She wasn't convinced that one young girl, in one small Scottish village on an entirely different continent could influence ivory poachers. However, she appreciated the sentiment. So far, neither of her two visitors had lived up to her assumptions about the Stùrrach youth and that was infinitely intriguing.

Ivor, hands wafting around her head for emphasis, was still talking. 'Just seems wrong like. I mean, have you seen what they do to those poor animals? It's barbaric, bloody barbaric. The poor wee things must be in *so* much pain and *so* scared. Then there's the wee ones left without their mummies.'

The girl ground to a halt and exhaled. Her tear-filled eyes met Jazzy's, daring her to contradict her. 'So, I'm Ivor.'

'Okay, Ivor it is then.'

With an unhealthy sounding clunk, Ivor turned the key to lock the car, whilst Jazzy scanned the street for unfamiliar cars or those idling with the ignition on and was reassured by the absence of both. Soon, at school pick-up time, the road would be jam-packed with vehicles, but for now, except for those belonging to her neighbours, and Ivor's monstrosity, the street was empty. She turned her gaze to the side road opposite her house but apart from a solitary parked Range Rover right at the far end and facing the opposite direction, it too was empty. Nothing to worry about.

With Ivor strutting ahead as if it was the most natural thing in the world, the unlikely trio walked towards Jazzy's house. Benjy fell into line beside Jazzy. 'She's a bit much but she means well, missus.'

'I heard that, Benj. Cheeky git.'

Jazzy opened her mouth to clarify that although she would give them the five minutes she'd promised, she wasn't letting this pair of reprobates into her home. However, that was before she noticed Benjy shivering. Ahead of her, the soles of Ivor's trainers flapped with every step she took and Jazzy was immediately back in primary school in her tatty, smelly clothes, with the taunts of the other kids ringing in her ears. *Five minutes in the warmth – that's all. Not a moment more!* Besides, she was intrigued about what they wanted to tell her. 'If you're going to be sharing information with me, you need to drop the "missus" okay? Either call me Detective or Jazzy – but definitely not missus.'

Chapter 15

Don't know what I was expecting, but it was more than this. After the excitement of yesterday? All the anticipation? This is more like a damp squib. A bit of an anti-climax. Rage simmers in my gut like molten lava ready to spew from my mouth – a river of death and destruction waiting to happen and Jazzy sodding Solanki better not be anywhere nearby when it erupts, or she'll pay the price sooner than anticipated and *that* would really piss me off.

The bitch always made out *she* was the clever one – the brainbox – but her actions, or should I say *reactions* today, would indicate otherwise. She's not risen to the crisis in the way I expected. Yes, there was that wee skirmish with Afzal and DCI Dick at the crime scene, but that was all it was – a skirmish. No passion, no flame throwing, no oomph. It's like she's diminished somehow. Has she lost it? Has her spark disintegrated?

All these years, I've enjoyed taunting her – dropping the odd reminder that I'm lurking nearby. Not that she knows who's been dropping off the cards. Not in her wildest imaginations will Jazzy Solanki guess what's in store for her. This is the culmination of years of planning. She might have buried her treachery so deep she can't remember it, but I've not and her punishment is inevitable. This is revenge for the broken promise, one that was written in blood, *our* blood. A promise made in blood.

When she looks back on all of this – if I allow her to, that is, she'll assume that it all started to go downhill when her misguided public interaction with Waqas Afzal culminated in that very significant face slap. That was the pivotal moment. Although it wasn't the starting point, it was when I decided that the time was right to move on to the end game. The beginning of the end. The start of her punishment. It's inevitable that being in the public eye – even for a short amount of time – would ensure her eventual destruction would have far-reaching ramifications and naturally it will be all the more public.

I still can't get my head round her misguided actions. Thanks to me that slap made the front pages of the *Daily Record*, so what did she expect? That Afzal would pull a few strings and bury it? That she was Teflon? No bloody way. I reckon Afzal decided to use it as a learning opportunity for Jazzy. A way to encourage her to lose the attitude. Wonder how that worked out for him? From what I saw earlier, although Jazzy might not be throwing actual punches at him, she was still sending him daggers. Of course, she was demoted. Boy, that must have hurt big time. A fall from grace and Afzal had the sense to hit her where it hurt her the most – her job. I couldn't have planned it better if I'd tried. She was lucky she didn't get sacked, really. But it was her personal and oh, so *very* secret relationship with Afzal that stopped *that* from happening and that gave *me* the opportunity I'd been waiting for to bring all of this into play.

Cashing in a few favours with some of my contacts down south to bring some of their trade up north was an inspired idea. Laying a few bread crumbs to divert the other MIT teams away from this area, yet leaving a trickle of crumbs leading to Stùrrach was trickier but doable. My only concern had been that Afzal and Dick might decide to employ uniforms to watch the Argy Bargy rather than Jazzy. I reckon, in the end, Afzal pulled rank on account of Solanki's experience and threw the bitch a bone.

As for the Clarks – well, you can call them collateral damage,

I suppose. A dispensable casualty in a much larger war. That girl was so easy to manipulate. Don't the parents teach them about privacy settings before letting their precious offspring loose in the big bad world of social media? I shouldn't complain though. That lapse made my job a lot easier.

There's a lad knocking at Jazzy's door. Wonder what he's after? Although I hadn't expected the bitch to clock me – I only followed her some of the way, just to prove I could, but she really should have spotted those two. Mind you, I suppose the chances of someone using that rust heap as a surveillance vehicle are slim, so maybe that's why she skimmed over it.

She's opened the door now and I wish I could hear what she's saying to the boy. Judging by the way his head hangs, she's giving him an earful. Then she's looking at the rust heap and following him down the steps to the car. As she bends down towards the door, Jazzy scans the road. Maybe she's not lost the plot after all. I grin, though, because never in a million years will she spot me. For a start the car I swiped has tinted windows, the engine's turned off and I'm facing away from her house. Nothing about this parked car shouts 'I'm stalking you'. Little does she know I've got strategically placed mirrors positioned in the rear window that afford me a comprehensive view of her front door, her car and fifty yards of street in either direction. Can you believe it, she's taking them back to her house?

A frisson of unease licks at my gut. What exactly do they want to talk to Jazzy about? A pulse throbs in my neck and I think back over the previous night. Everything had gone perfectly to plan. Everything. Nobody saw me – and certainly not anyone driving that rust heap. I exhale and rap my fingers on the steering wheel. They must have spotted her watching the pub. That's the only explanation. I settle down in my seat, eyeing them as they disappear inside. Maybe it's time to move on, for now. Besides, I need to get different wheels. Never does to keep the same car for too long.

Chapter 16

It felt strange inviting people into her home. The only person who had ever visited Jazzy, apart from her mum and dad, was Elliot and that had been under duress. She valued her privacy and didn't like feeling that her personal space was being invaded. Her home was exactly how she liked it and having visitors left her feeling exposed and vulnerable. As if they would crack open the chinks in her armour and disapprove of all the things she kept hidden.

For the first time since she moved in she considered her surroundings, imagining how Benjy and Ivor would see them. Would they think it a weird space? A home for an unloved spinster and her cat? As the teenagers kicked their shoes off and stood barefoot by the door, Jazzy, on automatic pilot, re-engaged the home alarms and slid the chain in place before turning to them. Instead of the mocking expressions she expected, what she saw was two uncertain teenagers, shimmying from foot to foot, as if to keep their sodden feet off her carpet. Their eyes skimmed the room and their mouths were near perfect Os.

With a frown Jazzy followed their gazes, wondering what had surprised them. Her walls were cream and dotted with A4-sized paintings of sari-clad traditional Indian dancers in various classical poses. She loved their vibrancy, but what did her guests think of them? A tall shelving unit to one side displayed a range of Lord Ganesh statuettes of varying sizes and sculpted from glass, wood, marble, sandstone or clay. For all her issues, Jazzy's birth mum had clung to her own strange brand of Hinduism until she died and when her mum's brother, Jiten, and his wife, Leila, Lillie for short, had taken her in, they too had celebrated their culture and religion and instilled respect for it in Jazzy. Although Jazzy couldn't commit to any religion – why would she after her childhood experiences? – she appreciated the soothing effect her new parents' faith had on them and revelled in the sheer vibrancy of her maternal heritage.

From the kids' expressions she deduced they were amazed with her décor choices. Elliot had been taken aback too and Jazzy wondered why her celebration of her Indianness with the bright colours and beautiful things that she'd been surrounded with throughout her teens would be so surprising.

Winky, back arched and tail swishing, marched along the hallway to greet the visitors, giving no indication that this was an unusual occurrence in this house. Distracted, Ivor fell to her knees and reached out making clicking sounds to entice the cat closer. Whilst his friend was occupied with the cat, Benjy edged closer to Jazzy and nodded to the alarm system and then the door. 'You kidnapping us or just really cautious about security?'

'Ha, bloody ha.' Jazzy grinned at him. These two were growing on her. Although her siblings would be older by now, Jazzy often wondered what they'd be like at different ages. Maybe they'd be as polite and funny as these two ragamuffin kids. She hoped so. 'It's a hazard of the job. You never know when someone you've put away might decide to take their revenge.'

Turning to Ivor who was now rubbing Winky's furry belly and eliciting deep, contented purrs, Jazzy said, 'Grab the cat and we'll go through to the kitchen. We might as well have a warm drink whilst you tell me what this is all about.'

The two hesitated, glancing first at their sockless ruddy feet and then at the expanse of cream carpet leading to the kitchen.

'Go on, you're not going to damage the damn carpet.' Jazzy followed the teens through to the kitchen remembering a moment too late that she hadn't secured the anonymous cards back in their drawer. Wide-eyed, the two kids gazed at the bundle of cards and envelopes contained in evidence bags and scattered over the table. *Shite!* As she bustled past the two skinny frames and gathered up the offending articles, shoving them back where they belonged in the drawer under the table, Jazzy kept her tone light. 'Pop the kettle on, Benjy. I've only had a couple of hours' kip and I'm gasping.'

With the cards out of sight she took some fresh coffee from the fridge and began to spoon it into her cafetière. 'Coffee or tea?'

After dragging a chair through from the living room, the three of them huddled round the small table with scalding drinks before them. Jazzy looked at Benjy. 'You saw me and my partner by the Badlands last night, that it?'

Benjy frowned, opened his mouth and then closed it again without saying anything. He cast a glance in Ivor's direction but she shook her head in a 'you're on your own' sort of way and began blowing on her heavily sugared tea. Blinking rapidly, Benjy pushed his own, equally over-sugared drink away from him and shrugged. 'I did see you and the fa . . .' he paused and thought for a second '. . . I mean, your partner staking out the Argy Bargy. But that's not what I want to tell you.'

He bit his lip, his eyes darting round the room, his fingers clenching and unclenching, and a lightning bolt shot through Jazzy. 'You saw something, didn't you? You saw something near the Clarks' house?'

When Benjy nodded, Jazzy ran her fingers through her tangled hair and exhaled. 'Shit, Benjy, you followed me from the Clarks' house to the police station in Livingston and you didn't come in and make a statement? What were you thinking?'

As soon as the words left her lips, Benjy slumped back in his chair. As she studied him, she realised that every other officer would have seen, first and foremost, a kid from Stùrrach. A kid from a marginalised community with no regard for the police or the law. A kid they would instinctively distrust. Therefore, he had no reason to trust them. Except, Jazzy *did* trust him. He'd gone to great lengths to track her down and that told her that whatever he had to share was worth hearing. She modulated her tone, taking care to eliminate all trace of doubt, accusation or judgement from it. 'Tell me, Benjy. Tell me what you saw that was so important you came here.'

Ivor reached over and squeezed his arm. 'You've come this far, Benjy. Just tell her. She's okay, for an oink-oink, I suppose. She'll listen to you.'

Benjy swallowed hard, his Adam's apple prominent on his skinny neck, and when he spoke his words spewed out at speed. 'I saw someone hanging around the Clarks' house at about half-fiveish this morning.'

Her first thought was to wonder what had brought Benjy out in blizzard conditions so early in the morning, but judging from the flush on his cheeks, that was a sore point, so she decided to shelve that for now. This was wonderful news. A tangible lead. A witness sighting of a suspect in the vicinity of the murders. This was explosive and, now, all she had to do was extract more details from Benjy. She should take a formal statement. In fact, she should escort both of them to the station, but this was a delicate situation. Relations between the police and the Stùrrachers were notoriously difficult to navigate and she'd been extremely fortunate that Benjy had taken his civic duty seriously. Keeping him onside and calm was her main priority.

However, the dickless wonder would be fuming that she had interviewed a witness in her home. He might even consider Benjy a suspect. Besides Imogen's boyfriend Danny Banik, Benjy was an ideal candidate to lay the murder on. Benjy had gone out of his way to share his information. He'd overcome his natural dislike and distrust for the police to seek her out and communicate what he'd seen. Had he kept quiet, they'd still be scratting about for a witness. Besides, his sighting helped establish a timeline of sorts.

But Benjy's mind wasn't on his own fate. 'Is Imo okay? I saw the police cars arriving and the plods put up crime scene tape and then you arrived and went inside. I knew that something serious must have happened. Then the police sent us away so I ran off pronto. We don't draw attention to ourselves, us lot. Too easy to blame us for shit, but I like Imo.'

Is Imogen Clark okay? That was a hard question to answer. Of course, she wasn't okay, but Jazzy couldn't share that with Benjy, so she opted for pragmatism. 'Yes, she's fine. But, how do you know her?'

'She's in my year at school – we both go to the academy.'

Whatever Jazzy had been expecting, it wasn't that. She'd been told that the kids from Stùrrach were home-schooled. She'd been guilty of assuming social services, rather than engaging in a battle they were destined to lose, turned a blind eye, but here was Benjy saying he went to school.

Ivor, face flushed, put her mug down. 'Our Benjy's a bloody genius you know. He's smarter than the rest of us put together. He's going to go to university. He's going to do science or something, aren't you? Tell her, Benj.'

Benjy nodded. 'She's right. Ivor's da is the teacher in Stùrrach, but I was too clever for him, so he and Ivor convinced my ma and da to let me go to the academy.'

'Do you like it there, Benjy? At the academy?'

'Well some of the kids are right dicks, you know? But Imo was always kind to me.'

Jazzy couldn't begin to imagine how the kids at the academy would react to Benjy and his inadequate, well-worn clothing, his neck tattoo and unkempt hair. She'd experienced being ridiculed when she was at school. Being the poor brown kid with the smelly clothes and decade-old hand-me-downs wasn't conducive to fitting in. But that was a topic for another day. 'So, you were creeping about in sub-zero temperatures in the middle of the night in the pitch-black?'

A nod.

'You do that a lot, Benjy? Wander about at night?'

A shake of the head.

Jazzy sighed. This was going to be a slow process. 'Okay, Benjy, I can ask you questions and you can give monosyllabic or even non-verbal responses, but that's not gonna get us anywhere very fast, is it?'

Again, with the headshake.

'Right, so you went to the bother to find me. So, just tell me what happened. What you saw, okay? I don't care if you were getting up to dodgy stuff. As long as you didn't do anything wrong, I'm not interested. All I want is to know what you saw, all right?'

Benjy nodded and with a look of tortured determination on his face, he garnered the courage to spit the first few words out. 'I snuck out of the house about fourish or thereabouts and I saw you and the fat – I mean your partner in the car with your lights out. First I thought you were a couple of lesb . . .'

'Benjy!' Ivor's voice was sharp and Benjy stopped and bit his lip.

Jazzy smothered her smile because she suspected that Benjy had initially assumed that she and Queenie were engaging in some illicit lesbian tryst. *In those arctic conditions – no way she'd be engaging in anything with anyone, let alone Queenie.*

'I soon realised you were staking out the pub and cause I know there's nothing going on there, I didn't bother telling anyone you were there. Thought it was funny that you were freezing your bollocks off for no reason. So, I skirted round your car and made my way up to Fauldhouse.'

'Back up a bit. Why were you sneaking about in Fauldhouse in the middle of the night?'

Benjy shuffled his feet, took a slurp of his tea and cast another glance at Ivor. 'I was . . .' His voice trailed away into an indecipherable murmur.

'You were what?' Jazzy's tone brooked no argument. 'Look, this is serious stuff. People have been . . .' Jazzy hesitated. She didn't want to use the word 'murder' and any other just seemed so far from the truth. Finally, she settled on: '. . . hurt. People have been hurt and you've seen someone who might be a suspect. You need to come clean with me.' She paused and sighed. 'I know this is hard, but I promise, I'll help you, Benjy. However, I need you to tell me the truth.'

'She's right, Benjy. Jazzy won't dob you in. Just tell her.'

Although she didn't like Ivor making rash promises that she might not be able to keep, Jazzy let it lie. Right now, she needed him to trust her and she hoped that the reason for his nocturnal jaunt would prove to be crime-free and innocent. But she'd cross that bridge when she came to it. Banish the image of Queenie, arms crossed under her boobs, shaking her head at her, her lips pinched in that way she had of telling you she thought you were weak and saying 'sucker'. Jazzy waited.

'Well, it's all because of Bobby Walsh. He's a right arsewipe. He's in my year at school and whenever he sees me, he slags me off. He's always with a whole load of other lads. He makes my life hell. Says I smell.' His eyes flicked up to Jazzy, but didn't quite meet her gaze and Jazzy was acutely aware that contrary to either Benjy or Ivor smelling, *she* was the whiffy one. 'But I don't.'

'Every day. Every single damn day he's there. Just when the Fauldhouse bus pulls in, his dad sweeps up in his state-of-the-art BMW and Bobby gets out and starts pointing out the holes in my jeans or how old-fashioned my hoodie is or something and his sodding dad just bloody laughs and eggs him on. I mean it's just not right. Everybody laughs and taunts me and, because I'll get the blame if I retaliate, I just keep my head down and walk away.'

Jazzy's chest tightened and her admiration for this kid increased. 'Aw, Benjy, that's crap.'

He sniffed. 'Well, who cares? Bobby fucking Walsh is a thicko.

He won't be the one earning mega bucks and in a good job in a few years' time, will he?'

A flicker flitted across Ivor's eyes and Jazzy thought she understood what it was. Ivor wanted Benjy to achieve his dreams, but she was scared of losing him. Again, Jazzy understood that sometimes the sacrifice of letting those you love go for their betterment was too much to bear.

'I decided that I was going to get my own back on him. I just wanted to bring him down a peg or two. Make him have to slum it on the bus with the rest of us, for a change. So, I snuck out in the snow with my shovel.' Benjy was wringing his fingers together now, his eyes focused on the table. 'It was harmless, like. Nothing too bad. I just wanted to . . .' Head bowed he fell silent.

'What did you do, Benj?' Jazzy hoped that whatever revenge he'd taken didn't involve malicious damage. She wasn't sure that a juvenile record would go down well on a university application.

'I buried his dad's car.'

Jazzy blinked a couple of times. 'Buried it? What do you mean buried it?'

'In the snow. I buried it in the snow. I shovelled as much over the car as I could, so that either Bobby would have to catch the bus this morning, or he'd be late.' He paused. 'But after what I saw, I didn't go to school anyway, so God knows what happened to Bobby Walsh.'

Relief flooded Jazzy. This was a prank and hopefully Walsh hadn't reported it, so she could ignore it. Besides she was more concerned with what Benjy saw afterwards. 'And, what did you see?'

'Well, I must have got too close to his neighbour's car or something because all of a sudden a car alarm went off and I split. I ran down the close between the two houses and ended up after a while in Imo's street. I was frozen and my chest was about to burst so I wedged myself between two wheelie bins, hoping nobody would have followed me, and that's when I saw him. All in black like a ninja sneaking round the side of Imo's house like he'd been in her back garden.'

The familiar tingle that came when she was on to something important flickered in Jazzy's gut before working its way up to her shoulders. Benjy had seen the killer. She was sure of it. 'What time was this?'

''Bout half-five.'

'What did he do?'

'He looked up and down the road then jogged down towards the Scotmid. He had a bag with him.'

'Right, Benjy, this is important. Really important. Tell me everything you can about him. His height, his stature, skin tone, hair, anything.'

'He was covered from top to toe. Even had these weird sorts of goggles on – like ski goggles, but he didn't have skis.' Benjy screwed up his eyes in concentration. 'He was huddled over – almost bent in half, so it's hard to tell his height.'

Goggles? The description crashed through Jazzy like a mallet. Could the person Benjy saw at the Clark home be her stalker? With shaking fingers she lifted her phone up, selected a still of last night's intruder and turned it to Benjy.

Before she could say a word, Benjy almost jumped from his seat, pointing at the image. 'That's him. That's him, Jazzy. You got him already.'

It was as if she'd just been booted in the gut. Her earlier concerns had become more acute now and a multitude of thoughts crashed through her brain. Was it really likely that her stalker and the person Benjy had seen in the vicinity of a murder were the same person? Her police training told her to question coincidences, but wasn't this one too far-fetched? She took a breath and, in her mind, replayed everything she'd learned from Benjy, her feelings about the Clark crime scene and the footage of the unidentifiable man in goggles.

No matter how she played this, the evidence was too compelling

– the goggles, the timing, Benjy IDing the man he'd seen at Imogen's house as her stalker, the way the crime scene had been set up – all of this eradicated all possibility of coincidence. Which highlighted the worry Jazzy had kept bottled up – that this person was personally known to her. The birthday messages, the beans, the mutilation. It all intimated that. But who? Who hated her so badly they'd plan and execute such a complicated crime? Would Dwayne Taggart go to all this trouble to avenge his sister? Could he have researched Jazzy's past in order to cause her as much pain as possible? Of course, for someone determined enough, the information was out there for anyone to access and he certainly hated Jazzy, but to go to those extremes . . .? Jazzy shook her head, wishing she could focus better.

At the crime scene earlier, she'd been triggered. That's why she'd spaced out. The problem was, her faulty memory made it hard for her to interpret her emotional responses. Composing herself and hoping they wouldn't hear the tremor in her voice, Jazzy explained to her guests that they would need to come to the station with her to make a formal statement, but that she was going to call her partner, to sit with them whilst she took a shower and got ready. She took bread, cheese, jam and marg from the fridge and set them the task of making toast whilst she phoned Queenie.

'Queenie, I need you.'

'Right now? You need me right now? I've got a bit of a domestic going on here. The wean's teething again and the hubster's nipped to the shops.'

Momentarily confused that Queenie had a child to deal with, Jazzy paused. How had she not known her partner had a child? A pang of guilt slithered into her heart – she didn't know even the basic facts about Queenie's personal life because she had never asked. She hadn't been interested. Still, she'd have thought Queenie's family would be all grown up by now. She must be younger than she looked or maybe one of those women who got caught out during the menopause. 'Never mind, Queenie. I'll cope on . . .'

'Aw, nae bother, JayZee, Craig just walked in. Truth is, I'll be glad to escape this mayhem. I'll see you in fifteen minutes. I only live in Cauther.'

That was something else Jazzy hadn't known about her – that she lived in West Calder, the next but one village along. Another thing she hadn't bothered to ask. It was only as she stuffed a butter-slathered slice of toast in her gob that she realised she hadn't told Queenie where she lived, but she supposed that Queenie had been more interested in Jazzy than Jazzy had been in her. 'My partner will be here in a minute. Eat your toast and let her in when she arrives. But check the camera first, you hear me?'

Chapter 17

A mere ten minutes later, Jazzy, ponytail dripping down her neck was tucking her blouse into her jeans when the doorbell rang. *Bloody busier than flies on a cowpat!* She grinned at her own grouchiness. After all, she had invited Queenie to her home; still, two lots of visitors in one day was pushing it. Yanking a jumper over her top, she marched into the hallway as the bell rang again. *Bloody kids, couldn't they answer the damn thing?* But the house felt empty and there was no sign of them hovering near the still-ringing doorbell. Heart stuttering in her chest, Jazzy's shoulders tightened as she strode towards the kitchen. It was empty. The little toe rags had done a bloody runner and the only evidence that they'd ever been in her small kitchen was a smattering of crumbs on the table, a pile of washed dishes by the sink and a note with a jammy smudge and a single word scrawled on top, sitting centre stage – *Sorry!*

Shite! The wee buggers had done a runner and now she could hear Queenie's not so dulcet tones yelling through the door. 'JayZee, open up. Got a delivery for you.'

With a deep breath, Jazzy cursed and marched to the door. She should have realised that two kids from Stùrrach wouldn't hang around to be taken to a police station to make a statement.

That was why they'd gone to the bother of following her and ambushing her at home. *I'm such an idiot! I should have realised they'd need more coaxing to make their statements official.* Where the hell did they think they were going to hide, though? Did they really think she wouldn't pursue them or did they think they could do a Thelma and Louise in that clap heap of theirs? *Shite, shite, pish and shite, I should have seen this coming a damn mile off.*

Queenie would be unbearable about this. She'd go on and on and bloody on about wasting time looking for them. As for DCI Dick? When he got wind of this, he'd destroy her and, knowing him, he wouldn't do it in private. What a bloody cock-up! 'I'm coming, okay. Give me a minute?'

Face flushed, she yanked the door open and was about to go on about patience being a virtue when she realised that Queenie wasn't alone on her doorstep. In that precise moment she could have kissed her, for there she stood, spiky grey hair awry, a splodge of something that might have been baby sick on her top and the arms of two chastened teenagers gripped tightly at either side of her. Her grin told Jazzy that she might never hear the last of it, but Jazzy didn't care.

'These two scrotes belong to you, by any chance?'

Ignoring Queenie's question, Jazzy glared at Benjy and Ivor. 'What the hell were you thinking? You weren't bloody thinking, were you? Did you think you could just eat my toast, drink my tea, dump a whole load of information critical to a murder investigation at the table and hop it the minute my back was turned?'

Still ranting, she stepped back to allow Queenie to frogmarch the pair back indoors. 'This isn't a bloody game, you know. People have been killed—'

Jazzy stopped mid-sentence as the expression on Benjy's face registered. *Aw shite! Could this get any worse?*

Benjy shook off Queenie's hold and took a step towards Jazzy. 'You told me Imo was okay? You said she was fine. You didn't say anything about murder. I thought they'd been burgled.' An angry flush spread across his hollow cheeks as he glared at her, apparently unaware of the tears that flowed freely down his face.

He was only a kid and she'd messed up big time. She reached out to touch his arm, but he yanked it out of reach and stepped back. His breath came in short pants. As soon as Queenie released Ivor, she ran to his side, rubbing his back and glaring at them. Shuffling from foot to foot, Jazzy looked at Queenie, who was silent for once. Then without a word, Queenie stepped forward and approached the distraught boy. 'There, there, Benjy son, it's all right. Everything's going to be all right, A-okay, right as rain. Your friend Imogen *is* fine. It wasn't her who was killed.' Like a magician she produced a crumpled tissue from up her sleeve and proceeded to wipe Benjy's tears away, murmuring in a soft, soothing voice as she did so.

'Imogen's really okay?' Benjy's words were muffled, but a small hopeful smile lifted the corners of his mouth.

'Aye, she's fine, son. But, you know DC Solanki – Jazzy – can't really discuss an ongoing investigation with witnesses. She didn't do anything wrong and . . .' she used two fingers to lift his chin '. . . she didn't lie to you.'

Benjy sniffed, grabbed the tissue from Queenie and blew his nose before turning to Jazzy. 'Sorry. We shouldn't have run away and we wouldn't have if we'd known that bloke I saw had murdered someone. It's just . . .' he shrugged '. . . nobody from Stùrrach likes having anything to do with the pigs, I mean the polis.'

'Aye, I know, son. But that's okay, because now you know, you'll help us, won't you?' All the while she was talking Queenie guided Benjy towards the kitchen. Ivor trailed behind them and Jazzy darted into the living room to get yet another chair so they could all sit down. Never before had so many people been in her house at one time. Her stomach contracted as it hit her that she cared what Queenie thought of her home. *Where the hell has that come from?*

Once sitting, Benjy proceeded to shred the tissue Queenie had given him, till it was nothing more than a snow-like pile on the table. As if by mutual consent, nobody spoke, allowing him time to process the last few minutes. It was a lot to absorb, after all. Queenie took control of making hot drinks for everyone and Jazzy, her legs like jelly, slumped in her chair. When a tear plopped from Benjy's chin onto the waterproof tablecloth, Jazzy stirred to action and pushed a tissue box towards him. Her eyes flicked to Queenie who, whilst wielding a kettle full of boiling water gesticulated with her free hand and jerked her chin towards Benjy.

Jazzy cleared her throat and tried to block out Queenie's increasingly enthusiastic antics. 'You feeling better now, Benj?'

The abbreviation of his name was unintentional and it startled her. *Now, I'm on nickname terms with the kid?*

Benjy raised his head and swallowed hard. 'If Imo's okay, then who's been murdered, Jazzy?'

As she held his gaze, Jazzy knew there was no way she could lie to him. The Clarks' names would soon be released to the press, if they hadn't already been leaked. No doubt the Clarks' bodies would have been transported from the scene to the mortuary and speculation would be rife. Hopefully, the precise nature of their deaths wouldn't be leaked because those details were an ace up the police's sleeves and could be crucial in making sure the killer was prosecuted. 'It was Imogen's parents, Benjy.'

Benjy nodded. 'I thought that must be the case.' He smiled his thanks to Queenie as she handed him a mug of tea. 'You think the bloke I saw did it? You think he killed Imo's parents?' Although his voice cracked on the last word, he took a deep breath and maintained his composure.

'We don't know, but we need as much information as we can. Are you okay to tell Queenie what you told me, Benjy? It could really help us.'

Twenty minutes later, with Queenie fully up to date, she and Jazzy escaped to the living room leaving Ivor and Benjy listening to the radio in the kitchen – that was Jazzy's attempt to drown out their conversation. Together, they scrutinised the anonymous cards Jazzy had received over the years and the security cam footage.

'Shit a brick, JayZee, you don't do things by half, do you? First you piss off the dickless wonder, landing us in the doghouse and then you don't share relevant information about a stalker who might be linked to the murders. Then to crown it all, you take statements from under-age kids in your home. How many more rules do you want to break? How many more lines are you going to fudge? How many . . ?'

'I get it, Queenie. I bloody get it, but what was I supposed to do when they turned up on my doorstep? I thought it was something to do with the Argy Bargy. I'd no idea it was to do with the Clarks' murders.' Jazzy threw herself onto her favourite chair. 'And, for your information, I didn't take a statement. I interviewed them in an unofficial capacity. Soon as I realised they had relevant information, I phoned you, didn't I?'

'Aye so you did, then you swanned off, leaving them unsupervised while you had a shower.' She glared at Jazzy. 'Not very professional now, is it?'

Despite realising the truth of Queenie's accusations, Jazzy couldn't stop herself. 'Professional? Professional? *You're* the one who was knitting on duty. You're the one who stabbed a prisoner with a bloody knitting needle. Besides, I was minging. I needed a damn shower.'

'Minging? Minging? I'll tell you what's minging. This whole entire investigation is minging and, if we don't do something about it, DCI Tony Dick is going to fuck it *and* us up big time. So, what are we going to do about that?'

Queenie sank onto the couch opposite, and allowed her gaze to drift over Jazzy's possessions as they pondered their predicament. 'What's that pretty wee thing up there on that shelf, JayZee?'

Jazzy followed her partner's gaze. How the hell had eagle-eyed

Queenie spotted it up there? Her auntie Lillie had given her the mandir when she moved out and it had lived, filled with its mini Hindu god statues and an incense burner, in every home Jazzy had ever lived. If Queenie was curious about that, there was no way Jazzy would confide that she kept a miniature Lord Ganesh – remover of obstacles – in her coat pocket. Not for religious reasons, but because her mum and dad had given it to her when she joined the police – to help her solve cases. 'It's a mandir. Hindus pray in front of it when they're not at the temple.'

Queenie snorted. 'Well, maybe you should bring it down and start using it. We'll need all the prayers we can to get out of this mess. Besides, it's lovely. Very ornate and bright. Uplifting really.'

Jazzy wanted to tell Queenie that her dad had made it for her, but something held her back. That lack of trust again. The same old unwillingness to reveal any of herself. 'We'll do what we said we would earlier as we were leaving the station. We'll make sure this case is solved. We'll take Benjy in, get an appropriate adult to sit with him and get Geordie to take a formal statement. Then, we'll take this to Dick and make identifying this guy a priority.'

Head to one side, Queenie considered Jazzy's proposal then shook her head. 'The image of your secret admirer tells us zilch. So . . .' She took a deep breath. 'I can't believe I'm going to say this, but I suggest we do everything you say, *except* for telling Dick about your stalker. I mean what would he do about that anyway? Sod bloody all, that's what. *And* it's not as if the camera capture gives us a solid ID on this guy.'

'You're suggesting holding back evidence, Queenie?'

Queenie raked her fingers through her hair. 'I don't want to do that. Christ, we're in the bad books as it is without doing anything else dodgy, but . . .' She shook her head. 'You're the subject of so much gossip as it is around the station. Do you really want to give them more?'

Queenie had a point. Every time she walked into a room Jazzy could feel the stares. Everyone was gossiping in corners about whether she and the chief super, Waqas Afzal, had been involved in a torrid affair. She was all too aware of that. She was also aware that her own actions had made her fair game for the gossip. However, could she wilfully cover up evidence pertinent to an ongoing investigation just to save herself from even more embarrassment? She was tempted, really tempted, but, 'No, Queenie. I can't do that. We need to bring all of this to the table and . . .' with a smile that didn't quite light up her eyes she added: '. . . sod what anyone says.'

Queenie released a loud whoosh of air. 'Thank Christ for that, JayZee. I didn't want to do anything dodgy, but for your sake I would. We're partners now after all. Come on, hen. Let's go and face the dogs.'

Jazzy's heart contracted. Queenie had been prepared to compromise her own principles for Jazzy's sake and that meant something. Especially when they hardly knew each other. Maybe, given the chance, they could make a good team after all. 'I'll talk to Fenton and Geordie and if my persuasive wiles don't keep them on side, I'll let you loose with a wrecking ball. Deal?'

Queenie grinned. 'Deal. Now let's get this show on the road.'

As they left Jazzy's house Queenie and Jazzy were on high alert in case her stalker was about. Queenie hurried the kids to her car whilst Jazzy scanned the area, before slamming the door shut on Benjy who was squashed in the back seat next to a rearward-facing baby seat. *So, Queenie does have a kid.* Before she could walk over to her Mini, Benjy cracked the window open. 'You looking for someone watching you, Jazzy?'

Prepared to reassure the boy, Jazzy smiled. 'Just a precaution, don't worry . . .'

'Well, there was a car earlier. It was down there facing the other way when we drew up, but I saw it following you from the roundabout. I thought it was a copper, but . . .?'

Every nerve in Jazzy's body vibrated as her head jerked up to rescan the area. Queenie was out of the car in a flash, also scanning the streets. 'God's sake Jazzy, bad enough you not noticing these two eejits in their bloody crapmobile, but not noticing your stalker tailing you is downright remiss.'

Satisfied that the car Benjy had seen was no longer nearby, Jazzy took a more detailed description of the vehicle – black, tinted windows, large – probably a Range Rover, with its plate obscured by muck. She'd send an officer to determine whether any home security cameras had recorded the car. Knowing when she'd picked up the tail at the Dedridge roundabout, a civilian employee would secure the footage. Hopefully they'd get a number plate and owner ID. In her Mini, Jazzy followed Queenie to the station, her eyes scanning the roads for any suspicious vehicles.

Chapter 18

On arrival at the station, Jazzy grabbed DC Geordie McBurnie and escorted the teenagers to the interview rooms so he could take Benjy's statement. Fortunately, it transpired that McBurnie had a history with Benjy's dad after helping him out with a minor incident a year earlier. McBurnie glanced away when Jazzy probed about how he'd manage to break through the notoriously private Albert Hendry's exterior to be allowed to interview his son. Chin up, he met her eye. 'I lived in Stùrrach for years, before I left to go to Tulliallan for police training.'

With his lips twisted in a sardonic grin, he added, 'Contrary to popular opinion, the Stùrrach folks don't all run amok, bay at the moon and deal drugs. They just want to be left to their own devices, but they've no objection to people leaving if that's what they want. Mind you that's not to say they're A-okay with Misty Thistle. They're fine with me being gay, but being a drag queen is, to some of the more traditional Stùrrachers, a step too far, especially in high heels.'

Jazzy laughed. She had trouble walking in shoes higher than an inch, but it intrigued her that once again she was learning something meaningful about a colleague. She couldn't begin to imagine the challenge the move from Stùrrach to Police Scotland must have been, but she was certain that Geordie McBurnie deserved kudos for making that step. As a gay man and a drag queen, Geordie had jumped from one frying pan into an even hotter one and it was testament to his strength of character that he handled the homophobic crap dealt out to him by the few Neanderthals roaming the station, with great aplomb.

Geordie lowered his voice. 'If it's all the same to you, though, I'd rather keep my connection to Stùrrach quiet or I'll end up being shunted there every time something happens that concerns that community. Don't want to be pigeonholed.'

Jazzy got it. She hated being paraded as one of the few brown-skinned women on the force every time they needed a 'diversity' representative. Glad that Benjy and Ivor were in safe hands, she hooked her rucksack containing the cards in their evidence bags onto her shoulder and, wishing she'd managed a few hours' more sleep and that her head wasn't filled with cotton wool or her eyes gritty and red-rimmed, went in search of DCI Dick.

She hesitated outside his office door to ground herself before knocking, took a deep breath and waited for his perfunctory 'Come'.

When he didn't immediately respond she realised he was with someone and her heart sank. She'd wanted to catch him on his own in the hope that she'd absorb most of his wrath in private, but it would be just like Dick to insist she tell him the purpose of her visit, no matter who was in the room with him. *Dick by name, dick by nature.*

The mumble of voices drifted on and Jazzy, assuming he didn't want to be interrupted, was on the point of beating a retreat when the door burst open and the chief superintendent, stood there. When were things going to go her way? The last person she wanted to witness her current fall from grace was Waqas Afzal.

Still talking to Dick, it took a moment for the super to register her presence and when he did, he stopped and studied her. His eyes raked over her face, down to her tense shoulders and back, no doubt noting the blush that covered her cheeks. 'DC Solanki?' A frown gathered across his forehead but his voice was calm and noncommittal. 'Come to tell us you've solved the Clark murders already, have you?'

Jazzy swallowed a lump in her throat and shook her head. 'No, sir, but I do need to speak with the DCI.' She paused and, hoping it would be enough to send the super on his way, added, 'In private.'

Waqas's frown deepened and his gaze fell to her hands and, too late, Jazzy realised she'd been wringing them. Why did he have to be so damn observant? Dick, being a dick, busied himself with paperwork on his desk and sighed. 'Can't it wait, Solanki? I'm a bit tied up at the moment.'

But, the chief super moved to the side and gestured for Jazzy to enter the room. 'Is it something to do with the Clark investigation?'

Wishing that she could say no, Jazzy offered a tight nod and resigned herself to being rollicked in front of her nemesis, for there was no way Waqas would leave them to it now. She was right. On shaking legs, she slipped past him. Waqas fell in place behind her and followed her to the front of DCI Dick's desk. He plonked himself down on the chair that he'd presumably left only moments earlier whilst Jazzy stood like a naughty schoolgirl before the head teacher.

Her boss threw the sheaf of paperwork onto the desktop and glared at her. 'Out with it, then. I'm all ears.'

With her entire face burning, Jazzy began the long tale starting with Benjy and Ivor tuning up at her home – but omitting the part where they ran away – and ending with Benjy recognising her stalker. By the time she ground to a halt, DCI Dick's face was an interesting shade of puce. The sparks flying from his eyes threatened to do serious damage to her. She swallowed, her throat feeling like a porcupine had taken up residence there. But it wasn't Dick who spoke first. It was the chief super, and his voice was gentle with an undertone of some emotion that Jazzy was unable to pinpoint. 'Sit down, Jazzy. That's quite a lot to take in.'

He pulled another chair over from the corner of the room and indicated she should take it. When she was sitting, he poured a glass of water and pressed it into her hand. All the while, Jazzy was acutely aware of Tony Dick's narrowed eyes, taking in his boss's movements. It didn't take a genius to work out that Dick was trying to figure out if the rumours about Jazzy and his big boss were true. Shite! Her relationship with DCI Dick was bad enough without him thinking she might expect favours from above his head. It was *so* unfair and as her throat tightened, she wanted to jump up and yell at both of them. For once, though, common sense prevailed.

Once back in his chair, Afzal, a pulse throbbing at his temple, quirked an eyebrow at Dick. DCI Dick cleared his throat and leaned forward, casting a nervous glance in Waqas's direction. Inside Jazzy groaned. That look meant that Dick would be civil – possibly even solicitous to her in his boss's presence – but it would come at a cost. A cost that would be exacted later on, when he could humiliate her the most. 'Well, eh, Jazzy, it's unorthodox to take statements from juveniles without parental consent.'

Jazzy couldn't help herself. 'I didn't take a statement. They went at great lengths to seek me out and were keen to pass on information. It was informal and as soon as I realised the importance of Benjy's information, I told them that we would need a formal statement taken in the presence of an appropriate adult – which is what's happening now. DC McBurnie, after contacting Benjy's parents – who agreed that his older cousin, eighteen-year-old Ivory Sturrock, could be his adult representative – is taking their statement.'

Afzal let out a short burst of laughter. 'That lad McBurnie must have a golden tongue if he convinced a Stùrrach family to entrust one of their own to us.'

'I believe Geordie has had dealings with Benjy's dad before, after someone graffitied the man's car in a Morrisons car park. Geordie managed to get reimbursement for the vandalism and everyone was happy. That made it easier for us.'

'Well, I hope you've written up a report about this and uploaded it to the server?'

'I'll do . . .'

'Wait a minute, Tony. If I'm not mistaken this information means that there's a very definite link between Jazzy's stalker and the Clarks' murders. You'll be holding a briefing to update the team, no doubt? And I'm sure you'll implement the necessary security measures to keep Jazzy safe in the interim.'

Dick opened his mouth, then snapped it shut again. His glare told Jazzy that her personal safety was low on his priority list.

Without waiting for a response, Waqas turned to Jazzy, his dark eyes unflinching in their scrutiny. 'What I don't understand though, Jazzy, is why you've never logged any of these anonymous letters before.'

Jazzy bit her lip. There it was. The question she least wanted to answer. There was no way she could tell Waqas Afzal that she'd confided in DI Elliot Balloch after the very first one arrived when she was still working from Gayfield Square in Edinburgh. Or that she'd convinced him to process the cards on the down-low. Or that, because she was so paranoid and untrusting, she communicated with Elliot only via burner phone. Or that, with their shared history, she had any sort of relationship with him whatsoever. These were secrets she wanted to keep to herself.

She shrugged. 'They were innocuous and unthreatening and over the last five years, they arrived so sporadically, I didn't consider them important.' She risked a smile. 'I mean who doesn't get threats from the public, eh? It's a rite of passage, isn't it?'

The chief super's eyebrows gathered, announcing a storm cloud about to break. 'We take each and every threat against a serving police officer seriously. You know that, Detective. Stalkers escalate. You know that too. It's part of your training. They can't just be left unmonitored – unlogged. It needs to be nipped in the bud or . . .' He wafted his hand in the air, but left his sentence unfinished.

Nobody needed to fill in the blanks. If she'd taken her stalker seriously and reported it in the first instance, then perhaps the Clarks would still be alive celebrating their daughter's birthday today. She took a sip of water to try to clear the blockage in her throat, then picked up her backpack from the floor where she'd dropped it when she sat down. 'I've got them all here. Every one of them.' She took the bundle out and handed them to Waqas.

As he sifted through them, DCI Dick looked at the captured home security cam footage, his lips pursed, making him look like a pouting fish. 'This is worse than useless. There're no clear features on display, no clear idea of body size or shape and the only thing linking this' – he shook her phone in the air – 'and our crime scene is the word of a scrote from Stùrrach. Hardly conclusive. My money's still on the boyfriend either on his own or abetted by the daughter.'

Jazzy's mouth fell open and all the disgust she felt for the man opposite crackled through her body. 'We can't dismiss Benjy's evidence, sir. The only reason I showed him the cam image was because his description of the man seen leaving the Clark's property was so similar to the one I'd spent hours looking at myself. He mentioned the hunch, the goggles, the face mask, the ninja clothes . . .'

'We've only got your word, DC Solanki, that he gave you that description *before* you showed him the footage and we've only got *his* word that this character was anywhere near the Clarks' house.'

Almost vibrating with rage, Jazzy jumped to her feet. 'Basic police work will confirm whether this Walsh character's car was buried in snow and whether a neighbour's car alarm went off at the time Benjy specified. Surely that's corroboration enough. He's got no reason to make this up.'

Dick clicked his fingers, a slow triumphant smile spreading across his moustached lips. 'Maybe *he* did it. Maybe your friend

Benjy needs to be scrutinised more deeply.'

'Enough!' The storm cloud had broken and Waqas's words pelted the room like hailstones. 'What the hell's got into you, Tony? As for you, DC Solanki, another charge of insubordination wouldn't look good on your record now, would it? Both of you need to rein it in. There's a clear personality clash here, but I won't allow that to interfere with the successful conclusion of this investigation.'

He got to his feet, glaring at each of them in turn. 'This man' – he shook the bundle of evidence bags in his hand – 'is clearly a person of interest. It's beyond the bounds of possibility to assume that two men dressed similarly would be wandering about in such a narrow vicinity on the same night and not be involved in those murders. Thus, as Sherlock Holmes himself would surmise, we have no alternative but to pursue this as an active line of inquiry.'

He strode round the room, leaving the other two in no doubt that his anger was still not spent. 'The biggest questions we have to address moving forward are why he chose to escalate to murder, now? Why did he choose the Clarks and what is the significance of this modus operandi?'

The atmosphere was arctic. Afzal's words hung in the air like frosty icicles about to break and shatter into a trillion pieces on the floor. The colour drained from Jazzy's face and as the import of Afzal's words cut through her like acid, she swayed on the seat. If anyone should be able to guess the significance of that crime scene it was her. As soon as she'd seen it – the ritualistically posed bodies, the chilling attention to detail, she'd suspected that this scene was somehow related to her.

But were her instincts spot on or was her imagination running away from her? She needed someone from back then to talk it through with. She was tempted to spit her thoughts and fears into the frigid atmosphere but, as if anticipating her reaction, the super narrowed his eyes and gave an almost imperceptible headshake. His eyes bored into hers, their meaning clear. *Now's not the time, Jazzy.* She closed her eyes, wondering when the time would be. She wished she could remember what had happened back then. Oh, how she wished Elliot Balloch would get back to her! He'd know what to do; he always did.

Tony Dick stirred, his moustache quivering as he spoke, his words clipped. 'We'll update the team. Everyone needs to be aware of this.'

In a rare moment of kindness, he turned to Jazzy and his tone softened. 'Half an hour, DC Solanki. You've got half an hour to pull yourself together before the briefing.'

Relief rolled over her and without glancing at either of them, she stumbled to the door intent on finding the nearest loos. As the door slid shut behind her, DCS Waqas's words followed her, his tone dark. 'What a clusterfuck. What a bloody clusterfuck this is.'

Gulping for breath, Jazzy tried to push away the thought that time was running out for her. Truth be told, time had always been running out for her. From the minute she decided to join Police Scotland her life had been like a huge egg timer with the sand trickling inexorably to the moment when everything she wanted to keep secret would become fodder, not only for her colleagues to gossip about by the water cooler, but for the press, the public and every damn criminal in Scotland. Her career would be over; the life she'd worked so hard to achieve would, in the blink of an eye, disappear. Moving forward, instead of being defined by her work ethic, her clear-up rate, her professionalism, she would be forever defined by something she couldn't even remember.

She burst into the ladies' toilets, did a quick check to make sure she was alone and then locked the door. Leaning over the sink, her head bowed, she gasped in great hulking breaths and tried to force her lungs to accept them. Finally, when the pain in her chest eased, she lifted her head and started at her reflection in the mirror above the sink. No wonder DCI Dick had taken pity on her. Her dark eyes were dilated and huge hollow bruises hung, like pendulums, beneath them. Her brown skin looked sallow and dull, and a pulse throbbed erratically in her neck. She lifted shaking fingers to it as if she could stop it pulsating, but of course she couldn't. She backed away from her reflection, wishing she could curl up and weep, not wanting to see how destroyed she was.

When her back hit a cubicle door, she pushed it open, lowered the toilet seat lid and collapsed onto it, cradling her head in her hands. Slowly, the lemony scent of bleach along with the sound of voices passing in the corridor outside penetrated her senses. She leaned back, resting her head on the wall, and allowed the soothing everyday sounds to lull her into a memory that she frequently had – one she could never make sense of.

She sits in front of a roaring fire playing with a baby doll. Her long brown hair is in pigtails and she's wearing leggings and a jumper. After setting her doll, Sally, lovingly on a cushion, she places the small wooden mandir on a large white hankie on the rug before her. She whispers and sings to 'her baby' as they play together. She is so engrossed in her make-believe world that she's unaware of her parents entering the room. They stand watching her. The man smiles, his brown eyes all sparkly – just like hers. His lips twitch as he listens to her sing. Although dressed in a suit, his large hands are all rough and scratchy when he tickles her.

Next to him, the woman in a calf-length dress, gathered at the waist to emphasise her slim figure, lays her hand on his arm. Her dark brown hair is curled into an elegant bob of sleek shiny curls. Her only make-up is a dash of pink lipstick on too-thin lips. Unlike the man, she frowns and purses her lips in a way that makes her look ugly. She thrusts her arm through his and glares at her daughter.

Jazzy screwed her hands tighter, willing herself to remember why her mum didn't like her, why she'd never liked her. Jazzy Solanki must have been an evil child – a naughty, misbehaving, evil child. That was the only explanation.

The man coughs and the little girl looks up.

'Daddy!' Her tiny face is flushed in the heat from the fire and,

smiling, she runs over to him, her doll momentarily forgotten. He releases his wife's arm and grabs the girl under her oxters, he swings her up and into his arms. Laughing, he twirls her round and round and round until the air is filled with high-pitched squeals of delight, and Jazzy is laughing so much she can hardly breathe.

Her mum watches, a frown pulling her eyebrows down, her eagle eyes scouring the room. When she sees Jazzy's 'picnic' on the rug, her face darkens, an ugly flush stains her cheeks and when she speaks, her voice is strident and cold. 'What do you think you're doing with my mandir?'

Dad lowers Jazzy to the floor, pushing her behind his legs. The little girl's lower lip trembles as she peeps round her dad's legs. He smiles at his wife and holds out placating arms. 'The bairn's only copying what you do, hen.'

'That's not the point!' she snaps, storming over to the rug and inspecting each of the god statues for damage. 'She's always helping herself to things that don't belong tae her.'

Jazzy's eyes sparked open. She knew what was going to happen, but she couldn't escape it. She'd seen this so many times and she could never stop it once it started.

With a sudden hand movement, her mum yanks the hankie, sending the mandir crashing over onto the rug. 'See what I mean? She's been snooping in our bedroom and stolen your new white hankie.'

Still hiding Jazzy behind his legs, her dad pats his wife on the arm. 'That's not my new one. Don't fret, hen. Ye'll get yourself all worked up again.'

Jazzy edges closer to her daddy. Her arms snake round his leg and cling on tightly like one of Tammy Forester's ferrets. She keeps her face hidden in his familiar tobacco-scented trousers, but her mum wrenches her by the arm and drags her away from him, screaming, 'Ye always take her side. Always! No wonder she's so naughty.'

Finding a voice from somewhere, the little girl, hands on hips, says in a wobbling voice, 'I wasn't being naughty, Mummy. I was only praying with Sally. We were praying for you to be happy.'

There is silence for a moment. Then . . .

Crack!

Although she'd expected it, Jazzy jumped, her hand jerked straight up to her cheek as if the slap had happened there and then.

The girl squeals and rubs at the angry red welt that appears on her cheek.

'For God's sake! There was no need for that, Hansa. If I don't mind her praying the Hindu way, why should you?'

'She's not a real Hindu. How can she be when you're Muslim?'

Her dad kneels down beside the crying girl and wipes her tears away. 'Yer mummy doesn't mean it, sweetie. She's not well.'

The mother, her face distorted, her chest heaving, moves closer. 'Ah didn't mean it, did I?'

She grabs the little girl, her hand circling her daughter's upper arm, and she swings her round throwing her onto the rug. Jazzy's head bounces off the fire guard. Tears stream down her face. She reaches up with a trembling hand and touches her head. When she looks at her fingers they're smeared with blood. 'Daddy.'

But her dad is busy trying to wrap his arms round his wife, who bats him away, swearing at the top of her voice as she struggles and kicks out at him. Her hands, clenched into fists, aim for his face. Her dad backs off, his hands extended in a placating gesture, his mouth tight. His glances keep flitting to his daughter, yet still he engages with his wife, talking in quiet soothing tones, like she is a wild animal. She doesn't listen though. Now he's let her go, she bends over and snatches the doll from the floor. 'Do you see this? Do ye? Do ye see it?'

The little girl nods, her bottom lip trembling.

'Well, this is what happens to dolls when wee lassies cannae behave.'

And ignoring both the girl's choked pleas and her husband's quiet, 'Aw don't do that, Hansa. The bairn loves that doll.' *She yanks at the doll's head. At last, it comes off in her hands. Without a second's hesitation she swings round, plucks back the fire guard and tosses the head into the middle of the flames. When she turns back to her husband and child, her eyes are bright, her lips turned up in a satisfied smile. 'Well that's a job well done.'*

She pats her hair to make sure it is in place. Daddy shakes his head and takes three backward steps, keeping his eyes low. He says nothing whilst his daughter mews like a lost kitten. Her small hands held to her cheeks, eyes as wide as picnic plates. Ignoring the blood trickling from her forehead, she kneels in front of the fire, watching the blue flames distort and melt Sally's delicately painted features.

When there is no more than a blob of blackened gunge to be seen in the fire, she curls up into the foetal position and weeps, hugging Sally's headless body, still wearing its woolly blue dress, against her skinny one. Her dad pats her head before he turns and walks silently out of the room with her mum.

Whilst the scene faded before Jazzy, the hurt and trauma remained. The same questions she asked herself every time she relived that scenario filled her head. Why had her dad left her with that woman? Why didn't he love her enough to take her with him? What had happened to her mum the night she died?

A commotion outside the toilet jolted Jazzy back to the present. Queenie yelling and hammering on the door brought her down to earth. 'You've got five minutes so get yer finger out yer arse and get a shimmy on.'

Jazzy got up and spent a few seconds splashing her face with cold water and pinching some colour into her cheeks before flinging her shoulders back and yanking open the door, to see Queenie, her face contorted into a worried expression, waiting for her. 'Come on, Solanki. Were you having a crap in there?'

Chapter 19

With Queenie by her side, Jazzy walked into the incident room. She kept her eyes to the front, refusing to meet the gazes of any of the officers and civilian employees who tracked her progress to the nearest chair. Although they didn't yet know what had prompted the briefing, her late arrival and obvious discomfort had sparked interest. She hated being the focus of attention and knowing that this group of people – most of whom she barely knew – were about to be given access to something she'd kept private for so long was upsetting. She was glad of Queenie's presence beside her and was aware of the scorching looks her partner was directing at anyone whose gaze lingered too long in their direction. This was going to be difficult, but she had to get through it.

When DCI Dick stood up at the front and cleared his throat, Jazzy cast a quick look round the room searching for the chief super, but he wasn't there. Her heart skipped a beat, which unsettled her even more. She hadn't actually expected him to offer moral support – particularly not after she'd publicly humiliated them both and caused a minor scandal that had prompted some very sordid rumours to circulate. So, why did his absence affect her so?

With her back erect, she bowed her head and listened as the

dickless wonder explained about her stalker and the link to the Clark murders as established by Benjy's witness statement. Her skin burned as two dozen pairs of eyes flicked towards her, stripping her bare. She wanted to jump up and run from the room as Dick's emotionless voice continued. Her cheeks became warm and her vision blurred. How would she be able to hold her head up high in this room again? Would she have to relocate to another force? Although most of the people present would sympathise with her, there would be the few Neanderthals who would blame her or find criticism of her decision to downplay the damn cards.

'Clearly, the information provided by DC Solanki and the additional witness account from this Benjy Hendry character sheds a new light on the Clarks' murders. You can read it in full on the server. The anonymous communications received by DC Solanki have been sent to the lab for forensic analysis, but copies of them have been made and uploaded too. You can access them at your leisure later. For now, I want us to look at the home security footage of DC Solanki's nocturnal visitor. The original has also been sent to the tech team for enhancement, with orders to expedite it.'

With the lights dimmed, Jazzy watched as the footage she'd already scrutinised a zillion times was replayed on the large screen at the front of the room. The sensation that she was revealing something very private sent a shiver up her spine, but she focused on the clarity of the recording, looking for details she'd missed in all her earlier viewings. Her stalker seemed more threatening on a larger screen. She doubted that the tech team would be able to enhance it enough to give them any additional clues to his identity, but it was worth pursuing. Now she could follow his movements more closely, his stoop appeared even more deliberate. She wondered if his body size was bulked out with wadding or additional layers of clothing.

Twice more they played the recording, and each time felt like a violation. Like they were plundering her very being. As if sensing her reaction, Queenie placed a hand on Jazzy's arm and squeezed. The human touch calmed her a little and she scolded herself. This was all part of the job. Nobody was intruding on her privacy and, if a few moments of discomfort shed some light on what was going on, then she was happy.

'That recording has also been uploaded to the server.' Dick's voice broke through the silence that followed the end of the final showing. 'Additional actions are as follows.'

He took a sip from a glass of water and, consulting a sheet of paper, updated everyone. 'One team will be searching for a link between the Clarks and DC Solanki. At this stage we don't know if there is a direct link or if the killer selected the Clarks for some other reason. However, no stone will go unturned. DCs McBurnie and Heggie are already underway with background checks on neighbours, work colleagues and any other contacts. One of our civilian operatives, Janine, is trawling HOLMES 2 for similar crimes. We're using the postmarks on the cards previously posted to DC Solanki to try to narrow the parameters a little.' He cleared his throat and glared in Jazzy's direction, accusation burning in his eyes. He didn't have to add that if she'd reported her stalker earlier, they wouldn't be in this position now. Jazzy flinched, then raised her chin and met his gaze. She had never backed down from a confrontation and Dick could hate her all he liked, but right now they needed her input.

His lips curled up in a snarl that made his moustache look like an undulating slug on his upper lip. Jazzy gave a humourless twitch of her lips. His eyes narrowed briefly before he turned back to the room. 'CCTV and ANPR between DC Solanki's home in Bellsquarry and Fauldhouse is being collected. The footage from her security camera combined with the statement from Benjy Hendry gives us a timescale to work with. We don't know how much time the killer spent with the Clarks; however, we know that Benjy Hendry saw him leave at around 5.30, therefore he had a good two or three hours and more to do whatever he needed to. Of course, Imogen discovered her parents at between 6.45 and 7 a.m.'

A disturbance by the door had heads turning and officers swivelling round in their seats to see what was going on. 'I'm really sorry to interrupt, DCI Dick.' The desk sergeant from downstairs ignored the curious glances and stalked towards Dick. 'I've got a reporter downstairs – a Ginny Bell – she's quite hysterical. Turns out someone's sent her some quite gruesome images from today's crime scene. She's asking for DC Solanki, but I thought she might be better talking to you. I got a constable to take her to one of the nice rooms.'

A wave of tension rolled through the room and every eye zoomed first to the sergeant and then to Jazzy, as if she was somehow responsible. Unless they had a leak – which seemed unlikely – the killer had contacted Ginny Bell himself. This could be another indication that their killer was escalating. If he wasn't already a serial killer then he was definitely one in the making, and so far he'd got the better of them. Conscious of the intense scrutiny, Jazzy focused on a point to the front of the room above the large white screen and tried to order her thoughts. Of course, many people – CSIs, police officers, lab techs, civilian employees – had access to the crime scene photos and, of course, the killer himself would have had plenty of time to photograph his work. The thought of him snapping away at the crime scene, treating it like a day out, made her want to scream. A ball of hot rage gathered in her chest and seemed to swell with every passing second.

Dick's arrogant tone brought her back to earth and she found his gaze was on her, his shoulders tense and sparks flying from his eyes. She was in no doubt that he blamed her for this mess, but more than that, he wanted every single person in the room to doubt her also. It was a cheap but effective trick. Jazzy kept herself to herself and – apart from her recently formed alliance with Queenie, Geordie and Fenton – she had few allies in the room. 'If, one of you is responsible for leaking confidential crime scene photos, I *will* find you and I *will* hang, draw and quarter you. Until I find who has done this or it is confirmed that the killer sent them, I will scrutinise every one of you who had access to them. I won't tolerate this sort of blatant betrayal on my team. Understood?'

A mumble of 'yes, sirs' filled the room and Jazzy was conscious of speculative glances landing on her. What a bastard Dick was. He smiled at her and continued, 'DCs Solanki and McQueen can take a statement from this reporter. I've got Danny Banik waiting in interview room two.'

Jazzy swallowed, a frown cutting across her forehead. He'd left that kid in an interview room whilst he held this briefing? What was Dick thinking? Of course they needed to speak with him, but it seemed heavy-handed, even for Dick, to drag a suspect down to the station for a first interview on little more than a whim and no hard evidence, then leave him hanging around for ages. He could have conducted an informal one at Banik's home, established his alibi, found out more about his relationship with Imogen and her parents and, if more evidence against the lad was forthcoming from his social media postings or interactions with Imogen, then they could bring him in. From experience, Jazzy knew the boy would be on high alert and would be less likely to open up at the station. Why the hell did Dick have to go in so hard? Was he going to drag Imogen Clark in from her hospital bed where she was still being treated for shock, too?

She scratted around for a way to redeem the situation and could only come up with one. She raised her hand and without waiting for DCI Dick to acknowledge her said, 'I'm wondering if it might be better if *you* speak with Ginny Bell, sir.' Jazzy forced herself to imbue the 'sir' with more respect than she felt. 'The information she has may well constitute a huge breach of protocol and we don't want that to get away from us, do we? Perhaps someone with your seniority might get more from her. Maybe Queenie and I could interview the Banik boy?'

Silence reigned for a nanosecond and Jazzy hoped he might grab her suggestion with both hands. But no such luck. Although he maintained a degree of composure, none of the people in the room were in any doubt of DCI Dick's anger. His puce face and clenched fists were a dead giveaway and although Jazzy maintained a placid expression, her legs were shaking. When he spoke, each of Dick's words dropped into the room like ice in a hailstorm. 'I've issued my instructions, Detective. Were they not clear?'

Jazzy clenched her hands, by her sides, but managed a nod. 'Of course, sir. No problem. Queenie and I will interview the journalist.'

Dick narrowed his eyes at her and held her gaze for an excruciating few seconds, before dismissing the officers. 'Right, if that's all, we've all got work to do. Get cracking.'

The subsequent flurry of activity was punctuated by some sympathetic glances being sent in Jazzy's direction, but that was balanced by almost as many scornful ones.

Jazzy avoided them all as she got to her feet, but before she and Queenie could escape, Janine – the civilian analyst – approached. Behind her large spectacles, her eyes were kind as she smiled at Jazzy, a slender hand extended. 'DC Solanki, we haven't met, but I thought that, as I'm going to be identifying and analysing potential crimes related to our current investigation, it might reassure you to know I am an experienced HOLMES 2 operative. I intend to use the cards you received to establish geographic parameters in the first instance. My name is Janine, Janine Gorman.'

Jazzy considered fobbing her off, but something about the calm way the woman spoke, her large blinking eyes behind her glasses and how she bit her lip made her hesitate. Not quite able to summon a smile, Jazzy took the other woman's small hand in hers and shook. 'I'm sure you'll do your best, Janine.'

Jazzy's voice was gruff, but the other woman didn't seem to notice. She stepped forward and gave a little laugh. 'DCI Dick's a bit of a grump, isn't he?'

Amused at the analyst's understatement, an unexpected grin broke over Jazzy's face. 'Yes, you could say that.' She made to walk past Janine and then reconsidered. Turning back, she quirked an eyebrow. 'Don't suppose you'd give me a shout as soon as you come up with anything, would you?'

Janine nodded. 'I would have anyway, DC Solanki. This is personal for you.'

Not used to opening up with strangers, but compelled to reciprocate the woman's friendliness, Jazzy, in little more than a murmur said, 'Jazzy. You can call me Jazzy.'

'Okay, Jazzy. You'll be hearing from me, in due course.'

Jazzy nodded, then frowned. 'One more thing, Janine. If this serial killer had committed identical crimes in Scotland over the last five years, surely it would have been flagged up already?'

'You'd think so.'

'Well, in that case. It might be worth your while to split down components of the crime to cross-match. Maybe this one is like a finale. Perhaps he's been practising elements of the final scene up to now. Maybe look for murders using specific limited criteria – like birthdays and murders or scenes where the killer left a message like "For You" or where the bodies have been muti-lated using kitchen implements, but no detached body parts. You understand what I mean?'

Janine scribbled in a note pad. 'Aye, I sure do. I'm on it.'

Jazzy caught up with Queenie. 'Good idea that, JayZee. We all know these serial killers spend a period of time refining their craft. Janine might be lucky.'

'I bloody hope so. We could do with a lead.' She strode ahead, causing Queenie to run after her on her shorter legs.

'Wait up, we're not all endowed with legs the size of a pit mule, are we?'

Jazzy waited and when Queenie caught up said, 'We should be interviewing Danny Banik, not him. Don't think he's ever heard of the word "nuance", far less employed it in his human interactions.

If that kid's innocent then he's gonna be scarred for life. The only saving grace would be if he was actually the killer, he might get nettled and let something slip.' She shrugged. 'Also, if it was him, then he's also my stalker and seeing me might startle him. Dick should be interviewing this reporter. We don't even know yet if the killer sent them, but that would be a fair enough assumption to make, wouldn't it? You know, killer craving attention, reaches out to the press – it's pretty standard stuff.'

'Aye, it's not unheard of for them to do that is it, though – taunt the polis. That's what happened in the last James Patterson book I read – psycho killer taunts the very attractive detective by sending stuff to a journalist. It's the norm, I've heard. And, just so you know, I'm the very attractive detective in this scenario.'

'James Patterson, really? You seriously think those books are anything like real murders?'

'Na, course not, just wanted to distract you from dwelling on the fact that everybody hates you.'

Chapter 20

Ginny Bell was waiting in one of the rooms they used for speaking with families or children. It was as different from the sparse interview room in which Danny Banik was currently being interviewed as it was possible to be. Jazzy, deciding that she'd watch the recording of the Banik interview before she went home that night, pushed it to the back of her mind and focused on the task in hand – gleaning whatever intel she could from Ginny Bell.

As soon as Jazzy stepped into the room, Ginny Bell flew across the space and all but jumped into her arms. Her face was streaked with mascara and her eyes were puffy. In one hand she held a sodden, dilapidated tissue. 'Thank God you're here, DC Solanki. I can't believe this has happened. I'm still shaking. Look.' She held out a hand that was indeed trembling.

Startled by the reporter's full-on assault, Jazzy glared at Queenie, who for once took the hint without demur and guided the distraught journalist over to the couch before plonking herself down beside her. 'There, there, hen. I'm DC McQueen, but you can call me Queenie. Me and Jazzy are here to look after you. Now, you've had a big shock, haven't you? But you're okay now. Perfectly safe here. Ye've got hundreds of Scotland's finest men and women in blue here to keep you safe, so just you sit there for a minute and I'll get ye a wee cup of tea and then, when you're settled, you can tell us all about it.'

Impressed and a tad envious that, despite her usual brusqueness, Queenie possessed a strange maternal vibe that soothed antsy witnesses, Jazzy remained by the door twiddling her thumbs. She didn't consider herself an intimidating figure, but she'd be the first to admit that shows of emotion left her feeling awkward. This in turn made her appear stiff and unapproachable. The crux of the problem was that whilst Queenie was happy to open herself up to people, Jazzy fiercely protected her privacy. Whilst Queenie looked at everyone with a healthy degree of distrust, she was also able to balance that by accepting that in every interaction there was at least the possibility of honesty and redemption. Which was why, even when dealing with the most obnoxious of criminals, Queenie was able to find a common ground – a little bit of empathy that allowed her to humanise them. Jazzy, on the other hand, took a lot more convincing.

Not that she considered Ginny Bell a hardened criminal, nor even someone with duplicitous intent – after all, the reporter had hotfooted it to the station to report the images she'd been sent. Still, past experience with journalists meant that Jazzy's opinion of the species was low.

Queenie patted Ginny's hand twice, then walked over to the door, opened it and yelled, 'A strong tea wi' two sugars and two coffees: one with three sugars and one black, nae sugar. Oh and some biscuits as well – no bloody digestives though, they go right through me.'

In awe of the way Queenie took charge of the situation and de-escalated the drama, Jazzy sidled over and sat down on the chair opposite Ginny. Although she was still sobbing, Ginny had now discarded her tattered tissue and was brushing the sleeve of her jumper over her eyes to soak up the tears.

'Here, Ginny, have a dry tissue, hen.' Queenie was back and poised on the edge of the chair, one arm round the weeping reporter. 'When the tea arrives, you, me and JayZee will have a wee talk about what happened, okay?'

The door opened and a constable, using her butt to open the door, backed into the room carrying a tray with three steaming drinks and a plate of custard creams. She smiled at Ginny, nodded to Jazzy and glowered at Queenie, who had already snaffled two biscuits and remained oblivious as, mouth full, she pushed the tea to Ginny. 'Drink up, hen. The sugar will do ye good after your wee shock.'

Sitting in the comfy chair, the smell of coffee redolent in the air, Jazzy wanted nothing more than to lean back, pull a cover over herself and hibernate till this investigation was over, but she wouldn't. She was a fighter and this fight was personal. She leaned over and grabbed her drink. The mere smell of the coffee made her feel better so she blew on it and took a sip before turning her attention to Ginny.

Queenie's ministrations had had the desired effect of soothing her and Ginny's sobbing had faded to be replaced by the occasional hiccup. She'd even managed to drink some of her tea despite baulking at its sweetness. Queenie, dunking yet another biscuit in her own drink, nodded at Jazzy letting her know she should begin.

'Can you tell us what happened, Ginny?'

The journalist puffed out a breath, which made her fringe waft up off her brow. 'I was getting fed up at the crime scene after I spoke to you and I was freezing cold. We'd been told there had been two suspicious deaths – which we could work out anyway because we saw the body bags leaving the house – and we knew from chatting to the neighbours that it must be the Clark parents because one of the neighbours said the girl had been taken away in an ambulance earlier. Anyway, I walked the two streets over to where my car was parked and got the engine running and whilst I was waiting for it to heat up I checked my emails.'

'Your personal one or your work's one?'

Ginny frowned, as if thrown by Jazzy's question, then shook her head. 'Sorry, I'm not with it. I'm freelance so my work and personal email are pretty much one and the same.' She took another sip of the tea, grimaced and pushed it away from her. 'Sorry, where was I?'

'Checking your emails, hen.' Queenie sniffed and gulped her coffee.

Ginny nodded and stared straight ahead, with her hands in her lap shredding the tissue, her eyes glassy. 'I wish I'd never opened it. Still don't know why I did. It looked like spam, but the subject heading was intriguing, you know?'

Queenie nodded and Ginny continued. 'It said: "For You, Happy Birthday".'

Jazzy's vision blurred. Hearing the words she'd seen smeared in blood across the Clarks' heads spoken aloud was like a punch to the gut. In an instant, she was back in that blood-covered kitchen, the smell and sights blaring in her head as Ginny continued chattering on. 'I mean, it isn't my birthday. I knew that, obvs, but it sort of caught my eye. Shite, I wish I'd just deleted it.'

Eyes filling with tears, she peeked up at Queenie. 'Why didn't I delete it? Why the fuck didn't I delete it?'

'There, there, don't fash yourself, hen. You weren't to know. How could you?'

'You don't understand though. I feel dirty. I feel like I'll never be clean again. Never be safe again. How can you do this? How can you look at that sort of stuff? I'll never be able to unsee that. It'll *always* be there. Those people – dead – their heads, the blood, the . . .' And she was off crying again, great gulping tears that tore at Jazzy's heart.

'Ginny.' Jazzy, her tone matter-of-fact, broke through the other woman's anguish. 'I really don't want to put you through any stress, but we need to see the images. This is time-sensitive. We need to look at your phone and we'll need to keep it till we've had our technical team check it over. Is that okay?'

Through her tears, Ginny nodded. The phone was lying on the coffee table near the tray of drinks. 'Take it. Take the damn thing. I never want to see it again. I'll get myself another. I'll get myself one with a new number and I won't use it for work.'

Jazzy lifted the iPhone and handed it to Queenie. 'Come on now, hen. We just need your finger to open it and then you don't need to touch it again, okay?'

Ginny averted her gaze and with a shudder extended her finger to allow Queenie to open the phone. 'There, there. What a brave thing to do. Now, don't worry, Jazzy here will change the PIN so we won't need to bother you again to get access.'

Handing the unlocked phone to Jazzy, she patted Ginny on the knee, then promising to return shortly, she and Jazzy left the interview room to view the images without Ginny being present. Moving several feet down the corridor, both women exchanged troubled glances. Neither Jazzy nor Queenie had any desire to view these images, but they had to determine if it was likely they'd been sent by the killer or by someone else with access to them. Within seconds of viewing them they had their answers. The first image was taken from an angle that included a corner of the dark garden outside. These were taken before the crime scene team and the police had arrived. The blood was red and shiny and only Bob Clark's head was detached and tossed onto the table. Shirley was clearly either already dead or at least unconscious.

'Zoom in, Jazz.'

Understanding what Queenie wanted to focus in on, Jazzy zoomed in close until the little corner of the window was in focus. There on the screen was a reflection of their killer.

'Got ya!' said Queenie, clicking her fingers. 'Got ya, you sick fucker.'

But Jazzy shook her head. 'He's messing with our heads, Queenie. Look. He's fully suited up, probably in an extra-large overall to hide his true physique. He's wearing a mask, gloves and those bloody goggles. There are no distinguishing features there at all. The bastard's goading us.'

Tension radiated across Jazzy's shoulders and down her spine. They were so close, but that sick bastard was playing with them like a lion toys with its prey. 'There's no point in looking at the rest. We'll get this to the tech guys and get them to enhance and print off the images as best they can. Perhaps they'll be able to get us something. The best we can hope for, is that he left a digital trace. But I wouldn't put any money on that, would you?'

Queenie grunted. 'Not a hope in hell.' She nudged Jazzy. 'But at least this confirms that the killer is responsible for the leak. That'll save us wasting resources investigating ourselves.'

Whilst Jazzy and Queenie had been discussing the email, Ginny had edged the interview-room door open. Now, head quirked to one side she said, 'You've no idea who he is, do you?'

Jazzy jumped and spun round. 'What the hell, Ginny? What do you think you're doing, eavesdropping like that?'

Ginny's voice trembled, her lips quivering. 'He's out there and he's got his sights on me. I'm in danger, aren't I? He could come after me next.' With each sentence, her voice increased in volume. 'He could do those terrible things to me. He could kill me.'

'Aw shoosh, hen. Don't you worry, we'll look after you. We'll get you to a safe house and have an officer outside keeping you safe, won't we, JayZee?'

Jazzy had her doubts about that. She reckoned that Dick would be reluctant to blow any more of his budget on protecting Ginny Bell than he had to – Police Scotland didn't have infinite resources and already they were being harangued over overtime expenses and operational costs. But now wasn't the time to reveal her doubts. Instead, she said, 'You look knackered, Ginny. We'll take your phone and we'll order in some food for you and then you can have a wee nap till we work out how best to look after you. Maybe you have a friend or relative you could stay with?'

But Ginny shook her head. 'Nobody. My family are all up north and I'm not putting my friends at risk.' A steely glint came into her eye. 'It's on you lot to look after me. To make sure I'm kept safe. Just imagine the sort of story I *could* write if I don't think you're treating my safety as a priority.'

With those words ringing in their ears, Jazzy and Queenie left Ginny Bell with a uniformed constable as they went to submit her phone to the tech team.

'What do you think of her, JayZee?'

Jazzy was conflicted. The woman had suffered a major trauma and had clearly been affected by the images she'd seen, still . . . 'Strange that after looking at the first one with Bob Clark's decapitated head rolling about the table that she would open the others too, don't you think?'

'Aye, bang on the money there. Yes, she was traumatised. Hell, you'd have to be a psycho not to be, but she still kept her eye on the ball. Still used her journo instincts. Wouldn't surprise me if she forwarded it to another email address.'

'Yep, I think so too. This is a scoop for her, after all, and she'll want to rake in the big bucks for it. We'll get the techies to check that out and I also want a background check done on her. I want to know exactly what she's reported on in the past, where she's lived, friends, lovers, past employment, even the colour of her knickers. The lot.'

Chapter 21

It turned out that DCI Dick was a formidable interviewer – it was just a shame that he was using his tactics on a twenty-one-year-old who had lawyered up and who, judging by the way his heel tapped on the floor and the frantic glances directed at the duty solicitor, was on the verge of clamming up completely. Dick, seemingly ignorant of the relationship between honey and bees, had performed an acrobatic interview – one minute glaring at the lad, then alternating between threatening him, interrupting him, switching up the questions and chopping and changing the topic – all with barely a gap to allow Banik to respond. It was a waste of time.

Even Jazzy, watching the recorded version of the interview, had lost track of what the DCI wanted to ascertain and it was as much a relief to her as it must have been to Banik, when the interview was cut short by the solicitor finally having the balls to say that as Banik's presence was voluntary, her client could leave at any time. *Too bloody late, you absolute incompetent bawheid.* Any other solicitor worth their salt would have ended the torment at least forty-five minutes sooner, especially when their client could provide an alibi for his whereabouts at the suspected time of death. Of course, Jazzy took that with a pinch of salt – it wouldn't be the first time a parent had provided a false alibi for their child, but as it stood they had nothing to dispute the veracity of his mum's statement.

With her headphones still on, Jazzy returned to the start of the interview to the parts where Danny Banik had spoken about his relationship with Imogen Clark.

'Describe your relationship with Imogen Clark.'

Banik's leg paused its endless juddering and something flickered in his eyes before he replied. 'We hung out a bit, you know? She was into me and that and we were . . .' He shrugged. 'You know . . . hanging out, having fun.'

Jazzy rewound and replayed the recording, pausing on Banik's face. *What were you thinking right then, Danny?* His eyes were wide and he kept blinking. Not for the first time that day, Jazzy cursed her boss. If he'd just hung fire, let uniforms take an informal statement and used the time before a second interview to scrutinise other witness testimonies about Banik and Imogen's relationship, they'd have got more from the kid.

Jazzy had come across Banik's kind before. He was a chancer, and judging by the reports that had steadily been added to the file during the day, he wasn't exactly the faithful type. Time and again, in the course of her work, Jazzy had seen players like Banik toying with vulnerable girls' emotions. *But, was he a killer? Did he have what it took to decapitate his girlfriend's parents?* Jazzy didn't know the answers to those questions, but she did wonder if Banik could have delivered the card to her home, either for someone else or off his own bat. She'd run his name through the database and could find no links to her, so she was inclined to dismiss that idea. Besides, when she considered his stature alone, she had to admit he didn't fit the bill.

Her stalker was devious. There was a reason he'd concealed himself for so long and a reason for revealing himself now. Jazzy wasn't naïve enough to assume that the person she saw in her security clip hadn't taken measures to thwart being identified, which of course didn't rule out Danny Banik.

She chewed on her lip, trying to work out if Banik had a role in any of this or if he was just an incidental actor in the narrative. Although he was a scrote of dubious morals, she suspected he wasn't their killer. He didn't present like he had a functioning backbone and Jazzy was convinced that the person responsible for killing Bob and Shirley Clark had confidence in spades. More than that, she was convinced that their killer, as well as having the intelligence and fortitude to embark on a long game, had the ability to escape detection. Judging by what she'd just seen, unless he was a talented actor, Danny Banik wasn't their man.

She cursed Dick again. His antics in the interview had all but obliterated any likelihood that Banik would come forward if he *had* noticed anyone scoping out the Clark house when he'd been waiting for Imogen to sneak out to meet him, or if Imogen had mentioned something relevant to him. Dick's strong-arm tactics may have lost them insight into Imogen's frame of mind. *What a fiasco!*

Jazzy had bumped into Banik as he was leaving the station with his lawyer – literally. She'd been rushing back to the incident room after dropping off Ginny Bell's electronics to the team and hadn't been looking where she was going. She'd crashed right into him as he exited the lift and it had taken a moment for her to realise who he was.

Banik had stopped and glared at her as if he held her personally responsible for his detention, before sliding a cigarette out of his packet and popping it behind his ear. 'Saw you on Insta, didn't I? You're the heifer who whacked that polisman. The high-heid wan?'

Jazzy had scowled and sidestepped him, slipping into the empty lift and pressing the button. Her cheeks had flushed as she waited for the doors to swish shut, the arrogant little sod watching her with a smirk on his disgusting face. Still, it showed an interesting contrast between his demeanour during the interview and his attitude to her. Was the interview all a big act? When watching the recording, she'd been careful not to allow her earlier inter-action with him and the 'heifer' insult to affect her perceptions. He'd been rattled during the interview. Jazzy frowned. Or had he? Still uncertainty niggled at her. She certainly wasn't ready to give Danny Banik the all-clear. Not just yet.

Lack of movement for the last couple of hours had tightened Jazzy's shoulders, so she rotated them now and threw her head-phones on the desk with a groan. As another wave of tiredness hit her, she massaged her forehead where the beginnings of a headache lurked. A yawn engulfed her and she straightened, rolling her head on her neck and grimacing at the resultant click. *God I'm dog-tired.* But the thought of doing all the little actions necessary to get her from her current position at the computer, into her outdoor clothes, through the station, into her car and on the road to her house, then into bed, just seemed undoable. Her desk was scattered with half-eaten sandwiches, half-drunk mugs of coffee and half a packet of prawn cocktail crisps. That summed her up – half a person, half a life! *I don't even like prawn cocktail crisps.*

With every limb seeming heavier than it had that morning, she stood up and looked round the incident room. A few of the night shift were pottering away at their PCs, but the room felt dead. She slumped back into her chair, took a final glance round and when she saw nobody was nearby, she took out her burner phone. She'd been so busy all day that she had forgotten to check it and now she saw she had a notification. Despite her better judgement, her heart sped up and she felt her lips twitch into a smile. At last!

> E: *You okay? Heard it's all gone to shite! Be careful!*
> J: *Yeah, it's bad. Can we meet?*

Clearly word had reached Elliot about what had gone down here, and she really could do with using him as a sounding block

151

right now. She didn't expect a reply – not straight away. Elliot was a busy man and she had no claim on his time. However, as she was slipping it back into her bag his reply came.

E: Tomorrow, Scott's Monument 7 p.m. Be safe.
J: Okay.

And just like that the dark cloak of anxiety she'd been battling with since she first saw the stalker on her home security lifted.

'You still here, JayZee? Away you go home.'

Jazzy jumped, her eyes shooting straight to her bag, checking she'd zipped the burner phone away securely. Elliot laughed at her insistence they keep their friendship so covert, but he wasn't plagued with Jazzy's secrets or her fears. Where she was all darkness, suspicion and pessimism, he was all light, trust and optimism. But Jazzy knew how things worked in Police Scotland. Where a male officer would be given a long leash, a female one was given one only long enough to strangle herself and a brown female officer was subject to even more scrutiny. She couldn't risk her past coming out, nor could she risk a repeat of the 'scandal' like the one with Afzal. No way did she want her friendship with Elliot Balloch coming to light. That could start a ripple effect linking her to the past she couldn't remember in its entirety, and that thought was horrific enough for her to want it to remain dormant.

'Just heading off now, Queenie. You?'

Queenie, her clothes rumpled, her coffee breath filling the air between them, scowled. 'What do you mean, me? I'm your escort. Don't say you forgot.'

Jazzy had forgotten that she was to be escorted to and from work for the foreseeable future and that frequent police drive-bys past her home in Bellsquarry had been authorised. She hadn't realised that Queenie was her self-appointed bodyguard. As she picked up her coat she studied the older woman. Queenie's eyes were rimmed with dark smudges and her face was pale. Jazzy could have kicked herself. The woman had a teething baby and – knowing Queenie – a long-suffering husband at home and here was Jazzy-no-mates idling away time at work because she'd nobody to go home to other than Winky, her cat.

'You should have gone home earlier, Queenie. Your daughter's teething, isn't she? She needs her mummy. I could have got one of the uniformed officers to follow me home.'

Queenie rapped her knuckles on the table top and shrugged. 'Only missed bath time and endless repetitions of *In the Night Garden*, no biggie.' She raised her chin and glared at something over Jazzy's shoulder. 'And Ruby's no' my daughter. She's my granddaughter. I'd have thought you'd have heard the gossip. After all you seem to know everything else about me. That bit of juicy goss not hit your ears?'

Wrapping her scarf around her neck, Jazzy shook her head and studied Queenie. Tension radiated off her from her twitching eye and jutting chin to her rigid shoulders and the persistent drumming on the table. Jazzy had looked at Queenie's recent history – the reason for her demotion – but she hadn't thought to look any further back. Now, she wished she had. Whatever story Queenie had to tell, was clearly one that cut her to the heart.

'Aye, wee Ruby's mummy – my daughter that is – was murdered in Glasgow when the wean was only a few months old, so Granny Queenie and Papa Craig are bringing her up.'

'Oh, I'm so sorr . . .'

Queenie's lip quivered as she exhaled and walked towards the door, not allowing Jazzy to finish her sentence. 'Come on, JayZee, let's get us Jazz Queens home safely, eh?'

After a second to absorb this information, Jazzy followed. How had she not known this about Queenie? Seems they both had secrets they'd rather not talk about. A wave of affection for the fiercely protective woman made Jazzy catch her up, wrap an arm round her shoulders and give a single squeeze, removing her arm before Queenie had a chance to shrug it off.

'You're all right, JayZee Solanki.'

'You too, Queenie McQueen.'

Queenie grinned and nudged Jazzy. 'Did you get the update on Imogen Clark? Her aunt and uncle – the dad's brother – have arrived from Inverness and she's been released from St John's hospital into their care. They're in the Travelodge over Tony Macaroni's at Almondvale for now, and will move to a better hotel in the morning. We'll be able to interview her tomorrow.'

'And Ginny Bell? Where's she landed? Don't say she's still here?'

'No, that jammy wee shite managed to nab a room in The Cairn Hotel in Bathgate. Disnae seem right to me that she's there in a bloody five-star and that wee lassie's slumming it in the Travelodge.'

Jazzy smiled at Queenie's indignant exaggeration – The Cairn Hotel was all right, but it certainly wasn't five star. She got her point, but it was Imogen's relatives who'd booked the hotel nearest the hospital last minute because they didn't know how long Imogen would be there. They'd be moved to somewhere more comfortable tomorrow and hopefully nowhere near Ginny Bell. She made a mental note to check that the Clarks were relocated to a nice hotel – maybe the MacDonald Houston House in Livingston – where they could have peace and quiet away from the prying eyes of reporters and gawky members of the public.

Day 2

Chapter 22

I wake up remembering a conversation from a long time ago.

'*What did Mummy do when it was your birthday? Did she bake a cake? Did you get presents?*'

I blink at the psychiatrist opposite, trying to judge what she wants me to say. She's all glossy, from her hair to her teeth to her shiny black shoes, and she's looking at me, smiling and nodding, like it's all so easy. But my head's not working again. It's all filled up with gunge and I feel bad that I'm letting her down.

'*Just have a little think. There's no rush. Take your time.*'

I keep my head bowed, but cast wee sneaky glances at her. When she moves, sweet fruity smells drift my way and I want to get up close to her so I can bury my nose in her hair. But that wouldn't be acceptable. I've learned that. Doing everything you want to do isn't always acceptable. People think you're weird if you say or do the things that pop into your mind. But sometimes, the urge is too strong and no matter how hard I try I can't button it down. Can't swallow my words. So, I just blurt out what I'm thinking. '*We made a promise. We made it in blood.*'

I know straight away I've said the wrong thing. She tries to keep smiling but her lips go all flat and tight, like when I stretch the worms out as far as I can between my fingers till they break. You can see their veins. *That's what her lips are like. All flat and veiny. Her fingers are all white and she leans away from me, like she's frightened of me. She should be. She really should be.*

That's the thing Jazzy doesn't get. Everyone leaves me eventually. But, on the plus side, everyone suffers too. All those who've leaned away, who've left me on my own – every single one of them suffers in the end; that's what it's all about. Making them suffer. Making *you* suffer. But at least I take care of them in death. Make it special for them.

I stretch and drag myself out of bed. I'm still tired from all the activity yesterday, but I've still got lots to do. As well as all my usual work commitments, which I have to fit in. I have plans. Plans that'll affect Jazzy Solanki. Plans that'll kick her right in the gut.

Seeing her up close and personal yesterday, being so close I could smell her shampoo and almost taste her sweat, was bittersweet. She'd no idea and that gives me a buzz. However, it's not enough. It was never going to be enough. Revenge is only satisfying if the stakes are high.

Today is the day I'm really going to make her sweat. Today is the day she'll rue ever betraying me. Today, my message will be short, sharp and hurtful. Jazzy Solanki will be on the back foot for once, and as we near the end game, she'll wonder what she could have done differently. It'll be no more than she deserves.

I leave my home and stride to the train station. A short ride and I'm in the vicinity of my stolen wheels. *Catch me if you can, Jazzy Solanki*, I think as I get in and head for my destination. Everyone likes a trip to the seaside, don't they?

Chapter 23

By lunchtime Jazzy was pulling her hair out. The only thing keeping her sane was the prospect of meeting Elliot later. She and Elliot had been thrown together by exceptional circumstances and it was those same circumstances that sometimes placed a huge barrier between them. Still, it was nearly Christmas and the Christmas markets were in full swing and she'd not seen him for ages. He'd be a good sounding board. He always was and besides, she deserved some downtime.

On her arrival at the police station, after being picked up by Queenie, she'd been tasked with paperwork. Whilst recognising the value of reviewing house-to-house, forensic and data analysis reports, Jazzy was fuming. This sort of task would ordinarily have been completed by a civilian employee and it was a waste of her skills to have her do this. She was champing at the bit to be on the streets, pursuing new leads, following up on interviews and the like, yet, under the guise of 'protecting' her, the dickless wonder had insisted she remain in the station. Jazzy saw clearly what his game was. This was payback for challenging him yesterday. Payback because the chief super had intervened on her and Queenie's behalf, ensuring they had a seat at the table. Queenie had escaped more lightly, and again Jazzy recognised that tactic for what it was. Dick trying to divide and rule – to break the blossoming alliance between Queenie and Jazzy. Which was why Queenie, not Jazzy, had been sent with a uniformed officer to interview Imogen Clark.

Meanwhile, Fenton Heggie and Geordie McBurnie were interviewing Imogen Clark's friends and teachers and again. Jazzy had been given implicit instructions to stay clear of the interview suites. Seeing everyone's sympathetic – or in some cases downright smug expressions – made Jazzy want to march up to the dickless wonder and challenge his decision-making all over again. However, she was on rocky ground – she had to keep her head down and get on with it or risk being completely alienated from the investigation.

She had hoped that Janine Gorman would have got back to her by now, but so far there was no news from the analyst. Jazzy supposed she was attempting to fit Jazzy's request in among the work assigned by Dick. The post-mortem report hadn't arrived yet and Jazzy was tempted to sneak over to St John's to see what Lamond Johnston could tell her in person. He was usually happy to provide first impressions and pointers, but all eyes were on Jazzy and she couldn't be certain she wouldn't bump into an officer up at the hospital who would be all too happy to report her transgression to the boss.

ANPR had come back with an ID for the car that Benjy had spotted following her. It had been reported stolen by its owner from a Morrisons car park on Portobello Road in Edinburgh and found abandoned in the Tesco car park in Bathgate. Unfortunately, the driver had been wearing a long coat, gloves, balaclava hat and dark glasses in both car parks. Between security cameras, unfortunately his movements after leaving the Bathgate Tesco had petered out and he hadn't been picked up again. This made Jazzy suspect he'd changed his appearance by turning his coat inside out or shoving it into the bag he was carrying when he dumped the car and melted into the streets nearby.

She'd repeatedly watched the recording of him stealing the car in Edinburgh and dumping it in Bathgate. What intrigued her was the way he leaned into the back seat and remained like that for a few minutes on both occasions. *What are you doing? Are you positioning something there? Something important?* In Edinburgh, he'd balanced on one knee as he leaned into the rear seat from behind the driver's seat. No matter how much they attempted to zoom in, it was impossible to see what he was doing. Then, before walking away from the vehicle in the supermarket car park, he'd repeated the movement. This time, when she zoomed in, it was obvious that he was carrying something that he then deposited in his rucksack. That puzzled Jazzy. Why would he waste precious time faffing about in the back seat? Time when he could be noticed by passers-by. Time that was registered on the supermarket's CCTV.

Once more she zoomed in and slowed the video right down. This time she thought she could discern a slender pole-like thing in his hand that seemed to have something attached at one end. She'd no idea what it was and with a sigh she shook her head. *No way I'm getting a clearer image than that one.* But she couldn't let go of it. Whatever it was, it was clearly important to the killer and, that being the case, it was important to her. It was something he spent time placing in the rear seat as soon as he stole the car and something he removed when he abandoned it. Whether he moved the item more than once was anyone's guess, but whatever it was, he had had no intention of leaving it behind. What could it possibly be?

Then, it hit her. Benjy had told her that the Land Rover he'd seen following her – the one now being processed by the police forensic team – had been facing *away* from her house. That was why she had dismissed it. Normally a surveillance vehicle would have obvious eyes on its target, but that one hadn't. It had been too far from her home, facing the wrong way and line of vision using the rear and side mirrors alone was restricted. In a single glance she'd taken in all those salient facts, but what if his view hadn't been restricted? What if the bugger used customised mirrors to ensure he could observe her home without looking suspicious? Mirrors that Jazzy wouldn't notice at first glance because they allowed him to park the vehicle further from her home.

Jazzy cursed herself for not paying closer attention to the vehicle. She'd ignored it even though she didn't recognise it and that had been a mistake. She could only hope it wouldn't prove a costly one.

She phoned Franny Gallagher, the CSI manager. 'Hey, Franny, Jazzy Solanki here. Could you do me a favour and make sure that whoever is processing the Land Rover found in Bathgate, checks the rear seats and the rear mirror thoroughly. I reckon this fucker used some sort of removable mirror contraption so he could park facing away from my house at a distance, but have eyes on me without drawing suspicion. Who knows, maybe he'll have left something of himself behind.'

'Cunning git, isn't he? I'll get it done, Jazzy. Don't you worry.'

Jazzy glanced round to make sure nobody was nearby before lowering her voice. 'You got anything you can share with me from the Clark crime scene, Franny? I'm being cut out and am relying on official reports hitting the files. Could do with any observations you have.'

Franny snorted. 'I wish I had something to tell you, but this bastard's so forensically savvy that I've got nothing really. If it's any help, I reckon he didn't venture anywhere other than the kitchen area, which makes it likely that he gained entry by the back door and also left that way. The door was unlocked and it looks like he either had a key or he was let in. Lamond reckons that the Clarks were immobilised before being beheaded – which is what I'd do if I was going to behead someone. He reckons some sort of narcotic was used – found an injection site on each victim's neck, but I don't think he's finalised his report yet and, as usual, the lab's backed up, so we're still waiting for results.'

'Thanks, Franny. I appreciate this. See you around.'

'As long as it's not with you as the body at the crime scene. You keep safe, Jazzy.'

She'd no sooner hung up than her phone vibrated and, desperate for a distraction, Jazzy grabbed it. *Queenie!* Thank God. Maybe she'd got a lead that Jazzy could follow up from here. The only information she'd been able to glean from the online files was more of what she'd already ascertained yesterday and, although her minor breakthrough with the mirror contraption made her feel that at least she was contributing something, she felt like a chunk of dead meat at a vegan barbecue. 'Hey, Queenie, how did the interview with Imogen Clark go?'

'Later. It's lunchtime. You're allowed to go out for lunch. Haggis is going to meet you in the car park and drive you to McArthur Glen. We're having the first Jazz Queen meeting in the food court. Get a move on.'

Before Jazzy could respond, Queenie hung up. But it didn't matter, Jazzy's heart was already beating a boppy tune and she could barely hide her grin as she grabbed her coat. As she passed one of the uniformed officers she said, 'I'm going for lunch. DC Fenton Heggie is my escort.' And she left the building.

As Fenton drove her the short drive to the designer outlet, Jazzy could hardly contain herself. It was like being one of the Thelma and Louise duo, although she wasn't sure which of the two Fenton would be. Wisely she kept that analogy to herself.

'She's doing my head in. Won't let up on the "Haggis this" and "Haggis that".' Fenton swooped into a parking spot in the multi-storey, glanced round as he exited the car and frogmarched Jazzy to the lifts. 'You need to get her told about the Jazz Queens thing. Neither me nor Geordie are happy at being called Jazz Queens, you know? Geordie's already a drag queen. He doesn't want to be a Jazz Queen too.'

Stifling a laugh, Jazzy nodded. 'You know she's toying with you, don't you? The more you get worked up about it, the more she'll say it. Just ignore it and she'll soon stop.'

Fenton snorted. 'I might strangle her before she tires of it, Jazz. The woman's a bloody nutter.'

'Yes, you're right. She is a nutter. But she's *our* nutter and she's fiercely loyal and she's a damn good copper. Better she's on our side than against us.'

Still scanning their surroundings as they got out of the lifts and headed to the escalator leading to the food court, Fenton sighed. 'Aye, I suppose you've got a point. Besides, she's not exactly had it easy has she, what with her daughter being murdered, leaving behind that wean and then her being demoted. Suppose I could cut her some slack right enough.'

So, even Fenton had heard about Queenie's daughter. Jazzy frowned. How the hell had it passed her by, but not Fenton Heggie? She stepped onto the escalator after him, still frowning. Was she so bloody bitter and twisted and introverted that nobody thought to share important stuff with her? She huffed, earning herself a startled glance form Fenton. Of course, she was. She shot down every overture of friendship like it was a personal affront.

In fact, now she thought about it, she'd barely spoken to half the people in the incident room before now. If she didn't have to communicate with them, then she didn't. She actively went out of her way to avoid any form of social interaction. She got off the escalator and saw Queenie with a bundle of McDonald's wrappers spread in front of her on a round table with Geordie McBurnie stuffing chips into his gob opposite her. *So, how the hell, despite my best antisocial habits, have I ended up part of this motley crew?*

'We got you both fish and chips,' said Queenie, pushing the packages across the table to Jazzy and Fenton as they sat down. 'You two eat, and me and the laddo here will fill you in.'

The aroma from the chips made Jazzy's tummy rumble and she realised she'd not had anything to eat yet today. No wonder she was salivating. As Queenie prepared to regale her with all the information she'd garnered that morning, Jazzy squirted vinegar and sprinkled salt on her chips begore slathering two sachets of ketchup over the lot. 'Bloody starving.'

'Right, well, I've just got back from interviewing that poor wee lassie.' Mouth drooping, Queenie shook her head. 'That poor bairn. I've no idea how long it'll take her to get over this – if she ever does – but it's not going to be easy. You know, I expected her to be hysterical – greeting and beside herself – but she was the opposite. All self-contained and vacant. Like there was nobody at home. She was so pale and her entire body shook the whole time I was talking to her, but she answered every question. It was like she was a robot though. Her eyes never wavered; in fact she barely blinked and her voice was monotone – no inflection at all. It was as if she was chilled to the marrow. That bloody animal did that to this wee lassie and on her birthday. How could he do that?'

The food in Jazzy's mouth was suddenly dry and unflavour-some. She pushed her lunch away. How could anybody want to eat when that poor girl was living the worst morning of her life again and again? Worse still, she'd not got her parents to help her through it.

'The auntie is a star, but Bob Clark's brother is in bits. He did the official IDs yesterday and it's thrown him big time.' Queenie grabbed one of Jazzy's chips and shoved it in her mouth, grimaced and swallowed it. 'Yuck! Vinegar? Really? Now get that grub down your gullet, Jazzy. You need to keep your strength up. Us no' eating won't help Imogen Clark. The only thing that will, is catching the sicko that killed her ma and da.'

The down-to-earth words were enough to have Jazzy stuffing a chip in her mouth. Then Geordie opened a portion of beans and her stomach lurched and her mind darted back to the coagulating orange mess on the Clarks' kitchen table. The sweet smell invaded her nostrils and, for the second time, she pushed her meal away from her, as she took deep breaths through her mouth. Queenie might be right. She'd already felt light-headed a couple of times that morning and she could do with something solid in her gut to soak up the shedload of coffee she'd drunk, but the beans had put her right off. 'Did she tell you anything new?'

Queenie shrugged. 'She recited how she'd found her parents as if she was on automatic pilot. Like it was something she'd seen in a film, not something that had happened to her.' Queenie paused, bit her lip, then blinked a few times as if to clear the memory of the traumatised girl from her mind. 'I'm not sure if that's a good thing or a bad thing, because at some point it's going to hit her that this is real and . . .' She banged her hands together emulating an explosion and, oblivious of the startled glances cast her way, she added an overloud 'POW!'

For long seconds the little quartet remained silent as normal activity resumed around them. Conscious of the tension in Queenie's jaw and the throbbing pulse at her temple, Jazzy wondered if her partner was speaking from experience. Was this how it had been for Queenie when her only daughter had been murdered? Had she withdrawn into a trance, not allowing the raw emotion – the loss – to cut through her?

On an impulse Jazzy reached over the table and squeezed Queenie's arm. Queenie's eyes drifted to where Jazzy's fingers gripped her arm and remained there. *Shit, I've overstepped the mark.* Jazzy, embarrassed and confused by her desire to reach out to Queenie, made to withdraw her hand, but Queenie's head jerked up, her eyes met Jazzy's and she nodded. Just once, but that single nod held a wealth of emotion and without a word uttered, an invisible bond was formed between the two women. Jazzy felt it reach out and circle her heart, squeezing the life out of her. For a second, she couldn't catch her breath and then the tension eased and instead of her usual frown, she found she was smiling. Not a full-on beaming grin, but a small offering of support.

Queenie exhaled and gave another nod before continuing. 'She'd been waiting upstairs in her bed for her ma to come and wake her for her birthday breakfast – it was their routine.'

Queenie's voice broke on the last few words and she dragged her sleeve over her eyes. 'Poor kid said she kept waiting, then she got a bit worried. So, when it got to quarter to seven, she decided to go to the loo, which was when she felt the draught from downstairs. She said that's when knew something was wrong. They were aye careful not to leave the doors open because they were trying to conserve energy. The poor kid went downstairs and turned to the kitchen. The door was open and she saw them straight away. She didn't touch anything, just ran to the front door, grabbed the key from the table next to it, unlocked it and ran over to the neighbour in her drive, without even putting on her shoes.'

Queenie dragged a tissue from inside her bra and mopped her eyes. Fenton leaned across and squeezed the older officer's arm. 'Come on, Queenie. We can't have our main Jazz Queen losing it, can we?'

Beside her, Geordie groaned. 'No, don't bloody go there, Haggis boy. Don't even hint at agreeing to be called a Jazz Queen. Just don't.'

The lads' banter had the desired effect and Queenie blew loudly in her tissue and studied the product of her effort before balling the tissue up and reinserting it down her cleavage. 'I'll get another blow or two out of that, yet.'

Jazzy shuddered and pushed her half-eaten food away from her. 'That's gross.'

Queenie waved Jazzy's protestations away and exhaled. 'I asked her about her relationship with Banik. She said she thought they had a special relationship, but now she thinks – and I quote "he's a dick" – nothing like the violent murder of your parents to put things into perspective, eh?'

'She reckon he had anything to do with this?' Fenton asked.

'Nah, she was definite about that. Said not to waste our time thinking about him.'

Geordie sighed. 'She have any suspicions? Did she see anyone dodgy around, or anything unusual?'

'She says not – no enemies, no arguments with neighbours, nothing! And to be honest by this point she was looking like she was about to keel over. I told her to phone if she thought of anything else.'

'So, nothing that will move the investigation forward.' Jazzy bit her lip, frustration making her keen to have something to do. She was convinced that if they didn't stop him, this killer would strike again. 'What about the images sent to Ginny Bell? Any luck tracing where they came from?'

Before she'd even finished asking, Fenton was shaking his head. 'No. This git's wise enough to cover his tracks. There's no way we can trace where they were sent from or correlate them with a real-life person. That email was bounced around the world and tells us nothing much. However, the lab is enhancing the images as we speak and have analysed each one. They've used recognition software, which appears with around 98 per cent accuracy to confirm that the killer and your stalker were one and the same. What's interesting though, is that one of the images shows the back door open and Mrs Clark lying unconscious on the floor nearby, whilst another one shows Mr Clark in a heap by the kitchen door. It looks like he injected them with something. Dr Johnston confirms an injection site on the neck of both victims.'

'He's taunting us. He's telling us exactly how he did it. Somehow, he got access to the Clark home and knocked them out. The only positive side of that is that they didn't suffer when they were beheaded.'

'Ach, hen. It's a bit much when we're looking for positives in a decapitation, though, do you no' think?'

Queenie was right – there were no positives, just a quagmire of depravity and violence. Filled with restless energy, Jazzy got to her feet, did a quick scan of the food court and paused. *Was that Philip Jamieson lurking over by Chopstix?* Anger surged through her. Here they were trying to catch a depraved killer and that wee scunner was scoping them out. She turned to her colleagues.

'Bloody Philip Jamieson – see him?'

But when she looked back he was gone and all four phones began to ring at once.

They each tensed for a second, then exchanging worried glances grabbed their phones. Whatever this was it wouldn't be good news and all thoughts of Philip Jamieson flew from her mind as she answered the call. 'What is it, Wullie?'

'Didn't know if you'd have seen it, Jazzy, but you need to check out Ginny Bell's blog. It's going viral and you're not going to like it. I've sent you the link. Keep yourself safe, now, won't ye?'

At Sergeant Hobson's words, Jazzy's heart plummeted. If Wullie was warning her about an online article, it couldn't be good. She risked a glance at the other three and saw that they too were flicking through their phones to check something out.

'Fuck's sake.' Queenie was the first to react. 'That Ginny Bell's got a lot to answer for.'

The colour drained from Jazzy's face when she saw the headline.

In a killer's crosshairs by Ginny Bell

But what was worse than the headline was the image Bell had used to accompany the heading.

'The bitch! Bloody irresponsible little cowbag. What the hell does she think she's playing at?' Queenie huffed and puffed and strode round their table like the wolf about to annihilate not just the three little pigs, but the entire universe as well. She glared at anyone who dared to approach the nearby seats. Her face was red and her fingers kept clenching and unclenching. 'She used *that* image. The one with the reflection.'

Queenie's words came out in a stuttering flow and the pain in her partner's eyes told Jazzy that the headline and the image had triggered something very visceral in her partner. Something personal? Something relating to her daughter's death?

Behind her Heggie was on the phone. 'Get it down. Get it

taken down right bloody now.'

He was talking to the tech team and Jazzy had no doubt they would take it down. She was also in no doubt that it would reinvent itself elsewhere. Now it was out there in the ether, there was no effective way to remove it completely. She gestured to McBurnie to look after Queenie whilst, after getting the number from her partner, she made one of the most uncomfortable calls she would ever have to make. However, there was no alternative and Queenie was too upset to do it. She had to make sure Imogen Clark didn't see that article.

'Is that Jane Clark, Imogen's auntie? I'm DC Jazzy Solanki from Police Scotland. I'm investigating your sister and brother-in-laws' murders. I'm afraid there's no easy way to tell you this so I'm just going to say it. The killer sent some images of the crime scene to a local freelance journalist who has uploaded them onto a blog post. We are working to get them taken down, but could you please keep Imogen offline. She doesn't need to see these things.'

Jazzy closed her eyes and braced herself against the onslaught of grief and anger that stormed down the line. She understood the aunt's need to vent and so she absorbed every barb, every cutting accusation, every iota of grief until the other woman was spent and sobbing quietly on the other end of the phone before speaking again. 'I really am sorry. I would have come to tell you of this development in person, but I felt speed was essential. Do you and Imogen have someone with you? Do you need anything?'

'Just leave us alone. We don't want to hear from you till you've caught this animal.'

Head bowed, Jazzy exhaled and squeezed her eyes tight shut. Imogen's aunt's anger hadn't been directed at her personally, but each thrust nicked Jazzy's heart nonetheless. Sometimes she really hated her job. 'Come on, Queenie, Ginny Bell's going to wish she'd never been born.'

She turned to McBurnie and Heggie. 'You two head back to the station. Your task is to pin Janine Gorman down. No way were the Clark murders his first. We're getting nowhere with forensics or witnesses, so we need to identify where he started. Janine's using the postmarks on the early cards sent to me as a starting point. Maybe a wee nudge wouldn't go amiss. We need to catch him before he does this again and we need a bloody lead.'

Chapter 24

The Cairn Hotel, where they'd housed Ginny Bell, was a mere fifteen minutes' drive away, yet Jazzy experienced every one of those minutes as if each lasted an hour. Queenie drove, yet the way she grated her gears made Jazzy wonder if she should have insisted on taking the wheel. 'You okay?'

Queenie glanced at Jazzy, her eyes fiery and her mouth pursed in a no-nonsense manner. 'Course I'm no' okay. Who the hell would be okay? That bloody whining reporter came into oor gaff yesterday – oor gaff – and she was all over the place, whinging and greeting like a banshee, and all the while the duplicitous, clarty, manky, vile lassie had taken the time to download the bloody images. She's taken us for fools.'

She indicated and overtook a bike, the rasping sound as she changed gears making Jazzy flinch. 'Poor wee Imogen. You telling me she'll no check for that blog post or those images in the future, even if they're taken down now? And when she does, she'll be right back there again seeing her folks dead in front of her.'

A tear rolled down Queenie's cheek. She sniffed and wiped it away. Jazzy hesitated, wondering whether to ask or not. Although she was getting used to Queenie's moods, she hadn't known her for long and hadn't worked out the boundaries of their fledgling relationship. Of course, the older woman had gone up in her estimation over the past few days and she was aware that Queenie knew secrets about Jazzy that she'd hoped never to have to share, but did that give her the right to probe into Queenie's private life? She studied the older woman's profile, noting the tension that made her neck veins stand out and the deep lines across her forehead and weaving from the corner of her lips. She could swear those had been absent the previous day. 'Queenie, did somebody post images of your daughter online?'

The silence in the car was claustrophobic. Queenie's fingers tightened on the steering wheel and Jazzy thought she'd gone too far. This was none of her business. She was about to apologise, when Queenie swung into the Cairn Hotel car park and, after parking haphazardly over two spaces, yanked on the brake. She turned to Jazzy, her normally blue eyes so dark they could almost have been black. 'Aye. The kids who found her. They did it. They posted the images online on Instagram and Facebook before they even called 999.'

She raked her fingers through her hair. 'Every time some joker decides to revisit Billi's murder it gets raked up again and does the rounds. We're never free of it, Craig and me. I don't want to see my wee lassie like that. But more than that, I don't want Ruby to see her like that either. It's Ruby I worry about. When she's older, she'll want to find out about her mummy and I can't bear the thought of her seeing those pictures. That's not Billi – that's no' her mammy. What sort of effect would that have on her growing up, eh?'

Jazzy got it. The few photos the press had of her as a child had fallen under the privacy regulations and her features had been blotted out. She doubted many people would make a connection between her and her mum's death. After all, her mum hadn't been murdered. Whilst her name had been withheld at the inquest, her mother's hadn't. But how would she have felt growing up if her face had been bandied about online? It was bad enough seeing the images of her mum – but there were only a few. Jazzy glanced at her watch. It was after three, but she had plenty of time to deal with Ginny Bell, get back to Livvy to pick her car up from the station and still make her meeting in Edinburgh with Elliot. 'Come on, let's make mince of Ginny Bell.'

They marched into the reception area and showed their warrant cards to the receptionist who sat behind a computer next to the sweeping staircase that led up to the rooms and Jazzy smiled. 'Ginny Bell. I believe she's in room 327.'

The receptionist, plastic smile in place and ponytail bobbing, nodded and responded in nasal tones. 'Just one minute, please.'

As Bobbing Ponytail clacked on the computer keys, Queenie – hands thrust into her trouser pockets – tapped her foot and glared around her. Whilst not the crème de la crème, the Cairn was a perfectly good hotel and right at that moment Jazzy considered it far more luxurious than Ginny Bell deserved.

'Oh, I'm sorry. You're too late.' Bright red smile still in place, ponytail woman – who according to her name tag went by the name of Tiffany – shrugged. 'She checked out about forty-five minutes ago.'

Queenie's groan filled the empty reception area and Tiffany's smile faded, her ponytail becoming less animated. 'Have I done something wrong?'

Quick to reassure Tiffany, Jazzy increased the wattage on her own smile. 'No, no. We just weren't expecting her to have left already.'

'But we bloody should have.' said Queenie. 'We should have realised she'd split as soon as she posted that blog article. Only an eejit would hang about after posting that.'

Jazzy pulled out her phone, cast another reassuring smile towards the receptionist and began to walk back to the car as she phoned it in. 'Hey, Fenton. She's gone AWOL. Checked out moments after she posted it. Can we have a BOLO on her?'

'Eh, Jazzy, DCI Dick's here. He'd like a word.'

Jazzy resisted the temptation to hang up and pretend she'd been cut off. That would only delay the inevitable bollocking. 'Sir?'

A faint echo made Dick's voice sound chillier than usual. Each word was clipped and his carefully controlled rage resonated down the line. 'DC Solanki, I believe I gave you explicit instructions to work from the incident room. Did you not understand them?'

Aw shite. In the heat of seeing the blog post, she'd forgotten all about her curfew. No that wasn't true. She hadn't forgotten, she'd decided to ignore it, but she couldn't admit *that* to the dickless wonder. Swallowing her pride, she closed her eyes and prepared to grovel. The last thing she needed was for Dick to complain to the super that she was insubordinate. She wouldn't put it past him to have her yanked from the investigation completely and, if he complained, Afzal would have little choice. There was only so long that he could protect her from herself.

'I'm so sorry, sir. I was out for lunch with DC McQueen when the notification of the blog post came in and I'm afraid I got caught up in the moment. We've ascertained that Ginny Bell has done a runner from the hotel and I'm on my way back to base right now to finish off my filing before I go home. Once more I'm sorry, but we thought time was of the essence.'

Beside her Queenie was pretending to stick her fingers down her throat whilst glaring daggers at the phone. Jazzy held her breath as she awaited Dick's response. You could never be sure which way he would go, although when it concerned her, it usually went badly. But this time she was in luck.

'Okay. We're short-staffed. Back to base, right now.'

'Will do, sir. On my way.' She grinned at Queenie after hanging up. 'Dodged a bullet, but we need to get back to the station. The uniforms can keep an eye out for Ginny Bell. No point in wasting any more time on her. Maybe Janine Gorman's come up trumps. I never got the chance to ask Fenton before Dick grabbed the phone.'

Unfortunately, Janine was ensconced in a meeting with DCI

Dick when Queenie and Jazzy got back, and she was still in it by the time Jazzy had to sign out. That, in itself, was a major operation, for Jazzy had no intention of telling Queenie where she was going or who she was meeting. With relief, she finally executed her escape from the car park and headed to West Calder train station to meet her blast from the past.

Chapter 25

After reversing her Mini between a Jeep and a Volvo in the West Calder station car park, Jazzy hotfooted it over the bridge and onto the platform at the other side. The train was approaching the station and she breathed a sigh of relief that operation Escape Queenie had been successful. Once on the train, she set to work on her phone. First step was to text Janine Gorman directly and beg her to put a rush on her search with the directive to forward any findings straight to Jazzy's email. Hopefully, she'd have something to work on at home after her meeting with Elliot.

That done, she checked for updates on the investigation and saw that the lab work on the Clarks had come back complete with the official post-mortem results. She scrolled down until she found what she wanted. Both the Clarks had midazolam in their bloodstream. Jazzy presumed it was an anaesthetic and a quick Google search confirmed that. According to Dr Google, the Clarks would have been rendered unconscious within minutes.

She scanned back up and looked at the post-mortem results. As expected both had died from blood loss and heart failure due to the wound that beheaded them. Dr Johnston noted that there were hesitation marks on Bob Clark's neck, but none on Shirley

Clark's, indicating that he had died first and that their assailant had become more confident by the time he came to Mrs Clark's decapitation. In his notes, the pathologist reported that the wound was consistent with any run-of-the-mill sharp axe. The wounds were delivered with force by a right-handed person whilst the victims were lying on the floor in a supine position.

Jazzy frowned and again consulted Dr Google. Yes, supine meant face up. So, what did that say about the killer? That he had no qualms at all about removing a head from a living person who was facing them, or perhaps he'd done his research and knew it was easier to remove someone's head from the front. Jazzy reckoned it was a mix of both.

As far as the pathologist could tell the mutilation occurred post-mortem. It was as if the perpetrator had wanted the beheading over with so he could take time with the bodies. Jazzy shuddered at the thought of Imogen Clark sleeping upstairs whilst her parents were being beheaded, their bodies manipulated by the killer until he was happy with the grotesque tableau he'd created downstairs. Jazzy quickly jotted down questions for the pathologist. *How easy is it to get a hold of midazolam? Could a single person working alone have manipulated the bodies from the floor and into the seats?*

As she typed the notes into her phone, her mind kept drifting to the mutilation. The pegs, the petals, the beans, the messages left on the victims' heads. Her iPhone screen blurred and she blinked. It was still fuzzy, so she blinked again, but it wasn't enough to dispel the images that intruded. A low groan escaped her lips. Jazzy knew what was coming and there was nothing she could do to stop it. So, fingers clutching her Ganesh, she rested her head on the window, closed her eyes and, hoping it would be short-lived, submitted to it, like she did every other time. It was the only way.

She creeps close to her mum's filthy body, lying on the old rug. The woman stinks. Her hair's all matted with blood and her

178

clothes are caked in poo and sick. The girl forces herself to touch her mum's cheek. It's still warm, but her eyes? Her eyes are dull – like the life has dribbled from them and the little girl doesn't know what to do.

Jazzy recognised that girl. She always did and, as the panic set in, a familiar sensation slithered up her body. It wound itself round her upper body robbing her of air and, like a boa constrictor intent on asphyxiating its prey, it squeezed tighter and tighter. As her chest compressed, the pressure built in her head. She was sure it was going to explode. She didn't want to see that girl anymore. Didn't want to feel those things.

Panting slightly, her breath misting the air before her, she opened her eyes and saw her reflection in the train window: a woman, long dark hair scraped back into a ponytail, eyes wide, her face gaunt – tortured even. But it kept morphing back into that girl – the skinny one with the shorn hair. *I'm not that girl anymore. Not that skinny little defenceless runt trying to look after my siblings when I can barely look after myself.* The silence outside made her eerie out-of-body sensation more profound.

She sensed a kid in a Hibs scarf staring at her with curious eyes before shrugging and looking away, lost once more in the thrum from those stupid earbuds they all wear these days. She ignored him and as the darkness beyond the train carriage flitted by, interspersed with white snowdrifts and merging with fleeting images of trees and buildings, taunting her with their twinkling lights, she forced her reflection to prevail and pushed those ghostly visions from her past away. But they were persistent and another image pushed past her defences.

Three children sit on an old tartan shawl by a burn. It's hot, really hot. Hot enough to melt the tar on the roads. The older girl, long hair pushed behind her ears, has one of the younger kids' feet in her lap. She's using a broken old knife to scrape the black gunge off the soles of his feet. 'I told you not to burst the tar bubbles. I told you, didn't I? She'll tan our arses.'

179

The little boy starts to snuffle. 'I'm sorry. Honest I am. Will she send me to the bogeyman, Jazzy? Will she split us up?'

The older girl stops scraping and pulls the boy onto her lap, throwing her arm round the other child, whose eyes have welled up too. 'She can never split us up. Never. No matter what happens we'll always be together. I'll always find you.'

'But how? How will you find us?'

She thinks for a moment, then a smile breaks over her face. 'I've got it. We'll make a promise, a special promise. But you need to be brave.'

The younger two look up at her, their eyes filled with love, filled with trust. 'What sort of special promise?' they ask in unison.

'A blood promise. That's one that can never be broken.' The older girl, in her tattered pink and white sun suit, slices into her palm with the knife and blood oozes out. She looks at her siblings. 'Ready?'

Wide-eyed, they nod and, scrunching their eyes tight closed, they extend their small hands, making barely a peep as the knife pierces their skin. The three, in turn, rub their open wounds against their siblings'.

'There. That's our promise. Our blood promise that can never be broken. We'll always find each other.'

Jazzy's fingers curled up and found the raised ridge on her palm. She stroked the scar and with tears threatening to fall, the image blurs until the young girl is replaced by the woman, whose wide and wild eyes frightened her. If, in her official capacity, she saw someone looking like that, she'd get medical help, sit them down, make them a sugary drink. But this wasn't someone else. This was her and she was well used to fighting her own demons, even though sometimes she had no idea what they meant. That girl in the vision wasn't her though. She was a Jazzy from another time, a Jazzy she can scarcely remember. One she doesn't know and certainly doesn't understand.

The reflection blurred and flickered before morphing into a skinny girl, with haunted, feral eyes and a shorn head again.

Another blink and she'd be gone, replaced by the serious girl in the pink and white sun suit. Another blink and she was gone too. Jazzy exhaled and waited, just in case they came back, but they didn't. Not this time.

Chapter 26

I've got an ace up my sleeve right now and I just need to decide when to best reveal it for maximum benefit. I could do it right now whilst she's on the train to Edinburgh, but that might be premature because I know who she's meeting when she gets there, and I'm looking forward to seeing the old team reunited. Mind you, it would be good to see first-hand how she reacts. I know getting on the train with her was risky and I'm tempted to spoil her night right now, but something tells me to wait. That a better opportunity will present itself, if I'm patient.

Does she spot me? No, she's too self-absorbed to look further than her nose and that suits me. She barely glances at the kid in the Hibs scarf, which gives me the chance to study her at close quarters, like she's a specimen in a science lab. She's troubled. At first, she's engrossed in work stuff, flicking through files on her tablet, checking stuff on her phone. Then something changes. I wonder if she's sensed something about me. But no. She's resting her head on the window, her eyes closed, then when she opens them she looks spaced out. Then, she looks teary.

As the train chugs away from Haymarket station heading towards Waverley, I lean back in and close my eyes, allowing my head to bob in time to the imaginary sound from my headphones, and I blend into the background. Jazzy Solanki, your time will come. Soon, your worst nightmare will be played out and I think I know just when to implement that.

Chapter 27

As the train pulled into the station, Jazzy, relieved to break away from the distorted image on the train window, jumped to her feet. Jostling through the crowds on the concourse, she headed for the Waverley toilets and once there took refuge in a cubicle. The sounds of commuters and tourists, hand dryers and running taps calmed her. She was beginning to make a habit of hiding out in public loos. All she needed now was for Queenie to hammer on the door yelling, 'Get your big girl panties on, JayZee, and get out of the crapper.'

What is happening to me? Jazzy turned her left hand over and rested it on her thigh. The scar was faint and she hadn't thought about it for years. *Why now?* Again, Queenie's voice inveigled itself into her head. 'Jeez oh, JayZee. You telling me you can't work that one out for yourself, hen?'

Jazzy rolled her neck, revelling in the cracking sound as she released some of the tension. This case was getting to her, dredging up half-remembered memories, playing on her vulnerabilities. But that wasn't her. She was a fighter and she needed to start acting like one. She took a wet wipe from her backpack, used it to wipe away the tell-tale signs of her distress and stood up, pulled her shoulders back and exited the loo. No more maudlin self-flagellation. She had this. With a grin she invoked her inner Queenie. After all, she *was* a Jazz Queen, wasn't she?

She was early for her meeting with Elliot, so decided to kill time wandering round the Christmas markets. Usually the bonhomie of Christmas music and crowds of people, all happy and full of festive cheer, filled Jazzy with despair, but after her experience on the train she was happy to be cushioned by jostling Christmas shoppers and to savour the enticing smells of fresh churros and spicy mulled wine as she wandered through the market. The Scott Monument was backlit and the shops along Princes Street had gone all out for the festive vibe. All of this combined with the softly falling snow and muted festive music was relaxing.

She only ever bought Christmas presents for her aunt and uncle – who were also her adoptive parents – slippers and a Marks & Spencer's voucher, usually, but something about the atmosphere compelled her to join in. She was anonymous in the crowds and, rightly or wrongly, that made her feel safe. Like she was part of something bigger than the ever-decreasing world of Jazzy Solanki. For once, she wanted to *not* be a bystander, but to throw herself into something normal. Something that other people did as a matter of course. Something that the feral shorn-headed child who had haunted her on the train wouldn't do.

One of the stalls was doing a deal on tartan glove and scarf sets and Jazzy smiled, imagining her wee auntie's smile if she found something totally unexpected in her Christmas gift this year. Jazzy selected a rich red tartan set for Lillie and a deep green tartan set for Jiten. Emboldened by her purchase, Jazzy drifted to the next stall and, with a warm feeling in her chest, selected a thick rainbow-coloured Shetland wool hat with ear flaps for Queenie. Moving on she opted for two, less brightly coloured beanie hats for Geordie and Fenton. She paused and as a last-minute thing, added another beanie to her purchases. She probably wouldn't give it to Elliot, but it wouldn't hurt to buy it. Just in case.

With her bags in hand and the strange memory from the train

fading, Jazzy grabbed two portions of churros and headed back to the Scott Monument. Elliot was already waiting. His hands stuffed into his pocket and his shoulders hunched against the breeze that whipped light snowflakes into the air. The sight of him made her want to run. Seeing him always took her back to the first time she'd seen him. It brought back all that fear and vulnerability. But he'd seen her and there was nowhere to run to; besides he was her friend – the only one she didn't have to pretend for. He'd seen her at her worst and was still there for her all these years later. Jazzy scowled and thrust one of the packs of churros at him. 'Here. Only got you these to stop you nicking mine.'

As he unwrapped the churros, Jazzy watched, amused that although he was completely unaware of it, he attracted his fair share of attention from passers-by. Detective Inspector Elliot Balloch was tall, broad and, even in the Christmas lighting, he looked very handsome.

Blue eyes twinkling, Elliot grinned. 'You taking no hostages, Jazz? Not even at Christmas? Not even when I haven't seen you in ages?'

Jazzy shrugged and avoided meeting his gaze. She hated when he got too personal. They were here to discuss what was going on. 'Let's go find a seat in the gardens where we won't be overheard.'

After using tissues to dry two bum-sized spaces on the nearest wooden benches, Jazzy sat down and began to chomp her way through her churros. Her gaze, as always, was drawn to Edinburgh Castle, which loomed over Princes Street Gardens. Its solidity, its history, its reliable presence always made her feel small and insignificant, yet so completely safe. She imagined the number of people who'd claimed sanctuary within its thick walls as well as those enemies who'd fallen foul of the Scots and lost their lives on the hill beneath and, by comparison, her problems seemed trivial. She had a good team working with her and supportive parents. Even today with a stalker threatening her and the strange thoughts that kept jumping into her head, she felt safe. Some of that was to do with Elliot's solid presence and was linked to their shared experience – *the* shared experience. The one they rarely talked about, but which hung there between them like an executioner's sword, ready to fall and shatter their fragile friendship.

Jazzy shuddered at the imagery *that* conjured and was transported back to the Clarks' crime scene – their severed heads so precisely placed on their kitchen table. A shiver iced her spine, making it feel brittle enough to snap. At every crime scene she visited, Jazzy remembered how young Elliot had been – it was only his first day on the job when he'd found her and her siblings. Was he as traumatised by it all as she was? She doubted it. Elliot was more pragmatic and he'd have dealt with any fallout head-on. Besides, her lifestyle, before her mum died, had consisted of a series of unresolved traumas, never mind everything else. By contrast, Elliot was from a loving family. He had a background of security to help him cope.

'Cold?'

'Nah, just thinking about the Clarks. The way they were displayed, the . . .'

Elliot, twisted towards her, his tone low and urgent. 'That's why you shouldn't be wandering around on your own, Jazz. Not till this bastard's been caught. You know it's all linked.'

Jazzy bristled, and shifted on the bench. She hated it when he got like this – all protective, like she had no autonomy. 'I'm not fragile, Elliot. Not anymore.'

He grunted, his lips tightening, yet he had the grace to look away with a nod. 'I know that, Jazz, but . . .'

Wafting a half-eaten churro at him, face red and eyes flashing, Jazzy shook her head from side to side. 'That's just it. You might think you *know* it, but you just can't quite bring yourself to believe it, can you, Elliot?'

'Course I do. It's just if you'd . . .'

Furious, she shook her head from side to side, her eyes flashing at him. 'Don't you dare. Don't you bloody dare, Elliot.'

'What?'

'You know exactly what I mean. Don't you think I know I should have reported all those cards when they first started arriving?'

He nodded, but before he could speak Jazzy went on. 'But that's all fine and well in hindsight, isn't it? At the time, it just seemed like a scrote trying to freak me out. And you know as well as I do that I, more than most, had to keep my head down to succeed in this job. Had to put up with more and expect a whole lot less. What do you think would've happened if I'd reported it? Yes, it would've been all official, but that wouldn't stop the haters from saying the brown girl couldn't hack it. That I needed to toughen up, take the good with the bad. Like I just accepted the bacon rashers stuffed in my locker – didn't even bother to tell the idiots that my family religion was Hinduism not Islam. I ignored the photos of the KKK left on my desk . . . I did the only thing I could to survive and *that* was to investigate on my own with your help. In case you've forgotten, by the way, we didn't find a sodding clue. So, reporting it would've done dick all and we'd still be here trying to work out my stalker's identity. I mean, how threatening can an unsigned card once or twice a year be?'

Although he tried to hide it, the whitening of his nose and the way he took an aggressive bite of the pastry told her how annoyed he was. No, not annoyed – worried. Her indignation scattered like the snowflakes in the breeze. Why was it sometimes so hard to communicate with Elliot? Why couldn't they find common ground? They were close – bound by their past. Yet, somehow, they couldn't get past it and that's what led to these tense, irritable interchanges. No wonder she mostly contacted him on the burner phone. It wasn't just about keeping her association with him off the radar, it was about protecting *his* career as well as her own.

He swallowed his food and in little more than a whisper said, 'Not threatening at all . . .' Then, louder, each word spat at her like bullets from a machine gun, '. . . until he surfaces and provides a wee birthday gift, just for you in the shape of two innocent victims with their heads severed.'

'We don't . . .'

'Of course, it was for you. We know it was for you so don't try to pretend otherwise. He selected that family purely because *you* shared a birthday with the daughter, Jazzy. You know that, I know that and Afzal knows that too. It's time to come clean about your past, your childhood and your mum's dead body. It's time to tell your team the truth and it's time to get to the bottom of this once and for all.'

Tears pricked at the backs of Jazzy's eyes, but she wouldn't give him the satisfaction of seeing them fall. All her earlier happiness at doing something normal like shopping for her new friends splattered on the concrete at her feet. How could she ever be normal? She should have known better than to try. Then something he'd said hit her. 'Afzal knows it too'. He'd discussed her with the chief super. Elliot, who was supposed to be on *her* side, had discussed her behind her back.

She threw her hands in the air. 'For fuck's sake, Elliot. You've been talking to him? To Afzal? About me? Like this illicit little triangle couldn't get any more sordid.'

Elliot shook his head. 'Jazzy, you need to try the hypnosis again. You need to . . .'

She sniffed. She'd hated doing hypnotherapy. It had thrown up too many awful memories and had left her depressed and unable to leave her house. No way would she try that again. Not even to find out the absolute truth about what happened back then. 'I don't *need* to do a sodding thing. I told you all that I remembered. I told you everything. I told them all everything. That should be enough. Why can't that be enough?'

Elliot reached out and squeezed her arm, but she yanked it away. 'You don't know what it's like to remember half of the stuff that happened but not all of it. To wonder if what you remember is a real or a phantom memory. If your damaged mind is taunting you.' Blinking rapidly, she inhaled and lowered her head, her voice so low, he had to lean closer to hear the words. 'You remember what you found in that room. Me?' Her laugh was hollow. 'I don't remember a thing. The flashbacks, when they come, jump about. Some of them are from well before you found us. Hardly any of them are from that time when we were alone in the house. They're all over the place. No chronological order, not neat little boxes, just a whole load of snippets that could belong to anyone. None of them are mine. None of them feel real.'

'I know, I know, Jazzy. Dissociative amnesia isn't easy to deal with. You have questions, I know you do.'

'Do you? Everyone seems to think they know what I think and what I feel, but it's not as easy as that. Maybe I don't want to know. Maybe I'm happy as I am. Maybe *you* lot should be content with me as I am. I mean am I so bloody horrible? So, fucking warped? So damn weird?'

Tears prickled her eyes, but she brushed them away. 'Or maybe it's that you think I did it? That I did those weird things. That *I'm* a psychopath. That's the truth isn't it, Elliot? You and Afzal have always worried that there's something missing in me. That's why you keep me on such a tight leash, isn't it?'

'That's not fair, Jazz. We've never thought that. There's never been any indication of that. You *know* we have to consider that the Clarks' murders are connected with . . .'

'Don't you say it. Don't you *dare* say their names. Just don't.'

Jazzy got up, her heart pounding, her throat thick with unshed tears, and gathered her shopping bags together. 'I wish I hadn't reached out to you.'

As she glared at him, he glanced away, the throb at his temple a dead giveaway, and realisation struck then. With a strangled half-laugh she shook her head. 'It wouldn't have mattered whether I reached out or not though, would it? You and Afzal had it all sorted between you, didn't you? He's filled you in on everything. It's out of my hands.'

A searing rage roared through her body from the soles of her feet right up to her head. 'I wish you'd never fucking rescued me. You should have left me there to rot, like my mother. I'd be better off dead like her rather than living like this.'

She chucked her half-eaten churros at him, spun on her heel and took off through the gardens, not caring if she knocked into people as she ran towards the Waverley station as if her worst nightmares might catch up with her. Why the hell had she come? Why had she thought talking to Elliot would be a good idea? And what the hell had possessed her to throw those last comments at him?

Chapter 28

When I opted to wait before putting the next part of my plan into action, I didn't anticipate the big bust-up in Princes Street Gardens. Wow! That temper? Whoa, I hadn't realised she had that amount of venom in her. Go Jazzy!

I'd expected to catch them snogging in the park, but this is *so* much better. I could never have anticipated this. I couldn't hear the specifics of their argument, but it isn't hard to guess what it's all about. ME!

I watch as she takes off through the gardens back to the station, her feet barely touching the ground, her demeanour enough to have people diving out of her way. There's no rush for me to follow. The next train's not for another ten minutes, so instead I sidle backwards and lean on a lamppost with my phone out as if I'm talking to someone. Elliot's shoulders slump and he leans forward resting his forearms on his thighs, his head bowed. Poor Elliot. Join the club of others Jazzy Solanki has let down. Surely, you're not dumb enough to be surprised by it. Our Jazzy is damaged goods, Elliot. You should know that by now.

I'd spent a long time wondering why Elliot became so obsessed by Jazzy. Why not me? Why didn't I capture his imagination? Then as I grew older I realised what it was. Elliot Balloch suffers from saviour syndrome. His genetic code made it inevitable that the skinny kid with the shorn head, the scabs and the bruises would be the one to capture his attention. It's a sign of his weakness and that doesn't concern me. He didn't betray me. She did.

I watch him for a while then amble over to the station. Now I see how tormented she is. How high her emotions are running, I'm glad I waited. Maybe when I implement my next step, she'll be knocked right off kilter. Maybe she'll break. After all, she's barely an episode away from an all-out breakdown.

Chapter 29

Dodging the traffic, Jazzy flew over the road and down the ramp to the station, pausing only to scan her ticket at the barrier, before darting through and managing to jump on the train as it idled by the platform. Huddled in a corner seat, her bags on her lap, phone in hand, Jazzy stared out the window, wishing the train would hurry up and leave the platform. Not that she thought for a moment that Elliot would follow her. That wasn't his style.

Her thoughts were in turmoil, her head throbbed and a strange heaviness settled on her shoulders. In all the years she'd known Elliot, she'd never left him feeling so utterly despondent. Of course, they often rubbed each other up the wrong way – with their shared history, her inability to open up and her innate prickliness, it would be hard for them not to irritate each other. This was different though. This felt like betrayal, not just a disagreement. It felt like Elliot was siding with Waqas Afzal and hanging her out to dry.

As the train filled, people sliding into the seats around her, she scrolled through her phone. She'd missed calls from Queenie and a lot of texts, each one punctuated by an increasing number of exclamation marks and capital letters.

Where are you, JayZee?
Forget I'm your bodyguard, did you?
This isn't on! Where are you?
Text me ASAP!!!!!
Get your flabby fingers out your arse and TEXT ME!!!!!!
ARE YOU OKAY!!!!!!!!
NOT FUCKING FUNNY!!!!!!!!!!!

Jazzy groaned. She should have texted Queenie. Of course, her partner would be concerned that she'd swanned off without telling her. It was no excuse that she'd intended to contact her when she got on the train in Cauther, but got caught up in the post-mortem report from Dr Johnston. Then she'd been blindsided by that weird memory followed by her argument with Elliot. None of that was good enough. Queenie was her partner and she should have let her know. The older woman was probably on the point of getting the search parties out. With a judder, the train began to move and with each second putting more and more distance between her and Elliot, Jazzy began to relax. Her fingers flew across her phone and she sent off a text to Queenie.

Sorry, Queenie. I'm fine. See you at the station.

Even with the throng of people in the carriage, Jazzy felt safe, snuggled into her corner seat, her bags filled with her Christmas shopping firmly on her lap. Still, she avoided looking out the window into the darkness beyond, just in case the flashing reflections triggered another memory vision. She was desperate to get home and lock herself in her little house, cuddle up to Winky and sleep till she could sleep no more. The carriage was uncomfortably warm and that strange smell of damp coats beginning to dry in the heat sapped the air from the confined space.

Jazzy wiped the steam from the window and peered out, trying to judge how far it was to the next station, but with crowds descending onto the platform the sign was hidden. At least the train was less busy. Her phone rang and she almost ignored it, assuming it was either Elliot trying to smooth things over or Queenie determined to chew her ear off, but it was an unknown number. Not in the mood for a cold caller, but aware that she'd been out of contact for a few hours already and reluctant to miss any urgent calls, she hit answer. 'Yes?'

When she heard the robotic modified tones drift down the line she froze.

'I think you'll want to check your WhatsApp, Jasmine. Tick tock, tick tock.' The call ended abruptly.

She had wondered if the killer would contact her, but now that it had happened it chilled Jazzy to the bone. Cold sweat dotted her brow and her hands shook as she swiped to her WhatsApp. The same unknown number had left a video. Dread twisting her heart, she slipped her earbuds in and downloaded the recording. When she saw her mum sitting in her kitchen, Crumble by her side, Jazzy's heart hammered in her chest and she stopped breathing for a few seconds. Then, with a gasp, she tuned in to her mum's sweet tones. 'Can you tell me again, what is the award Jazzy's up for? You know she deserves an award, does our Jasmine. She works tirelessly and she's been injured in the line of duty a few times.' On the screen her mum poured their drinks from a teapot with a tartan tea cosy on.

The altered voice was chilling. 'It's the Lothian and Borders police merit award for outstanding dedication to duty.'

Jazzy strained to see if she recognised the speaker, but of course the voice modulator had put paid to that. As her eyes raked over her mum's smiling face, a wave of anger surged through her. There was no trace of strain or fear about Lillie, but that didn't reassure Jazzy. She'd seen what this monster could do and he'd clearly had time to edit this recording before sending it to her, so there was no guarantee her mum was alive. If she ever got her hands on the person sitting in her parents' kitchen drinking tea, then Jazzy wouldn't hesitate to kill them.

'Och well, she deserves that. She really does. Now, what do you want from me?'

'Just a bit of background really, you know about her adoption and why you chose to adopt her and not her siblings? How she settled in with you and suchlike.'

On the screen, her mum frowned. 'We did try to adopt all three, but it was believed that with them being so young . . . but, what's that got to do with her award?'

Lillie frowned and hesitated. She cast a sideways glance towards the door as if doubting the wisdom of letting this man into their home. 'What polis station did you say you were from?'

The man stood up, towering over her aunt. His back was to the camera when the recording cut out.

Shit, shit, what the hell was that? Hands shaking, Jazzy phoned first her mum's mobile – no reply. Then her dad's – again no reply. Finally, she phoned the landline, but again it rang out and when she went to leave a message it was full up. All thoughts of her earlier bust-up with Elliot dismissed, she dialled his number.

'No burner phone this ti . . .?'

'No time for that, Elliot. He's got my mum. He's got Lillie. Sent me a WhatsApp video. You need to get there. I'm stuck on the train. Get uniform there and . . .' Her breath caught in her throat, almost choking her. She gulped. 'Just get there, Elliot. Just get there. I'll forward you the video.'

'I'm on it. I'll head there right now. I'll get the locals there too.'

Clutching her phone to her chest, Jazzy glared out the window and was relieved that they were passing West Calder primary school. Not long now, approaching. Quickly forwarding the video to Elliot, she grabbed her bags, forced herself to breathe slowly and moved to wait by the door, ready to jump out as soon as the train stopped.

When the doors opened, Jazzy – in her haste – fell out and almost landed on Queenie who was pacing up and down the platform, her unzipped coat flapping behind her like a cape. 'Where the hell have you been, JayZee? I'll tell you where you've been: AWOL. Bloody magical disappearing woman, that's you. Out of bloody touch. That's where you've been. We've got a dangerous and violent killer on the loose and you decide to shake off your protection and wander off Christmas shopping in Edinburgh.'

No time for Queenie's shenanigans, Jazzy brushed past her and headed towards her car, her mind burling with thoughts of all the things that could be happening to her mum and dad right now.

'Hey wait up. You can't just swan back into circulation and drive off into the sunset in your Matchbox car without an explanation, or an apology. I've been bloody frantic waiting here for you.'

Jazzy opened the driver's door, tossed her bags into the back seat and, barely holding her tears back, glared at her partner. 'Get out of my way, Queenie. I don't have time for your dramatics.' Her next words caught in her throat. 'The bastard has my parents. I've got to go.'

Queenie barely hesitated before grabbing Jazzy by the arm and dragging her towards her Land Rover. 'You're in no state to drive, JayZee. Get in. Where are we going?'

Realising that Queenie was right and that her Land Rover would rattle through to Portobello more quickly than her wee Mini, Jazzy locked her car and climbed into Queenie's passenger seat. She hardly managed to close her door before Queenie skidded out of the car park and up the hill to join the A71 towards Edinburgh, where they could catch the bypass to Portobello.

Chapter 30

On the edge of her seat, Jazzy alternated between phoning Elliot Balloch and phoning her mum and dad's phones. 'No reply. Nobody's picking up. Elliot should have arrived there by now. Surely, he's there by now. What if . . .?' She couldn't finish the sentence.

Queenie, with her foot to the floor, kept her eyes on the road, peering through the dark blizzard and looking like a shorter Jackie Stewart on steroids. 'Who is this Elliot bloke?'

'A friend. A DI from Edinburgh. He's closer to Porty than us.'

Queenie nodded. 'Right, tell me what happened.'

Jazzy exhaled and tried to focus. 'He sent this recording via WhatsApp. It's of my mum and it's taken in their house in Porty. The bastard tricked her into letting him in. Told her he was from Police Scotland and they were doing some sort of award for me.'

Jazzy played the WhatsApp recording for Queenie, drinking in her mum's smiling face and trying not to think about the damage her stalker could do. She'd never forgive herself if anything happened to her mum or her dad. Not after everything they'd done for her. Not after they'd sought her out after her birth mum died, against her grandad's wishes, rescued her from foster care and brought her up as their own daughter. They'd not been allowed the twins. Social services recommended that because of their youth and the mystery around the post-mortem mutilations that it would be better to give them a new start in life away from each other.

'But you've phoned it in, yeah?' Queenie recklessly overtook a Transit Van, and pulled in narrowly missing the oncoming Citroën, which tooted at her.

'Yeah, I phoned Elliot and he took care of it. He should be there by now. Why has he not contacted me?'

With her thoughts all over the place, Jazzy hadn't considered how she would explain Elliot's role in this to Queenie and she'd blocked their earlier argument from her mind. Elliot didn't bear grudges anyway. 'Can't you go any faster, Queenie?'

Rage and anxiety made it impossible for Jazzy to sit still. Every sinew in her body, every nerve ending was on fire. If she thought she could reach her parents' house any quicker she'd have jumped out of the car and run there. Instead, she squirmed on the edge of her seat, as flashing car lights illuminated the car's interior. She cursed herself for not identifying her folks as vulnerable. She should have known that they could be a target and she'd left them alone and unprotected. If anything happened to either of them – if one hair on their heads was even displaced, she'd kill him.

For the first time since she'd begun to link the Clarks' murders with her stalker, Jazzy fully accepted that her past and the Clarks' murders were linked. The beans at the Clarks' crime scene, the mutilation using everyday household items – all of it linked her stalker to her birth mother's death and there were only three people there when Hansa Solanki died: herself, and the twins – Mhairi and Simon. The unthinkable thought that she'd pushed down since she'd first attended that crime scene broke free. All the memories, all the nightmares – every one of them pointed to her brother Simon – after all he'd been the one she'd seen leaving the bedroom, his hands covered in blood, and now he had her mum!

It was her fault. She should have acted on this sooner. She

should have taken her half-submerged memories seriously and heeded their warning. She replaced the image she'd held in her heart of her light-haired half-siblings with their trusting brown eyes and uncertain gap-toothed smiles, with the image of the man caught on her home security camera. Could it be her half-brother?

She's cold – freezing and the door's open. There's only two of them curled up on the mattress. She knows where he is. He's always sneaking off there. Somewhere inside her a raw burning begins as she stands up. She doesn't want to know what he's doing. But why is he always there? She wraps the blanket round Mhairi and crawls over the lobby to the other bedroom. Her legs are all wobbly, but she takes a deep breath, pushes the door open and shines the torch in. He's only little, his eyes blinking against the glare, his hands covered in gunge and he's got pegs in his hands . . . Oh, Simon!

Jazzy blinks the memory away. Was that real, or did she imagine it? Even now she's never entirely sure which of her flashbacks to believe. All those years ago, when her birth mum died leaving three frightened kids to fend for themselves in that freezing house – all alone and unprotected – a sequence of events had begun leading her to this precise moment in time. Like a lightning flash an image of herself as a ten-year-old disturbed her thoughts, taking her out of the present and back fifteen years.

The girl, with her long black hair and brown skin, sits atop a three-legged stool on a sea of newspaper, her head down, letting the barrage of insults and curses roll over her. At least she isn't hitting me – not yet, anyway. A woman – her mother – yanks the girl's ponytail up from her scalp and attacks it with rabid, stabbing scissors, gouging out chunks of hair by the roots, scraping the blades across her scalp, jabbing the points into her skin. She is uncaring – maybe even oblivious of her daughter's squeaks of pain and her squirming body on the stool.

Two younger children scrunch together on the couch, weeping and pleading for their mummy to stop, as one wavy lock after another of their sister's hair falls onto the newspaper. The girl keeps her head bowed, biting her lip as the stink of booze on her mother's breath rolls over her and the scissors jab her scalp with increasing savagery, bringing tears to her eyes.

'Stop, Mummy. It's Jazzy's birthday. Don't hurt her on her birthday, please don't hurt her.'

'Birthday? Birthday? Mucky little cows who get nits don't deserve birthdays. Now you two shut up or you'll be next.'

The twins huddle closer together, their bright eyes wide, their pupils dilated, the thought of going through what their big sister was going through petrifying them into silence.

Scalping complete, her mum grabs the stool in one hand and her daughter's skinny arm in the other. With her fingers pinching the skin, she drags her daughter through to the kitchen, her voice slurring as she yells to her other children. 'You two get that fucking mess cleared up and put in the fire before we all get infested.'

The girl tries her best to keep up, but her legs are too gangly and, as her mum stumbles through the narrow gap between their small living room and the tiny kitchen, she bangs her head against the bottom of the overhead worktops. Still, her only sound is a startled yelp as she is hoisted up by one arm onto the stool which her mum places before the sink.

'On your knees you mucky fucking scrote. On your fucking knees.'

The girl scrambles up and kneels with her head scrunched down over the sink. She's too tall for the stool now, but her mum doesn't care as she begins the delousing. Foul-smelling cream drenches her hair and her mum's talon-like fingers claw at her scalp, relentlessly working the lotion into each follicle until it nips her skull. Head still bowed over the sink, she braces herself as cupfuls of ice-cold water are thrown over her head, again and again until her breath comes in gasping gulps. All the while her mother's muttered imprecations punctuate each savage stroke. 'Dirty little cow. Disgusting filthy bitch.'

With the girl's patchy hair dripping all over the sticky kitchen floor and threadbare carpet, the mum yanks her off the stool and *back through to the living room.*

'Get on the bloody stool, you dirty little animal, and don't bloody move.' To punctuate her instruction, she grabs her daughter by both arms and shakes her. 'Got it?'

The shivering girl, her scalp stinging, avoids her mum's glazed look and holds her breath against the boozy fumes. Her too-small, stained and faded T-shirt is sodden and she wonders if she'll ever get warm again. Of course, there's no money for the leccy meter because her mum has drunk it all and the only food she and her siblings have are the few tins of beans she's hidden under the bed in their bedroom. That will have to be enough till Monday – if she even lets them go to school. The girl crosses her fingers and places her hands under her thighs so her mum won't see and prays that she'll let them go to school. At least there they'll be warm and they'll all get something to eat and she knows her siblings will be safe.

Her mum bangs about in the kitchen cupboards, mumbling drunkenly as she searches for her next instrument of torture. When she returns, her eyes are even more glazed than before as she grabs the scruff of her daughter's neck with her bony fingers and pushes her head forward, till her neck won't tilt any more. Knowing what is to come, the girl keeps her eyes shut to contain the tears as her mum scrapes the metal fine-tooth comb through the patchy stubble on her scalp. The sporadic ping as the remaining nits land on the newspaper on the floor sounded like rain dripping on the roof of Mr Murray's fish van.

Curious to see the creatures that are at the root of her torture, the girl opens one eye. Tiny, dirty, brown insects crawl over the letters on the page, making it look like the writing is moving. They are too small to blame for her predicament so, blanking out the pain in her scalp as her mother combs, she begins counting them in her head, stopping occasionally to give the larger ones names. When she wriggles on the stool, her mother raps her hard on the head with her knuckles. 'Sit still – I'm no' done with you yet.'

Off she stumbles, clattering against the fridge door, then bouncing *against the cupboards, before grabbing the half-full bottle of lice killer and a grubby towel and weaving her way back to her daughter. She glares at her eldest child in disgust before opening the bottle. Her lips are pinched and, despite the drunken glaze in her eyes, the girl can see she's enjoying herself. Once more, she pours the liquid over her scalp, rubbing it in so that each gouged track on the girl's head nips like hell. It smells like syrup of figs, castor oil, and tripe mixed together. The girl's eyes water and tears stream down her cheeks, but her mum isn't satisfied till all of the foul-smelling stuff is on her head. With a final grimace she wraps the soiled towel round her daughter's head and tucks it in place. Beneath the fabric, the burning continues and the girl's eyes water, both with the fumes and with the pain.*

Her mum prods her in the chest. 'Maybe that'll teach you not to get nits.'

Then, she steps away, flinging her head back as a phlegmy laugh gurgles from her throat, making her convulse in a coughing fit. 'Hope it stings all night, you minging little cow. Now, get to your bloody beds, the three of you.'

The younger two are at the door leading upstairs in a nanosecond, but the older girl hesitates for a moment to settle her shaking legs. She wishes she was brave enough to tell her mum to stop. Brave enough to tell someone about what goes on in their home – what she and her siblings have to put up with. But she can't. She just can't. Instead she jumps up, eager to get away from her mum, eager to unwrap her head and eager to sneak into the bathroom to see the damage that's been done to her hair. How can she go into school like this on Monday? She'll be the laughing stock and not for the first time.

As she jumps off the stool, her foot catches the crossbar and she stumbles. She misses and instead tumbles head first into her mum. Her mum totters, her hands waving in the air as she tries to regain her balance, but too much alcohol has made her incapable of catching herself. With her daughter watching her – making no attempt to catch her – she falls backwards, her head crashing into the metal corner of the gas fire before she continues downwards to the floor where her skull cracks against the edge of the fireplace with a sickening sound.

Jazzy's breath was like acid in her chest. Hyperventilating, she threw her arms around her body, desperate to rouse herself from this nightmare. Her eyes won't open. It's as if the nit lotion from her dream is stinging them, forcing them to stay shut. Just out of reach, Jazzy sensed reality. A coarse yet kind voice is saying her name over and over again.

'JayZee, JayZee. You're all right, hen. Your auntie Queenie's here. You're all right, just take deep breaths, that's it.'

But she couldn't escape the dream. On and on it went . . .

The siblings stand stock-still, waiting for their mum to get up and lambast them. But, she lies there unmoving. The eldest child, eyes wide, her heart beating like a thunderstorm in her chest, glances at the scared faces of her siblings. The two smaller kids huddle together for a moment, tears trickling down their rosy cheeks, before they edge closer. The older girl's gaze moves from her siblings back to the drunken heap before her. Her mum's eyes are wide open, but vacant. Her head rests on the scratty rug and blood oozes out around her skull like a halo of raspberry sauce. The girl's nose crinkles in disgust and she covers her mouth with her hand. Her mum has peed herself and soiled herself too. It isn't the first time she's done that, not by a long chalk, but it always makes her even angrier when she does – like it was somehow their fault, that she's an alky.

The last thing the girl wants is to be there when her mum wakes up, for she knows her backside will be red raw from the spanking she'll get. As she looks at the dark liquid soaking into the carpet, her heart skips a beat. Will her mum ever wake up? For a moment her shoulders feel light – as if a burden is lifted. Then reality sets in. What would happen to them, if her mum was gone?

'What if she's dead?'

The other two move closer, holding hands now, curiosity making small frowns form across their brows. Her brother speaks first.

'Wouldn't miss her if she was. She deserves to die. We're better off without her. I'm glad you killed her, Jazzy. We'll be okay, us three.'

Almost as one, her two siblings raise their free hands and wipe the tears from their cheeks as they step closer, their eyes fixed on their mother's still form.

But Jazzy's not sure. She shrugs. 'Dunno. It might be worse for us if she's dead. They might split us up.' She doesn't know what to do. Should she be trying to shield them from the sight of their mum with blood coming out her head?

Holding her breath to stop herself gipping, she prods her mum's shoulder, but she doesn't move. She looks at the twins and then repeats the action, this time just a bit harder, Still no response. A smile breaks out across her brother's face and, before she can stop him, he lifts one foot, pulls it back and delivers a mighty kick to the silent woman's side. Jazzy holds her breath, waiting for her mum to rise and grab the hairbrush to whack them with. But she lies there, unmoving and silent.

Hands on hips, her brother nods, his lips pursed. 'Told ye' so. She's dead. If she wasn't she'd be moving by now.'

Jazzy creeps forward and looks at their mum's filthy form, her hair matted with blood and her stinking torso caked in shit and puke. She forces herself to touch her mum's cheek. It's still warm.

'What are we going to do?' This is the first words her younger sister has uttered since she's seen their mum fall, and Jazzy can think of nothing to say. She bites her lip, trying desperately to work out a response, but it is their brother who answers. 'We'll drag her up the stairs and shove her on her bed and we'll stay in our room till Monday and then we'll go to school. It's all right, we've got our promise.' And he holds his palm up and in turn the three of them bump their hands together.

Jazzy thinks about it. She knows the promise won't work. She's killed her mum and now the three of them might get separated. But only if someone finds out. They can go to school like normal and nobody needs to finds out . . . not ever. 'Let's do it.'

Chased by visions of three skinny children tugging and yanking with all their might at the enormous corpse, Jazzy finally pulled herself from the flashback. Her fists clenched so tightly that her fingernails gouged her skin.

'Thank Christ you're back, hen. I thought I was going to have to stop. You okay now?'

Jazzy heard Queenie's words as if through water as she unclenched her fists, noticing the bloody half-moon marks cutting over the scar on her left hand. Her breath hitched in loud, strangled gasps and she wondered if she'd die there. Queenie was speaking, her face morphed into scrunched-up burrows of tension, her words rapid, but unintelligible to Jazzy whose ears were filled with a whooshing sensation.

Sensing the car slow down, Jazzy shook her head, and waved her hand in a keep-going gesture. 'Don't . . . stop. I'm okay.'

Queenie's face tensed even more, but she pressed her foot down on the accelerator and, as the car picked up speed, Jazzy focused on slowing her breathing down, desperate to get to her mum in time.

Chapter 31

Her phone rang. *Elliot!* 'You there yet? Are they okay?' Jazzy switched the phone to speaker. 'You're on speakerphone. My colleague DC Annie McQueen is present.'

'Calm down, Jazzy. They're okay. Your mum and dad are fine. The bastard was taunting you. He visited Lillie earlier today. Looks like he waited till Jiten went to the club before approaching the house. Gave her the story about you being up for an award and Police Scotland wanting a few personal anecdotes to include in the presentation speech. We're getting CSIs over to see if he left any trace evidence, but my bet is he wore gloves and . . .'

'Let me speak to her. Is she okay? Is Dad okay?'

Her mum's voice came on the phone. 'Don't you fret, Jasmine. I'm right as ninepence. Take more than a chancer coming the ham to get the better of me.'

Jazzy sent a silent thanks to Elliot for not telling her just how much danger she'd been in.

'But, I think you should come and live with us for a wee while. Just till Elliot catches this bugger. I don't like to think of you on your own in that wee village.'

Blinking back tears, Jazzy smiled, not caring for once that her mum seemed to think Elliot was more capable of catching her stalker than Jazzy herself. 'Aw, I wish I could, Ma, but it's easier to commute from Bellsquarry to Livvy than it is from Portobello.'

Her mum tutted and Jazzy could imagine her lips tightening as she sighed in resignation. 'Well, Elliot's all for us moving into a hotel for a few nights and your da's in agreement. Maybe a wee spa break would be just the thing. Though if that bugger turns up again he'll get a walloping with my rolling pin.'

Jazzy's grin widened. Her mum was ferocious, and the rolling pin threat was one she'd used on a burglar a few years ago. It had worked too. The kid – a known criminal – had run from the house petrified and been caught an hour later. 'Aye, okay, Mum. We'll talk in a bit. We're nearly there, me and my friend Queenie.'

As she hung up, Queenie nudged her. 'Friend eh? I'm yer mate, am I? Yer pal? Yer bestie?'

Jazzy, knowing that her family was safe, let out a bark of laughter. Bestie indeed – she didn't have any other friends so by default, that might make Queenie her bestie. 'Aye the most annoying BFF ever.'

Now that she'd had time to process the events of the last hour or so, she looked at Queenie, eyes narrowed. 'How did you know I was getting off the train at Cauther Railway station, anyway?'

Queenie began fiddling with the radio controls and took a sudden interest in the vehicles behind them.

'Queenie . . .?'

'Och, well I was worried about you. I know yer all that independent way and I knew it was only a matter of time before you'd try to ditch us so . . .' She shrugged. 'You can't really blame me.'

'Queenie?'

'I put a tracker on yer car.'

Jazzy blinked. 'On my car?'

'Aye. Yer car?'

'So, how did you know I was in Edinburgh or that I'd be on *that* particular train?'

'Well, I might have dropped one in your bag too. Just to be sure.'

'Queenie, for God's . . .'

'Just as well I did though,' said Queenie pulling into Jazzy's parents' cul-de-sac. 'Or you'd still be on the A720, wouldn't you?'

There was little point in responding to Queenie's logic because, annoying though it was, she was quite right.

'Anyway . . .' Queenie beamed at Jazzy as she drew in behind two police cars outside her parents' house. 'At least we'll get a proper ID on this arse – maybe a photofit, because there's no way he wore his ninja wear when he was interviewing yer mum.'

Jazzy shook her head. 'That's just it, Queenie. He waited till my dad went out and my mum is blind, so we're no further forward in terms of ID. He thought this was just another easy way to taunt me.'

After the fifteen minutes it took for Jazzy to be sure her mum and dad hadn't suffered any residual trauma from their experience or panic at two sets of police constables, followed by Elliot turning up on their doorstep, Elliot, Queenie, Jazzy and her parents, with Crumble sitting between them, her head resting on Jazzy's mum's thigh, congregated round the enormous rustic kitchen table and drank hot drinks.

Jazzy cast glances in Elliot's direction but he ignored her, focusing his attention on her mum and dad instead. 'I'll remember his voice though, Jasmine. So, when you catch him I'll be able to confirm his identity.'

Jazzy patted her mum's arm. 'Yes, you will and that'll be crucial. Now why don't you and Dad get packed for your enforced spa break. One of the two officers are going to drop you at a hotel. I need to speak with Elliot.'

A huge grin broke across Lillie's face as she turned to Elliot and Jazzy felt the weight of Queenie's curious glance. 'It was good to see you again, Elliot. Don't make it so long till your next visit.'

'Aye, it's been grand to see you too, Lillie, and you too, Jiten.' He turned to the round-faced constable who was hovering near the door. 'You want to give Mr and Mrs Solanki a hand with their bags, Ali?'

When the Solankis had left the kitchen, the other three sat for a moment before Queenie broke the silence. 'So, your adoptive parents are . . .'

'Also my aunt and uncle.'

Queenie frowned. 'Actually, I was going to say Highlanders. Your parents are from the Highlands. I could hear that Highland burr when they spoke. You have it a wee bit too. Just on some words, but that explains it. So, how are they related to your mum?'

Jazzy had been asked that question before, so it didn't come as a huge surprise. 'Jiten is my birth mum's brother, but my mum had been estranged from the family for a long time when she became pregnant with me. My grandfather disowned both her and me. He now has nothing to do with my mum and dad either because they took me in. It took a long time for Mum and Dad to fight through the foster care system to adopt me – I was thirteen when it all became legal – and I owe them everything. They sacrificed a lot to take me in.'

Queenie, seemingly happy with the explanation, nodded, then turned to Elliot grinning. 'So, Inspector Balloch, how do you and oor JayZee know each other?'

Elliot's mouth twitched, but he just shook his head and directed his next words to Jazzy. 'I was going to tell you this earlier, Jazzy, but . . .' He rolled his hand in front of him to indicate that things had got out of hand, before continuing. 'I'm telling you now. I've been drafted in as SIO on the Clarks' murders so that DCI Dick can focus on his overall duties coordinating both the A and B teams. It's all kicked off and they need somebody on hand who can liaise effectively with forces up and down the country.'

He held Jazzy's gaze, his eyes never wavering as he delivered his next words. 'Tomorrow will be a day of revelations, so I suggest you two get back to Livingston, grab yourselves a good night's kip and be prepared for a difficult day tomorrow.'

Before Jazzy could reply, he was on his feet, nodding at each of them, and then he was gone, leaving Queenie speechless and Jazzy fuming.

Elliot's parting words filled her with foreboding. There was nowhere to hide. He'd made it clear that everything about her siblings would be revealed in the morning and the only reason she didn't just throw in her badge and walk away was that she knew innocent lives could be at risk and she couldn't countenance being responsible for that.

Day 3

Chapter 32

Despite activating her alarm the minute she entered her home, Jazzy was on edge. She'd been tempted to take Queenie up on her offer to stay over at her house, but knowing that Queenie had a baby granddaughter and a husband awaiting her at home made Jazzy force a smile and manufacture a false, but hopefully convincing yawn. 'Honestly, Queenie, I'm knackered. All that adrenalin knocked me out. I'm going to have a hot chocolate and curl up in bed with Winky. I'll be out for the count in seconds.'

Queenie had scrutinised her for long uncomfortable seconds, but Jazzy had been resolute. 'Right, JayZee. But if you need me, I can be here in ten minutes – nah, scrap that – five minutes tops. None of your usual misguided "I can look after myself" crap, "I'm all Ms Independent" rubbish, "I'm not letting any bugger, far less a serial killer frighten me" nonsense.' Each statement was punctuated by Queenie's stubby fingers making jabby speech marks in the air.

Jazzy, her joints creaking like a gallon of WD-40 wouldn't go amiss, had slid out of the Land Rover and, although she didn't look back, the thrum of Queenie's engine as she walked up her path was reassuring. Like her, Queenie had scrutinised their surroundings when they pulled up and despite knowing that the increased police presence around Bellsquarry would be a deterrent, Jazzy couldn't shake the feeling that the killer – her stalker – was watching her every move.

She'd opened the door, turned with a swift wave to Queenie and closed the door behind her, reactivating the alarm as soon as the door was shut. After a quick but thorough walk-through, checking doors and windows, she went into her bedroom, threw off her clothes, climbed into her warmest pyjamas and snuggled under her duvet. Winky purred beside her, the rhythmic sound lulling her to sleep before she knew it.

Later, the weight of the darkness – combined with a dream that pierced through her consciousness making her toss and turn as if the duvet was stealing her breath and wrapping icy tentacles round her frozen limbs – drew her from a deep sleep to a tortured semi-consciousness and sent Winky scurrying from the room. She fought, her entire body wrestling against the memories that flooded her exhausted brain, as she tried to make sense of what was real and what was imagined. Like a film unspooling, the memories continued, vivid despite being in monochrome – a desperate blockbuster finally making the big screen, a home video gone tragically wrong as the flashback from earlier played out again, except this time sleep rendered her unable to escape it.

Tears streamed down Jazzy's cheeks dampening her sweat-drenched pyjamas even more, until eventually reality woke her fully. She leaned over and flicked the light switch on. She wouldn't sleep any more tonight. The flashback in the car had been worse than her wildest imaginings. *She'd* killed her mum. She'd always thought it had been an accident, but now she wasn't sure. Did she push her on purpose? Did she mean to end her mum's life? Heart hammering, Jazzy swung her legs round till she perched on the side of the bed. With her head bowed, she tried to make sense of the dream.

Over the years she'd been told to be wary of assuming these dreams were accurate – that they offered the truth. Psychiatrists had implored her to consider these flashes of memory with some distrust. All sorts of things – her life experiences, the cases she'd worked, her guilt at being separated from her siblings – could impact on how the memories played out. But this one felt real to her. It felt authentic. She'd let her siblings down all those years ago and because *she'd* killed her mum, one of them – or so it seemed – had become a monster. Jazzy had created her own Frankenstein. Maybe it was *she* who was the monster. Maybe *she* deserved to be punished alongside them.

The thought of having to reveal this to her colleagues was overwhelming. For a moment she wondered if she should just disappear. Leave them all to it. Let someone else sort out this entire mess. But that wasn't in Jazzy's make-up. Her sense of responsibility was too strong. When she'd killed their mum – whether deliberately or accidentally – she'd set in motion a chain of events that led to their current situation. She'd broken her promise to her siblings that she would always be there for them. She'd deserted them when they needed her most and, now, innocent people were paying the price.

The more she thought about it, the more convinced she became that her brother was responsible for murdering the Clarks. They'd identified her stalker as male, Benjy had verified that in his witness statement and her mother had identified her intruder as male. She pondered that question, trying to think back fifteen years to her six-year-old siblings. Had there been signs even then that Simon might become a monster? They'd been so sweet – so beautiful, so full of love and life. She'd have done anything for them. She'd tried her best to protect them from their mother's wrath after their dad had left them. Bad enough that Jazzy's father had left her, but for the twins' dad to leave too? Well, that had unleashed a whole new level of destruction and hatred – most of it directed at Jazzy.

Now, the only thing she could do for her siblings was to find them both. Who knew whether he would target her sister too?

After all, Jazzy's memories had shown him progressing from mutilating their dead mother's body to committing vengeful acts of murder to punish her. Shivering in the dawn frost, Jazzy sighed. This was her job. No matter the cost to herself professionally or personally, she had to stop the killings and that meant sharing what she knew. Besides, if her sister was at risk, then she had to do what she could to protect her.

She leaned back and tried to clear her mind. She had to remember something that could help them. Winky, sensing that the drama had ended, returned and curled up on Jazzy's lap. Absently, she stroked his soft tabby fur, allowing his rhythmic purrs to soothe her – to keep her grounded. She'd already relived her birth mother's death in the space, so now she made herself imagine the front bedroom – the one where she and Simon and Mhairi had holed up until they were rescued.

When her chest tightened, she forced herself to keep her body relaxed and her breathing slow and measured and with the purring cat for company and the ticking of the central heating kicking in, she allowed fleeting images to flit through her mind until one took hold and settled there. Her heart stuttered, but she pushed the panic away and forced herself to loiter in that image, repeating in her head a mantra that she hadn't used in years. 'It's in the past and you survived. It's in the past and you survived.'

Mhairi is snuggled so close to Jazzy that the stale smell of her little body is a relief from the stench of the crap and piss in the bucket. Jazzy knows she should empty it, but the thought of leaving this little safe haven they've created in the front bedroom makes her heart thump. It's dark – only the street light from outside allowing her to identify the familiar shapes in the room – the broken dresser, the dripping wallpaper hanging off the wall, the bucket with its offensive stench. She wiggles out from under the blankets, shivering against the frigid air and then stops. Where is, Simon?

She crawls off the mattress, the hair on her skinny arms standing upright as she edges towards the bucket. She doesn't want to deal with it, but she is the biggest and the twins are too small. Last time they'd tried to do it together Mhairi had spilled it all over her clothes and Jasmine had been forced to strip her and give her some of her clothes instead.

She lifts the bucket. It's so heavy. She's still wondering where Simon is. She told him to stop going in there. Told him it wasn't right, but every time she dozes off, he sneaks out. She braces herself against the even worse stench in the lobby and pushes the bedroom door open, holding her breath, putting off the moment when she'll gasp in the taste and smell of her mum's death. The door opposite opens a crack and a skinny frame slides out. Anger that he's forced her to open her mouth so soon, gives her words an extra edge. 'What the hell are you doing in there, Si? I've told you not to. You're sick, going in there. Like a monster.'

In the near dark, Simon's dark eyes hold hers and without replying he brushes past her into their haven, letting the door shut behind him. Tears well in Jazzy's eyes.

With a groan, Jazzy wrenched herself out of the memory and rubbed her fingers over her eyes. Realising that, unless this was one of those manufactured images the psychiatrists had warned her about, she could now be certain it was Simon who had mutilated their mother. Despite the warmth of her bedroom, Jazzy was chilled to the bone. She wanted to deny that either of her siblings could be capable of stalking her, far less the callous murders of Bob and Shirley Clark, but the similarities between the mutilation carried out on her mother, the coincidence of the murder being carried out on her birthday – the day when her birth mother had died and Benjy's sighting of her stalker at the scene were too compelling to be ignored. The details of the mutilation were known only to the investigating officers at the time, various psychiatrists and the three children.

Of course, records could be accessed, but in light of the similarities between what was done to her mother and the presence of those taunting beans spilled all over the table, she knew she was right. Beans were the only food they had in the house whilst her mother rotted in the next room. The smell had been horrendous – human waste and decomposition. Both her siblings had witnessed her distress as she tried to force the small mouthfuls of bean down her gullet. Their small hands had patted her back when her eyes watered as she tried to keep them down. They were the only two people who knew how much she hated them . . . and why, and how much seeing them at that crime scene would affect her. The team needed to locate both of her siblings and in order to keep the innocent one safe, Jazzy was prepared to sacrifice her peace of mind and her privacy.

Heavy-limbed she got up and shuffled through to the en-suite shower room. Turning the heat up as high as she could thole, she stepped in and allowed it to excoriate her skin, knowing that this would never be punishment enough for the deaths she was responsible for.

Chapter 33

Here I am again, bright and early with yet another shrink. They never last long. The longest was just short of a year and, no surprise, that didn't end well – for him that is, not for me. As always, it ended fine for me. This one will fare no better than the last.

I ponder that time. Trying to tease out emotions I'm not sure I ever had. Regret? No, that's doesn't feel right. Sadness? Again, I come up blank. I can mimic it easily – glimmering tears, the furrowed brow, the anguished hand-wringing, the slow head-shake. It's all very convincing. I've always been clever like that. What is it they say these days? *Fake it till you make it?* I'm the master of that. I've always needed to be. Especially after the big betrayal . . . But I won't go there. Not now, not yet.

The one emotion I *can* muster, though, is anger. That visceral, destructive rage that takes me over body and soul. That's not a pretence – that's the real me. A whirlwind of fervent hate and focused fury. When it comes it's brutal – I'm brutal. I've had to work really hard to conquer it, to control it and I've learned and adapted and survived.

Over the years, they've all been happy with their misdiagnosis of post-traumatic stress disorder – my disorder. I love that word

– for that's what I crave above all else. Disorder. Punishment and revenge for past betrayals. I'm playing the long game. Have been for a while now and soon, very soon, even more disorder will descend. But for now, I want to have some fun. So, here goes.

'That's how you typically start these sessions, isn't it?' I make my smile wide – all teeth and crinkly eyes – like I've seen other people do.

Dr Clarice Cameron frowns – a gentle, puzzled one. One designed to portray confusion not criticism. 'Not sure I'm with you. Can you explain?'

I lean forward, head to one side, and imagine my smile spreading right across my face. The only way I can make it seem real is if I imagine it. Imagine me making it happen, like I'm an artist drawing the smile on my own face. I keep my voice light and fluffy like the girl in the Costa coffee near my house. The painted-on smile and the memory work together. 'Tell me about your childhood? That's how you usually kick off a first session with a new client, isn't it?'

She smiles, her lips glossy and slick, her teeth straight and shiny. Perhaps she thinks she's made a connection with me. Perhaps it's one of those mimicking strategies I read about – show empathy by 'aping' the client's body language.

'Is that what you want to talk about? Your childhood?'

Of course, she's read my file – or the parts of it I wanted her to read. Probably thinks she knows all there is to know about me. *Post-traumatic stress disorder brought on by a traumatic childhood experience.* Poor little me. Poor pitiful me. At least I've put the time spent in these sessions to good use. Used my experiences to hone my own skills and now, *I'm* the one doing the head-shrinking. That amuses me, appeals to my macabre sense of humour. Shrinking the shrink's head is a game to me.

I cross my legs. My grin deepens as she, again, copies my posture, her smile widening too. The thing I'm one hundred per cent sure of is that her smile would fade in an instant and she'd take to her spindly high heels if she could see into my soul. I'm enjoying this game. Enjoying playing with her, teasing her. I prop my elbow on my knee and place my chin on my fist. The same fist I imagine clenched tight and driving into her smug face. The image of blood spurting from her mouth, her teeth tinkling like pearls from a broken necklace onto the carpet is so powerful I can almost taste the blood as I imagine her nose bursting open, spraying me in blood. My tongue darts out in a sideways sweep over my lips. Again, the memory of the metallic taste takes over. Her tongue, a cotton-wool-furred snake, escapes her lips. Her gaze drifts up and meets mine. Her tongue stills and retracts; a flash of confusion darts over her face. *Maybe she's seen something behind my façade?*

Bored with the game, I shrug and stand up. I walk to the bookcase and let my fingers trail over the ornaments before picking up the snow globe as if I didn't already know it was there. It's got pride of place, right in the centre of the shelf. A special memento. A treasured gift, but I already know all about it. 'I like this. Was it a gift?'

I turn, cradling the ornament in one hand and quirk an eyebrow at her. 'Who gave you it?'

Again, with the frown, but her smile stays in place. 'What do you like about it? Does it remind you of something? Maybe someone – a special person? Or a significant time?'

I toss it from hand to hand, relishing how her shoulders tense as her eyes follow the movement of the fragile globe. I fake-drop it and she jumps. Her pupils dilate and a sweet little breath hitches in her throat, to be replaced by a slight tightening of her lips when I catch it with a laugh. My gaze never leaves her face. Not for a second. 'Oops. Butter fingers.'

Her eyes focus on the globe as I continue to bat it from palm to palm. A pleasurable flicker tickles my spine and across my shoulders. This is fun. 'What did you ask me?'

She hesitates, then. 'I asked if the snow globe reminded you of something, or someone.'

I purse my lips and pretend to let the thought take hold. Then, I shake my head, moulding the hesitant frown to my forehead, knowing she'll catch it – she comes highly recommended after all. 'Nooo. No, not really.'

She nods, her head tilting to one side, inviting more. So, I oblige. 'But *you* do. You remind me of someone . . .'

A frown mars her brow momentarily, surprised at the direction the conversation has taken, before disappearing behind her professional mask. Yet she can't hide her pallor or the nervous way her fingers flutter to the single pearl-shaped diamond, dangling from her neck on a gold chain. When she speaks, her breath catches in her throat, her words coming out all breathy and uncertain. 'Who? Who do I remind you of?'

I place the snow globe on the very edge of the shelf, making sure to balance it just so. It wouldn't do for it to fall now, would it? I turn around, lean both fisted hands on her desk and tower over her. 'My mum . . . That's who.'

Chapter 34

Despite every bone and nerve ending in her body telling her to turn and run and never look back, Jazzy, with Queenie by her side, lifted her chin, straightened her back, threw back her shoulders and inhaled deeply outside the open-plan office that was generally the domain of the detective inspectors. The general briefing consolidating progress around the Clarks' murder investigation had finished by the time Jazzy arrived. In an abrupt text early that morning, Elliot had told her to skip it and she'd been happy to. This meeting was dedicated to unravelling her stalker's history after being armed with the full facts of Jazzy's personal history. It had been considered prudent to run two parallel investigations: one dedicated to pursuing leads around the Clark murders; the other to establish timelines, links and patterns between the Clarks and possible previous crimes as well as identifying the current whereabouts of Jazzy's siblings.

The latter was being conducted on a need-to-know basis with DI Elliot Balloch in charge. For now, Jazzy was allowed to contribute. She wasn't stupid enough to assume that her role in the investigation into her brother would last beyond the end of the day. They'd pump her for information and then leave her out in the cold while they pursued her brother and tried to protect her sister. *This is so fucked up.*

Although she had the beginnings of a throbbing headache mithering at her temple, there was a degree of relief at the prospect of finally being able to offload everything she'd kept so tightly coiled inside her for years. Well almost everything. Over strong coffee, she'd decided that although she owed a lot to the investigation and to her siblings, she didn't owe them either her soul *or* her sanity.

With her Mini still parked in the West Calder train station, Queenie had picked her up and spent the short journey to Livingston insisting that the way to bolster Jazzy's confidence was to use a theme tune to buoy them up. In Queenie's words, they'd 'kick ass', as they braved the lion's den. However, with her mind veering towards 'Bat Out of Hell' – particularly, as Queenie would no doubt sing, the *'gone, vamoosed hopped it'* refrain, Jazzy had been dubious about it. Then Queenie, bouncing in the driver's seat, slapped her hand on the steering wheel. 'I got it, JayZee. "Killer Queen" – we're the Jazz Queens, aren't we? So, for a limited time only – because you can't always be the boss queen, you understand – *you* can be the *Killer Queen.*'

Right up until she parked at an angle, taking up two parking spaces in the station car park, Queenie, having created the new lyrics, loudly sang her version. By the time they entered the station, *JayZee Queen. Top-notch, cool and mean. Hot stuff with a killer gleam. This girl's gonna whoop your arse,* echoed like a subliminal and persistent earworm in Jazzy's head and she found she was striding in time to the beat. Maybe Queenie's idea wasn't as daft as it sounded.

She thrust the door open, and allowed the rhythm to propel her inside. With her eyes straight ahead, she blanked the chief super, the dickless wonder and Elliot Balloch, and strode to the front. Using her annoyance that her future lay in the hands of the three men sitting behind a table to bolster her resolution, she kept her chin up and never faltered in her step. Of the three, she knew that DCI Dick would be advocating to either sack her completely, or at the very least to sideline her from the investigation. Her only hope of remaining an integral part of this inquiry relied on three things – her ability to demonstrate how her insights would be integral to progressing the investigation, the impartiality of the chief super, and the new DI's support, which – particularly after her behaviour in Edinburgh the previous evening – was an unknown entity. Her best hope was that with the killer – her brother – targeting her parents, he would want her on board.

'Ah, DC Solanki. We wondered where you were. We were about to begin.' Waqas Afzal regarded her with a steady gaze, only the slight frown gathering at the bridge of his nose indicating any unease on his part.

Jazzy nodded, but worried her voice would break if she spoke, she satisfied herself with a taut smile, as she neared the front of the room.

Elliot lowered his voice so only she could hear. 'Okay, Jazz?'

As she tried to regulate her breathing without anyone else noticing, she nodded. A sideways glance at the dickless wonder clued her in on the extent of his suppressed anger – although whether with her or with the fact that he'd been ousted as SIO and replaced by an incomer from Edinburgh was anyone's guess. Even his moustache seemed to quiver as he glared at her. His entire being so tense that Jazzy wondered if he was in danger of shattering into a zillion pieces. 'Better late than never I suppose.'

Jazzy allowed his words to roll over her. In the overall scheme of things, he was an irritant and now he had lost his SIO role, he had little power over her. Or so she hoped. Apart from the three bosses, herself and Queenie, there were only DCs Heggie and McBurnie in the room. Cheeks burning, Jazzy hesitated, unsure whether to join the men at the front – after all, she'd been ordered to update the investigation on their new working hypothesis – or sidle into a chair opposite them.

Maggots wriggled in her gut again as the prospect of their

reactions to her upcoming revelations taunted her. How could they trust her after this? She hadn't shared all the information with them and now secrets from her murky past – guilty secrets, secrets that filled her with shame and anxiety – could wreck the tenuous relationship she had just begun to build with her colleagues.

As if sensing her discomfort, Afzal gestured to the empty chair next to the one Queenie had just occupied. 'Take a seat, Jazzy. Elliot's about to get started.'

Rather than address her boss, Jazzy hesitated. She and Queenie had discussed how Jazzy should handle this meeting on the way over. Whilst the temptation to allow Elliot to explain everything to her colleagues was strong, both Jazzy and Queenie had agreed that, if she was to garner any respect from her colleagues then she was duty-bound, no matter how painful, to make her own explanations. There was no way she could control other people's responses, but hearing the entire story from Jazzy herself made it more personal. As Queenie said, she had been able to witness Jazzy's vulnerabilities and to see the truth in her words. Hopefully, Queenie's kindness would be replicated by the others in the room.

Instead of sitting next to Queenie as instructed, Jazzy stepped forward and, turning around to face her colleagues, she rested her bottom on the edge of the desk – mainly because if she didn't, she feared she'd fall over. She forced her lips into a tentative smile, which she directed at the other people in the room and was pleased to see them return her smile, albeit hesitantly. Before she spoke, she reminded herself that these officers – Geordie and Fenton – were her colleagues, perhaps even her friends and were nothing if not professional. She hoped that after her revelations, she'd be able to maintain the working relationship she had recently established with these people. The flutter in her chest told her how important that was to her, but now wasn't the time to dwell on 'what might happen'. Without looking at the three senior officers behind her she said, 'It's *my* story, boss, I've got it from here.'

The sound of a chair scraping made her glance back. Elliot half standing – a frown gathering above the thunderclouds that were his eyes – glared at her, his mouth open, ready to intervene. But the chief super put his hand on his arm and shook his head. 'It's her show, Elliot. Let her explain.'

The heat of Elliot's gaze scorched the back of Jazzy's neck and she wished she hadn't gathered her hair in a topknot as heat seeped from her nape onto her cheeks. Sweat gathered under her arms and her mouth was unbearably dry. Queenie with an almost maniacal grin, which Jazzy supposed was meant to be encouraging, nodded at her and handed her a bottle of chilled water. Then, allowing her grin to slip from her lips, Queenie glared first at Elliot, then at DCI Dick and finally at Waqas – her warning clear. *Butt out!*

In different circumstances, Queenie's loyalty might have cheered Jazzy, but here and now it filled her chest with so much gratitude that she feared she'd unravel. So, taking a moment to allow the refrain *JayZee Queen. Top-notch, cool and mean. Hot stuff with a killer gleam. This girl's gonna whoop your arse*, to bolster her, she straightened her shoulders and stared over the heads of her audience.

Chapter 35

Aiming her words at a spot to the right of the door, Jazzy began the revelation that would lay her soul bare to her colleagues. 'You're all aware that various pieces of evidence – circumstantial and actual – including the taunting visit to my parents' home yesterday, have led us to the conclusion that the person who has been delivering cards to me at intervals over the past few years, is also the main suspect in the killings of Bob and Shirley Clark. Ergo, it seems there is a tangible link between these instances and me.

'As experienced officers, we know that the level of precision, planning and mutilation present in the Clark murders would be practically unheard of in a first offence. Clearly, the severing of their heads and the post-mortem mutilation appears to be a dramatic escalation from sending anonymous communications to me. In turn, logic has led us to believe that somewhere, over the past few years, this killer has been active – honing his craft, if you will, and that we, in Police Scotland have failed to identify this activity.'

The only sound in the room was the creaking of chairs as their occupants moved. Four pairs of eyes focused on Jazzy's face from the front, and yet, it was the three pairs boring into her from behind that unsettled her the most. She stopped and took another swig of water, wondering how water could be so dry, and risked a glance at Haggis and Geordie. Both nodded at her and Haggis even offered a small smile, whilst Geordie gave an almost imperceptible wink. Jazzy could have hugged them, yet she was aware that the hardest part was still to come. She inhaled and plunged on.

'Certain aspects of the Clark murders have made it expedient for me to share something I had hoped would remain firmly in my past.'

A burst of laughter from outside the office mocked her. Although not the most sociable of people, Jazzy would have given anything to be out there sharing a laugh at the coffee machine rather than in this room baring her soul, but she blocked out the sounds and focused on the room. 'In order to progress the investigation, it is important that you are privy to any and all information that may pertain to it and so, to that effect, I hope you will bear with me as I share something that is likely to have bearing on it and that may offer us a more detailed scope of inquiry.'

Jazzy closed her eyes and ordered her thoughts, her fingers clasped tightly before her. A burning sensation started in her gut and radiated outwards and upwards, making every part of her skin feel on fire. Sweat seeped through her T-shirt and broke out across her brow, but there was no way she could stop now. She'd come too far and the only option was to plough on. So, head down, letting the chips fall where they may, that's what she did. Her gaze fixed straight ahead, her mind on another plane as if looking down at her colleagues waiting with bated breath to hear Jazzy Solanki's tragic story, she began.

'On my tenth birthday myself and my two younger half-siblings – whose dad jumped ship when they were only babies – became orphans after my mother died in our home. It was my birthday – the 14th of December – which as you all know is the same date

231

that the Clarks were slaughtered. We were rescued a few days later. According to post-mortem reports she died as the result of a fall, which resulted in her banging her head. The number of empty alcohol bottles found in the house indicated that her fall was alcohol-related. This was corroborated by numerous accounts by neighbours and teachers alike and ultimately by the post-mortem. Myself and my siblings entered the social care system and were separated. I was eventually adopted by my mother's brother, Jiten, and his wife, Leila, Lillie for short, and lost touch with the twins who were also, at the recommendation of various psychiatrists, separated from each other. Lillie and Jiten had wanted to adopt them, but again this was vetoed by social services. At present we are awaiting information regarding their adopted names and their current whereabouts, especially in light of my mum being targeted.'

'Okaaay?' Haggis – his face scrunched up in a puzzled frown – elongated the word before continuing. 'But how does this relate to the Clarks?'

Jazzy looked out the window, only vaguely aware of the buffeting snow outside. 'Well, here's the thing. When we were discovered huddled up on a mattress on the floor in a cold damp room, we were nearly out of food. The only thing we had left were tins of beans, which I was sharing between my siblings and myself. The only reason I know that is because I've been told. You see, since then I've suffered from dissociative amnesia, which basically means that most of what happened from before my mother's death and until we were found is distorted or out of order or sometimes even just plain inaccurate.'

Jazzy paused trying to work out how best to describe it. She found it hard to get her head round her condition, so she had little hope of her audience understanding the ramifications of her memory loss. However, she had to try. She had to make them understand why she didn't have all the answers they wanted. 'It's like a series of flashbacks that aren't always chronologically

232

correct. The events of my birth mother's death and the subsequent period before we were rescued – six days according to the post-mortem – hasn't returned to me, although I do have occasional flashbacks that may relate to that time.'

Now that she was nearing the part that was truly horrific, the maggots in her gut begin their dastardly dance again. She closed her eyes, allowing the song to calm her. *JayZee Queen. Top-notch, cool and mean. Hot stuff with a killer gleam. This girl's gonna whoop your arse.*

She wished she could slay the squirming insects in her belly before she vomited all over the floor. She raised her bottle to her lips, but couldn't make herself drink any. Her mouth was filled with cotton wool, yet she had to go on. She'd come this far and she could do it. 'This is important because, you see, whilst they discovered that my birth mum's death occurred in the living room, when she was found her body was in her bedroom. Forensic reports indicate that we – myself and my half-siblings – dragged her through to her bedroom and hefted her onto her bed. It seems we closed the door and lived largely in the second bedroom using a bucket for waste, until the smell alerted the neighbours to something being amiss. At that point they contacted the police. However, when the young police constable . . .' Jazzy risked a taut smile and turned to Elliot '. . . the, then PC, Elliot Balloch, found the three children and their dead mother, he discovered something darkly disturbing.'

With the mention of Elliot's name everyone's attention diverted to the brooding figure hunched at the desk behind Jazzy. Elliot lumbered to his feet, scowling at the room in general and moved to stand beside Jazzy. 'My mum's body had been mutilated – pegs had been pinned on her nose and tongue, gashes made to her skin, cutlery stuck into her eyes and things stuck up her nose. The twins clammed up and refused to speak. Or perhaps they couldn't articulate what had happened. They were only six-year-olds after all. As for me? Well, I was so traumatised that I couldn't remember what had happened and I still can't – not fully. My gut says I didn't mutilate my mum's dead body, but deep down I couldn't, until now that is, believe that either of the twins did either. They were babies and I was the one who looked out for them.'

Gasps filled the room and any courage Jazzy had left drained from her body as the faces that had seemed so sympathetic before now seemed filled with doubt and accusation. *Who could blame them?* Jazzy was filled with a plethora of conflicting emotions and no amount of therapy or reassurances that she had *not* been the one to mutilate her dead mother convinced her. Not entirely. If she couldn't state categorically that she had had no part in her mum's mutilation and death, then how could she expect her colleagues to believe her?

'Over the years various psychiatrists have worked with me and have attested that they believe it is unlikely that I participated in the mutilation. Which means it was one of the twins and we all know that childhood cruelty is considered a serial killer trait. However, some psychiatrists were of the opinion that rather than an indication of a violent nature, the "mutilation" was more a way to say goodbye – a sort of warped funeral rite, if you like. That appears to be why the authorities deemed it beneficial for the twins to be separated. Because my mum's death was ruled accidental and because of the tender age of my siblings, they were given new identities and entered the care system anonymously. Their records have remained sealed and we are currently trying to unravel the red tape surrounding that in order to establish their whereabouts over the last fifteen years.'

Jazzy took a sip of water. 'Of course, with the video footage of my stalker, Benjy Hendry's witness statement, my mum's evidence, it's clear that my brother is responsible for both stalking me *and* for the Clarks' murders. It's imperative to locate him. It is also imperative to locate his twin sister because she may be at risk.'

Now it was time for the hard part. 'Last night, I forced myself to think back to the period when Simon, Mhairi and myself lived in that front bedroom. It won't be admissible as conclusive proof, but I dislodged a memory of my brother leaving the back bedroom, his hands covered in blood, whilst I was emptying the waste bucket. Of course, I repeat the caveat that this memory could be distorted or even false. It could be a product of suggestion; there's no way of knowing for sure. I can't stress enough that we need to find my siblings quickly. My brother, I am convinced, is my stalker and a murderer, and my sister is a potential victim.'

As stunned silence replaced the earlier flutter of disbelief, tension entered the room like a thundercloud intent on rupturing and destroying everything in its path – all the respect Jazzy had gained as a dedicated police officer, her focus, her job, seemed to disintegrate in its path. It was DCI Dick who finally broke the silence, his venomous words like shrapnel to Jazzy's sensitive skin. 'Can you *believe* that she ever got through the police psychological test? With *that* sort of history? She's one of the ones that should have been weeded out from the start. Police Scotland doesn't need the likes of her.'

Face smarting, Jazzy lowered her head, blinking away the tears that nipped at the backs of her eyes. Behind her, a chair scraped across the floor, the chief super's voice tore into the room, his tone curt, each word slicing through Dick's arguments. 'And yet she did. DC Solanki has a stellar record – well almost. Her psych results were better than most officers – including your own, Tony, but more than that, DC Solanki has seen fit to be honest about her past although there was no need for her to do so, as her juvenile records were sealed. Not only that, she submits voluntarily to regular psychological assessments. Also, contrary to *your* opinion, DC Solanki is exactly the sort of dedicated, incisive officer Police Scotland needs in its ranks. I'm sure you have a lot to catch up on with the drug and human trafficking investigation your other CID teams are involved in, so I'll not take up any more of your time. DI Balloch is more than able to move this investigation forward. You're dismissed.'

Electric tension thrummed through Jazzy's body, making her fear that she would combust. Had the chief super just stood up for her in public? Despite the worry of the ramifications for her when *that* snippet of gossip got out, a not altogether unpleasant sensation settled on her chest – like the one she felt when she stroked Winky and heard his guttural purring vibrating up her leg. The dickless wonder's chair clattered backwards, smashing into the wall before falling over. Still, Jazzy averted her gaze. She had no desire to open herself to his animosity. His feet thudded towards the door, its slam telling her he was gone, but, despite Elliot's reassuring presence beside her, Jazzy was done.

She exhaled and glanced at Elliot, a slight shake of her head telling him she'd had enough. He edged closer and put his arm round her shoulder, squeezing tightly for a moment, but she pulled away, glaring at him as if he'd slapped her. *What the hell is he thinking?* She didn't need his hugs. She didn't need any more speculation about her personal or professional life. In this room, at this moment, he was her boss. Not her friend, not her rescuer, not her knight in shining armour. Just her boss.

Half stumbling, Jazzy landed in the seat beside Queenie. Under her breath, Queenie sang, '*JayZee Queen. Top-notch, cool and mean. Hot stuff with a killer gleam. This girl's gonna whoop your arse.*' Before adding, 'You did good kid. You did damn well good. You smashed it, bopped it out the park . . .' Then as if realising her trio of examples were inappropriate, her voice faded and she rested her hand on Jazzy's thigh, squeezed once and then removed it. The fact that Queenie, usually so flamboyant in her gestures and words, restrained herself from going OTT and hugging Jazzy tight to her large chest, made Jazzy's eyes well up even more.

Elliot cleared his throat. 'Right, where were we? Ah, yes, as Jazzy said, the day she and her siblings were rescued was my very first day on the job and I had no idea what would happen when I carried those three wee mites from that disgusting house. Of course, being an inexperienced beat bobby at the time, I was excluded from the resultant investigation, but something about the haunted look in those kids' eyes made me check in every so often.'

He scrunched up his nose and a frown flitted across his brow before he shrugged and smiled. Jazzy, observing him despite her lowered gaze, grimaced. His blue eyes held the darkness of a cloudy day and, despite his smile, Jazzy knew he was right back in that horrific house, with the stench and the flies and the mutilated body of her mother. It had taken Jazzy a long time to accept that her birth mother's death had afforded her a second chance at life. A life devoid of beatings and hatred and venom. A life also devoid of the presence of the twins. In moments of clarity, she accepted that all their lives should be improved by the death of their mother. If she'd lived, any one of them may have died by her violence and, if they'd survived growing up with a violent alcoholic mother, what would the future have held for them?

Deep down Jazzy wondered if she'd helped her mother on her way to hell. In her rare moments of honesty, she admitted that if she *had* indeed been instrumental in her mum's fall, then she held no regrets for it.

Elliot had never doubted her. He'd been the rock to which she had clung even after she'd been first fostered and then adopted by her aunt and uncle. His presence in her life provided much-needed ballast in the turbulent waters in which she often floundered. The fact that the twins – cute and unfettered by any signs of guilt – were adopted separately upset Jazzy. They'd always been so close.

In fact, she'd spent her entire life being saddened by the aftermath of the entire affair, but now, scrutinising Elliot as he prepared to reveal how he'd found them fifteen years ago, she realised that *his* life had been tarnished by the memory too. The way he drew his brows together as if concealing his emotions. The tightness at his lips and the tell-tale way he drummed his three fingers against his thigh as if he sought comfort in the familiarity of pretend – playing his euphonium told her that.

237

Her heart fluttered and she regretted not allowing him his moment of contact with her earlier. She realised now it had been as much for himself as to support her. She raised her head, met his eyes and smiled. When he returned her smile, the squirming in her gut finally stopped and it was like the sun had come out, the blue in his eyes reminiscent now of a summer's day in Porty as he started to speak, explaining how he'd rescued three children from the house after finding the mutilated body of their mother in the back room.

'You can read the files from that investigation. Our civilian analyst Janine Gorman here has made them available on the server, so I don't want to dwell on that too much here. Afterwards, all three kids, as a result of the post-mortem mutilation, were subjected to extensive psychiatric assessment – which was when Jazzy got her associative amnesia diagnosis. However, even after extensive psychiatric input, it couldn't be proven which of the children had partaken in the post-mortem mutilation. All three children's child protection files were sealed after they were taken into care.'

He inclined his head towards Jazzy who took up the tale. 'My aunt and uncle, whom I consider my mum and dad, were keen for me to recognise my Indian roots. They appreciated how hard it would be for an Indian kid growing up in a relatively small Scottish town, with hardly any other people of colour there. Jasmine was my birth name. As for the twins – my half-siblings – they were born Simon and Mhairi Smith. I have no idea what became of them. I don't know if they were adopted, if they had any lasting psychiatric damage from their childhood trauma, if they ever met up or stayed in care for the rest of their childhoods. I'd no idea and, until now, it didn't seem important.'

Jazzy shook her head. 'I assumed that, like me, they had grown into adulthood relatively happy and I hoped that because of their youth they suffered fewer lasting traumas than I did. I suppose I wanted to put distance between myself and those experiences and

I also didn't want to drag them up again for Simon and Mhairi if they were well adapted. Those were hellish times that no one should have to relive.'

Again, the only sound in the room was shuffling feet, creaky chairs and the occasional voice echoing from beyond the closed door. But Jazzy knew there would be questions. How could there not be? It was Geordie who asked the first one. 'What about your father, Jazzy? Or the twins' father? Weren't they around? Or other family?'

Jazzy's head jerked up and she blinked first at Elliot and then at Waqas Afzal. The maggots were back, silently squirming. 'I have vague memories of my birth dad as a child. I think he was driven out of the family home by my mother's alcoholism.' Jazzy looked at her fingers as they plucked at invisible threads on her jeans. 'I have memories of him being kind to me. I think he loved me, but to be honest, I have no idea which memories are true and which are distorted. In hindsight, I suspect that my birth mum had post-partum depression too – although that can't be proved. My memories are sketchy, but suffice to say, I bore the brunt of her aggression even after she hooked up with the twins' dad – not that he hung about for long either. They both left us with a woman who was unfit to be a mother and that is something they have to come to terms with. As for other family – my mother managed to alienate her father – my granddad – after her mum died, when she became pregnant with me out of wedlock. The fact that my birth father was Muslim, whilst my mum was Hindu, appeared to create an even deeper wedge between them and she was disowned. As a result, we were isolated as a family and she was vulnerable. She drank too much – way too much.'

For long seconds the silence pulsated in the room. Jazzy bowed her head, not wanting to catch anyone's eye. Every muscle in her body protested against the rigid way she held herself and she thought that if she didn't relax them soon, she'd never be able to unclench them again.

When DCS Afzal stood up, flashed his too bright smile round the room and flicked imaginary dust from the sleeve of his jacket, Jazzy heaved a sigh of relief. At least now the attention was diverted away from her. She wondered if he'd done it on purpose, for her benefit – that would be typical of the Waqas Afzal she knew – the kind man. The one who through her own insecurities and inner rage, she'd exposed to public scrutiny. He'd laughed it off, saying he was old enough and experienced enough to weather a minor turbulence. His concern had been more for her benefit than his own and though he'd been reluctant to publicly punish her, his advisers had left him no option. Demote Jazzy or sack her. Public insubordination at that level could not be seen to be condoned, no matter what the real story was and, of course, the real story would never see the light of day.

Doctored images on the front page of a tabloid were nothing new and Jazzy's union rep had advised her to keep her head down and let the story run its course. So, for the sake of her relationship with the DCS and her career, that's what she'd done. Although he'd known how hard it was for her to bite the bullet and allow the falsehoods to stand, Afzal had been insistent she remain silent on the matter. For her sake, not his.

Sensing that this small cohort of colleagues had got over the story and were totally focused on the investigation, Jazzy allowed herself a rare moment to study Afzal. He was tall and handsome. The wings of grey hair above his ears lent him a learned look that suited him. He'd fought hard for his current position in Police Scotland, being only one of a handful of officers of colour in the force, and he was determined to leave a legacy that involved recruiting a more diverse cohort, moving forward. His slight Highland burr was melodic as he spoke. 'Right, I think you've all learned a lot today and you're all clear that your part in this investigation is twofold. One, to identify DC Solanki's siblings and locate them and two, to investigate links between the Clarks' murders and any similar crimes – either solved or unsolved. We know damn well that this fucker didn't start his killing career with the Clarks and he'll be a hell of a lot easier to locate if we trace his previous criminal activity. I'll leave you to it.'

He turned to Elliot. 'Can I have a word, please?'

Elliot hesitated and glanced at Jazzy, his blue eyes raking over her face making her feel completely exposed. She glared back at him, pursing her lips, and then looked away, annoyance that he'd risked drawing attention to her clouding her eyes. As if whatever he saw in her face had reassured him, Elliot shrugged, and before leaving the room with Afzal, he looked at Queenie. 'In my absence, you're in charge, Queenie. I want you to brainstorm any actions we can implement. Make sure we've covered all bases. When I get back, we'll work on the case files the civilian analyst has compiled.' He paused, then added, 'DC Solanki is here purely in a consultative role. Is that clear?'

He glared first at Jazzy and then at each of the other officers in turn before striding after the chief super.

Chapter 36

With Elliot absent from the room, the atmosphere lightened and everyone began flicking open folders as Queenie took control. 'To summarise, our working theory, based on existing evidence, is that Jazzy's stalker and the killer are one and the same. The similarities between the Clarks' crime scene and the way Jazzy's birth mother's body was mutilated post-mortem, alongside other circumstantial evidence like the significance of the date of the Clarks' murders, the leaked crime scene images, and the way the killer is engaging with Jazzy all indicate that the perpetrator is most likely her brother and that the Clarks' murders aren't his first rodeo, yeah?'

Queenie's words might have been blasé, but the expression on her face was not. Her lips were turned down and the lines etched around her mouth and across her forehead testified to the strain she was under. When Jazzy looked at her other colleagues, she realised that both Fenton and Geordie bore the weight of both her revelations and the enormity of the task ahead of them in their tensed shoulders and gritted teeth.

All Jazzy could do was agree with Queenie and attempt to maintain her professional persona. With a taut smile, she nodded. 'Which is why Janine Gorman, the civilian analyst, has compiled this list of possible previous murders. That's one of our jobs for the day. The other is locating my siblings as soon as we get the warrants to unseal their records.'

Haggis drummed his fingers on the plastic casing of his phone and shook his head forcefully. 'That's not enough. We should also focus on identifying Jazzy's brother. He *must* be in the vicinity. Someone must have seen him out of his ninja disguise, so surely it can't be that hard.' He turned to Jazzy. 'Wouldn't you recognise him, Jazz?'

The same thought had been running through Jazzy's mind. She ought to recognise her own brother – but the truth was, she wasn't sure she would. The idea that she might have walked past him in a supermarket or shared a passing smile with him sent a chill coursing through her veins. Jazzy omitted to tell them that for the first years after their enforced separation, desperate to find them, she'd scoured crowds scrutinising any children who looked about the same age as her siblings. Guilt had hung heavy with her and she'd wanted to reassure herself that they were fine. That they were living better lives away from her than they had when they'd been together. That they were thriving and moving on. She hadn't cared if they'd forgotten all about her, as long as they were well and being looked after. Now, the irony of that struck her. Even when she'd first joined Police Scotland she'd dedicated a few months of her time trying to locate them again, but even her finely honed detective skills hadn't borne fruit.

'I don't know, Fenton. For years now, I've given up looking for him or Mhairi either, for that matter. Who knows how much he could have changed in fifteen years? I mean, he was only six when I last saw him and that crappy recording is misleading. It gives us no idea of his height or even his physique. Shit, Fenton, he could be *you*, for all I know.'

Fenton blinked at her, his face paling as he swallowed hard. 'It's not me. I mean I'm not . . .'

'For the love of Jesus, Haggis. Nobody thinks it's you. Jazz was just using you as an example, that's all. No need to get yer panties in a fankle. A Jazz Queen wi' fankled breeks is unacceptable.'

Glad of Queenie's humour, Jazzy nudged him and grinned. 'She's right, Fenton. I think I can cross you off my list of possible siblings.'

He gave a tight smile. 'Aye, I see what you did then, Jazz. But . . .'

He scrunched up his face in a way that Jazzy was becoming familiar with and exhaled. Contrary to popular opinion among the other detectives, his tortured expressions weren't indicative of a lack of intelligence, but more a reflective expression indicating he was giving something great thought. As she'd come to know the younger officer, Jazzy had come to appreciate his solidity – the way he made measured, considered deductions. Okay, he wasn't a quick thinker like some of the hotshots on the A and B teams, who no sooner thought of an idea than they were out the door chasing their tails and more often than not, landing on their arses. In contrast, Haggis was a plodder who took his time and pondered things from all angles. He was methodical and that often paid dividends and sometimes, in the long run, saved time and produced results. She'd take three of Haggis on her team any day rather than the supercilious arrogant gits that the dickless wonder seemed so fond of.

Jazzy gave him time, watching the way his thoughts played across his face in a series of frowns, lip twitches, gurning motions and rapid blinks, before finally emerging in a conflagration of flushed cheeks and a self-deprecating grin. 'Stands to reason that he'd want to hang about around the crime scene though, doesn't it? More than that, he'd want to be near *you*, Jazzy. This is all directed at *you*. Everything he's doing right now is with *you* in mind. *You're* his raison d'être. All of this is about *you* and for *you*.'

He fluttered the fingers of both hands around the room like he was about to burst into some weird rendition of 'Twinkle Twinkle'. His grin was wide and oozed the triumphant pleasure of someone who'd reached an acceptable conclusion. Although his words were like a knife through her gut, Haggis hadn't said anything she wasn't already aware of, so Jazzy swallowed down her emotions along with the ever-present bile that lurked in her throat. Queenie, though, wasn't so magnanimous. 'Eh, now you just wait a minute there, Haggis boy. None of this is JayZee's fault.'

Her chest thrust out like a puffed-up robin redbreast, her offensively bright and misshapen red cardigan – which Jazzy suspected she'd knitted herself – adding weight to the comparison. 'You can't say that. She . . .' Queenie jerked her thumb towards Jazzy, but glared at Haggis with eyes that threatened to strip the skin from his bones more painfully than an acid bath '. . . is *not* responsible for any of this. Got it? *Not. Responsible. For. Any. Of. This.*'

Haggis flinched, his grin slipping from his face, his brow furrowing as rapid blinks betrayed his struggle to work out where he'd gone wrong.

Jazzy wanted to scream at them. All the emphases on *she* and *her* and *you* was doing her head in. They were talking about her like she wasn't there. As if she were some irrelevant onlooker or, worse still, a victim. Someone they could dissect at their leisure with no consideration. A familiar heat started in her gut and radiated outwards, spreading through her body. It was so strong and so hot and so powerful she thought she might explode with it. How *dare* they sideline her and treat her like she was part of the problem but not necessarily a part of the solution. None of this was her fault, but then again none of it was *their* fault either. These were unusual circumstances for everybody and, if they were to work together effectively on this – and she knew she was lucky she hadn't been bounced from the team already – then she needed to smooth things over.

Puzzlement spread across Haggis's face. His lips pulled downwards and his eyebrows huddled together. When he shook his head furiously in denial it looked like he was attempting to rub noses with Queenie. The heat ball that had reached Jazzy's chest by then dissipated as she observed the ridiculousness of her colleagues' standoff. A gurgle of laughter escaped her lips as she watched the pair.

Geordie, clearly also seeing the ridiculousness of it all, glanced in her direction and winked, before stating in his usual slow drawl: 'Get a room, you two. The rest of us have got a killer to find and your shenanigans are distracting.'

Queenie turned to Geordie. 'Eh? What you on about? We've got a bloody room.' She spread her arms out to encapsulate their surroundings. 'This one no good enough for you? What do you want? An en suite with a gold-plated throne? Piped music playing through carefully hidden speakers? A lavender-scented aromatherapy candle frae Jo Malone? We're investigating a serial killer, for God's sake not having a day out at a spa.'

Jazzy glanced at Haggis whose frown had deepened. His head swayed between Queenie and Geordie trying to keep up with whatever nonsense was going on. Taking pity on the lad, she placed a hand on his shoulder. 'Just ignore those two and tell me what you're thinking.'

Still frowning, Haggis swallowed and edged away from Queenie. 'I didn't mean that *you* were responsible, Jazzy. Course I didn't. I mean you've not killed any . . .'

'I know that. Just bloody spit out what you're thinking before Queenie goes off on one again.'

'All, I was trying to say was that I think it'd be worthwhile going over the video footage Wullie took from the crime scene and cross-referencing it with any camera in the vicinity of both you and your parents' houses. You said yourself that those sickos sometimes revisited the scene of their crimes. Sometimes they try to insert themselves in the investigation. It won't take a team of civilians long to go through the footage and compile a list of men in the correct age bracket in more than one vicinity. We can also look at witness statements from the door-to-doors and see if any of the neighbours have seen someone matching the stalker's description. Hell, maybe one of them is your broth . . .'

He stopped, tried to catch the word back and failed. 'Eh, I mean the suspect.'

Geordie slapped his colleague on the back. 'Good idea, Haggis. I reckon you should add anyone from the crime scene log who fits the parameters. Best to be thorough.'

For a moment the four of them looked at one another in silence. Geordie had verbalised what they'd all been thinking. What if Jazzy's brother *was* one of them? A police officer or a CSI or a paramedic? It was hard to digest the possibility but impossible to ignore.

Jazzy nodded. 'Geordie is right. You okay doing this, Fenton?'

Heggie puffed out his chest and moved over to a bank of computers lining the back wall. 'On it. You can count on me.'

'One more thing, Fenton. Can you check to see if the other team has managed to locate Ginny Bell? I'm becoming concerned about her. I thought she'd have checked in by now, but she hasn't and she is on the killer's radar isn't she?'

'I checked earlier, Jazz. No recent sightings. We traced her car to Livvy North station car park and then nothing. Her phone is offline – she's probably using a burner. She's not at her home address and neighbours haven't seen her. I'll keep on it.'

A sinking feeling settled in Jazzy's gut. Ginny Bell had betrayed her trust when she uploaded her blog post, but that didn't mean Jazzy wasn't concerned for her welfare. That girl, she was sure, was dicing with death. She only hoped she hadn't got too close to Simon, for that did not bode well.

'Right, now that we've got Haggis sorted, the rest of us better stop slacking and get on with finding something we've missed.' Queenie slapped her hands down on a desk, turned her chair round and mounted it like she was a cowboy at a poker game, resting her arms along the backrest. All she needed was a cigar and a pair of cowboy boots to round off the image.

Chapter 37

When Elliot returned with Janine Gorman in tow, minutes later, Jazzy and the others were scrutinising files and analysing reports generated by the other team. Fenton and Geordie refreshed their screens every few minutes as they waited for the records of Jazzy's siblings from their time in social care to be released.

Despite trying to block out their frequent surreptitious email checks, Jazzy was ultra-aware of them. The realisation that the two younger officers would be privy to details about Simon and Mhairi and their lives after their mum's death unsettled Jazzy. Although she'd not had access to any of her siblings' confidential psychiatric reports, she had applied prior to joining Police Scotland under Article 15 of the General Data Protection Regulations to be allowed access to her own medical records in their entirety. This included psychiatric reports and transcripts of sessions with mental health care professionals, including child psychologists, social workers and psychiatrists. Initially, fearful of what she might discover about herself, she'd been reluctant to open that can of worms.

Subsequently, she'd discussed it with DCS Afzal, who had encouraged her to read them in order to better understand the actuality of her experiences, rather than be victim to the disproportionate account her imagination may have created. In some ways the clinical accounts had reassured Jazzy. Their factuality left no room for hysteria and although her heart went out to the child she had once been, the piercing revelations she had anticipated hadn't come. However, it was reassuring to read in black in white the conviction from professionals that she displayed only the expected trauma of an abused child and none of the sociopathic tendencies she'd been concerned her experiences might have seeded in her developing psyche.

Whilst in the previous fifteen years she'd tortured herself periodically, wondering how the twins had turned out and what the reports from the professionals working with them might reveal, she was relieved to be spared the experience of reading their files. With her self-awareness at an all-time high, Jazzy was conscious that she'd be unable to avoid comparing her own files with those of her siblings and that, no matter how hard she tried, she would be unable to combat the self-flagellating thoughts that would lash her mind with every sentence read.

Thrusting thoughts of her siblings to one side, Jazzy smiled at the civilian analyst as Elliot introduced her. 'Thanks to Jazzy's guidance on search parameters, Janine has unearthed a glut of similar killings over the past five years. These years coincide with Jazzy's stalker's activity but that doesn't mean that we will ultimately limit the search only to that time period. Make no mistake – this killer is escalating and with escalation comes irrationality, increased risk-taking and ever more desperate actions in order to maintain the buzz he needs. This killer won't sit meekly waiting for us to catch him. He will already have found his next victim and planned their murder. He's in free fall and the adrenalin from challenging Jazzy will make him rash, violent and bloody dangerous. We need to identify him and stop him fast.'

A momentary silence filled the room as all eyes turned to the analyst. Janine stepped forward and began distributing folders. 'These are the murders that I think may be most relevant. I've uploaded them to the servers too so you can access them in whatever format you prefer. Ask me if you need anything else.'

Despite the dark blue smudges under his eyes and the tension along his jawline, Elliot smiled at Janine who, fresh in her smart skirt and jumper, was the only one of them who looked like she'd managed a full night's sleep.

A silent buzz of electricity zapped through the room and everyone – regardless of lack of sleep, emotional distress or anxiety – flung their shoulders back and sat up straighter in their seats as Elliot cleared his throat. 'You okay to annotate our thoughts as we scrutinise the files while I use the interactive to highlight notable details, Janine?'

Janine nodded and stood beside the first whiteboard, marker in her hand.

'Right, we've got five possible cases so far, all with significant similarities to the Clark murders. The earliest one took place five years ago and we're working on the premise that this might – unless Janine finds any earlier murders – be the first one.'

As a series of crime scene images appeared on the interactive screen, Jazzy pushed the paper files away, leaned back, arms crossed and scrutinised each one, searching for details that linked the Clarks' murders with this one, whilst beside her Queenie, Fenton and Geordie did the same. If Elliot and Janine were right, the crime scene they were currently viewing could signal the starting point for their killer. The murder that had been brewing in her brother's head, perhaps for years, perhaps for a lifetime, perhaps since the moment he saw their mother expire in a bloody mess on their living-room carpet.

Jazzy shuddered. There were no glaring beacons that could be identified as proof that a serial killer had started their life's work at that specific point. No definitive marker that linked this five-year-old murder with the Clarks', yet never had the sense of evil at a crime scene been stronger. Jazzy glanced at Queenie, who with her photographic memory had absorbed the crimes scene images in seconds and who now sat, head bowed and eyes closed, her grey pallor expressing her distress more clearly than any words could. She leaned over and squeezed Queenie's arm.

At that moment Jazzy would have done almost anything to flood Queenie's brain with happy images, but she knew that her gift – or her curse as she herself called it – might flag something up that would set them on the trail for a serial killer. Queenie exhaled, opened her eyes and smiled at Jazzy. 'I'm okay, JayZee. Don't worry about me. The memories are never quite as intense when it's images. It's the actual crime scenes that cause me more problems.'

Elliot, slowly flicking through the slides briefed them. 'Elsbeth Tait was murdered in Nairn. A single mother found dead in the family bungalow by her daughter, Naomi, after school. Elsbeth adopted Naomi when she was six. Cause of death was a stab wound to the back of the neck, which severed the spinal column. Although there was no bloodletting, mutilation of the body, removal of body parts, scattered petals – fresh or plastic – or clothes pegs attached to the nose, earlobes or tongue, three things earned this crime its place on our list.'

He paused and met Jazzy's gaze. 'CSIs found a single clothes peg in the hallway. Forensic analysis found traces of the victim's saliva and cells from her tongue on it, causing them to surmise it had been attached to the victim's tongue. The position of the peg by the drag marks on the carpet, appeared to indicate that it had fallen off the body during its removal from the kitchen.'

Elliot flicked to a new slide showing the scene from the kitchen along the hallway towards the open bedroom door. 'Elsbeth was dragged from the kitchen, post-mortem, through the house, past the living room and into her bedroom where she was then positioned on her back on the bed, hands clasped in front of her.'

Jazzy's mouth went dry as she leaned forward, her eyes raking over the crime scene photos on the large screen, desperately seeing all too clearly the things that could link this scene to either the

Clarks' murders or her own mother's. The birthday cake, with its '16' candle still stuck in the icing on the kitchen table convinced her that this was a good catch by Janine. 'You said three things spotlighted this crime. I assume the presence of the birthday cake, although interesting, could be coincidental. The second being the single clothes peg; so, Elliot, what is the third red flag?'

Elliot flicked to an image of a young teenager in school uniform with braces on her teeth and a shy smile on her lips. A pulse throbbed at his temple as he avoided meeting Jazzy's gaze. 'You're sort of right about the cake, Jazzy. On its own, the cake could be considered a coincidence. However, the significance of the date of the murder elevates this to more than a fluke.'

Jazzy's eyes narrowed as they darted to the bottom of the slide and homed in on the date, magnifying it. Queenie frowned, following her gaze. 'That's not your birthday, Jazzy. Maybe this is . . .'

But Jazzy was shaking her head. 'No, Queenie. This is linked. Elliot's right. It's got to be linked. June the 10th is the twins' birthday, and five years ago, they would have been sixteen.'

Acid gathered in her throat. Even though this was their first tangible link, that their working theory was correct and it would provide them with a starting point for their ongoing investigation, it didn't detract from the overpowering guilt that chilled her. She was the catalyst for this. She and her siblings were somehow responsible for the chain of events that had started fifteen years ago in Inverness, then visited death at this crime scene in Nairn and hopefully ended in the one in Fauldhouse.

But Queenie, still playing Devil's advocate, frowned. 'You can't be certain of that, JayZee. That could just be a coincidence. A correlation of three random things don't a certainty make. I mean, there's more missing from the scene than is present. Where's the cutting on the skin, the petals, the kitchen items, the beans, the cryptic messages? There's none of that, is there. We're still piecing things together.'

Jazzy jumped to her feet. 'There's too many coincidences. You know that. Besides, if this was his first killing, we wouldn't necessarily expect him to have included every element from the Clarks' killings, would we? In the beginning, he'd be evolving, trying to refine his . . .' she grappled to find an appropriate word and in the end all she could come up with was: 'craft . . . his fucking craft. But even without that, there are loads of indicators and we can't ignore them.'

She began pacing the room, counting them off on her fingers, her words becoming harsher and more staccato with each point made. 'One, we were living in Inverness when *it* happened. Two, Naomi was adopted when she was six – Mhairi was six when she went into the social care system and was presumably adopted. It's logical that someone nearby would adopt my sister and, of course, she would be young enough to cope with a name change easily. Three, Naomi's adoptive mother was murdered on Naomi's sixteenth birthday. Four, the body was dragged through to the bedroom. Five, the clothes pegs . . .'

'What are you suggesting? That Naomi Tait is your half-sister?' Queenie exclaimed.

Jazzy dragged her fingers through her hair. 'Yes . . . no . . . I don't know. I just don't know.'

'Okay, okay.' Geordie had listened to them with Elliot, Fenton and Janine watching speechlessly on, but now he moved between the two agitated women. With his hands extended, one towards each of them, he allowed them a moment to calm down. When he finally spoke, it was with quiet insistence. 'There are *two* things we need to bear in mind here. We need to acknowledge that you want to protect Jazzy from this, Queenie, and we *equally* need to be aware that you're very personally involved in this, Jazz.'

He turned to Queenie and held her glare with one of his own. 'Which means that *you* need to start acting like a detective and not a friend. You can't protect her, Queenie. This is horrid, but Jazzy will be better served if we respect her right to experience this crap without being mollycoddled. I mean, for the first three months I worked here, I could barely look at her without kecking ma breeks. She's the last person that needs cosseting. Agreed?'

A flush suffused Queenie's cheeks, but she gave an abrupt nod. Jazzy folded her arms and scowled at Queenie, but Geordie wasn't done. He swivelled so he was eye to eye with Jazzy. 'And *you* need to allow *us* to challenge your gut reactions and that means questioning some of your conclusions to be sure your perspective hasn't been clouded by your residual guilt and your proximity to all this.'

Jazzy opened her mouth, then closed it again, her eyes never wavering from the younger officer's. On the one hand, she wanted to screech at him but on the other she was impressed that he'd found the courage to step between her and Queenie like that. Perhaps his demotion to D team had been as undeserved as her own. She bit the inside of her lip. His allegations that guilt was clouding her judgement were accurate, and it hurt to hear it exposed. She offered her own version of Queenie's earlier nod and smothered her smile when she saw the tension in Geordie's shoulders ease as he exhaled a breath. *So, not as tough as you make out after all, Geordie?*

Queenie sidled up to her and nudged her with her bony elbow. 'You're right, JayZee. Too many coincidences.'

Elliot cleared his throat. 'You're all overlooking something, though. We need our suspicions confirmed. We need to find out if Naomi Tait is your sister, Jazzy, and that's a waiting game for now, until those damn records are released. But there's one other possibility we can't ignore.'

He paused and waited for it to sink in. 'If she is your sister and not some random girl who shared Mhairi's birthday, then we have to assume that she might have been involved in her mother's murder. No matter how unlikely, until proved otherwise, we need to keep the chance that she's complicit in this on the table. We can't at this stage rule out that she helped him then and may still be helping him now.'

Jazzy shook her head as an image of sweet little Mhairi flashed into her mind. The dimples on her chubby cheeks, her trusting look. She couldn't bear it if Mhairi was involved. It was hard enough to realise her brother might be responsible for this, but surely not her sister too. 'No. No. She wouldn't . . . she couldn't.'

But even as the words left her lips and she slumped onto a chair, her professionalism prevailed. She turned to Haggis. 'Get those adoption records for Naomi Tait, pronto. I don't think for a minute that Mhairi is involved, but we need to know if that girl . . .' she jabbed a finger towards the screen where an image of Naomi Tait remained '. . . is my sister or not.'

With an abruptness that was akin to a salute, Fenton nodded and started rapping on his PC as Elliot scrolled through the remaining photos. A line of police cars, an ambulance and a group of people all wearing shoe covers and protective overalls flashed onto the screen. In the forefront of the image two uniformed officers escorted a teenager from a house. Naomi Tait, slim and angular, wore baggy pants that sat low on her hips and a crop top revealing a glittery real or artificial navel piercing. There was no way to tell from the image if she still wore braces. Her shoulder-length black hair was too dark to be natural. With one hand up, as if to shield her face, the girl looked expressionless – numb maybe.

Jazzy drew closer to the image, her eyes raking over the girl's face, desperate to see something there that reminded her of her six-year-old sister. Was this Mhairi? Could this Goth child be the sweet little girl who once had gripped Jazzy's hand *so* tightly, she thought the blood would be cut off? She couldn't tell. Nothing about this image sparked a memory. Nothing about this girl made Jazzy place her beside her in that god-awful house, with the stench of her mother rotting in the bedroom next door.

Elliot moved on to the next crime scene. Four more murder cases with similarities with the Clarks' – four more sets of images showing the brutality of it all. First the addition of a birthday cake, then in the next one clothes pegs on ears, nose and tongue. With each subsequent murder, Jazzy was aware that the actions of this killer were crescendoing to the decapitation witnessed at the Clarks' crime scene. All at once bile burned her throat and she scraped her chair back from the desk and raced from the room, making it to the toilet with mere seconds to spare. On her knees in a cubicle her stomach contents splashed onto the ceramic toilet bowl, her muscles straining in protest as the heaves continued long after there was anything to throw up. *I really need to stop ending up puking my load in loos.*

With the door closed behind her and uncaring of the dubious hygiene, Jazzy lowered the lid and, without the strength to stand, she rested her forehead on top, savouring its coolness on her brow. Although her eyes nipped, she was beyond tears. Her limbs were heavy and cumbersome as shiver after shiver racked through her body. With her eyes closed, each of the images Elliot had projected onto the whiteboard played through her mind like one of those old-fashioned cinematic reels. The only difference was, instead of being in muted black and white, they were in full-colour horror. Each one a testament to the suffering of the victims. Each one a testament of the depravity of the killer. *How can this be the work of Simon? How can he be responsible for this?*

A tap at the door made her jump. She'd been so lost in the horror of it all that she hadn't heard the main toilet door opening. She had no need to ask who it was; it could only be Queenie and when she heaved herself to her feet, and sank onto the toilet seat, she saw the tips of Queenie's scuffed Doc Martens poking under the door. She imagined the older woman, with her ear stuck to the door, one hand running through her spiky short hair making it stand out like Oor Wullie's and the image almost brought a smile to her lips. Almost, but not quite. Jazzy wasn't recovered enough for that yet. Still, the fact that Queenie was here, by her side, looking out for her, released the tears that had been frozen inside her.

'You okay, JayZee?'

The use of the nickname made the tears hitch in Jazzy's throat and nothing could stop them as huge gulping sobs broke through, tearing through the near-silent bathroom. Within seconds, Queenie kicked the door open, bashing it against Jazzy's knee before it bounced back almost whapping her in the face. Hunched over, her arms wrapped round her trembling body, her shoulders heaving as torrents of long-held tears flowed down her chin, Jazzy sat and let it all out as Queenie stepped in and took over.

'Aw, you poor wee mite. Look at you.' Queenie somehow managed to shuffle onto the loo seat beside Jazzy, the only thing keeping them on the seat being the confines of the cubicle wall.

As Queenie's arms wrapped round her and her head was pulled onto Queenie's ample chest, a momentary gurgle of laughter rose in Jazzy's throat at the ridiculousness of her short friend calling her a 'poor wee mite'. But it was short-lived as the enormity of everything that had happened over the past few days kicked in yet again. Her stalker, her mum being targeted, the guilt that *she* was responsible for all these deaths, all this pain and suffering. She collapsed against the solidity of maternal comfort that was Queenie. She savoured the scent of the older woman's minty shower gel mixed with the faint baby smell that Queenie always carried with her. She was safe in the warmth of her embrace, the strength of her arms around her body and the softness of her substantial boobs. All the while Queenie mumbled inconsequential but soothing words in a tone that she probably used with her small granddaughter. Using the sleeve of her misproportioned cardigan, Queenie wiped Jazzy's tears away and together they sat there squashed in a bog in Livingston police headquarters till Jazzy's sobs receded and her tears dried up.

'Right, JayZee. You ready to face the troops again now are you? Cos my arse cheek is bloody throbbing! I'll be getting Craig to rub the arnica cream on it tonight, mark my words, and no doubt he'll take that as a sign that he's in for some rumpy-pumpy.'

Jazzy, giving Queenie a slight push to get her onto her feet, grimaced. 'Yuck, Queenie. TMI!'

'Yeah, you're right. Maybe I'll get Haggis to do it for me. He can wear gloves if he wants.'

Jazzy followed Queenie from the cubicle and moved over to the sink to study the damage done to her face. As she splashed water on her swollen eyes and red cheeks, Queenie stood just behind her, hands shoved in the pockets of her jeans and rocking back and forth on her heels. 'You're not a pretty greeter, JayZee. In fact, you're probably one of the ugliest greeters I've ever seen. Maybe you need to slap some make-up on or something.'

Jazzy glowered at Queenie's reflection. Why did she have to spoil it? Why couldn't Queenie just admit she was a softie at heart and stop with the brusqueness? She opened her mouth to respond, but was interrupted when Queenie's phone rang. Raising one finger in the air in that universal hold-on gesture, Queenie lifted it to her ear. Jazzy saw the moment Queenie's mouth fell open and her gaze flitted away from Jazzy as she edged her way towards the door. 'Aye, boss. We're on our way back. We just needed a minute, that's all.'

Jazzy quirked an eyebrow. 'Elliot?'

'Aye. So, you need to get your substantial arse back in there. That dopey Haggis has come up with the goods and compiled the pertinent details into a chart – a fucking chart would you believe? The laddie's heid's no as fu' of haggis as I thought – mince, aye, but not so much haggis.'

258

Chapter 38

Most of the time I'm patient. I've had to be. All these years waiting, all those years planning and plotting and imagining what it would be like when I finally punish her. To see her face. To feel her anguish, her guilt when she realises what she's caused.

Today though, it's almost unbearable. Hanging around, knowing that they're dissecting my life might be satisfying in its own way, but I want to see what's going on. The anticipation of her being called out to my next little offering is what's keeping me going. It'll be so good. Just when they think they're catching up with me, I throw them another curve ball. Like all the best detective novels, it's good to keep the twists coming.

The strain on their resources must be taking its toll. After all, there's A and B teams rounding up the dealers in one of the biggest drug catches Police Scotland has ever seen and a major murder inquiry headed up by the dubious Team D – named, I hear, specifically because they're considered the Dunce Team. No arguments from me on that score. DCI Dick even skipped using the letter C just to kick Jazzy in the guts. It amuses me that they've enlisted their knight in shining armour, DI Elliot Balloch, to bail them out. No doubt he played down the fact that he nearly shat himself when he found us. That he could barely bring himself to lift us out of the cesspit we were drowning in. That he nearly puked his load when he saw Mummy all squirmy and maggoty and smelling like an abattoir.

Yep, it's definitely not the A team chasing me, but I have high hopes for Jazzy. I think given the right incentive she'll rise to the occasion. So, whilst I wait for my next little act of degradation and chaos to come to light, I'll crack on with sorting out my next moves. Planning is my thing. The thing I'm best at. I imagine her as I've seen her so many times before with her hands shaking and then, the tell-tale sign – She curls her fingers up and strokes the scar on her palm. It's like we have a connection. I smile as I stroke the one on my hand.

Chapter 39

Hours passed and each of the subsequent files that Janine Gorman had put forward for their perusal added to the chill in Jazzy's bones. As the team scrutinised images from the five most likely murders, she sat with a mug of long-cold coffee cupped in her hands. All she could think about was whether Naomi Tait was her sister or not. If she had been religious, she would have prayed to both her birth parents' gods, but she wasn't. So instead, she raged internally against the systems that had let her and her siblings down so badly.

A tension headache engulfed her entire head, making her squint as image after enlarged image demonstrated the escalating progression of a murderer's extreme fantasy. Whilst each of the subsequent crimes identified by Janine Gorman had enough superficial aspects to make a link between them plausible, there was no conclusive lightbulb moment when a piece of evidence flashed up that said, 'Yes, these crimes are all the work of the same perpetrator.' Instead there was the slow-burning certainty that so many coincidental links couldn't be ignored.

It was frustrating because, setting the need for incontrovertible evidence aside, it was clear that if the killer's progression was plotted on a graph it would show the development of their sick mind as each scene became more finessed. The main problem was the lack of conclusive forensic evidence to confirm that a single perpetrator was responsible for all the murders. No transfer of evidence between the scenes, no stray hairs or skin cells or handy deposits of bodily fluids to link the scenes, no witness statements or footage to isolate a figure similar to Jazzy's stalker – nothing but assumption, surmise, experience and gut instinct. None of which would convince the Crown Office and Procurator Fiscal Service that they had a viable case or indeed a likely suspect. Not unless they could find their killer and work backwards to link him to these crimes too.

Whilst there were elements in each of the cases that added to Jazzy's conviction that they were on the right track, the inconsistencies made proving it impossible. The team had identified six key elements present in the post-mortem death scene at Jazzy's old home that were present, either in isolation or in a small cluster, at the crimes they were scrutinising: the clothes pegs pinned to nose, tongue, lips, earlobes; eyes gouged out or mutilated; the presence of kitchen household items inserted into facial orifices; scattered petals fresh or plastic; small cuts done post-mortem; death caused by an injury to the neck or upper body by a sharp object.

To take into account escalation over time, they added severed body parts to the list and, on Jazzy's insistence, they also added elements from the Clarks' murders that hadn't been present when Jazzy's mum's body had been discovered: the tin of beans, the birthday cake, the message written in blood on the victims' foreheads and the significance of the dates of each killing. Whilst these lists focused their attention, they also illustrated inconsistencies and still, that crucial link between them all was missing.

Elliot, sweat stains under his arms and a strained expression on his face, dragged himself to his feet. Jazzy thought she might be the only one in the room to identify the exhaustion threading through his clipped words when he spoke, because he hid it so well. Every new line etched across his brow, every heavy movement, every swallowed sigh told her he was finding this hard to deal with and her earlier annoyance with him was put on the back burner – for now.

'Right. I feel like we're chasing our tails here. You've all had ample time to go through the files; let's brainstorm. We're not leaving this stinking room till we come up with something we can roll with, okay? So, I suggest starting again and taking it all step by monotonous step.'

When nobody replied, he cricked his neck, rolled his shoulders and exhaled. 'Apart from Hansa Solanki – Jazzy's birth mum – and Elsbeth Tait we've got five possible victims of our killer. Two of the murders took place four years ago: Matt Fraser, a forty-four-year-old corner shop owner, stab wound to the gut on the 9th February in Stobswell, Dundee, almost eight months after Elsbeth Tait's murder, and then the double murder of Francis, a civil servant, and his wife Ellen Gillies, a foster parent, forty-five and forty-three years old respectively. COD for Francis was a stab wound to back of neck whilst Ellen died of manual strangulation on 15th March in Biggar, barely a month after Matt Fraser's murder.'

He paused, rolled his shoulders again and continued, 'Then we've Ged Pollard a thirty-eight-year-old high school teacher from Broughty Ferry killed by a stab wound to the chest over a year later on the 10th of June. The last incident was another double murder of Stuart and Mick Delaney-Smith, twenty-five and twenty-three respectively in Edinburgh. Stuart managed a small art gallery on Rose Street whilst Mick had a couple of part-time jobs as a bouncer by night and barista by day. Their murders occurred over two years later on 18th of September and of course, if we're right the next murder was that of the Clarks, which was fourteen months later. What do you think? Is this all a waste of time or do we have something here?'

Queenie who, despite her better judgement, had been looking at the photos from each crime scene, chucked a pile of glossy, sickening images, taken from every conceivable angle onto the table and glared at Elliot. 'Think? Think? My heid's going to bust. This is . . .' She exhaled, sending some of the images wafting further away from her and dragged her stubby fingers through her increasingly spiky hair, then in a voice softer than Jazzy had ever heard her use before said, 'This is crap. I know you've got your hopes pinned on me gleaning something from the glossies, but although I'm trying, there's so much to sift through and sort out and . . .' She swallowed and shook her head.

It was Fenton who reached over and squeezed her arm. 'Aw, Queenie, you need to pace yourself. It's hard for us, but for you . . .?' He shook his head. 'Just do what you can. That's all you can do, Mama Jazz Queen.'

Queenie extracted a well-used tissue from her bra, blew her nose like a trumpeting elephant and offered Fenton a watery grin. 'For a Haggis, yer no' a bad man, son.'

'Fenton's right, Queenie. Just do what you can. But you're part of a team, so . . .' Elliot looked at the others. 'Any of you lot got thoughts on this?'

Geordie cleared his throat. 'I was thinking about the chronological closeness of these first three murders. I mean eight months between Elsbeth and this Matt bloke, then only five weeks till the next and then over a year till the next. I'm not sure that adds up. Don't serial killers start slow and build momentum?' He beat a tattoo on the table with his fingertips. 'Maybe we're missing some murders? Also, the dates trouble me. I mean we've got Hansa Solanki's death on the 14th of December, Jazzy's birthday, and we have the Clarks' murders then too, which sort of links. We've also got two of the single murders on the 10th of June, which we've ascertained is the twins' birthday, so they again add up. But what about the others? Double murders 15th of March and 18th of September and another single on 9th of February. You'd think bearing in mind the significance of the dates of the other deaths that those, if they're linked, would also be significant dates, too, wouldn't you?'

Jazzy had been listening with her head bowed. A nagging headache gnawed at her temple and her stomach was protesting too much caffeine and not enough food. She massaged her head, with her eyes shut to avoid the effects of the artificial lighting. 'I'm not sure about the other dates, but the 15th of March was my birth mum's birthday. Maybe the significance of the other dates will become clear when we have access to Simon and Mhairi's records. Still no joy, Geordie?'

Geordie shook his head. 'It's like they're working backwards. Bloody annoying. We really need them to make sense of this.' He screwed up his nose. 'If there's any sense to be made of them, that is. This could all be the proverbial pissing-in-the-wind scenario. I mean look at the range of murder sites, the variation in them. None of it makes sense.'

Jazzy glared at the chart that Fenton had put on the board summarising the similarities and differences between each of the six crime scenes and the details of how her mother had been found. Whilst the likenesses convinced her that they were on the right track, various things troubled her about the discrepancies and she was keen to know what everyone else made of it. Even now with evidence mounting up, Jazzy wanted her suspicions about her brother to be proved wrong. She was shamed that her job necessitated reducing the victims to a chart on a bloody interactive screen in a police station. However, Fenton had done a great job.

It was easier to scrutinise it in a compact form like this. With Geordie's comments in mind, Jazzy studied the chart. 'I can see links between these murders. We all can, but the superficial simi-larities aren't enough. My main gripe is if these murders are linked then why did no one in Police Scotland put this together before now? Why are we the first to make any connections? Any takers?'

Geordie exhaled and scratched his head. He'd pulled himself so his legs were right under the desk, but they were so long they

265

protruded from the other side as he slouched in his chair. 'Well, that's easy in some respects. Your mum's death' – he tilted his head towards Jazzy, his shrug apologetic – 'was accidental so it wouldn't be on the radar at all. As for the others, well, they were committed in towns and cities in different police divisions. Elsbeth Tait in the Highlands and Islands, Matt Fraser in Tayside, the Gillies in Lanarkshire, Ged Pollard back to Tayside, the Delaney-Smiths in Edinburgh and then ending up here in Lothian and Borders. Quite a trail to unravel and few similarities in the victims, which would have made it difficult to lump them together.'

Fenton shuffled on his chair, the bloom blossoming on his cheeks an indication that he had something to contribute.

'Oot with it, Haggis heid. What are you thinking?'

If anything, Queenie's 'encouragement' brought even more fire to the young detective's chops, but he gamely rose to the occasion, flinging his shoulders back and inhaling audibly before adding his thoughts to the melting pot. 'Yeah, the age differences in the victims and the fact that some were murdered as couples, and some not, would throw a spanner in the works. And although some of the dates are significant and draw a line to Jazzy's mum's death, we've no idea whether the other dates are significant or not. I mean the celebration cakes sort of indicate they are but' – he shrugged – 'we don't know, for sure.'

That had bothered Jazzy too. That both the twins' birth dates and Jazzy's birthday popped up twice was too coincidental to dismiss – that four murders out of the six occurred on a date significant to Jazzy just couldn't be chance. Still, the other dates didn't ring any bells with her – perhaps they meant something to the killer.

She was convinced that Elsbeth Tait's death was linked to her sister. Whether Naomi was her sister or not the birthday coincidence was compelling. Perhaps Simon targeted the Tait family because Naomi shared a birthday with him and his twin or perhaps Naomi was his twin. Perhaps his aim had been to kill her too. The fact that Nairn and Inverness were within spitting distance of each other was another compelling factor.

The indisputable fact was that, on her birthday, her stalker – or someone very similar – was witnessed in the vicinity of the Clarks' home near the time they were murdered. That, together with the taunt in the card, the visit to her parents' home and the pegs and other stuff at the scene, was a link back to Elsbeth Tait's death. She was convinced it had been laid out like that for her benefit. Had the decapitations happened purely to shock her? Was it her fault that grotesque act had happened? She closed her eyes and pinched her leg. *Don't be so stupid, Jazzy. None of this is your fault. The only person to blame is the one who murdered those people.* 'Go on, Fenton. What else are you thinking?'

Although he started off with a tremor to his voice, Fenton soon warmed to his theme. 'In the scenes identified, some wounds were to the chest and some to the throat – with one of each of the double murders involving manual strangulation too. Stab wounds are pretty frequent – nothing that unusual about those . . .'

'Tell that to the victims, Fent.' Geordie nudged his colleague.

But Fenton was on a roll and ignored him. '. . . So that wouldn't flag anything up. Of course, the clothes pegs should have flagged an alert or even the petals and leaves – but they weren't present at every scene. What muddied the waters was that some of the murder investigations were closed, so nobody would ever look at them again. Matt Fraser's attack was considered a burglary gone wrong and lumped in with others in the area. Another shopkeeper had been stabbed and died from his wounds a few days later. They thought they'd found their culprit – but maybe they were wrong. That's what *we're* saying now, but we've only got the benefit of hindsight for that. There's a note in Fraser's file that, the culprit, a Jimmy "Hardass" Nails, consistently denied being responsible for Fraser's murder, but he still went down for it.'

'You've got a point there, son. Jimmy Nails? Aye, there's a blast from the past. The Nails are renowned in Glasgow.' She stared into space for a moment then shrugged and continued flicking through a file, her stumpy fingers jabbing at points on the page as she read. 'The drugs and paraphernalia at the Gillies' scene were enough to direct that investigation towards a couple of their previous foster kids who'd become embroiled with local drug gangs. The coppers narrowed it down to a scrote called Clarence McLaren.' Queenie snorted. 'Clarence Bloody McLaren? What were the parents thinking, calling their laddie that? No wonder he ended up in deep shit.'

She flicked on a few pages, scratching her armpit as she did so. 'Oh, aye, they weren't really thinking right much. That laddie's ma and da were junkies too. Poor sod never really had a chance, did he? No that that's an excuse for offing yer foster parents, like.'

'But if he went down for their murders and he didn't do it . . .' Geordie's voice trailed off.

Queenie took over, her chubby cheeks jiggling. 'Then, right enough, he's in Barlinnie for no good reason, other than being a scrote, that is and that's no' reason enough to be in there. But, don't get yer violins out just yet for Clarence – we still have to prove it.'

Jazzy had grabbed another file as the others spoke and flicked through it. 'Looking at the Delaney-Smith file – apparently Mick Delaney-Smith had a gambling problem and had racked up a substantial debt and then borrowed heavily from Loanie Gibbs.' Loanie, Lionel, Gibbs unsurprisingly was Edinburgh's leading loan shark. 'Although E division couldn't tie a specific culprit to the murders, they were convinced it was one of Loanie's gang who'd done the deed and with nothing concrete to go on, they had more or less unofficially closed the case, pending getting one of his minions to squeal – it's open but inactive.'

'So . . .' Geordie tapped a biro on the table top, his scrunched-up face reflecting the degree of concentration he was using to get his head round everything. 'What we're saying is, if the wrong guys are locked up for *some* of these murders then our killer was savvy enough to set it up that way?'

Every one of Geordie's words was laced with doubt – doubt that Jazzy shared. He flicked the pen so it hit Fenton on the shoulder. 'I mean, when Matt Fraser was killed, your siblings would have only been seventeen. Would either of them really have been on the ball enough to set this up?'

Queenie's snort rent the air. 'For God's sake, laddie. We're no talking aboot the bloody Von Trapps here, are we? It's not the Partridge Family, or the damn Brady Bunch.'

'The Fun Traps? Who the hell are they.' Fenton's puzzled frown earned him a scowl that immediately had him drawing his neck in like a startled tortoise.

'Bloody *Von Trapps*! You hear me. *Von Trapps* not Fun Traps – we're not talking some sort of weird swinging club.' She glared at Geordie, who also shook his head. 'Fuck's sake, what's the world coming to when we've got polis who've never heard of the Von Trapps? Bloody *Sound of Music*, you heard of that?"'

Both men nodded in unison, although Jazzy suspected that was more to do with deflecting Queenie's ire, than actually having heard of the musical. But there was no stopping Queenie now that, as Jazzy's mum would say, her gander was well and truly up. 'Beautiful film. Lovely songs. All about families working together, being a team, cooperating. A bit like us really.'

A grin slid over Geordie's face as he spotted an opportunity and with feigned nonchalance, he gave a small 'I'm only asking' shrug. 'Thought mebbe we could call ourselves the Von Trapps instead of the Jazz Queens. I mean that might be better, eh? With us being like family and all.'

Queenie's brows drew together, her eyes dark as thunder only to clear as she slapped her thigh. 'Oh, you're joking, Geordie. Course you are. Nah, don't you worry we're The Jazz Queens, our little quartet. Nothing will change my mind about that so don't you fret.'

Before Geordie could respond, and much to the horror of her

three colleagues, Queenie, her eyes glazed over as if she was in another world entirely, broke into a beautifully and unexpectedly sweet rendition of 'The Hills Are Alive'.

Fenton curled over, till his head rested on his keyboard, his arms covering his ears. 'Make it stop . . . please make it stop.'

With no sign of Queenie's rendition coming to an end any time soon, Jazzy intervened. 'Right that's enough, Queenie. We need to focus, okay?'

As Queenie faltered to a stop, she glanced round at her colleagues and rubbed her hands down her trousers, a slow bloom gathering on her cheeks.

So, Queenie could be embarrassed and *the woman could sing! Maybe Geordie could drag her up on stage with him one Friday for a duet? That would be a sight for sore eyes!* Delighted by that thought, Jazzy stored it away for future scrutiny as she drew the team's attention back to their discussion. 'What were you going to say before Julie Andrews inhabited your body, Queenie?'

Still rubbing her hands down her legs Queenie shrugged. 'Just, don't underestimate those bairns. How many kids younger than that have we caught red-handed doing horrific crap?' She blinked rapidly a few times and her jaw tensed. Queenie had a point, youth was no barrier to intelligence and planning and they'd do well to consider that. Unfortunately, it was also no guarantee against evil and inhumanity.

'They can be devious when they want to and let's not forget, either one of these two suspects has had a traumatic childhood experience. Ye can never tell what that sort of thing can do to a bairn's psyche. Whether it'll warp and twist them into monsters.' She shrugged. 'Mind you, the faffing about wi' a dead body when they were six is a pretty good indicator that at least one of their brains was mashed a long time ago. It was only going to get worse.'

With that ominous proclamation ringing in her ears, Elliot cleared his throat. 'Of course, we'll enlist the relevant divisions to re-interview the next of kin and any suspects they flagged up in light of our suspicions, but that's all padding until we find a cohesive link.'

Jazzy cricked her neck. Her earlier meltdown had left lingering tension in her body as well as the starts of a throbbing headache. She walked over to the screen. 'So, we're no further forward really, are we. We've spent an entire day, up to our neck in this and we've nothing to show for it.'

Queenie exhaled engulfing them all in a garlicky breeze. 'So where does this leave us, eh?'

At this point, Elliot, decisive and calm, took control. 'Right, we need to interview Jimmy Nails and Clarence McLaren in light of our suspicions – see how credible their denials are and see if they can come up with any names. Find out if they knew Naomi Tait. Geordie, you could do that and take one of the PCs with you. Then, there's the time gaps between murders – either our killer lay dormant for ages, or there's other victims out there.'

He looked round the room frowning. 'Where's Janine? We could do with her doing a deeper dive to see if there are any other possibly linked cases out there.'

No one had seen Janine leave, so Elliot nodded at Fenton. 'Get her on that when she gets back, will you?'

Jazzy had just drawn up a chair to record the actions Elliot wanted carried out by the PCs, when the trill sound of his phone rung through the incident room. The effect on the team was immediate as everyone froze, all eyes on Elliot as he answered.

He listened for what seemed like ages, the tightening of his jaw the only indication that what he was hearing was unpalatable. When he hung up, his eyes went straight to Jazzy.

Her fingers gripping the edge of the desk, Jazzy closed her eyes for a second and threw her shoulders back before opening them again. 'Another one?'

He nodded. 'Make sure everything we discussed is in progress and we'll meet you and Queenie at the scene. I'll text you the address.'

He grabbed his jacket, and darted from the room, leaving the others stunned for a moment. As Jazzy exhaled and stood up, both Geordie and Fenton's phones emitted a beep. Both dived to see what the notification was. Jazzy only needed to look at their grinning faces to see that, finally, they'd received her siblings' unsealed records and so with mixed feelings she left the incident room knowing that on her return her life would be irrevocably changed.

Chapter 40

Jazzy and Queenie drove along South Street, past a busy butcher's shop, a Chinese restaurant that was showing signs of getting ready to open for the evening and the Armadale community hub where a bunch of kids gathered, their hoods pulled up against the cold as they lobbed slushy snowballs at passing vehicles. The children's innocent shrieks and laughter made a mockery of the scene that awaited them just down the road. Queenie indicated and turned into Barbauchlaw Crescent, where a red-nosed officer waved them through. The road had been closed at the far end and this was the only entry point for those needed on site. Queenie nodded at the road sign. 'That's the auld name for Armadale, you know? Barbauchlaw.'

Since moving from Edinburgh to Bellsquarry, Jazzy hadn't visited Armadale and hadn't known what to expect, but the main street, in the dying daylight, was bustling and the Christmas decorations and lights gave the town a homey feel. 'Why change the name?'

Queenie shrugged. 'Centuries ago some poncey landowner from Sutherland wanted it named after him. Probably up his own arse like most of the landed gentry – sticking his label on the toon. Like a dog pissing to mark his territory.'

With a half-smile at Queenie's reply, Jazzy looked around her. The police activity and the gathering crowd left her in no doubt where they were headed, and Queenie, spotting a space a couple of blocks down from the police cars and CSI vans, pulled in. As she got out of the car and hugged her coat around her, the gentle wafting snow turned into a blizzard that all but obscured Jazzy's view of the street. Although mainly residential a few of the two-storey red-brick houses had been converted into business premises. Jazzy made a particular note of the brightly lit café with steamed-up windows opposite. If they were delayed at the crime scene for any length of time, that would be a godsend. Her toes were already tingling with cold and knowing a warm drink was available was reassuring.

Conscious of her ravaged face, after her earlier emotional upheaval, Jazzy was glad that the deteriorating weather provided an excuse for her raw cheeks and swollen eyes. Although, to be honest, thoughts of her appearance didn't occupy her mind for very long as she leaned against Queenie's Land Rover and considered what lay ahead. With the memory of the Clarks' scene still fresh, she was hesitant to visit this one, for there was no doubt it would be as bad, if not worse than the previous. This was sure to be yet another escalation and that meant nastiness.

Official vehicles lined the street and already rows of reporters, smartphones at the ready, huddled together, their eyes flitting over the activity beyond the makeshift barrier. Pedestrians holding takeaway coffee cups mingled with neighbours cupping their own mugs in freezing hands. Jazzy's eyes flicked over them – a crowd of nebby nosy parkers feeding off someone else's misfortune like vultures at a battlefield. *So much for the spirit of Christmas.* Not even the weather was going to stop them getting their thrill as they shuffled in the cold, collars pulled up to their ears and scarves wrapped round their chins. If the killer was here, there was little chance of recognising them – not in this weather.

At the back of her mind, the notion that someone involved

in the investigation might be the killer – might be her brother – lingered like a bad smell. Would she recognise him after all this time? She thought not. Why would she? He'd been six when she last saw him. Now, at twenty-one, he'd look completely different. She'd no idea of his height, or his stature. As for hair and eye colour? Either of those were easily altered. She cast her mind over the CSIs and constables that she'd worked with many times before, wondering which of them slotted into the correct age range. Had any of them given off any strange vibes? Had they looked at her askance? Harbouring these thoughts was self-torture and, although it took effort, she thrust them aside and tried to prepare herself for what lay ahead. 'You ready, Queenie?'

Queenie, hands stuffed deep in her pockets as per usual, was also scouring the scene. She gave one of her offhand shrugs that could have meant: *Yes, raring to go*, or equally: *Nah, I'd rather hoick my eyes out with a crochet hook*. 'Come on, JayZee. No point freezing our arses off out here. Let's get shuffling.'

Together they trudged towards the crime scene tape that demarked the inner cordon that sectioned off Clarice Cameron's office, the houses adjacent and the entire road as far as the fences around the houses opposite, from the rest of the street.

Clarice Cameron, a therapist, had advertised her business premises with an A-framed sign detailing her services – hypnotherapy, CBT, Dynamic Talking Therapy, to mindfulness and courses to help with weight loss or addiction therapy. The garden was neat. Twinkling lights decorated three bushes and multi-coloured tree-shaped lights lined the path up to the door. The door was ajar. Light blazed out, illuminating the CSIs as they erected a tent to obscure the scene from the looky-loos. Another Christmas tree shone from the large front-room window, making Jazzy shiver at the incongruousness of it all.

Before getting suited up, Jazzy made a beeline for Sergeant Hobson and instructed him to ensure that footage of those loitering about was captured and sent to Fenton. As she spoke her eyes trailed over the crowd. Although she had a clearer view of them from inside the inner cordon, visibility was still poor. 'Shit, this weather makes it near impossible to identify anyone.'

Annoyed, she kicked the tyre of a nearby police car and, eyes narrowed, tried to focus on identifying anyone with the body shape of her stalker. Of course, he was too clever to reveal his true size and the weather offered the perfect excuse for anyone to bulk up with layer upon layer of clothing. As Queenie signed them in to the crime scene and obtained their shoe covers and overalls, Jazzy focused on the journalists. She recognised most of them. Philip Jamieson was there, broodily glaring at a uniformed officer who had moved him back.

She scanned the crowd to see if she could identify Ginny Bell, but there was no sign of her. Maybe she was keeping a low profile after her provocative article or, more likely, she was making sure she was just another indistinguishable blob. If she'd any sense she'd not want to be on the receiving end of either Jazzy or Queenie's wrath after her underhand stunt. *Should I be concerned at the reporter's absence?* Jazzy wasn't sure. Regardless of her duplicity in doing that blog post, Jazzy would have expected her to be here, in the thick of things. She raked her eyes over the hordes again, then shrugged. This was a waste of time. Bell was either there or she wasn't. Either way, now wasn't the time to think about how she'd deal with her.

Snatching her coveralls from Queenie, Jazzy struggled into them, 'Hey, Wullie, let me know if you spot that reporter Ginny Bell, will you? I have a long-overdue meeting with her lined up and I want to catch her by surprise. Let me know if she shows up, and if she looks like she's leaving before I've had a chance to speak to her, detain her on some pretence or other – just make up some excuse. I don't care what.'

Ducking under the tape, Jazzy trudged through slush up to the door. The building was quaint, with red bricks running around the bottom and pebble-dashing on cream covering the rest of the facia. It looked clean and well cared for, like the other houses in this street. Queenie shuffled along behind her, looking like a dumpy snowperson who'd lost their carrots and coal. Her hood was pulled up over her spiky hair. It's tightness around her face made her cheeks seem even more bulbous than usual. The legs were too long for her short frame and she kept yanking them up at the knee, but they were still soaking wet. 'You don't have to come in, Queenie.'

But Queenie was already shaking her head. 'Aye, hen, that's *exactly* what I have to do. You know that. I might no' like it. I might wish I was eating an ice cream on a beach in the Bahamas, or having a wee snoggin' session wi' his nibs in the back row of Cineworld or . . .'

'Okay, Okay, I get the picture . . .'

'. . . or riding a donkey at the seaside with Ruby.' She puffed out a gust of pure garlic and folded her arms under her boobs. 'But that's no gonna happen, is it? So, I'll go straight to the crime scene and then I'll work my magic on my own back in the car and hopefully, after going through all of that, I'll be able to tell you if anything in there matches or links to both the Clarks' murders and the various ones Balloch showed us earlier.'

She sniffed, making gurning movements with her mouth in an attempt to loosen her elasticated hood. 'It's my job, hen, and I'm going to do it.'

With the tent up now, Jazzy and Queenie trudged through and following the metal plates, entered the property. The hallway was spacious and led to the right into an office area, which housed the large tree Jazzy had spotted from outside. Around the perimeter, matching padded chairs lined the walls, a coffee table with a supply of magazines and a potted plant, in front of them. A reception desk was positioned to the rear in front of an arch leading to a small kitchen area.

Two bulky figures, engrossed in an animated discussion, stood by the stairs. Although Jazzy had expected DI Balloch to be there, she was momentarily flummoxed when Chief Super Afzal also turned to greet them. What the hell was he doing here? This was well beneath his paygrade. It felt like he was stalking her, keeping an eye on her every move and it pissed her off. No wonder the rumour mills were churning, like Duracell bunnies on overdrive. While Elliot's gaze seemed to rest on Jazzy's face a little longer than necessary – probably trying to apologise for not warning her of Afzal's presence, Jazzy focused on the reception area. Was it just her or had the CSIs and the PC sitting in the corner with an older woman who was weeping, stopped what they were doing to look at her?

Heat flooded her face and she wished the floor would open up and snatch her from this debacle. Afzal, on the other hand, seemed oblivious to Jazzy's emotional state as he raked his fingers through his thick dark hair and offered them a brusque nod. 'Straight up the stairs, you two. Victim's office is on the left. Prepare yourselves – it's not pretty.'

As Queenie inhaled loudly, Jazzy brushed past them and followed the activity above. As she stepped onto the first stair Jazzy glanced into the reception area again. The woman still sobbed into a disintegrating tissue. This was probably the receptionist who, Jazzy had been informed, had arrived late for work after being delayed due to a slashed tyre. Poor woman found her boss eviscerated upstairs. *Slashed tyre? Was that deliberate? Had that been due to our killer's forward planning? Nothing would surprise me. Another needless victim!* Another person who would forever see dark and shadows, even in the brightest sunlight.

Chapter 41

By the time they'd reached the top of the stairs, the smell of blood was present – not overpowering, but still there and still disturbing. Queenie shoved her fists under her oxters, glowering at her bootee-covered feet as if they were responsible for her current predicament. 'Come on then. Let's get this bloody done with.'

Jazzy exhaled and nudged the door open with her elbow so she could view the room without actually entering. She moved, allowing Queenie easy exit should she need it. Even by comparison to the previous scene, this one was bad. Dr Clarice Cameron had been positioned behind her desk, facing the door as if ready to greet her next client. The only trouble was that her head was on the desk, the tongue protruding and, once more, clothes pegs clung to the revolting pink appendage as well as her eyelids, nose and earlobes. Her hands had also been severed and lay palms upward, her fingers pointing to her gaping mouth. Cradled in them, like some sort of comedic offering, was an ornate snow globe. The room seemed awash with blood, and Jazzy understood enough of blood spatter to realise that the swathes of red streaking the walls and ceiling were the result of the strokes causing the decapitation and the resultant blood spray.

'Fuck!' There was little else to be said really and Jazzy was in no mood to either modify her language or come up with another word. As if to emphasise her anger she added a 'fuck, fucking bastarding hell.' Before closing her eyes and turning her attention to Queenie.

Although ashen-faced, Queenie's eyes flitted across the room. To a casual observer it may have looked like she was making a cursory inventory, but Jazzy knew Queenie's incredible brain was logging and noting and memorising every aspect of the crime scene. There was no part of this scene that Queenie would forget, no detail that would be too inconsequential to note. When she saw her partner gip and sway on her feet, Jazzy laid a hand on her arm and guided her away from the room. 'Go and get some air, Queenie. You've done your bit. Go downstairs, hydrate and we'll compare notes in a little while.'

With barely a nod, Queenie, pupils dilated and her gaze glassy as if attempting to obliviate what they'd just witnessed, backed away and trotted down the stairs, her head bowed and shoulders hunched. Jazzy watched as she ripped her overalls off before she'd even reached the front door, her stumpy fingers grappling with the fabric like she couldn't bear for it to engulf her for a second longer. When Queenie lurched through the open door and made it past the cordon before bending over, hands on her knees and gasping huge breaths of cleansing air, Jazzy released a breath she hadn't realised she was holding. Satisfied that her partner would be okay, she inhaled, cleared her mind and turned back to the abattoir, dreading what she was about to encounter, knowing she had to analyse it in all its grotesque ugliness.

Unbidden, a flicker of an image – a memory – flashed before her eyes, causing her to stop and raise a gloved hand to her forehead. *Not now. Please not now!* But her treacherous mind wasn't content to allow her to do her job. Instead the images flooded her – rolling out before her, eyes like an Instagram reel slowed down to maximise the trauma. Her chest tightened and she gasped, leaning her hand against the doorframe for support as like a fly on the wall she observed her younger self – her ten-year-old self – shielding her siblings.

As soon as she hears the hammering on the door she knows it's the polis. She jumps up and together with Mhairi creeps from the front bedroom. Mhairi's fingers are sticky and she wants to pull her hand away, but she's the big sister. It's her job to hold her sister's hand. She should make her have a bath – not just her, all of them – but it's scary in the toilet and the big tree outside the window looks like the bogeyman trying to get in. Where the hell is Simon? They need to stick together – the three of them.

She pulls open the door at the top of the stairs and hears voices through the big door – a man's and some women – Mrs Wood from downstairs. Crabbit auld bitch that she is. Interfering like she's better than us – well that's what their ma used to say. She didn't really mind her cause she sometimes gave them sweeties – sherbet lemons – and they'd hide them in their room and sook on them for hours.

'Get in there, numpty. See what's going on, will you?' The man sounds nasty and the little girl feels scratches going up her back, like when Ma scrubs her with the nailbrush. She doesn't want him to come in. Please don't let him come in. But someone else answers him – a different voice – one that sounds smooth as tablet. 'Aye, nae problem, sir. I'll kick it in.'

Mhairi tugs at her arm. 'What do they want, Jazzy?'

Even though her heart's all flippety flip, Jazzy smiles and pulls her close. 'Probably nothing, but where's Simon?'

Just then, Simon, releasing a stench of rotting meat, opens Ma's bedroom door. He's got his hands behind his back. They'll be covered in gunk, but she's no time to tell him off so she glowers at him and whispers, 'What have I told ye' about going in there, Simon? It's disgusting and it stinks.'

'He's always in there,' says Mhairi, her smile relishing the thought of getting her brother in trouble.

'Am not, Mhairi. It's you that's always in there.'

But Jazzy can hear battering at the door and she knows they

281

don't have much time. 'Ssh, you two. We don't want them to hear us, do we?'

As Jazzy drags the children back into the room, Simon closes the door behind them, replacing the rags they'd put along the floor before kneeling beside the girls. 'Should we hide, Jazzy?'

The hammering's louder now. It'll no be long till Mr Tablet voice is through. She scrunches her eyes tightly closed and covers her ears as the sound of splintering wood rings up the stairs. 'Come on. We need to hide. Quick. Get back in our room. We'll hide under the covers and he'll never notice us.'

'Jasmine? . . . Jasmine? DC Solanki, are you with us?'

Jazzy glanced at the CSIs who'd paused in the middle of processing the scene. The pathologist, Lamond Johnston, studied her with a slight frown puckering his forehead. 'You were in another world, then, Jasmine.'

With a forced smile, Jazzy waved her hand in the air. 'Hey, Lamond. Just taking a moment to wonder about the sort of person who'd do something like this.'

'Aye, it makes you wonder, indeed. I think Rabbie Burns had it right when he spoke about man's inhumanity to man.'

Lamond Johnston often spouted verses from his favourite poet's works, but Jazzy wanted to get to work. Determined to distract the older man from a protracted recital of *A Man's A Man For A' That*, Jazzy asked, 'You got anything for me?'

Even behind his mask, Lamond's smile was evident, his eyes lighting up and making them crinkle at the edges. No matter how bad a crime scene or how bad a person's death had been, Lamond somehow found a way to power through it with his temper intact. Jazzy had once wondered aloud about it in the presence of the chief super and been told that Johnston's home life was idyllic – whatever that meant – and that the doctor's faith gave him an outlet for any lingering troubling thoughts he might have.

Personally, Jazzy couldn't wrap her head round that. Every crime scene she saw served to convince her that no humane God would allow this sort of hurt to happen and therefore the only logical conclusion to be reached was that there was no higher being. Not that she grudged Johnston his beliefs. In fact, she envied him. She'd give anything to make sense of the depravity and horror that humans inflicted on their fellow humans.

Still reeling from her earlier memory flash, Jazzy wondered if maybe she should check out Lamond's church. God knows she needed something to help her make sense of this. But she wouldn't. Communal therapy wasn't Jazzy's thing. Besides, she was too moody to be around optimists for long. Her birth mum, despite being estranged from her parents over her own life choices, had retained her Hindu faith and tried to instil it in her three children – not easy as a single parent in an all-white neighbourhood and harder still for one as fucked-up as her mother was. Jazzy wondered how that had gone for the twins as they were bandied about in the foster care system.

Chapter 42

Queenie lurched towards the car and hauled herself into the driver's seat. She'd ignored everyone and would be hard pressed to say how she'd managed to drag herself over the slippy ground without falling over. Her movements were heavy and uncoordinated as if great weights were attached to each of her joints. Now ensconced in the car – away from the crime scene – the images of what she'd seen wouldn't let her go, regardless of the physical distance she'd put between them and herself. They hurled around her like great flapping ominous bats, intruding on her sanity with a relentless determination she couldn't deny.

Conscious of the sweat droplets across her forehead and regardless of the shivery spasms that racked her body, Queenie wrapped her arms round the steering wheel, gripping it tightly as she lowered her brow to her hands and gently bumped it against her frozen knuckles. She savoured the discomfort, channelling the physicality of it as a distraction to her mental anguish until a clatter outside the car jolted her upright to peer through the swirling snow, her breath coming in pants. When she realised, it was a minor spat between one of the constables and an over-exuberant journalist she swallowed and exhaled.

Reaching down she turned the key in the ignition and activated the vehicle's central locking. Although she was safe here, with all the officers nearby, the insistent feeling that the killer was nearby wouldn't go. She switched the wipers on and peered towards the building where Dr Clarice Cameron had died, taking in the row of small businesses – a hairdresser, a bakery, a café. They were closed for business although in some, twinkling Christmas lights combined with the warming glow from the streetlights to offer an incongruously merry ambiance. Despite the snow and the festive decorations, this was no Christmas card scene. How could it be, when a woman had died terrified and alone in a place where she should have felt safe? How could it be when the merriment of December had been tainted by police cars, CSI vans and the comings and goings of a team that signified tragedy?

The throngs of reporters and ghoulish passers-by added to the incongruity of the scene. Some of the journalists Queenie recognised, but in her current state she couldn't identify them. The crime scene still played before her eyes and would not be denied. Queenie sighed. The only thing she could do – the only thing she *should* do – was give it her full consideration. *That* was how they would catch this killer. She had to focus, but first, she needed just a little slice of normality – a touch of joy to ground her in reality. She jostled her phone from her pocket and swiped to open her gallery. At the sight of her husband, Craig, his black hair speckled with grey, his eyes crinkling in sheer joie de vivre as he posed cheek to cheek with their granddaughter, Ruby – their daughter's child – some of the panic left her. The little girl who, since Billi's death, was their responsibility. Ruby brought joy to their lives every day, but she was hard work – sometimes too hard for her and Craig to cope with. But not coping wasn't an option. Not coping wasn't something either she or Craig would give in to. Just like neither of them would rest till they knew who killed their daughter.

Queenie, focusing on the images of her savagely reduced family, smiled at the photos of Ruby – in a tiara and bright yellow Wellies, in a dinosaur outfit, in a nappy, at bath time, reading a picture book with focused concentration. Then there were the images of Billi – cuddling Ruby, in her Goth phase, as a baby, dressed for her prom with Queenie and Craig looking on in proud happiness.

With a sniff, Queenie put the phone on the dashboard, cranked the heat up and leaned back on the headrest. She blanked out the darkening sky and the outside activity and allowed her impressions of the scenes that had distressed her so much, to reveal their secrets. At times like this, when the images were so brilliantly clear – so horrifically vibrant in her mind – she felt like Tom Cruise in that film where he stood in front of a screen and used his hands to pull images to the front and send others offscreen. This was exactly what Queenie did as she filtered image by image seeking out anomalies, noting similarities and storing them in various labelled cubbyholes in her mind. Snatching out nuggets from other scenes, other cubbyholes her truly magnificent mind had visited in the past. Duplicating information verbatim and thrusting it to the forefront of her brain. That was her true skill. The ability to uncover the important stuff and dispatch the trivia.

Whilst she was doing this nothing else intruded. It was as if a translucent shield slotted between the images and her emotions – creating a sort of fuzzy disconnect that, for now, allowed her to use her curse, her superpower, for the greater good. Of course, later on when the lights were off and sleep was just about to embrace her the shield would dissolve and the monsters would invade. It was then that her superpower drained her and became the curse. It made her vulnerable, physically and emotionally. It was then she was most at risk of throwing herself over the edge and ending it all. But not anymore. Not now there was only herself and Craig to look after Ruby.

Nobody watching Queenie would realise the dark places she went to in her head, but she was oblivious to that as she unleashed the data her amazing brain had stored. A cropped image of the snow globe cupped in Clarice Cameron's amputated hands insistently shuffled every other one out of the way, telling Queenie that this was her priority for now. But what did it mean to the investigation? Its persistent presence told Queenie it was important, so she allowed her thoughts to wander, asking herself questions and considering different angles.

What had that ornament meant to Clarice? Perhaps its importance to the victim was what had prompted the killer to use it as a prop? An impulsive gesture, to throw them off track? Was that what her mind was telling her – that the globe was a red herring? She frowned and shook her head. No, that wasn't right. It was important and that's why it had obliterated every vision in order to grab her focus. That's how this worked – she knew this well enough by now. She changed tack and considered why the killer had chosen the globe. What had it meant to the killer? What was their motivation in using that specific prop? It seemed unlikely that the killer had brought it with him, but who knew? Perhaps he had – they couldn't discount that as a theory yet. Which meant she had to consider *why* he might bring a prop like that with him – because it had significance to both him and Clarice? Or was it a message for Jazzy? Definitely worth finding out the history of that globe – but Jazzy would be on that.

For now, Queenie focused on whether the globe linked in any way to the Clarks' murders, Jazzy's mum's death or any of the other killings they'd identified as possibly being committed by their killer. She shifted her mind's eye to various mental folders and, starting in chronological order with Jazzy's mum's crime scene photos, she scrolled through the images of the various victims she'd become acquainted with over the past few days. She was convinced that if a link could be drawn between the murders, then the snow globe might be the catalyst that plotted the murderous route from Hansa Solanki's death fifteen years ago to those of Elspeth Tait, Ged Pollard, the Delaney-Smiths, Matt Fraser, the Gillies, the Clarks and now Clarice Cameron's.

Although Jazzy's mum's death had been classed as accidental, there was a proliferation of crime scene photos from the entire house. Queenie selected the correct folder from her mind and began to filter out the irrelevant ones – those from the sordid cell Jazzy and her siblings called a bedroom and the ones that catalogued the blood seepage in the living room and recorded the subsequent journey the kids had made when they dragged their mother from the living room down the hallway and into her bedroom. She pressed a mental pause button there, sent the other images flying back to their respective folders and slowed the scrolling to a snail's pace.

When she'd first witnessed these photos, a searing rage had surged through her as she imagined the horror that Jazzy had experienced. No bairn should ever experience something like that. This time, the anger that thrummed through every sinew was just as sharp, just as poignant but somehow Queenie swallowed it down and focused on her job. That was the best way to help her newfound friend and colleague.

When the images showed the bloated figure of Hansa Solanki sprawled on the filthy double bed and the familiar post-mortem mutilation with the clothes pegs, Queenie zoomed in and studied the image inch by inch. Whichever of the twins had passed the time by mutilating their dead mother's body – Simon, most likely, according to Jazzy – they'd been almost reverential in some aspects of their care. The way a hairbrush was positioned next to the head and the tangle-free hair indicated that time had been taken to brush it. The smattering of plastic petals around the head and over the chest, again spoke to an almost religious type funereal activity.

Juxtaposing that though, were those bloody clothes pegs, grossly attached to Hansa Solanki's tongue, nose and earlobes – what was that all about? Queenie flitted her attention to Hansa's hands, but there was nothing there – no ornament, no photograph, nothing that hinted at a link between the subsequent murders – the only thing were those pegs. Those pegs, Jazzy's stalker, the significant murder dates and the tin of beans at the Clarks' crime scene.

She thought for a moment. *Perhaps it doesn't need to be the hands.* She brought the images from the other crime scenes and nodded. The only one with a prop positioned in the victim's hands was at Clarice Cameron's crime scene. She brought the Solanki scene to the forefront and continued her perusal. It took a while, but then it hit her.

She homed in on the item on the dressing table behind Hansa Solanki's shoulder and smiled. She'd seen something similar before – in Jazzy's home, tucked away like a guilty secret on a top shelf in the corner of her living room. She'd asked Jazzy about it and was told it was a mandir – a small ornate replica of a Hindu temple that followers of the religion used for prayer at home. Jazzy had said her parents had given it to her when she moved out of their home and Queenie realised she was talking about her adoptive parents, not her birth mum. Now, the presence of a mandir in Hansa Solanki's bedroom combined with the immature religious aspects in the way Hansa had been looked after in death, took on new meaning.

Although the globe still felt significant to Queenie, this new information seemed more pertinent. Excitement overtook her anxiety as she retrieved images from each of the other crime scenes. This time though, instead of focusing on close-ups of the corpses and their immediate surroundings, she panned out and took a mental inventory of the wider area. Exhausted, but satisfied, she finally whammed her hands on the steering wheel, before doing a wiggly sitting-down dance that shook the car. She didn't care. She had something worth sharing with the team – with Jazzy. Something that they could use to track their killer.

Now with absolute certainty, she knew these crimes were linked – every single one of the murders that Janine Gorman had highlighted shared a common characteristic. This wasn't random. It was personal. Personal and significant to the killer *and* to Jazzy, although she hadn't picked up on it because they'd been blindsided by the personal items positioned near the bodies: Clarice Cameron's snow globe, the photo of Elsbeth Tait with her daughter, the broken mug with Best Teacher on it beside Ged Pollard, the Home sweet Home sign near the Delaney-Smiths, the huge glass jar of penny sweets beside Matt Fraser and the syringe and pill bottle beside the Gillies. Although Queenie was convinced that each of those held significance for the killer, they were already there, in the victims' homes. Their purpose was to deliver a message to the victims.

However, Queenie was convinced that what linked each of these murders to the others was what the killer *brought* to the scene. The importance of the overarching religiosity, as demonstrated by the offerings in the form of flowers and gifts and the ritualistic positioning of the victims, was consolidated by the fact that Queenie had identified religious artefacts that she was certain had been left by the killer. It was that act – the act of bringing something to the scene and then leaving it behind that was conclusive. He'd brought a religious item to each scene that, for whatever reason, held significance for him. Perhaps he was religious or perhaps, like his sister, Simon was railing against the futility of faith. The logic of it didn't matter. What did, though, was that solid police work would be able to link these items to their killer. He'd made a mistake!

Just to be sure, Queenie shut her eyes and went through the images she'd isolated from each scene. In Hansa Solanki's bedroom the mandir, nestled with its incense holder and small statues of Ganesh and Lakshmi amid a flurry of plastic petals similar to those scattered over her body, were a clear demonstration of the dead woman's faith. Even in children so young, their mum's faith had been part of their developing belief systems. Queenie knew Jazzy wasn't religious. That she pushed against it and who could blame her? Her childhood had been hellish. However, her attitude might not be one shared by her siblings.

Perhaps, as he grew older, Simon's fascination with death and religion became integral to his way of life.

Certain that she was right, Queenie cast a last sweep over the images she held in her head and nodded. Hidden among a range of ornaments on the shelves in Elsbeth Tait's bedroom was a small ornately carved wooden crucifix – the only religious artefact in the entire house. Peeking from beneath the counter of Matt Fraser's shop, like they had been ripped apart, were scattered rosary beads. Beside the TV in Francis and Ellen Gillies' home lay a framed bodhi leaf, glass side up, which Queenie knew was a Buddhist symbol of enlightenment. Tucked half under the fruit bowl on the dining table in teacher Ged Pollard's home was a ceramic plaque decorated with a small brightly coloured footprint. Queenie had seen similar ones on the wall in Jazzy's kitchen, each with a different Hindu symbol on them.

A Google search told Queenie that this one was a symbol of prosperity attributed to the Goddess Lakshmi. A blank postcard featuring an image of the Vatican stuck by a jaunty bagpipe magnet now seemed incongruous beside the torn-off shopping lists, the recycling schedule and a well-worn recipe for chocolate muffins in the Delaney-Smith household. In the Clarks' kitchen the killer had left a rotund Buddha beside the aloe vera plant on the windowsill, his benevolent eye horrified by the carnage inside and in the latest scene in Clarice Cameron's office, there for all to see but so easily ignored was the Ichthys or Jesus fish decal on the window among the twinkling Christmas lights.

The forensics for each of those items would be reassessed and witnesses from each of the individual cases re-interviewed to confirm Queenie's suspicion that these items had been brought to the scene by the killer. It was all about joining dots and formulating a cohesive and watertight case to ensure that justice was served for each of those victims.

As exhaustion hit after her adrenalin rush, Queenie took a moment to reconnect with the present. She closed the crime scenes down, sending them to their respective storage units. Then, as if to lock them firmly away, she stuck her earbuds in, selected a track and, with her eyes closed, matched her breathing to the calming sounds of waves rolling onto a beach and allowed the toxicity of the previous half hour to drain from her body. When she felt better – more in her own body and mind, she picked up her phone and dialled Jazzy's number. 'I've found the links – we just need to piece it all together now. But just check where that globe came from. It was important to her, but it was also important to the killer.'

Chapter 43

'So?' Queenie's tone was abrupt, her glare accusing as she hurled the word at Jazzy before she'd even swung her long legs into the passenger seat, far less slammed the door shut.

Under the guise of unfastening her coat and getting comfy in the overheated vehicle, Jazzy took a minute to observe her partner. Queenie stared blankly through the windscreen, tapping the steering wheel in sharp jerky movements whilst her leg kept time with her fingers, juddering up and down as if to expel all the excess energy surging through her body. In profile, the tension wrapped round her was palpable. Her lips were thinned, emphasising the wrinkled dips and lines that bore testimony to past traumas and that radiated from the sides of her mouth as if gouged there by rivers of molten lava. The same effect was replicated around her eyes and forehead and her spiked hair drooped as if deflated. If she could just let go of the tautness in her upper body, Jazzy was sure her shoulders would slump in a slithery heap.

She got it. Queenie was barely holding on to her control. Adrenalin had kept her going and allowed her to do her job, but now that the urgency was gone she was in danger of collapsing.

Jazzy rummaged in her coat pocket and extracted a bottle of

water, which she offered to Queenie. 'Here, this'll help. You need to hydrate.'

Queenie's scowl deepened as she turned, chin raised, and snorted. 'Water, fucking water? You think that's what I need, JayZee. No, you're wrong, hen. What I need is to get these bloody images out of ma heid.' She thwacked her knuckles three times, hard on the top of her head, then with a tut that spoke volumes, accepted the water.

Jazzy waited until she'd downed half the bottle and a satisfying flush of pink had spread over Queenie's cheeks before speaking. 'You were right, Queenie. You smashed it! The globe was gifted to her by . . .' she grinned and nudged Queenie with her elbow '. . . a previous patient. One, according to her partner, she'd always felt she let down. With Fenton and Geordie having access to the twins' records, it was easy to discover that Clarice Cameron was Naomi Tait's therapist for a few months before Naomi was re-fostered after Elsbeth's murder . . . it's all beginning to make sense, isn't it?'

Queenie nodded. 'And the religious stuff?'

'I sent the details to Fenton and Geordie, so hopefully by the time we hotfoot it back to the station they'll have managed to contact relatives or officers or acquaintances of the other victims to confirm that they didn't belong to the victims. I doubt we'll get much if any forensic evidence from them. They may not have been examined in detail because there were so many other items at the scenes. They may not have been kept, but who knows? We might get lucky. You're a star, Queenie. A bloody star.'

Although Queenie's grin wasn't up to her usual hundred-watt offering, Jazzy was satisfied that she was recovering – at least physically – from her deep delve into the crime scenes. She wasn't naïve enough to assume that her partner could just switch off what she'd seen or that those images wouldn't creep up on her and bite her when she least expected it. No, she'd too much experience of sweat-sodden sheets, hammering hearts and laboured middle-of-the-night breathing after jolting awake in the dark to an intrusive memory that somehow seemed more vivid and threatening than every other midnight monster. Just as well Queenie had such a supportive husband waiting for her at home. Jazzy had no doubt that Craig McQueen had responding to his wife's night terrors down to a fine art.

The knowledge that her sacrifice had paid off revitalised Queenie – or maybe it was the water? Jazzy didn't care. The lines etched in her face seemed to smooth out and even her previously floppy hair had perked up as Queenie exhaled a long breath. 'Right, Jazz Queens, get this show on the damn road.'

Chapter 44

They were back in the incident room in Livingston. Elliot, caught up in meetings with the high-heid yins had instructed Queenie and Jazzy to update the rest of the team. The journey from Armadale back to Livingston had calmed Queenie – or maybe the speed at which she drove or the non-stop cusses and gripes about the ineptitude of other motorists had helped dissipate the adrenalin. Whatever it was, Jazzy had been relieved when they arrived back safely and glad that, at least on the surface, the old irascible Queenie was back.

After Queenie's lengthy update, Fenton, a frown puckering his brow, said uncertainly, 'So, we're *certain* it's the same killer. No doubt at all?'

Jazzy opened her mouth then, unsure why Fenton sounded so doubtful, she closed it again, with a shake of her head. What was he thinking? *That the decapitations at both the Clarks and Clarice Cameron's crime scenes were random? That they had two sick fuckers roaming West Lothian?* She glanced at Geordie, whose lips were a twisted grimace and then back to Fenton who, seemingly oblivious to the stupidity of his question, waited for a response.

Hands pinching her waist and legs spread wide as if to cement her to the floor, Queenie resembled a fully clothed sumo wrestler.

Her voice boomed through the room, each word dripping with sarcasm. 'What do you mean are we sure? Are *you* not looking at the same crime scene photos as us, Haggis, son? Ah mean, does the decapitated heid no' give ye a wee clue, like? Or maybe where you come from lopping off body parts is standard behaviour. Hanging clothes pegs on a victim's tongue is routine, eh? Leaving stuff at the crime scene is normal? Is that it? Every murder scene you've ever attended has that degree of brutality, does it? That visceral cruelty? That depraved detail? You never heard of an MO? MO . . . DUS OPER . . . AND I?' With the stretching of the last two words, Queenie's voice crescendoed enough to shatter glass. 'That is, in case you're not certain, the specific wee sick tweaks the killer performs at a crime scene. Never heard of it, eh?'

Taking pity on Haggis whose distressed plump face resembled a squashed tomato, Jazzy intervened. 'It was rhetorical, Queenie. Give him a break. Fenton knows what an MO is and he knows that the crimes are linked.'

She looked at Fenton, the slight gathering of her brow indicating that she wasn't one hundred per cent convinced of her assertion. 'Don't you?'

Fumbling for words, Fenton began nodding so fast it looked like his head might fall off. 'Aye, rhetorical like. Course it was. I'm no' stupid, you know? I just meant . . .' He splayed his hands in front of him, his frantic nods now replaced by a slow headshake, his words delivered on a melancholy sob: 'I've never been to a murder scene before. Never been on a murder investigation either and . . . what sick bastard would do the likes of this? It's beyond sick, it's like a horror movie gone wrong. I've never seen anything like this. *Never!* And statistics say it's unlikely two separate killers killed the Clarks and Clarice Cameron. I get that. But . . . for one person to do all this . . .?' He exhaled, his frown deepening.

Queenie clouted him on the shoulder. 'You know, I'm seriously reconsidering letting you join the Jazz Queens. Not sure you're either JayZee *or* Queenie enough to be part of oor troupe. Not like Geordie here.' She turned her attention to the taller lad. 'He's whipping into shape reasonably nicely, that right, son? You'll make a good Jazz Queen in time, eh?'

As the grin faded from Geordie's lips, Fenton's squashed-tomato face bloomed into an explosion of beetroot purple.

Jazzy sighed. 'Redeem yourself, Fenton. Tell us something that your weird computer-magic has come up with. Something that will make us think your place on our supposedly dunce team wasn't, in fact, well earned.'

Fenton flinched and ducked his head as if to avoid one of Queenie's nudges or worse a skelp round his lugs. 'I mean like. I know it's the same killer. I'm just saying we need to *prove* it, don't we? That's our job, isn't it, and well – there are . . . whatchamacallits?'

He looked at Geordie, snapping his fingers as if he expected the taller lad to magically supply the words he was looking for, but Geordie – looking blank – shrugged. 'You're on your own, mate. No idea what you're on about.'

With a nervous glance at the glowering Queenie, Fenton swallowed hard, his words spilling out in a rush. 'Inconsistencies, that's it. There're inconsistencies and we need to look at those, don't we?'

Queenie narrowed her eyes and rocked on her heels. 'Ah, so my wee Haggis has got balls, does he? Go on then, Haggis. I'm all ears.'

Still looking like a deer in the headlights, Fenton swallowed and slugged a gulp of water, wiping away the drops that trickled down his chin. 'Well, some of the scenes didn't have the clothes pegs, did they? Delaney-Smiths and the Gillies' ones. Just wondering what that means for the MO?'

That little gem hadn't escaped Jazzy's notice either. They had discussed it when they'd initially perused Janine Gorman's list and scrutinised the crime scene photos, but the feel of the scenes, the other mutilation of the bodies, had convinced her to keep them in the mix. Now, with the items that Queenie had homed in on, she was glad she had.

Queenie snorted as Fenton puffed up his chest and took a moment to collect his thoughts. 'Right. Well, as soon as you sent me the victim ID, I searched for any mention of the artefacts DC McQueen specified.' He turned to check his tablet – and listed the religious items Queenie had flagged up.

Queenie glared at him. 'And?'

On a roll, Fenton bounced on his chair. 'Well, they were noted in each evidence log as being found in the vicinity of the bodies; however, there was no forensic follow-up on them – probably because the investigators assumed they belonged to the victims and they had so much to process from each scene. Also, because each incident was treated as an isolated crime, they didn't consider any serial killer traits or behaviour.'

Haggis risked a glance at Queenie, which sent his colour skyrocketing again. He swallowed audibly, his Adam's apple wobbling, before he continued with his stammering explanation of what he'd discovered. 'I decided, well we . . .'

He glanced at Geordie, his eyes pleading with his mate to intervene, but Geordie just grinned from where he was rocking on the back two legs of a chair. 'You got this, mate. On ye go.'

Again, with the swallow and the jiggly Adam's apple. 'Me and Geordie decided that – you know like? In the interests of expediency to sidestep the investigative team and go straight to the next of kin or the key witnesses to see if they can provide additional information in light of our findings. We're reaching out to witnesses from all these cases and DI Balloch sanctioned us requesting that local uniforms make initial contact. That's ongoing and we're awaiting their reports.'

He looked up, clearly eager to share his last nugget with Jazzy and Queenie. 'With the Gillies couple being foster parents, I've requested more detailed background checks on not only them, but on their former foster kids. Their initial murder investigation didn't throw up any drug-related crimes and because the SIO on that investigation couldn't work out the significance of the pills and syringe, they brushed it off as an unrelated coincidence.'

All but bouncing on his chair now, Fenton shook his head. 'You go, Geordie.'

Geordie stretched, his T-shirt coming away from his jeans, exposing two knobbly rows of ribs. 'Aye right. Well, Simon Smith's unsealed social service records revealed that after entering foster care, Simon was given a name change. He became Josh Bentley. He was in and out of foster care, group homes and in a lot of trouble – petty theft, breaking windows, under-age drinking – until, on his sixteenth birthday, he dropped out of the system completely. Now this is the interesting thing. His records show that he spent a two-year period between the ages of eight and ten with the Gillies family. But, we haven't been able to get a current ID on him yet. We're working on that. So, we have a definite link between him and two of the previous five cases – Elsbeth Tait was his twin's – you're siter Mhairi's – foster mum and the Gillies were his foster parents.'

Fenton grinned. 'So, Queenie reckons that the killer brought the religious items with him, but that he selected a personal belonging from the murder site as some sort of message. This got me thinking about Matt Fraser. He owned a corner shop that mainly catered for the nearby school, selling sweets and stuff, plus, his shop was near a school so he probably got lots of schoolkids going into the shop. Maybe Simon intersected with him there.'

'Good work. That's a possible point of contact. Fenton, you need to check if Simon attended that school or another nearby one, or lived near Matt Fraser.' Thinking back to the community centre they'd passed in Armadale she added, 'Or a community centre, for that matter. There's no doubt Simon intersected with each of these victims at some point. His link to Elsbeth Tait is obvious. She was his twin sister's foster mother, but there must be a link to the others too.'

'So . . .' Geordie paused, shuffled on his chair. 'Erm, Jazzy, confirmation has just come in that Naomi Tait or Mhairi seems to have gone off the grid. Perhaps changed her name again. Wouldn't be surprised, after having her foster mum murdered too. We're working on locating her.'

Momentarily annoyed that Geordie hadn't led with that information, Jazzy glared at him, then relented. It wasn't an easy thing to have to tell her, but he'd done it now. She wasn't sure how to deal with that information. It was hardly a surprise to her, yet it felt strange. Her heart went out to the sister who had lost not one but two mums in such awful circumstances and she prayed they found her before Simon did. For a few moments silence reigned. Then Jazzy thrust that to the back of her mind. She couldn't let that affect how she did her job. She'd consider her emotions later on when she was at home alone.

As she sipped her water, Jazzy did a mental run-through of everything they need to follow up on. She snapped her fingers. 'Okay, how are we getting on with the list of people connected with the Clarks' murder investigation who could conceivably be Simon?'

Fenton raised a hand. 'The team scrolling through the footage that Wullie Hobson took outside the house also looked at neighbours and the Clarks' acquaintances. The first list came up with a quite a few possibilities, including some of our own and by that, I mean CSIs, officers, paramedics. To be fair, the parameters are pretty wide – twenty-one-year-old male with no specifics on height, body type, distinguishing features or anything else. I then used an algorithm to exclude people whose history shows definitively that they've either always lived in West Lothian or have never been in the foster system. Here's the names.' He pressed a key on his laptop and a list appeared on the white screen at the front of the room.

Jazzy moved closer and scrolled down the names. A couple she recognised as CSIs. Alongside one police officer, whose name she didn't recognise, was a familiar one – Geordie McBurnie. She met his gaze, noticing that his sculpted cheekbones were pink. Geordie, gangly and slender didn't appear anything like the image of her stalker she'd seen on the security recording. However, Geordie was a drag queen in his spare time and was into amateur dramatics. Could he conceivably be the killer? Her gut said no. She liked Geordie. But a flicker of doubt persisted. Calmly she quirked an eyebrow at him. 'Well?'

Geordie's lips tightened for a second, then he flung his hands up. 'I entered the foster system at six, just like your brother. But my ma died of a drug overdose. It wasn't long till my auntie found me and took me to Stùrrach where I lived till I turned sixteen. I'm not your brother and I've already done a DNA test to prove it, but I insisted, in the interests of transparency that Fenton keep my name there. I'll remove myself from the team if you want.'

Jazzy studied Geordie. His gaze was unflinching as he met hers, but his right leg bobbed up and down, revealing his nervousness. She exhaled and shook her head. 'I can't lose you from our team. Queenie would never forgive me if I reduced the Jazz Queens quartet to a trio, especially when you're the only one who can hold a tune, bar Queenie. Besides, no way was my brother ever going to be as tall as you.'

She turned her attention to the other names on the list:

Danny Banik (Imogen's boyfriend)

Philip Jamieson (the reporter)

Dwayne Taggart (brother of a rape victim who blames Jazzy for the rapist getting off)

PC Conrad Lee (first officer on scene at the Clarks' murders)

Jazzy visualised her interactions with each of the people on the list. Which one of them wanted their revenge on her? Which of those young men hated her so much they were prepared to go to such lengths? A shiver rattled up her spine and those damn maggots started their dance again. *When the hell is this going to end?*

Fenton clearing his throat alerted her to the fact he wanted to add something, so Jazzy exhaled and then nodded. 'On you go, Fenton.'

'Thing is, Jazzy, I then wondered if the reason Simon has reappeared in your life now, after no contact for over a year, is because his twin is also nearby, so, in order to cover all bases, I widened that algorithm to include all staff.'

Jazzy frowned. 'You think Mhairi's nearby?'

Fenton shrugged. 'Just niggled me a bit that after a lengthy break, Simon's come back with a vengeance. Wondered if something triggered that. Then, I thought, if Simon can find you so easily then Mhairi can too. I mean, you haven't changed your name and there was . . .' he wafted his hand in the air and looked at his PC rather than Jazzy '. . . that newspaper crap. I just thought she might have been curious about you, that's all, and he might have followed her back to you again. After all, he killed Mhairi's foster mum, didn't he? Who's to say the possibility of her reconnecting with you wasn't the catalyst for this massive escalation?'

Jazzy thought his logic a bit far-fetched, but he clearly felt he had found something. If she'd been able to identify either of her siblings, she would have reached out to them, but she'd have made sure she found out more about them first. Could her sister have done that? Could she, after all the trauma she'd suffered, finally have found Jazzy and wanted to reconnect? Whilst not definite it was something to consider. 'Go on. What did . . .'

Before she'd finished speaking a list of women appeared on the screen – all of them known to Jazzy:

Ginny Bell (journalist)
Ivory (Ivor) McCafferty (Stùrrach resident)
Franny Gallagher (CSI Manager)
Janine Gorman (Civilian Analyst, Police Scotland)

Each name was like a body blow to Jazzy. She hadn't realised that so many of her acquaintances had been in the foster system. This was bizarre! As she stared at the names she considered Fenton's logic.

Could any of these women – women she'd met and interacted

with – be her sister? 'Have we located these women yet?'

'Working on it, Jazzy. Franny was at the crime scene in Armadale, and is being escorted here. DI Balloch says he'll interview her when she arrives. We're sending someone to Stùrrach to check on Ivor, Janine Gorman's on a break and Ginny Bell is still AWOL since her blog post.'

'Shite, JayZee, she's a likely candidate, isn't she? After all, she was the only journalist the killer contacted. Maybe that was the sick bastard's way of reaching out to his sister. She could be the one. Where the hell has the sneaky wee bitch gone?' Queenie shoved her hands in her trouser pockets and rocked back and forth on the balls of her feet.

Queenie was right. Of all of them, Ginny was by far the most likely candidate, but Jazzy was unconvinced, although she was concerned over the journalist's safety. When she thought about it, Ginny had reached out to her at the Clarks' crime scene, which fitted Fenton's hypothesis. It was another avenue that had to be explored, no matter how unlikely it seemed. Jazzy wouldn't forgive herself if any of these women died because of her. Still, that didn't mean she was Jazzy's long-lost sister. In fact, Jazzy couldn't see anything in the journalist that reminded her of Mhairi – but it had been a long time, after all.

'Locating Bell is a priority – whether or not she's my sister, she is at risk. The killer has been in contact with her and she may well be his next victim. Get on that, Geordie.'

With Franny accounted for, that left Ivor and Janine. 'Is Janine in the building?'

Fenton grimaced. 'She's not replied to my emails and when I went to find her one of the other crime analysts said she was at lunch.'

On any other day and on any other case, this might not have been overly concerning to Jazzy, but today it jarred. She exchanged a glance with Queenie who rubbed her palm up her nose, her frown one of concentration. 'What are you thinking, Queenie?'

'I'm thinking what you're thinking, hen.'

'Which is?' Geordie raised his voice as the pair of them headed for the door. 'You gonna share it with us?'

But he was talking to thin air as the door slammed behind them.

He turned to Fenton. 'Well, that was just rude!'

But Fenton, still in a huff with his mate for his earlier defection to Camp Queenie, shrugged and turned back to his screen.

Chapter 45

Scurrying on her shorter legs to keep up with Jazzy, Queenie kept up an annoying monologue about how stupid they'd been.

'Too good to be true. All that sooking up with her analysis and being your new best friend and magicking those cases out of her arse quick as a magician with a wee bunny rabbit like she was a bloody genius. That woman knows who you are and that her twinnie is a sociopathic killer and now the chances are she's either gone after him for killing her mum or he's caught her.'

Jazzy ignored her and ploughed on through any obstacles in her path. She could have pointed out that not two minutes earlier Queenie had been convinced Ginny Bell was her sister, yet now she was convinced Janine was. At this point Jazzy didn't know either way; however, she had a duty of care to all the people on Fenton's list and she wanted to be sure that Janine was safe – finding out if they were related would come later. Her brain felt fried with too much information. Why hadn't Mhairi – whatever her new identity was – reached out to her? Surely, she'd know that Jazzy would help her. Why all the cloak-and-dagger stuff? An ice-cold shiver started at the base of Jazzy's spine and worked its way upwards. The weight of responsibility was dislodged by a bolt of chilly anger. How could her sister have been so irresponsible?

'Should've fucking known she was a duplicitous cowbag. Imagine the information she could have shared. The time we could have saved.' Queenie's tone was becoming angrier and angrier with every step they took.

With fear smouldering in her chest and fanned by Queenie's incessant mithering, Jazzy barely managed to smother the desire to scream in the faces of fellow officers and personnel staff as she elbowed them out of her way in her haste to reach the analyst's office.

'You can't trust civilians. Always said that. They're a' the same. After all that's when most of our clientele come from isn't it. The civilian population? If it wasn't for civilians being criminals, we wouldn't have a job.'

Panting now, Jazzy ground to a halt outside the door to the open-plan office where Janine Gorman was based and tried to slow her breathing. No point in going in all guns blazing – especially not if Gorman was still AWOL. 'For God's sake, Queenie, give it a break. We don't know which, if any, of the women on that list are actually Mhairi. This isn't an exercise in blame; it's about making sure they're all safe. That's all.'

But Queenie wasn't listening. 'Civilian implies civil, orderly, well behaved, but judging by most of the scrotes and bawbags we encounter on a frigging daily basis, that's a bloody gross misnomer, a bloody travesty, a damn word designed to lull us polis into a false sense o' security. We never should have let the buggers infiltrate our ranks. Never. Phew, civilian staff? Bloody might as well open the prisons and recruit from there, eh?'

Jazzy glared at Queenie. 'Will you just shut the F up, Queenie? You're doing my head in and I can't think. You need to wheesht.'

Mouth open, Queenie glared back at Jazzy, then taking time to emphasise her displeasure, she worked her shoulders up and back, folded her arms under her chest and gave a slow eye-roll that any teenager would be proud of. Lips pursed, she huffed and then made a huge show of exhaling so hard, it caused Jazzy's fringe to waft. 'Ah was only saying. No need to get yer breeks in a bloody fankle, is there?'

Jazzy ignored her and pushed the door open. 'Let me do the talking, right? We don't want to worry anyone.'

Another eye-roll, but Queenie lifted her fingers to her mouth and twisted them as if locking a door. At a glance, it was clear that Janine's desk was empty, but what chilled Jazzy even more was the fact that it was almost entirely bare, as if its owner had no intention of returning to it. What was going on? If Janine had tidied her desk for the holidays, she hadn't mentioned it. Jazzy strode towards the desk nearest to Janine's and ignoring the fact that the man sitting there had headphones on and was clearly engrossed in his work, she tapped him on the shoulder. His exaggerated jump, hands raised to his chest, his mouth half open as he swung his chair round was, for the degree of surprise emanating from a slight shoulder tap in a busy workplace, unwarranted. 'Oh my God, you startled me.'

No time for niceties, Jazzy got to the point. 'We're looking for Janine. Any idea where she is?'

Mr Surprised frowned, his mouth pursed in a moue of distaste as if she'd just asked him what colour his underwear was. 'Janine?'

He tapped one well-manicured finger on his lower lip and tilted his head to one side before replying seconds before Jazzy shook a response from him. 'She's gone.'

'Give me fucking strength . . .' Queenie's low rumble from behind Jazzy drew Mr Surprised's attention. His eyes widened and he rolled his chair backwards, clearly under the mistaken belief that that would protect him from the wrath of Queenie. Casting nervous glances in her direction, he spoke to Jazzy. 'She left around lunchtime. She's popular today – I've already had to tell another detective that.'

'Okay, so where did she go?' Although she had never felt less like it, Jazzy forced herself to smile, but she suspected that it was the way Queenie moved abreast of her and squared up, her flashing eyes making it clear that she meant business that encouraged his speedy response.

'No idea. She didn't say and to be honest, she keeps herself to herself.' He pursed his lips. 'She's a bit standoffish, you know? Wouldn't take part in the office Secret Santa. Can you believe it? Soooo antisocial and' – he wafted his hand round the room – 'we're such a friendly lot.'

'If you're that friendly, maybe one of you might know her home address?'

'Oh well, that's confidential stuff. I'm not sure . . . You could ask . . .'

Queenie took another step closer, crowding him, a low growl emanating from deep in her throat like a dog about to attack.

Flushing, he turned to his computer. 'Aye, right. I could save you the time. I mean it is official business isn't it, so I'm not breaking any rules? We've got one of those bad-weather round robins so we can give each other lifts in an emergency.' His fingers flew over the keyboard and a document opened on screen.

Jazzy stepped forward and ran her finger down the list till she got Gorman's home address. 'Punching it into her phone, she swung away from Mr Surprised throwing an abrupt 'Thanks' over her shoulder, and, with Queenie, retraced her steps.

'She lives in Dedridge. Not too far away. Let's hope we've got this wrong and she's home with flu or skiving off Christmas shopping or something. I'll get a uniform to check it out.'

But before she had a chance to issue her order her phone rang. *Benjy!* She was tempted to let it go to answerphone, but reconsidered. They still had no word on Ivor's safety and she'd promised him he could ring her at any time. Maybe he had something important to share. She flipped her phone to speaker. 'Hey, Benjy. Can't talk long but . . .'

'It's Ivor. She's been taken or . . .' The sound of wheezing came over the line, obscuring Benjy's next words.

'Benjy, Benjy, stop walking. You're breaking up. Stand still and talk to me. Where are you?'

'Same man . . . sure of it. Almost certain.'

'Shit, Benjy, stop. Tell me where you are. We'll come to you.'

'. . . in . . . car . . . not sure . . . Stùrrach.' Then the line went dead.

Fuck. Cold dread focusing her, Jazzy pushed Queenie towards the lifts. 'You head to the car; I'll grab our coats and update the others.'

Not waiting to see if Queenie was obeying her orders, Jazzy took off, her long legs making short work of the distance back to her office and, within minutes, she was sliding into the passenger seat beside Queenie and bundling their belongings on the back seat. 'Step on it. You get us there as quick as you can. Fenton's sending a couple of officers to check out Janine Gorman's address and another couple to Stùrrach. I'll keep trying Benjy.'

But every time she tried Benjy's phone it rung out and as the slush-filled roads and snow-covered fields sped by, Jazzy's heart sank lower and lower. What had happened to Ivor and Benjy? Had the killer targeted them because of her? Had Ivor been taken by the killer? Was Ivor her sister? *Come on, Benjy, come on, Ivor, you've got to be okay.*

Chapter 46

By the time Jazzy and Queenie arrived at Stùrrach, darkness had fallen, casting a freezing air over the creepy deserted village. Light from the Argy Bargy illuminated the white sleety street, throwing strange shadows over the Badlands, giving the discarded fridges and deserted vehicles the look of huge threatening statues. Queenie drove past the space where they'd parked only a few nights earlier, whilst Jazzy peered through the windscreen, looking for any trace of either Benjy or Ivor, but it was impossible to see clearly.

Before Queenie had fully braked, Jazzy flung her door open and jumped out, striding through the snow, towards the pub. Within seconds, she thrust the door open and strode inside only to grind to a halt. *What the actual hell?* The Argy Bargy was nothing like she'd expected. There was no spit and sawdust, no choking smoky smell, no latrine aroma, no dark dingy corners, no sticky lino. Behind her, Queenie tumbled into the room, almost knocking Jazzy flying in her haste. 'Jeez. Oh, I wisnae expecting this, were you, JayZee?'

A woman with a riot of auburn hair and a wide smile looked at them, a mild frown gathering on her forehead as she placed the glass she'd been polishing down on a gleamingly clean bar.

Hands on hips, head to one side, she dialled back her smile. 'Can I help you?'

'Is that mince and tatties I smell?' Queenie sniffed the air like a hunting dog scenting a fox and rubbed her belly. 'Ah've no had mah lunch yet.'

It was true the fragrant scent of mince and tatties filled the room, making even Jazzy's tummy rumble, but that wasn't why they were there. They needed to find Benjy. Yes, the pub's gleaming interior with its hint of lemon floating in the air was appealing.

She nudged Queenie and stepped forward, glancing at the few customers dotted at tables around the bar. They all looked like the Stùrrachers she'd come to expect, yet in this context, even their tattoos looked mellow and non-threatening, their body language relaxed and loose-limbed – at ease in their home setting. Jazzy got that. As one of only a few Asian police officers and a woman to boot, she understood the need to be on your guard when in an unfamiliar environment, in case some dick or other decided to hassle you for not being like them. Likewise, she cherished being able to fully relax when in her own space.

When they caught her eye, they nodded as politely as if she was in the Railway Inn in Cauther. This was a pub that rarely saw outsiders, let alone two police officers – one a lanky woman whose long hair was half scattered over her shoulders with only a few strands caught in her scrunchie and a stocky, spiky-haired, and equally spiky-natured, pugnacious one. Clearly, they hadn't made them for polis yet, which was good and you had to give them credit for not running a mile or chucking them out! Despite her thumping heart and the niggle at the back of her neck that radiated her fear for the young lad, Jazzy tried out a smile and hoped her voice betrayed none of the anxiety she felt. 'Anybody seen Benjy? I was on the phone to him but we got cut off. Just checking in to see . . .'

Ms Auburn Hair behind the bar, gave a soft snort. 'So, you trailed all the way out here to check on our Benjy, did you? You're not profiling him, are you?'

So, our police identities didn't go unnoticed. Despite the bar manager's smile, Jazzy doubted that Ms Auburn Hair would let them off the hook lightly and she was right. 'I've heard of you lot profiling kids. Targeting them, making assumptions based on where they live. That what you're doing with Benjy, is it? You jumping to conclusions because of . . .'

'Oh no!' Hands splayed before her, Jazzy shook her head. 'Course not. We're friends of Benjy's.'

A snort from behind her had her spinning round to meet the gaze of a huge man who lumbered to his feet, dwarfing even Jazzy. Behind her, Queenie had retreated to the bar and was mumbling something about 'Mince and tatties to go', so Jazzy was on her own. The man, as he slowly unfolded himself, took on the proportions of Hagrid, yet his narrowed eyes destroyed any notion of a gentle giant. 'Benjy isn't friends with the polis. None of us are, so maybe you should get on yer . . .'

A kerfuffle to the far side of the bar stopped him. Instead of continuing, he tutted and rolled his eyes. A door slammed and then Benjy was there, his cheeks rosy, dragging a coat onto his shoulders and glaring at the big man. 'Och, Uncle Pedro, they *are* my friends. Be nice.'

It was all Jazzy could do to stop herself from rushing over, gathering the boy up in her arms and hugging him. She'd been convinced something awful had happened to him. However, as she saw his rosy cheeks and his more than robust health, relief gave way to annoyance. 'What the hell, Benjy? We got cut off and I've been trying to phone you. What happened?'

Benjy shrugged and mumbled something. His reply was distorted by the giant sitting back down with a thunderous racket of scraping chair legs on the wooden floor. Jazzy suspected, judging by his insolent grin, that was deliberate. She ignored him and turned back to Benjy. 'What?'

'I needed a crap, okay? All the panic about Ivor made me need to go and I wasn't going to stay on the phone to you when I was having one so, I hotfooted here and left my phone at the bar.'

Ms Auburn Hair picked it up and threw it to Benjy after glancing at the screen. 'Aye, right enough, you've got a wheen of missed calls there, Benjy.'

Benjy caught it and, looking at Jazzy, his face a crumpled pie of ruby-red misery, he stepped closer and lowered his voice. 'I'm sorry, okay? I am worried about Ivor, but . . .' He glanced round the bar where everyone was watching the proceedings with avid interest, pint glasses of beer at different levels sat untended in front of them as they drunk in the entertainment. Grabbing Jazzy's hand he dragged her over to a door in the corner. 'Come on, over here. We'll go in the snug so that . . .' he raised his voice and glared at them '. . . none of these nosy bastards will be able to hear my business.'

As if his words had broken the spell, the customers launched back into whatever conversations had been interrupted and a low-level hum of background noise ebbed and flowed throughout the bar. As she followed Benjy, she heard Queenie say, 'Aye just three half portions, hen, and a Diet Coke each for us and the laddie. He looks like he needs feeding up.'

The snug was cosy with a real wood fire burning in the grate. It was then Jazzy realised how cold she was. She extended her sodden boots to the fire, enjoying the tingling sensation in her toes and watched the steam gently rise in the air. As Queenie nudged her way onto one of the comfy seats in the sectioned-off area, spilling Coke over the table, Jazzy glared at her. 'We've no time for food, Queenie. We need to find out what's gone on with Ivor and then . . .'

But Ms Auburn Hair was already there with three plates, two on one arm and a third on the other. The aroma was like nectar and as Queenie winked at her and began shovelling the mince and tatties into her face, Jazzy's stomach emitted a gargantuan rumble. *Aw fuck it, a girl has to eat!* She yanked the plate closer, unwrapped her cutlery and pointed the knife at Benjy. 'Speak. I want to know every sodding thing there is to know about what you saw with Ivor?'

Benjy dragged his fork around his plate and lifted a small bundle of mince to his mouth and chewed for a second before replying. 'We were supposed to meet up. We were . . .' He bit his lip. 'I mean we were . . .' His eyes went up and to the right as he considered what excuse to make.

Through a mouthful of food, Queenie spluttered, 'Don't you give us it, laddie. You and Ivor were going to do some amateur sleuthing. Am I right?'

He nodded.

'Yous were going to Armadale? You'd heard about the other murder?'

Again, with the nod. 'We're not nosy, we just wanted to see . . .'

'Aye, aye, aye.' Queenie wafted her fork in the air. 'Never mind that, just get on with your story.'

'We'd arranged to meet after school and I was on my way back from the bus stop to Stùrrach when I saw her in the distance. She was standing beside her car, just near the Badlands waiting for me like we'd agreed. Then another car drew up. The driver got out and approached her. I yelled but she didn't hear me. I wasn't worried until she went over to *his* car and got in the passenger seat and they drove off. Why would she do that?' Benjy's fork clattered onto his half-eaten food and he began kneading his hands together. 'We were supposed to meet up – why would she go into someone else's car and not wait for me?'

Jazzy gave him a moment as she ate her meal, before prompting him: 'Then?'

'Well, I ran towards the car, but it was driving away from me towards Whitburn.'

'What about the driver? Did you get a good look at him? Or the car? Did you get a good look at it?' Queenie's tone was encouraging. The one she used for her granddaughter, no doubt.

'Not really. But he was dressed in black . . . like that bloke in the car and in that photo you showed me. Like the one I saw at Imogen's house and he was all stooped, like that bloke in that video you showed me – like he was trying to make himself smaller. He kept looking around like he was keeping an eye out. She wouldn't just leave me hanging. Not Ivor.' His voice was higher now, piercing and laced with unshed tears. 'Why won't you believe me?'

'We do believe you, Benjy. But we have to ask questions. You know that. Now, could she not just have decided to go for a drive with a friend instead of meeting you?' Jazzy hated asking it, because it didn't ring true to her, yet she had to know.

'No, no. Ivor wouldn't do that. If she arranged to meet me, then she would. Besides, if something cropped up, she'd phone. But she hasn't. Something's not right and you two are here stuffing your faces on mince and tatties instead of looking for her. I thought you were my friends. I thought I could trust you.'

Jazzy pushed her plate away and squeezed his arm. 'We are your friends, Benjy. That's why we're here. Now, what about the car? Can you describe it? Make, reg number?'

But Benjy was shaking his head, a tear rolling down his cheek. 'I looked at the number plate, but it was covered in mud. It looked like a black or navy hatchback. That's all I can say.'

'Okay, that's fine. It's a start. Queenie, put out an APB with descriptions of the car, Ivor and the driver and get CSIs and officers along to the place where she was picked up. We might be lucky. There might be tyre tracks in the snow, or footprints or better still security cameras that caught them and, if so, we might be able to ascertain the make of the vehicle from those.' Although all of that was true, Jazzy was saying it mainly to reassure Benjy. Truth was, these things took time and the maggots in her gut told her they didn't have a lot of that.

Whilst Queenie wandered off to make her calls, Jazzy squeezed Benjy's arm. 'We'll find her, we will.'

But Benjy jumped to his feet, clicking his fingers, a wavering smile pulling his lips wide. 'I'm such an idiot. Such a bloody idiot. We've got trackers on our phones. Just me and Ivor, see?'

He fumbled with his phone and opened the app. 'Look. There's her phone you can see, she's . . .' His face fell. Ivor's phone app was active but it showed its position as a hundred yards from where Benjy said Ivor had been picked up.

Before Jazzy could console him, her phone rang. She checked the caller ID and froze for a moment. Then, with a tight smile she patted Benjy's arm. 'I need to take this. Wait there, I'll only be a tick.'

With the still-ringing phone in her hand, she rushed out of the pub and into the freezing night air. Taking time for a deep breath, she set her mobile to record before answering, her tone belying the frenzy of thrumming and drumming going on in her chest. 'Yes?'

Jazzy wasn't surprised when the strange robotic voice she'd heard before responded. 'Hello, sister dearest. Are you looking for me?'

Chapter 47

It's such a thrill to see Jazzy rushing from the pub, glaring at her phone as if she'd like nothing more than to throw it as far into the snow as she could. It doesn't take a genius to know she'll answer. Whilst *she* studies me to work out *my* modus operandi, she's only just realising that *I've* been studying *her*. My fingers run over the familiar bulbous glass shape of the charm on my necklace. It gives me comfort to touch the small Ganesh pendant so similar to the statue I left at Elsbeth Tait's home. Our mum always told us that Lord Ganesh was the remover of obstacles – turns out she was right. He certainly removed that useless piece of crap from our lives and over the years I've found that he's helped *me* to remove other obstacles from *my* life. Now, it's nearly time for the final obstacle to be destroyed, and I can't wait.

Seeing Jazzy close up through the binoculars is weird. Of course, I've observed her before, but this time it's different. This time, she knows I'm around, can sense me in the vicinity, and that gives me such a rush. True enough, she lifts her head, her eyes darting all over as she executes a slow spin to scope out the area. She sniffs and I laugh, my breath steaming before me. Maybe she can smell me? Maybe the familiarity of my scent has caught on the breeze and her animalistic wiles have registered it. Either that or she's got a sniffle.

Although I'm well hidden from her field of vision, I pull my mask over my nose, just in case. No point taking chances. Besides, some doddery old fool might stumble along and I don't want to be forced into any unnecessary killings. Not today, anyway.

As Jazzy answers, I wonder if they've found my other little offering. Nothing like scattering the troops with an attack from left field. Let's face it, they're not very bright in the first place and my pièce de résistance will surely blow their tiny minds.

'Yes.'

Even with the passage of years the sound of her voice is as familiar to me as my own. Of course, unbeknownst to her, we've interreacted many times. I feel like an invisible line joins us by our umbilical cords, pulling us together like magnets, and I wonder if she feels it too. Her curt one-word response is designed to get me talking and I'm okay with that. It's why I phoned her, after all. No matter how long I stay on the line, given time, they'll manage to isolate and trace this burner phone. They'll do that weird triangulating thing where they work backwards from her received calls and hook up to phones in the area or something – I've watched *CSI*.

'Hello, sister dearest. Are you looking for me?'

She hesitates, her gentle breath drifts over the line, slow and calm, as if she's forcing herself to relax. Her body language tells a different story, though. Out there in the cold, without her bulky coat, she shivers and wraps her free hand round her middle. A strange spasm in my chest tells me that her vulnerability has elicited an emotion in me. Not the usual anger or frustration I normally feel, but something quite different, something less grounded. It's not often that happens so I try to catch it, try to make it linger, but as usual it drifts away out of sight – an ice-blue cloud in a red sky melting in the heat from a burnt amber sun.

My therapist – well one of them, can't remember which one – taught me to visualise these rare sensations. Poor sod thought it would help me adjust and become more social, more able to react appropriately to different circumstances. It hasn't done so far and I doubt it ever will. My instinct – even now – is to laugh at a sad film. Of course, I've become adept at hiding it. Through the binoculars I continue to study her. It irks me that she's not replied to my question. I understand that it's part of her training to keep me off balance, but still it irks and the spasm I felt earlier is but a distant memory as rage swoops in, gripping my heart like a vulture's jaws, squeezing poison through my system. I *hate* her. I hate that woman, that Jazzy Solanki. She let me down. Not just me, but my twin as well. When *we* needed her she set us adrift, to navigate a world we were ill-equipped for. She allowed us to be separated, allowed us to become part of a system that hated us whilst *she* thrived.

The worst thing was, she never once looked back. *She* was our big sister; *she* was full of false promises, full of lies, full of treachery and she never *once* looked back.

An arm stretches round my shoulder pulling me into a tight embrace. My twin's scent, comforting as my tears are gently wiped away followed by a kiss on my nose. With a last squeeze of my arm, my twin nods. Behind us, faint moans and groans waft from the van, and I wish the girl with the weird name would shut up. Maybe we should have drugged her. As I look at my mirror image, so nearly identical to me, I speak to our older sister. 'No answer, Jazzy?'

I pause, expecting the token silent protest, but I can't be bothered waiting. 'Well, it's fine. You've got till three. One . . . two . . .'

'Okay, okay. What do you want, Simon? Do you have Ivor?'

'Tut, tut, tut. That's not how we play the game, Jazzy. *You* know that. Don't you remember the game? Simon Says – that's the one. So, let's play, shall we? I'd hate to have to hurt your new little friend . . .'

Again, with the silent treatment. So boring, it makes me want to scream. 'Or, I could hang up . . .? Your choice.'

'No, no, I'm listening.'

'Say it then, Jazzy. Play the game properly.'

Her swallow is audible and the vulture inside me releases its grip as she speaks. 'What does Simon say . . .?'

That's more like it! Chin resting on my shoulder, my soul mate grins. We're getting *so* close to the end now and the anticipation is thrilling. The quiver in Jazzy's voice eases the vulture's grip even more. 'Sorry, I didn't quite hear you?'

'I'm listening, Simon. It's just, for a minute, I was back there. Back under the covers with you and Mhairi playing our game.'

Bitch! Does she really think that crap will work on me? That fifteen years of betrayal and neglect will be swept away with a few bittersweet memories? 'Don't give me that crap, *sister* dearest. You're fifteen years too late. Stick to the script, Jazzy, and we'll see if you can save a life. Just stick to the FUCKING script.'

My chest is tight, but thank God, I'm not alone. My twin's sweet words calm me. I put the phone on mute to give myself time to recover. To give Twinnie time to soothe me. When *I'm* good and ready, I speak. 'Say it then, Jazzy. Play the game properly.'

But can you believe it, the bitch thinks she's still the boss, acting all big sister on me?

'Do you remember that time when you said, "Simon Says steal Mummy's vodka and pour it down the sink"? Do you remember that, Simon? We did it. Together we . . .'

Bitch! She gave up the right to call the shots years ago. 'PLAY THE GAME!'

I don't know if it's my anger that makes her capitulate or if she's playing me. It makes no difference because the outcome remains the same. 'What does Simon say . . .?'

'Sorry, I didn't quite hear you?'

A little louder. 'What does Simon say?'

'Well done, Jazzy. That wasn't so hard, was it?'

She's pacing now, kicking the wall of the pub. Pinching the bridge of her nose with her free hand. This is so good. So enjoyable. If things continue to go to plan, then we're heading for a huge climax with a fanfare of trumpets and drums and ra-ra dancers. It'll be perfect. Then, like she's exhausted after her little tantrum, she falls back against the wall, her head bowed. 'No.'

Twinnie's nose scrunches up, just like it did when we were kids. Head tilted to one side, the shrug towards the van is just so 'us'. 'Come on. We need to get this party started.'

Twinnie's right, so before I issue my instructions we get into the car, ignoring the struggling woman tied up in the back. After all, we need to get to the spot before Jazzy does. With a last look at Jazzy, leaning on the pub wall, dejected and beaten, I drive off. 'Good. We're on the same page, so *here's* what Simon says. Get the fat cow's car keys, and drive towards Whitburn. Don't tell your police mates what's happening. You'll be hearing from me. Got it?'

Her voice trembles as she answers. 'Yeah, got it.'

'Oh, and be aware, I'll know if you deviate from my instructions because I've bugged your partner's car.'

Chapter 48

Her brother's words chilled Jazzy to the core. The vice around her heart was nothing compared to the claws shredding her insides. The desire to vomit was so strong she bowed her head and pinched her nose, trying to inhale silent breaths that wouldn't alert him to her turmoil. If he thought he'd got to her, that would give him ammunition and she was determined to maintain the upper hand.

Her back prickled with the idea that his eyes were on her – like they had been when he was stalking her. When she left the pub, she'd scoped out the area to see if she could spot him, but visibility was so poor, she could hardly see a foot in front of her. She hoped the blizzard would disrupt his visibility too, although of course he could have binoculars. Who knew? She swallowed, and as a shiver racked her body, she wrapped her arm round her middle and waited. She wanted to unnerve him. Hoped her silence might provoke him into saying more than he intended.

'No answer, Jazzy?'

There was a trace of a smirk in his tone – a taunting arrogance that she'd never discerned when they were kids – but then, he'd only been six years old then. What should she do? Should she reply or should she go back inside and alert Queenie?

As she considered her options, he got impatient, forcing her to respond to his ultimatum and leaving her with no option but to comply with participating in his manipulative Simon Says game. Memories flood in, yanking Jazzy by the throat, robbing her of breath – the three of them huddled under the covers playing Simon Says whilst their mother lay in a drunk heap in the living room. She blinked, trying to dislodge the memories. There was no time for sentiment. The monster on the phone wasn't that sweet little Simon with the flushed face and the sticky-out ears. Not anymore. *He has Ivor.*

She racked her brains wondering how she should play this. This interaction – their first direct one with him – was crucial. He had a hostage, possibly more – they still didn't know where Janine Gorman or Ginny Bell were – and their safety was paramount. She blanked out the 'if they're still alive' that jabbed at her brain like an insistent woodpecker and complied with his sick request to play the game. What choice did she have? With no hostage negotiation training, Jazzy focused on exploiting their shared experiences. If she could connect with him, she might learn something important, but more to the point, when she sent this recording to her team, maybe *they'd* be able to use it. She had to keep him talking. She had to lull him into revealing something, anything that could help. But Simon cut her off dead.

Provoking him further might send him spiralling out of control. If pushed too far, what was he capable of? Who was she kidding? She'd seen first-hand only too well what he was capable of. She'd never forget the abomination he'd inflicted on the Clarks and on Clarice Cameron, never mind his previous victims. So, Jazzy made the only decision she could and capitulated. Like the sociopath he was, all trace of his previous anger evaporated and his tone became smug. Simon wanted his pound of flesh. He wanted Jazzy subjugated.

In a surge of rage, Jazzy kicked the brickwork hard. She was so angry that the pain shooting up her leg didn't register. Quelling the desire to slam her fist into the wall, Jazzy slumped against it, wondering how this would all play out, as Simon issued his instructions. As he spoke, she worked through every possible way she could make this work and when he'd finished she didn't hesitate. There was no time. The bastard had Ivor. Her heart hammered as she spun round, re-entered the pub and strode over to the snug. Thankfully, Queenie was still engrossed in her phone calls, so Jazzy grabbed her coat, snatched the car keys off the table and left before Benjy or her partner could react. Her long legs made short work of the icy road and before Queenie had make an appearance at the Argy Bargy entrance, Jazzy was already pulling away in her car.

Queenie's horrified expression in the rear-view mirror made her gulp. What was she doing? This was stupid. She knew it was stupid. She fumbled for her phone and WhatsApped the recorded call to Queenie with a message warning her the car was bugged. Queenie would get the troops together, in double-quick time, but Jazzy couldn't risk her brother realising she hadn't followed his instructions. She had to get to Ivor before it was too late.

Chapter 49

Still on the phone, Queenie dashed after Jazzy as she flew from the pub and was in time to see Jazzy driving down the road in her vehicle. As she caught Jazzy's eye in the rear-view mirror, her phone buzzed with a WhatsApp notification. She broke off the call with Haggis, and took a moment to absorb Jazzy's message. Panic surged in her chest, threatening to stop her heart mid-beat, but she thrust it aside and forwarded Jazzy's message to Fenton. He'd know what to do. Then, spinning on her heel, she barged back into the bar. 'Right. It's Police Scotland here. I need one of yous to give me the keys to your vehicle.'

She glanced round the motley crew, who looked at her like she'd been dragged in on their shoes and realised that wasn't going to work. 'The bloke who killed the Clarks and that woman in Armadale has got Ivor and my colleague. The tall, skinny, uglier one of us, is chasing them on her own. Now who's gonna give me their keys?'

Six shovel-sized hands thrust car keys towards her, but it was Benjy who grabbed his Uncle Pedro's and, bouncing on his feet, yelled, 'Come on, for God's sake the killer's got oor Ivor. Hurry the feck up.'

He scurried from the bar, Uncle Pedro's massive frame

lumbering after him and Queenie taking up the rear. When they got outside, she found Benjy standing by the passenger side of a Discovery arguing with his uncle. 'You can't drive. You've had a pint. Queenie will drive. You get in the back. We've no' got time for this.'

The large man looked set to argue until he saw Queenie square up to him, chin angled pugnaciously in his direction and her hand extended to receive the keys from Benjy. 'He's right. I'm driving, but you two are not coming. I'm not taking civilians into possible danger.'

But Uncle Pedro had already squashed himself into the back seat and was peering between the two front seats as Benjy hopped in the passenger seat.

'Oh, for fanny bawbag's sake.' Queenie jumped in and thrust her phone at Benjy. 'Get the tracker app up. She's got one in her handbag and on her phone, so we can follow at a distance.' As she started the engine and accelerated over the frost-covered road, following Benjy's instructions to head towards Longridge on the B7010, she told him to get his phone out so she could contact Elliot Balloch and the rest of the team. The thought of telling Balloch that she'd lost Jazzy made her nauseous.

When the call connected, Queenie, her voice hoarse, swallowed hard before speaking. 'That you, Elliot? I've a wee bit of . . .'

'She's got me on speakerphone, Queenie. On that burner of hers. I can hear what's going on. She's heading towards Longridge. I'm on my way with Geordie and I've teams converging on the area. Fenton's coordinating things from back at the station. We've still not got a definite ID on this fucker, but Fenton's got officers trying to locate each of the men on that list. Not that it matters who he is at this stage – we need to stop him in his tracks. The chief super has ordered a firearms team to the area too, but we're all going to hang back till we know what's happening. Where are you?'

'I'm on her tail, boss. I borrowed a Discovery and I'm tracking her position as we speak.'

'Right. Keep in touch. We're not using police comms in case he can intercept them.'

'Aye, I will, boss.' Then almost as an afterthought, Queenie, added, 'I'm sorry, lad. I should've . . .'

'Never mind could'ves and should'ves, Queenie. Just get her back . . . or else.'

That 'or else' hung in the air as she drove. They were only minutes – no more than five – behind Jazzy, but in the countryside, away from busy roads and populated areas, if they got too close they would be visible. Queenie's fingers gripped the sticky steering wheel, but she didn't care about that – or about the weird odour that clogged her throat. What the hell did Uncle Pedro transport in this bloody thing?

'She's turning right onto School Road. That road leads to nowhere. Where the hell is she going?'

Benjy leaned forward, stretching his seatbelt as he peered straight ahead. 'We've got to get Ivor. Don't know what I'd do without her.'

Uncle Pedro, his humungous head thrust between the seats, his unruly beard tickling Queenie's cheek every time he moved, reached his hand over and squeezed the lad's shoulder. 'Don't fret, son. We're all here. We'll not let anything happen to our Ivory. Look . . .'

Queenie glanced in the rear-view mirror and groaned. How had she only just spotted the motley range of cars from Stùrrach following them. Most didn't even look roadworthy. 'For God's sake, what are they doing following us? They can't come with us. This isn't a bloody hillbilly outing, or an excuse to step we gaily tae a clan wedding or a convoy of Yorkie chomping gorillas . . .'

But Benjy nudged her arm. 'Right! Turn right. Jazzy's just passing the Ploughman's Poet Cottage. I reckon he's taking her to the Hens Nest Road. There's a few deserted farms out that way.'

'Ring that number again, Benjy.'

When Elliot answered, Queenie was glad to have information. 'We reckon he's leading her to the Hens Nest Road. Benjy says there's a couple of deserted farm buildings around there. Can we get eyes on them from the air, do you reckon?'

'We'll keep the police helicopters on standby, but it's so secluded out there, they'd see them before they got close enough to be useful. We're going to hang back till Jazzy gives us an indication of her probable final destination.' Voice grim he added, 'We'll only get one shot at this, so we've got to make it count. Just keep trucking on, Queenie.'

Queenie rolled her eyes. *Aye, just keep on trucking on with my convoy of amateurs and imbeciles.* She hoped this wouldn't go horribly wrong. Uncle Pedro broke the momentary silence. Unlike his earlier abrasive tones, this time his voice was low, sympathetic even. 'You need to let me get out here, hen. The roads are getting narrower and this isn't a nippy ride. Charlie's got my bike on a trailer back there. I'll be better off on it.'

Queenie met the large man's eyes through the rear-view mirror. It was a sackable offence, to allow a civilian to participate in a police operation without permission from on high but Queenie – and Jazzy and Ivor – were out of options. A motorbike in these conditions would have better and swifter access to Jazzy. With an abrupt nod, she braked and waited till the large man had struggled out of the Discovery. 'You need to stay close to me. Don't go all Robocop on me. You wait till I give the word, okay?'

Uncle Pedro's grin wasn't in the least bit reassuring, but Queenie was out of options. She had to rescue her friend by fair means or foul, legal or illegal, motorbike or Discovery. She only hoped this gamble paid off.

Chapter 50

As she drove, the Five Sisters shale bings looming before her eerily through the mist, Jazzy kept an eye on her surroundings. She'd no idea where Simon was and didn't know if he could see as well as hear her. As far as he was concerned, with the precautions he'd taken – the bug on Queenie's car, his insistence on keeping the call between them live, the possibility of him having eyes on her – Jazzy was on her own, isolated from her colleagues and heading into unknown territory with no backup.

Jazzy could only hope that wasn't the case. Under cover of retrieving Queenie's keys and with her call to Simon still active, Jazzy had called Elliot from her burner, leaving the call on silent in the hope that he wouldn't hang up on her when she didn't respond. Providing the tracking device Queenie had put in her bag was still active, and that Queenie had the presence of mind to catch on to Jazzy's meaning after listening to the recording, her partner would be able to track her current location and could follow at a distance. If Elliot was still on the line and could hear the instructions dictated by Simon, he too would be on his way.

'You're going to drive past the Ploughman's Poet Cottage in a moment, Jasmine. It's beautiful, don't you think? Picturesque. But just keep driving.'

Jazzy's eyes flicked to her rear-view mirror. Was anyone out there for her? For Ivor?

'Can I speak to Ivor, Simon? I need to know she's okay otherwise there's no point in this charade. No point in me continuing.' She braked, slowed down and indicated as she glided onto the snow-covered grass verge. Heart hammering against her breastbone, she waited. This was her chance to discover if he had eyes on her, but it was a risky manoeuvre. It wouldn't take much for him to flip and take his anger at Jazzy out on Ivor.

'Oh, no, no, no, Jasmine. You don't get to call the shots.'

Jazzy released the breath she hadn't been aware she was holding. His tone, although difficult to judge with the robotic voice modifier, seemed fairly calm. More amused than angry.

'I suggest you start driving again, Jazzy. Don't want you to get stuck on that soggy grass verge, do we? For that *would* certainly result in injury to your wee friend.' He laughed. 'I'm not stupid, you know. I know perfectly well that you staged that little demand so you could work out if I can see you. Well rest assured, sister dearest, I can see you only too well. Which makes me think that you're the stupid one. However, as a show of good faith – after all, we both question the importance of faith in our lives, don't we? – here's your strange friend Ivor.'

'Jazzy, Jazzy, don't come near – they'll kill you.'

Ivor's voice was cut off and the sound of skin connecting with skin followed by a muffled yelp filled the air. Jazzy closed her eyes. Ivor's use of the word 'they' had given her key information – Simon was not working alone. She scanned the fields to either side, hoping for some indication that help was nearby. The windy, narrow road behind was depressingly empty of traffic too. She had to proceed on the assumption that Ivor's and her own safety relied on how she handled this situation. She braced her hand on the steering wheel, engaged the clutch and began driving. Her only real option was to upset their equilibrium. Knock them off balance.

'So, your other "sister dearest" is with you, Simon. That's intriguing. Are you two working like the needy little tag team you always were?' She raised her voice a little, allowing the sarcasm to flow through her words. 'Care to say hallo to your big sis, Mhairi?'

As Jazzy approached Ploughman's Poet Cottage, the only sound except the wind whipping the hedgerows to either side of the narrow lane was Simon's heavy breathing. She crossed her fingers, hoping she hadn't overplayed her hand. Praying that her attitude wouldn't impact on Ivor's safety. When he spoke again, he'd regained control of himself. 'Not long now, Jasmine. Slow your car right down because you're taking a right two hundred yards after the cottage. You'll need to look out for it. It's barely visible from the road. Not long now till our reunion, sis. Not long now.'

Dusk was falling as Jazzy edged past the cottage, her eyes peeled for the overgrown lane. She didn't want to miss it. She had to get to Ivor. She shivered as she saw the potholed single-lane track. Bulky imposing evergreen bushes lined each side of it, forming an eerie tunnel that led only to darkness beyond. Her headlights had little impact on the almost impenetrable gloom and, as she edged the Land Rover onto the track, jaggy branches and spiky car-eating leaves eviscerated the paintwork. The shrubbery was so dense that Jazzy knew her brother had got to his destination by another route, probably a much quicker one, so that he was fully prepared for her arrival. As she slowed to under ten mph, Jazzy wondered if she'd still be alive to receive Queenie's tongue-lashing when she saw the state of her car.

Every fibre of her being was on high alert as the car crept steadily forward. With the brooding presence of murky vegetation, came a sense of foreboding. Her only protection was the tiny tin Tonka toy in which she sat and, in the here and now, Queenie's Land Rover felt as insubstantial as a will-o'-the-wisp. In fact, right now Jazzy would gladly pay for the company of a spunkie because at least then, as she was led to her doom, she wouldn't be alone. It seemed that Simon no longer wanted to talk. Instead he beat a funereal tattoo on the edge of his phone. *Always one for the jokes, eh Simon?* Ahead, a glimmer of light shimmered and in the crazy darkness Jazzy almost believed that she had indeed conjured up the sprite with its treacherous lamp.

Sweat made her hands slick, so she rubbed them down her jeans, before gripping the steering wheel tightly and braking. This was her last chance to work out a strategy before her encounter with Simon and his co-conspirator. Curiosity at finally being able to identify her brother and possibly her twin sister, vied with her desire to reverse back down that creepy lane as fast as she could. Now that her brother's identity was on the cusp of being revealed a strange sadness settled in Jazzy's chest. She'd loved him, protected him from their mother's wrath, looked after him from the moment he was born until he and his twin had been forcibly separated from her.

Over the years she'd wondered what had become of them, and placed her faith in the hope that they'd lived better lives than they otherwise would. Now, she knew that the aftermath of Hansa Solanki's death hadn't been the release it should have been – not for them, perhaps not for any of them. Faces from Fenton's list bounced in front of her eyes. Which one of them was her brother? Which her sister? Which one of them had grown from an innocent child into a monster? She'd find out soon enough.

As far as she was aware, Simon had only ever used a knife or an axe to kill his victim, which meant that Jazzy had no reason to suspect he would be in possession of a firearm. Of course, this was by no means a certainty, but, she shrugged, certainties were over-rated. Right now, she had to go with the odds and that meant that it was unlikely he'd shoot her. So, as long as she remained inside the car, she would be safe. Could she accelerate at speed and run him over? She doubted it. He'd keep Ivor close to him – she was his protection – which left only one plausible option. Simon would use Ivor to entice her from the car, and the only thing in Jazzy's armoury, once she left the car, were her car keys, which she could use as an improvised knuckle duster and the small, illegal mace canister she'd found in Queenies glove compartment. Neither of those would be any good unless she got up close and personal with Simon. She had her wit and agility, but against two assailants her chances of surviving and rescuing Ivor were slim.

Before she moved forward, Jazzy took the time to send two mental messages. She didn't believe in telepathy, but this might be her last chance to express her emotions, so she closed her eyes and conjured up an image of Elliot. Her rock for so many years. She should have told him how much she valued his friendship. How much his presence in her life meant to her. How much she'd miss him if she never saw him again. Uncaring that Simon could hear every word, Jazzy, hoping he could hear her, spoke aloud to the picture of Elliot in her head. 'Ell, If I get out of here alive, I'm going to live life for the moment, like you always told me to do. I'm going to be more spontaneous, more like you.'

As his image faded, her heart contracted and her eyes prickled. *No time for this, JayZee. Get a grip.* Queenie – small, dumpy, abrasive and with the biggest heart of anyone she'd ever met – replaced Elliot in her mind's eye. *You're no' died yet hen. Give it bloody laldie and kill the fuckers!* Jazzy grinned. Queenie was right. She wasn't dead yet and she'd use every ounce of strength to keep it that way. Besides, she might not have religious faith, but she had faith in Queenie and Elliot. They wouldn't let her down. 'Tell Queenie she's a Queen and I'm honoured to have worked with her. Also, tell her I'm sorry about her car.'

As she drove closer to the glimmery exit, the area beyond the tunnel opened out onto an overgrown slush-covered farmyard, beyond which stood a dilapidated building. A combination of disintegrating sandstone walls and patchy barbed wire enclosed them. To the side of the building the vehicle, as described by Benjy, facing towards another wider and less overgrown track. *A getaway route?* Beside it was a quad bike also facing towards the track, but what drew Jazzy's eyes was the tableau in front of the farmhouse.

A figure in ninja black, masked and wearing his trademark balaclava, stood, one arm encircling Ivor's neck, whilst the other held a knife to her throat. A few feet behind Simon, was another identically dressed figure dangling an axe from one hand. This one was slightly hunched and looked off to the side as if distanced from the scene. As expected, there was no way to weaponise the car without hurting Ivor, so Jazzy discarded that idea and focused on taking note of the environment as she opened the car door and stepped onto the boggy ground.

Ivor's eyes widened. Her hands and feet were bound, her mouth covered with an old rag; still the girl struggled against her captor. In warning, he nicked the girl's neck, drawing blood, his eyes never veering from Jazzy. 'Come closer, sis.'

Jazzy stepped closer, straining her ears for any indication that backup was on its way and swallowing her disappointment at the deadly silence that prevailed. Deliberately keeping her tone casual, she thrust her hands in her pockets, positioning the keys in her right hand and the mace canister in her left, and took another step. 'Long time, no see, Simon. How's life treating you?'

The spurt of amplified robotic laughter made Jazzy jump. Adrenalin surged through her veins, making her hands and knees shake. She stepped closer. Only thirty yards separated them. Simon dragged Ivor forward, narrowing the gap further, and pressed the knife tip deeper into the girl's neck. Tears flowed down Ivor's cheeks and Jazzy wanted to beg and plead for him to stop and just take her instead. But that wouldn't work. There was no way both she and Ivor would escape here alive unless *he* ended up dead.

Jazzy turned her attention to the other figure. 'That you, Mhairi? Not going to say hallo?'

Mhairi shook her head and edged closer to Simon, which allowed Jazzy to keep an eye on both of them. There was no way to disarm him without Ivor being hurt, so she opted to play for time. 'What's with the voice modulator and disguise? Surely we're past that now?'

Simon let loose another eerie chortle and pierced another area of Ivor's neck.

'Come on, guys. This is a family reunion. Let the lassie go.'

Simon shook his head and as Jazzy became aware of a faint sound from beyond the fields to her left, said, 'Why one or the other, when I can kill both of you?'

And with that he drew the blade across Ivor's throat and let her fall to the ground.

Jazzy dived towards Simon, but Mhairi, the slighter figure, lurched in front of him. Jazzy sprayed the mace in her direction, closing her eyes and diving through the toxic mist, car keys aiming for her brother's eyes, but not making contact. Out of nowhere, the air was filled with sirens, a growling motorbike revving and a range of papping car horns coming from two different directions. When Jazzy opened her eyes, Simon was sprinting towards the quad bike. She glanced at Ivor, clutching her neck, her wide eyes terrified and beside her, also on the ground coughing and spluttering as tears soaked into her balaclava was Jazzy's sister.

Help was on its way, so Jazzy rushed to Ivor, whipping off her coat to staunch the blood, but before she could apply it to her neck, two large hands forcibly lifted her from her kneeling position and thrust her to the side. 'I'm a doctor. I got this. You take my bike and catch that bastard.'

Not waiting to work out where Benjy's Uncle Pedro had come from or to register her surprise that the huge man was a doctor – time for that later – Jazzy grabbed the handles of the motorbike and jumped on. It had been a while since she'd last ridden one, but she knew what she was doing. She aimed for the quad bike, which was now heading cross-country. Anger and frustration fuelled her to push the old motorbike to its limits, as she took off after Simon. No way would the police vehicles or indeed any of that haphazard line of civilian ones led by Queenie – *is that an ice-cream van at the back?* – be able to navigate this terrain. Chasing her as she headed towards the figure on the quad bike was the strains of the nursery rhyme from the ice-cream van. Their ominous message made her shudder. She'd always hated nursery rhymes.

> *Girls and boys come out to play.*
> *The moon doth shine as bright as day.*
> *Leave your supper and leave your sleep.*
> *And come with your playfellows into the street.*

As she always knew it would be, this final battle was one between Jazzy and her brother.

Chapter 51

Elliot, eyes raking the area for signs of Jazzy and the killers, screeched to a halt on the spot where the quad had been only seconds earlier. Through the still connected burner phone he could hear the roar of the motorcycle and having heard a gruff male voice telling her to 'take my bike and catch the bastard', it was fair to assume that Jazzy was in pursuit of her brother.

From a narrow tunnel of darkness, a never-ending convoy of vehicles emerged, Queenie's at the front. She jumped from the car, leaving the door open behind her, and landed in a puddle whilst Benjy, with more finesse, exited the passenger side. Both of them rushed to the two prone figures on the ground. Through the discordant sound of screeching quad, roaring motorbike, sirens, car engines and the eerie, tinny sound of *'girls and boys come out to play'* cutting through them all, cut the young lad's high-pitched yell.

'Ivor, Ivor, I'm here. Uncle Pedro will sort you. You'll be fine.' Benjy skidded to a halt beside his uncle, gazing down at the rapidly growing pool of blood and with an anguished squeak he kneaded his hands together. However, Uncle Pedro was having no histrionics. 'Either find me a pen or some narrow tubing, Benjy, or sling your hook. You're no use to Ivor if you're a mess.'

The starkness of his uncle's tone galvanised Benjy and, as Queenie approached the other figure, the lad pulled a pen from his pocket and handed it over. Tears pouring down his cheeks, Benjy covered his ears and, as he fell to his knees beside his uncle, yelled, 'Shut the ice-cream van down. Please, someone just stop that fucking song.'

After a few seconds, the strangled metallic tones drifted to a halt mid-sentence '. . . *leave your sleep. And come with your playfellows into the street.*'

Benjy fell forward clutching Ivor's unmoving hand, his breath coming in ever faster gulps, until a constable put an arm round the lad's heaving shoulders and stayed with him.

Not stopping to consider whether 'Uncle Pedro' was qualified to do whatever he was about to, Elliot was on the phone requesting that the standby helicopter with its paramedics on board 'park their tails in the field and get over here to save a life, pronto'.

With no sympathy for the blubbering black-clad figure and seeing no resistance from her, he took a moment to take in the wider scene. *Where the hell have all these vehicles come from?*

'Christ, boss, what a mess.' Queenie's eyes homed in on the chase across the fields. The quad, followed by Jazzy, her long hair loose from its usual ponytail, flowing behind her as she gained on her prey. As Elliot followed the direction of her gaze, his face blanched. 'Fuck, that's Jazzy.'

He took a step towards the rapidly disappearing figures in their respective vehicles, then reconsidered, instead calling in for immediate motorcycle backup.

He stepped forward, ready to caution the cowering person at their feet, then looked at Queenie. 'You do the honours.'

'With pleasure.' Queenie leaned over to roughly grab the balaclava, as the writhing figure on the ground tried to bat her hands away and yelped as if she was scalping her. 'Aw, no you don't, hen. There's no escape for ye. Let's see who you really are.'

Without further ado, she yanked the woollen covering off. Both she and Elliot paused, staring in disbelief. Despite their bloodshot eyes and swollen lids, the person grinned up at them. 'Surprise! Not as smart as you thought you were, are you?'

Elliot wanted to smash his fist into Philip Jamieson's raw face.

The reporter's lips curled into a sneer. 'You'll never catch her, you know. Mhairi's far too clever for you. She's got plans and that bitch' – he jerked his chin towards the fields – 'is about to be punished.' He laughed like he'd never stop.

Elliot sensed a different texture to the atmosphere around him as he leaned down to heft Jamieson to his feet. He hesitated, his eyes drawn to the undulating snow-covered field where the quad bike had stopped and turned to face Jazzy in a standoff. One foot on the marshy ground, Jazzy revved her engine, whilst her opponent, knife held high in the air like some sort of modern-day jouster, let out an exultant whoop before accelerating at speed towards Jazzy. In response, Jazzy, revved and set off to meet her nemesis.

Elliot didn't hesitate. He thrust the still-laughing reporter towards Queenie and took off over the fields to Jazzy. Meanwhile, the quad rider increased her speed as she raised the knife into the air, hooting and howling.

Sweat pooled in Elliot's armpits as he ran. His winter coat impeded his movement so, not slowing down, he slipped it from his shoulders and increased his pace, pumping his arms as he went. The two women circled each other, each seeking an advantage to press home, each desperate for this standoff to be over.

Still Elliot pushed onwards, his heart thundering, his breath casting puffs of mist that dispersed around him as he plunged forward, his eyes never leaving Jazzy. Mhairi feinted to the left at the last minute, her knife hand descending towards Jazzy's arm as she attempted to ram the side of the quad. *Had she hit her?* Jazzy skidded round, ready to face her combatant, and this time she held something in her hand. With limited control over the bike now, Jazzy's approach was slower, but no less determined.

The more cumbersome quad took a wide circle to re-enter the combat head on. The two charged forward with Jazzy's roar filling the night sky.

A hundred yards away, Elliot looked around for a weapon. A branch, a stick, something he could use at a distance to impede Mhairi's attack. Nothing! A thunderous noise rent the air. His eyes were immediately drawn back towards the battle. Mhairi had caught Jazzy's back tyre sending her off balance, her front wheel slamming into a dilapidated drystane dyke. As if in slow motion, he saw Jazzy, bike still between her legs, propelled into the air and over it, only to skid over the frost-covered grass and clatter against a pile of bricks and rubble. The bike landed on top of Jazzy, the sound of it bouncing onto her slender frame, chillingly loud. The wheels spun and a plume of grey smoke surged into the darkness.

Still whooping like a banshee, Mhairi rode right up to her fallen foe, raised her knife and sliced it downward. Elliot yelled, the sound hoarse and guttural, as she raised her hand to repeat the action. 'Noooooooo!'

She paused, whipped her balaclava off and turned to grin at him. Stunned, he stared into the eyes of Janine Gorman. Gone were the spectacles and the pleasant smile and in their place was a triumphant sneer as she leaned from the quad, ready to strike again, but before she could, another unfamiliar sound swooped in. The helicopter had released a drone and was directing it towards Gorman, who, realising she was in danger of being caught, turned the quad round and sped over the fields to the forest, where the trees would render the drone ineffective.

'Hang on, Jazzy, I'm coming.' He reached a gap in the barbed wire and pushed through, uncaring of the barbs slicing his skin. He willed himself to go faster. When he reached the dyke Jazzy had crashed into, he vaulted over, not breaking stride until he slid to a breathless stop in front of the wreckage. For a moment, all he could see were plumes of smoke and the massive bike. Then as the acrid stink of petrol hit his nostrils he moved forward, pulling and pulling at the bike, until finally, it moved and he could access Jazzy's body. Sinking to his knees, he did a rapid survey of her injuries. She was unconscious, blood pouring from a wound to her head, her arm at an impossible angle. The petrol smell was stronger now and he could hear it dripping from the tank.

There was no time to do anything but yank her free and hope he didn't cause her additional injury. Not looking at the bike, he hauled her inch by inch away from the treacherous vehicle, until he could go no further. Panting, he cradled her in his arms, covering her broken body with his as in one mighty explosion, the tank blew, filling the night sky with flames and smoke and detritus.

Chapter 52

Jazzy woke to rolling blue lights, a bonfire smell, a cacophony of sounds, each one indistinguishable from the other, and a heavy weight pinning her to the hard, freezing ground. She blinked, then blinked again, trying to make sense of where she was and what had happened. From nowhere a wave of panic overtook her and she began writhing, trying to escape from whatever imprisoned her, but then the pain overtook her and she subsided into a frightened stillness, afraid to move lest the agony struck again. Sharp lights flashed into her eyes, unfamiliar voices telling her to be still, that they would help her. None of that helped.

A series of disjointed images played out in her mind as she scrunched her eyes against the blinding torches that insisted on resting on her face. A motorbike, Ivor, blood, a cut throat, an axe, the chase, the grinning, taunting whoops of the person on the quad and all she could think was that she'd lost Queenie's mace and would be in big trouble. Then, as if the thought had conjured her from nowhere, her coarse tones sliced through the soothing ones of the anonymous figures. 'JayZee, JayZee, you better no' be deid or I'll bloody kill you.'

All at once the panic dissipated, and the shadow of her spiky-haired friend loomed over her, growling her annoyance. 'Ye've fucked up ma car big time, JayZee. Hope you're bloody insured.'

Then the weight across her body was moved. Jazzy found herself stretching out with her good arm trying to make them put it back. 'No, no.'

'There, there, lamb.' Queenie's voice was all soft and tablety again. 'They're just checking him over.'

The panic was back and, as she tried to focus, in the seconds before she lapsed back into unconsciousness she remembered. *Elliot!*

Three days later

Chapter 53

'You shouldn't be here. You know that don't you?' Queenie was wheeling her through the corridors of Livingston police station as if she were competing at Brands Hatch. Her annoyance at Jazzy's insistence on coming into work making her movements so jerky that Jazzy regretted agreeing that she only be allowed in the building under supervision and in a wheelchair.

'Rest and recuperation. That's what they said. Not, go into work to get your neon pink stookie signed. Not, subject your battered body to a whole load of busybodies. Not, let's go and pander to a serial killer who demands an audience with his big sister . . .'

Bollocks to that! Jazzy was perfectly capable of getting around, albeit slowly, on her own and it annoyed her that the chief super had seen fit to put Queenie in charge of her. On the one hand she accepted that it had been a wise decision on his part, because Queenie was probably the only person in the whole of Police Scotland who could convince Jazzy to do as she was told. Still, it was a mean trick. 'I'm better off doing something, Queenie. You know that. Besides, we need to get whatever information we can from that scrote Jamieson.' Not able to think of him as her brother – not yet anyway – she stammered over the name.

'It's personal, Queenie. You *know* that. We know what my

sister is capable of and she has to be stopped. We have to find her before she kills anyone else.' Jazzy was still coming to terms with the revelation that Janine was her sister and that she's been the main instigator, using Simon as a pawn in her twisted game. There had been no sightings of the ex-analyst since she disappeared into the forest and the team were desperate to locate her.

'Hmph, that's if she *is* the killer. We've only got his word for that so far and he's a lying, duplicitous, dishonest bawbag.'

All of that was true, but something compelled Jazzy to confront him and the powers that be – well, the chief super – had agreed. The thought of Afzal's motivation in agreeing to this interview was another thing that left Jazzy cold. The last thing she wanted was to be beholden to him.

After a couple of narrow escapes, Queenie trundled her into the empty incident room and left her there saying, 'I'm fair parched, so I'm off for a drink. You're no lightweight you know, JayZee. Could do with shifting a few pounds. Hefting you around has got me peching like a couple of shagging pigs.'

In Queenie's absence, Jazzy manoeuvred herself to the edge of the chair and using her good arm managed to stand up. She did a quick inventory of which body parts were aching. Her arm, protected in its fuchsia cast, was good. The stitches on her thigh where Mhairi had sliced her were pulling, but the worst pain was the dull persistent throb in her ribs and chest. 'Try having Elliot Balloch yanking you from under a motorbike and then landing on you himself, if you want to know about heavy,' she chuntered under her breath, as she hobbled over to the incident boards.

Behind her the door opened, and she braced herself for the solicitous greetings from everyone. Her house was filled with vases of flowers sent from her colleagues. The biggest and typically most ostentatious was from Afzal, but she'd binned those on principle. She hadn't realised so many people cared about her. There were offerings from the Stùrrach residents, the CSI team – no doubt organised by Franny Gallagher – Lamond Johnston, even DCI

Dick and the A team had sent some. The massive cake with *To Jazz from the rest of the Jazz Queens* written on it – organised by Queenie – had made her laugh. Geordie and Fenton, though, had been inventive in their get well soon gift – a night out at Misty Thistle's Christmas Party. She looked forward to being driven by Limo to The Pond in Leith on Christmas Eve to see Geordie perform in his drag persona.

'Hey, Jazz, you okay?'

Jazzy tensed. She hadn't expected Elliot to be around. They hadn't had a chance to talk alone since she was whisked off to hospital and, although she'd rehearsed loads of things to say to him, now she had the chance her mouth had gone dry. Eyes closed, she blinked away a tear. Her last thought before they moved him off her in the field was that he was dead and she'd miss him so much. He was her first ever friend. Now that she had the chance, the words wouldn't come, so instead she did a Queenie. 'What do you think? I'm battered black and blue. Next time you want to jump on top of me, do you think you could do with shifting a few pounds first?'

His laugh, textured like sunny days and candy floss, rolled over her. She grinned and turned around, taking in the cuts on his face and his bandaged hand where he'd burned it. 'Thanks, Ell. That's the second time you've rescued me and I really appreciate it.'

Elliot nodded. 'It'd take more than a madwoman on a quad bike to kill Jazzy Solanki.' He folded his arms over his chest. 'Mind you, let's leave it at least another fifteen years before I have to rescue you again. Now, if you're up for it, he's waiting for you. You ready for this?'

Of course, she wasn't ready for this. Who would be? On the drive over, she'd schooled herself not to think of Philip Jamieson as her brother. To focus on him as a damaged but very dangerous man who was, at the very least, culpable in the murders of many people. For the victims, she'd hold it together. For them, she'd accede his narcissistic demand to talk to her. For them, she'd play his games in the hope he'd reveal a clue to their sister Mhairi's whereabouts. Then, when she'd done that, she'd succumb to Queenie's insistent ministrations until she was fit to come back to active duty. 'Let's go.'

Chapter 54

As she enters – her bright pink stookie testament to how close we came to destroying her, I scrape the uncomfortable plastic chair away from the table, swing my legs up, and rest my feet, crossed at the ankles on top. As I cross my arms over my chest, my entire body loose and relaxed, I maintain eye contact with her. I admire the way she returns my gaze. Her eyes, the mirror image of mine, despite the slight colour variation, don't narrow. Her brow doesn't wrinkle with distaste; her mouth remains loose, her lips moist. No quick tell-tale lip lick from Jazzy Solanki. Even her shoulders remain relaxed. My smile widens. She's putting on a fine act of being in control, but I know she's not. Somewhere inside, she's buried all her tension – all her fear and rage and anger and hate – for later. There's no way she's the ice queen she portrays. Not our Jazzy, not my sister. But how deep are her emotions buried?

I allow the silence to lengthen, toying with her, using the time to scrutinise her. Of course, she's older now and, round her eyes, she bears the faint lines of her twenty-five years. I doubt they're laughter lines. She's not had it easy, our Jasmine – but still a lot easier than me and Mhairi have had it. She can't be unaffected by what's happened, by what we've done. By what *Mhairi's* done. By what Mhairi could still do. Not Jazzy. Not our mother hen Jazzy.

Then I get it. All the tension I can't see isn't buried that deep at all. It's there underneath the table, in her hands. If I dip my head down and take a peek, I bet her fingers will be clenched tight in her lap, her fingernails bitten down to the quick, no polish, no manicure – just ratty, scraggly, old nails. I bet she's touching her palm where her blood promise scar is.

Now that I've sussed that out, my smile widens, revealing my teeth. I deliberately make it look more like a snarl than a smile, in the hope it'll tease a quiver in her lips or a flicker in her eye. But no, the lady's not to be drawn. The silence lingers, then the older bint, sitting next to her. The one with the short grey hair and a face that looks like an earthquake zone, DC McQueen, stretches over and switches on the recording equipment and without looking at me, she completes the necessary preamble of dates and names and ranks of those present.

The recording runs and the video records, yet still no one asks a question. A flicker of fire begins in my gut and rises up through my chest till my entire body is engulfed in a warm, humming glow as I rise to their challenge. They are good – very good. Their strategy might work for someone less used to playing mind games, but what they don't realise is that they're up against an expert at this.

I nod and allow my gaze to drift over Queenie McQueen. I know her – useless, demoted, lazy and incompetent. Mhairi and I have laughed long and hard that this useless old turd is Jazzy's partner. My lip curls as she glances up and meets my eyes for a nanosecond before, with a tightening of her mouth, becoming engrossed once more in the file in front of her. I can't see what she's reading – what she thinks is so important in that file, but I don't need to know.

I look at Jazzy and find her dark eyes still on me. She blinks steadily – not too fast, not too slow – just enough to send out an 'I'm not ruffled' message. I wonder how she's managed to snag this interview. I wasn't sure that even their desperation to find my twin would guarantee me this opportunity with poor DC Jazzy Solanki – demoted, like her sidekick, unfairly in her case – because her brown face and chequered past alongside the unfounded scurrilous rumours about her sex life didn't quite fit. Poor old Jazzy. I exhale, making it seem like a bored sigh, and remove my feet from the table. I've given up my right to a solicitor. I'm smarter than any duty solicitor they'd find in the bowels of Livingston, anyway. 'Remember when we used to share beans straight from the can, Jazzy?'

I relish the way her shoulders tighten for a spilt second before loosening and quirking into a rueful shrug. The barb hit home. She hates beans and I know *why* she hates them. Why they make her want to throw up. I know a hell of a lot more about Jasmine, Jazzy, Solanki than she does about me and that's why I'm the favourite to win this little round. Mhairi would be proud of me.

Ting, ting, the bell peals in my mind, but before she replies, I continue. 'So, what do you want to hear about first? How she used an axe to chop off the Clarks' heads? Or how she took great pride in displaying them for Imogen to find? How she inserted different things in their orifices? How she talked to them the entire time? Telling them all about our poor little horrid pasts? About how she got inside their house, how she made sure you got the message this time? Or maybe you want to hear about the Gillies couple? About the clues she left behind? About the little gifts, just for you, Jazzy? Or Elsbeth Tait, her own foster mum? How she took real pleasure in putting a line through that episode of her life?'

God they're cold. The bitches don't respond to any of my taunts. Their eyes, bland and unemotional, match mine and I can't resist slamming my hand down on the sticky table top. Anything to get a reaction. The little one jumps, but the only response from Jazzy is a slight headshake. God, I remember that from when we were kids. That minuscule movement that carried so much disapproval. Well, she can disapprove all she likes, I'm not in her thrall anymore.

'Mhairi always knew it would end like this. This is how she planned it. For years, she's been setting things up. That other wanker, Balloch, tried to talk me through some of Mhairi's little projects.' I lean forward. 'How did it feel when you discovered you'd been housing a viper in your midst? That your trusted civilian analyst in her big specs and tentative smile was actually your little sister and you didn't recognise her? That she knew every step you made? God, we laughed when you set that Ginny Bell up in a hotel. Mhairi could have got to her at any time. As it is, we got her out of the country. Italy, I believe. The alps are nice at this time of the year. Still, she was a nice little red herring to keep you on your toes. Well, this is nice, but I really asked you here to see if you had anything you wanted to ask me. Maybe a few questions about Mhairi and her plans?'

I quirk my head to one side and when she opens her mouth to respond, I cut her off with a hand wave. 'Thing is, Jazzy, I really want to help. You are my big sis after all and that's what families do, isn't it? Help each other?'

I wait for her nod, then: 'WRONG! You've never helped us, have you, Jazzy?'

To give her credit, she doesn't jump, doesn't even flex a muscle – although, predictably, Queenie does. Those fingers of hers must be clenched so tight they'll cut off her circulation.

'But, where was I? Oh yes, talking about the Clarks and Clarice Cameron. Do you want to know what she told them, what promises she made, before she sliced off their heads?'

I lower my head and lean in towards her, near enough to see the barely concealed shadows under her eyes, close enough to smell her perfume and, before collapsing into hysterics, I whisper, barely loud enough for the microphone to pick up, 'I can't, Jazzy. I can't tell you. Not because I don't want to, but because unlike you I take our blood promise seriously. I won't betray her. Not my Mhairi. I'll tell you three things about my twin: one, she's determined; two, she's patient; and three, killing you means more to her than her own survival. Which means, at the end of the day, sister dearest, you're fucked.'

I collapse in a heap of uncontrolled hysterical laughter. I'm playing to the audience. Making my case for my insanity plea, just like we planned. Yes, I'll feed them the information that clears me of the actual killings. That's what Mhairi wants and, let's face it, Mhairi always gets what Mhairi wants. No matter how often we play Simon Says, Mhairi always holds the trump card. Mhairi always wins.

Jazzy gets to her feet and, without another word to me, leaves the room. Her bestie scrapes her chair back and ends the recordings.

Chapter 55

Jazzy opened her front door and stared at the man standing on the doorstep from behind the chain.

'You going to let me in, Jasmine?'

A whirlwind of emotions hurtled through her in the moments it took to unhook the chain, step back from the door and beckon him to precede her into her home. It was strange seeing this man – one she only ever saw at work – in her living room, looking at her, eyebrow quirked as he waited for her to offer him a seat. She gestured to the sofa and he sat, stretching his legs out before him, whilst she occupied the seat furthest away from him.

'I hear your recovery is going well. That you'll be back at work in the new year – on light duties initially, I'm told.'

She nodded and felt a spurt of satisfaction when a flicker of a frown sped across his forehead. She'd no idea why he'd decided it was appropriate to visit her at home, but whatever had prompted this social call, she wasn't going to make it easy for him. She owed him nothing. He deserved nothing – not from her anyway.

With a sigh, he raked his fingers through his perfect hair and crossed his legs. 'Jasmine, I understand why you're being like this. I understand your anger, your irritation with me, but I want to make amends. I really do. I want to be part of your life.'

Eyes flashing, Jazzy jumped to her feet, immediately regretting it when her ribs protested, but nothing could stem the words that flowed from her mouth like a machine gun taking no prisoners. 'You *understand* my anger? You *understand* my irritation? Pity the great wonderful Waqas Afzal didn't *understand* his four-year-old daughter's need for a father before he left her with a deranged, vicious, alcoholic mother. Pity he didn't *understand* his obligations to that ten-year-old daughter when her mother died leaving her unwanted, alone, and scared, until her uncle and his wife stepped in. Pity he didn't *understand* his responsibilities to that girl throughout her childhood.'

She stood shaking in the middle of the room, her eyes slicing him with contempt.

He splayed his hands in front of him. 'I'll do anything, anything at all to make it up . . .'

'Ach, SHUT UP.' Jazzy clenched her good fist by her side. The desire to pummel him for all the years he'd denied her, all the time he'd spent with his second family, all the distress and abuse he'd left her to cope with on her own, was overpowering. She inhaled sharply, recentring herself and when she was calm she continued, her voice low and with only a trace of a tremor. 'It's too little, too late, sir.' She spat the last word at him and saw it hit its mark.

'We will occasionally have to interact at work – that's inevitable. I expect and need no favours from you. All I want is for my sergeant rank to be reinstated. I lost that through no fault of my own and I deserve it back. Other than that, all I want from you is an update on the investigation, then you can leave.'

Waqas Afzal looked at his daughter, something indefinable in his eye and nodded once. 'Okay, if that's how you want it, Jasmine. I can't expect any more from you.' He cleared his throat and gestured that she should sit back down.

Something inside Jazzy's chest twanged – *her heart?* Couldn't he have tried a little bit harder? But no. Even now, even after all these years. Even after all she'd been through, the work she'd put in on this investigation, he still didn't consider her worth fighting for. Shoulders tense, she looked unflinchingly at him as he updated her.

'We've had a psych assessment done on Simon and it's likely that he'll end up in a secure psychiatric unit rather than prison. However, since your visit he is cooperating and, so far, it seems that he can prove that Mhairi is the mastermind behind the murders. We've got a substantial team working on verifying any claims that could confirm his account. In terms of Mhairi? Well, we found the quad abandoned at the edge of the forest she disappeared into after causing your accident. As you'd expect she had an escape vehicle waiting and, so far, we've had no sightings of her. If Simon's intel is accurate, she has enough funds to disappear indefinitely and we know from experience that she's got the smarts for it. However, we know she'll never let go of her ultimate goal.'

He stopped and looked straight at her. 'She'll come back for you, Jasmine. Maybe not soon, but unless we catch her, at some point, she'll come back for you.'

'And when she does, I'll be ready for her.' Jazzy stood, indicating the conversation was over. Afzal hesitated, then, tight-lipped, he got up and walked past her.

Hand on the door handle, he hesitated. 'We'll *all* be ready for her, Jasmine, beti. You may not want me involved in your life, but I will protect you to the best of my ability. The whole team will.' And he was gone, leaving only a rush of frigid air and a turmoil of emotions behind.

Epilogue

Christmas Eve

Having luxuriated in a white limo, sipping prosecco and trying to control the butterflies in her stomach on the drive from Bellsquarry to Leith, Jazzy hovered by the entrance to The Pond. She wasn't used to interacting with her team socially – who was she kidding? She wasn't used to socialising full stop, but tonight marked a change in dynamics for her. A step into a brave new world where, having been reinstated as a detective sergeant, she was team leader of the motley 'D' team who had proved themselves over the past couple of weeks to be more than mere colleagues. She wasn't sure how to handle this alien situation, but at least she'd managed to admit, if only to herself, that she was willing to try. Which is why she stood there in high heels and a sparkly mini dress, which almost perfectly matched the fuchsia stookie on her arm, gripping a bag filled with Christmas presents in her other.

That afternoon, she'd been struggling with Sellotape and scissors when the doorbell rang signalling the arrival of the little helpers – in the form of Ivor and Benjy – whom she'd invited for mince pies and the spicy Indian tea her auntie Lillie had shown her how to make. Physically, Ivor was recovering well. The dressing on her throat was smaller now and although her voice was croaky and faint, she was able to speak. However, her pallor and the nervous way her eyes darted around the room, told Jazzy that she'd have a long road ahead of her. She'd need support and Jazzy was determined to be part of Ivor's network of friends and family.

The afternoon had been fun, with Benjy protective of his cousin and Ivor loosening up when she saw Jazzy re-engage the security system. Rather than ask the pair to wrap their own Christmas gifts she'd had Elliot buy from the Christmas market in Edinburgh, she handed them over with a 'Merry Christmas, guys.' They'd immediately donned the beanie hats, Ivor's eyes lighting up when she saw the bright colours. They'd surprised Jazzy with a gift of their own. She unwrapped it and then, tears threatening, she swallowed hard. Ivor had painted Jazzy wearing a sari, her head held high, her waist-length hair flowing freely behind her, dancing beneath a sky filled with stars.

She didn't know what to say, so instead she jumped to her feet and removed the central framed images of an anonymous Indian lady dancing in the night and replaced it with the one Ivor had created. 'It's beautiful, Ivor. I'll treasure it forever.' Then they'd settled down to wrap the other gifts for her to bring to The Pond.

Now, as she scanned the room, an elegant vision in glittery green with a Santa hat atop her raven curls descended on her, flashing impossibly long red nails, each sporting a tiny reindeer. 'Hi, I'm Georgia and you must be Jazzy. Oh, you are as delectable as Misty led me to believe. Come on, darling, your group are over here.'

Unaccustomed to her heels and the dress, Jazzy smiled and allowed herself to be guided in a cloud of Chanel towards the front of the room nearest the stage. Although, with Queenie's voice thundering over the desultory conversation and background music like a herd of stampeding bulls, there was no real need for the escort. 'That you, JayZee? In a frock? Jeez. Oh, I didn't know you had legs.'

A blush drifted up Jazzy's neck to her cheeks as everyone in the room stopped and turned to stare at her. Feeling cumbersome and self-conscious in her stookie and carrying the bag of Christmas gifts, Jazzy stumbled forwards, eyes to the floor, and slid into a seat hoping the room would resume its earlier low-key buzz of camaraderie. Queenie, however, clearly having downed a couple of drinks already, clapped her hands like an overexcited sumo wrestler and grabbed the bag from Jazzy's hands. 'Yaay, you bought us all gifts.'

She turned to Fenton whose hand was linked with an impossibly beautiful woman with an amused smile on her lips. Clearly Queenie's overexuberance hadn't fazed her. 'You owe me a tenner, Haggis. I told you she'd bring us aw pressies.'

Haggis shrugged and grinned at Rebecca, his girlfriend. Next to him, Geordie's partner Guy released a guffaw that shook the glasses on the table. 'I'm Guy. Let me get you a drink. I find chaos always looks less daunting with a prosecco inside me.'

Queenie's husband Craig grinned at Jazzy as his wife handed out the gifts. Jazzy was glad that she'd thought to buy gifts for her friend's partners and for Queenie's wee granddaughter, Ruby. Then, she was looking at Elliot. She hadn't been sure he'd be here tonight, so she was glad she'd brought his gift too. He accepted it from Queenie, never taking his eyes off Jazzy as he pressed the soft bundle. 'Football for me, Jazzy?'

There was no time to reply as the lights went down and a spotlight hit the stage. A husky voice boomed over the microphone, hitting the corners of the room with sensuous undertones and a hint of sass. 'Welcome to Misty Thistle's Christmas Party. This first song is a tribute to my boss. She's one of the fiercest, most fair and fabulous people I know. To Jazzy Solanki. You are my . . .'

Misty stepped onto the stage, in a long sequinned purple dress, her blonde hair cascading down her back, her make-up

361

immaculate, her smile vibrant and, one hand in the air, her index finger circling to cue in the live band. All trace of her alter ego's gangliness was replaced by sheer vivacious sensuality and genteel elegance. Jazzy's heart sang with joy as the realisation that despite everything that had happened, moments like this were to live for.

The opening strains of a familiar song filled the room and Misty winked at her as she spun in a complete circle. '. . . Killer Queen and I'm proud to be a Jazz Queen,' Misty sang to an enthusiastic audience, then the spotlight fell on Jazzy, and Misty sang their improvised chorus, accompanied by Queenie. '*JayZee Queen. Top-notch, cool and mean. Hot stuff with a killer gleam. This girl's gonna whoop your arse.*'

Much later, as Craig poured Queenie into Jazzy's limo ready to go home, Jazzy smiled. These people might be mad as hell. They might not be your typical coppers, but they were *her* coppers. Her team, and every step along the way of this investigation they'd had her back. Sliding into the seat next to her partner, Jazzy wondered if that unfamiliar feeling in her chest was love? Friendship? Trust? One-handed Jazzy attempted to straighten the hat she'd gifted Queenie so that both ear flaps covered her ears rather than her face and the back of her head, but Queenie was having none of it. 'Fuck off, JayZee, you're no' getting it back noo, hen. No chance.'

Jazzy exchanged a grin with Craig as the limo sliced silently through the night sky. It was actually Christmas day now and for the first time in forever, Jazzy had a bag of gifts of her own nestling at her feet. She was an adult, but this Christmas felt like it was the first she'd celebrated free from fear or the shackles of guilt she'd carried for most of her life. Both would return. But not tonight.

Three-quarters of an hour later, she waved the limo carrying her friends on to West Calder away and crossed the road to her little home. She faltered, her heels slipping a little on the frosty pavement as she glanced at her Mini. *What was that?* She got her phone out her bag, dialled Elliot's number and, as she waited for him to answer, she approached the envelope tucked under the windscreen wiper. With a shaking hand, phone tucked between her shoulder and cheek, she freed the envelope. The call to Elliot rang out in the dark night. She ripped the envelope open and read the message on the inside of the Christmas card.

Jazzy,
   Justice is never far away.
   It might take months, it might take years, but trust me, we'll meet again. For now, though, watch your back and make sure those you care about watch theirs too.

Dear Reader,

I'd toyed with the idea of setting a series in Scotland for a long time, but never in my wildest imagination did I realise the emotional whirlwind that would go into setting a series in the place where I grew up. Researching the area around my home village of West Calder was both educational (you see things differently when you have your writing hat on) and poignant, with nostalgic memories of people and places no longer with us. I think that's why I've put so much of myself into this book. Neither of my parents lived to see me achieve my doctorate, nor did they see me published, so it felt only fitting to put a little bit of them and others who were important to me growing up, into *The Blood Promise*. One of my recurring characters, Elliot Balloch, was named using my dad's family name (my maiden one) and my granny Balloch's maiden name. Another character, Lamond Johnston is named using a combination of my mum's family name and her mum's maiden name. They were strong personalities who always made sure I had a book in my hand and helped to nurture my love of reading.

So, with this sentimentality in mind, it was only natural that some of the scenes were set in areas I was very familiar with growing up and that some of my own childhood memories informed snippets that made their way into the book – my lovely pink and white sun suit for one.

Setting the series in and around West Calder reinforced my pride in my Scottish heritage. As they say – 'You can take the lassie oot o' Scotland, but you can never take Scotland oot o' the lassie.'

Writing *The Blood Promise* allowed me to reconnect with memories, experiences, places and people from my past, but more than that, it allowed me to pay tribute to those who are important to me.

The research for my Creative Writing PhD focused on inclusion and representation in the crime fiction genre and explored the nature of my writing process, during which I concluded that every experience, memory, encounter (whether in person or vicariously through anecdote, newspapers, etc.) contributed to my plot ideas and, in writing *The Blood Promise*, this has been especially true.

My niece Jaina's inspirational journey through sight loss and seeing the freedom having her guide dogs Laura and then Kath gave her, inspired me to include a blind character in my series and of course this gave me an opportunity to use my writing to highlight the work done by Guide Dogs UK and to be one of the many who adopt a puppy in training. Jazzy's mum's guide dog, Crumble, is my version of the fully trained adult guide dog inspired by the puppy I sponsor. Here's Crumble's story

The Blood Promise was a trial of emotional highs and lows, poignant memories, self-doubt, laughter and joy, but ultimately it has been the book I've enjoyed writing more than any of my others. Writing *The Blood Promise* was like coming home. I hope you enjoy reading it as much as I enjoyed writing it. Of course, if you loved getting to now Jazzy, Queenie and the team, then please do leave a review, shout about it to your friends or talk about it on social media.

Until the next Jazzy and Queenie adventure, keep safe. Best wishes,

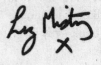

Last Request

When human remains are discovered under Bradford's
derelict Odeon car park, DS Nikita Parekh and her
team are immediately called to the scene.

Distracted by keeping her young nephew out of trouble,
Nikki is relieved when the investigation is transferred to the
Cold Case Unit, and she can finally focus on her family.

But after the identity of the victim is revealed, she's soon drawn back
into the case. The dead man is a direct link to her painful past.

As the body count begins to rise, Nikki must do everything she
can to stop the killer in their tracks before anyone else gets hurt –
even if it means digging up secrets she had long kept hidden . . .

**For readers of Angela Marsons and LJ Ross comes a gritty new
crime series featuring bold, brave and ferocious DS Nikki Parekh!
This rip-roaring thriller will have you reading long into the night!**

Broken Silence

When Detective Felicity Springer is reported missing, the countdown to find her begins . . .

On her way home from a police training conference, Felicity notices something odd about the white van in front of her. A hand has punched through the car's rear light and is frantically waving, trying to catch her attention.

Felicity dials 999 and calls it in. But whilst on the phone, she loses control of the car on the icy road, crashing straight into the vehicle ahead.

Pinned in the seat and unable to move, cold air suddenly hits her face. Someone has opened the passenger door . . . and they have a gun.

With Felicity missing and no knowledge of whether she is dead or alive, DS Nikki Parekh and DC Sajid Malik race to find their friend and colleague.

But Felicity was harbouring a terrible secret, and with her life now hanging in the balance, Nikki can only hope that someone will come forward and break the silence . . .

The next gripping crime thriller in the DS Nikki Parekh series, for fans of Angela Marsons and LJ Ross!

Dark Memories

THREE LETTERS. THREE MURDERS.
THE CLOCK IS TICKING . . .

When the body of a homeless woman is found under
Bradford's railway arches, DS Nikki Parekh and her
trusty partner DC Sajid Malik are on the case.

With little evidence, it's impossible to make a breakthrough,
and when Nikki receives a newspaper clipping taunting
her about her lack of progress in catching the killer, she
wonders if she has a personal link to the case.

When another seemingly unrelated body is discovered,
Nikki receives another note. Someone is clearly
trying to send her clues . . . but who?

And then a third body is found.

This time on Nikki's old street, opposite the house
she used to live in as a child. And there's another
message . . . underneath the victim's body.

With nothing but the notes to connect the murders,
Nikki must revisit the traumatic events of her childhood
to work out her connection to the investigation.

But some memories are best left forgotten, and it's going
to take all Nikki's inner strength to catch the killer . . .

Before they strike again.

Acknowledgements

Writing a novel is one thing, but whipping it into shape, ironing out the kinks and making it reader ready is another and is down to team work. Huge thanks to the HQ Stories team who have worked so hard to get *The Blood Promise* to publication. There are too many to mention, but a huge shout out goes to Aud Linton, my editor, whose eagle-eyed attention to detail and complete faith in my book and in Jazzy and Queenie has been so humbling. Helena Newton and Michelle Bullock worked tirelessly to iron out my mistakes – thanks so much.

Many thanks to the cover designer, Anna Sirkorska, who has truly excelled themselves in creating a distinctive, eerie cover with a flavour of Scotland incorporating the West Lothian landscape.

My agent, Lorella Belli at LBLA, saw the potential in my madcap pair of detectives from the start and flawlessly guided me through to publication with good humour and encouragement.

My early Beta readers Carrie Wakelin, Anne Hampson, Lynn Hampson, Maureen Webb, Lynda Checkley, Anita Waller and Alyson Read, to name a few, are a source of constant support and eagle-eyed suggestions. Their support means the world to me.

Fellow Awesome Authors, Tony Forder, Malcolm Hollingdrake, Anita Waller, Tom Reid, Mike Hollows, Maggie James, Andy

Barrett, Kerry Richardson, Eileen Wharton, Mark Tilbury, Jim Ody, Neil Lancaster, Nadine Matheson, Roz Watkins and so many more, have lent shoulders to cry on, practical advice, hugs (Andy in particular), stern words and absolute encouragement. You rock and I love you!

My online crimey groups, especially UK Crime Book Club and Crime Fiction Addict, are a source of constant entertainment and provide a safe space to interact with readers and fellow authors. Thanks to the Admin teams of both groups.

My family too have, as always, been amazing. They know how much I cherish being a crime writer and see the joy it brings me and are always there for me. My husband, Nilesh, in particular, goes the extra mile to make sure I can do all the writerly things I want to do. Huge thanks and much love to them.

But, my most heartfelt thanks go to you, the reader, for without you there would be no reason to write.

If you're reading these acknowledgements, it's because you've decided to give the Jazz Queens a chance. I hope you enjoyed your reading time with them as much as I did my writing time. Humungous thanks for taking the time to get to know Jazzy, Queenie and the team.